S0-BAD-142

我始終還是愛你的。

鍾小嵋
Amy Chang

content

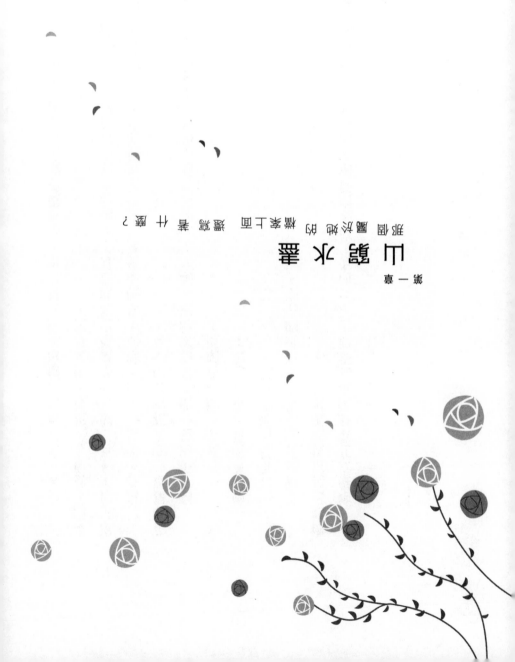

山藍水羅

第一章

那個圖形分割的　深深烙上黑　還算著什麼？

1

她凝立在歌劇院走廊那塊告示板前方，垮著兩個細瘦的肩膀，一動不動，就彷彿她已經這樣站著很久了。

那張長長的名單上沒有她的名字。

一如所料，她落選了。

她咬著嘴唇，跟自己說：

『不過就是一齣歌舞劇罷了。』

啊，不過是一齣她很想演的歌舞劇罷了。裡面有個小角色——劇中那個惡魔的花園裡眾多吃人花的其中一朵。

也許，要是一年前，她並不那麼渴望演這種佈景板般的小角色。可她已經很久沒工作了。有三個月吧？還是已經四個月了？她記不起來這段漫長的日子總共有多少回，就像今天這樣，她又落選了。

今天一大早來到這個歌劇院的舞台上，她戰戰兢兢地試著跳一段舞。由於她沒

見過吃人花，她張牙舞爪地，盡量跳出一副吃人不吐骨的可怕模樣。然而，舞跳到一半的時候，她瞥見坐在台下負責選角的副導演突然朝她張大嘴巴。

她以為他想喊停。原來，他是在打呵欠。

那一刻，她明白自己沒機會了。

可她還是抱著一絲希望回來。

她腳下像生了根似的，依舊杵在告示板的前方，固執地望著那張無情的名單，彷彿只要再這樣多看幾回，也許會有奇蹟出現。她會突然發現自己的名字原來一直也在上面，她剛剛不知道為什麼沒看見。

但是，今天不會有奇蹟了。

很久以後，她終於動了一下，跨出一步，然後又一步，戀戀不捨地離開那塊告示板。

這時，一陣風吹起，那份名單的一角捲起了，露出底下第二頁。她沒看見。

直到許多年後，她才知道她的名字在上面。

她推開歌劇院的玻璃大門時，一陣冷風灌進來，她趕緊把頭上那頂毛線帽拉低了些，打開手上的雨傘，孤零零地走在霏霏雨霧中。

她個兒嬌小，右手白皙的手腕上戴著一只綠橄欖石串成的手鐲。毛線帽下一雙黑亮的圓眼睛露出做夢般的神情。這雙眼睛好像一直都看著遠方不知名的某一點。

她臉色有點蒼白，髮絲紛亂地貼著臉龐，那頂毛線帽的帽緣有個破洞。她身上裹著一條單薄的羊毛裙子，裙腳的地方已經走了線，腳上那雙深紅色的尖頭麂皮短靴已然磨破，肩上掛著的那個大如郵袋的包包也很破舊了。

二十四歲的她正值荳蔻年華，這個年紀的女孩子都愛美，她看上去卻有點邋遢。但她的邋遢並不使人討厭，而是像一隻披著雪白羽毛的小鳥不小心掉到一窪污水裡似的，使她那張清純的臉蛋益發顯出一份飄零無依的感覺。

2

她像朵枯萎的鬱金香那樣低垂著頭，在賓館的樓梯上踱著。又髒又舊的樓梯兩旁丟了些垃圾，轉角處一個香爐裡插著幾支正在燃燒的香枝，灰燼如飛絮般掉落在她那雙紅色短靴的鞋尖上。她沒理會。她爬上二樓，推開賓館那扇黏膩膩的泛著油

光的玻璃門進去。

昏黃的走廊上彌漫著一股汗酸味，幾個非洲男人蹲在那兒，朝她露出白晃晃的牙齒。她沒看見。

她從他們身邊經過，掏出一把鑰匙，朝最後一個房間走去。當她走近了些，她看到她那只小小的行李箱孤零零地給丟在門外。

她連忙走上去，蹲在地上打開行李箱，翻開裡面塞得滿滿的東西看。她一直翻到底，沒有她要找的東西。這時，一把聲音在她背後冒出來。

那把粗啞的女聲說：

『我早跟你說過，今天再不交租就得給我滾！』

她轉過去抬起頭，望著中年女房東那張蠟黃的大臉胚。

她張開嘴想說話，唇上長著鬍子的女房東搶白說：

『你別再擺出一副可憐相！』

她站起來，焦急地說：

『我還有一樣東西在裡面！』

她說著抓住房間的門把，想用她那把鑰匙開門。孔武有力的女房東這時從她手

上搶走那把鑰匙，瞪著她說：

「你的東西全在這兒了！」

「不！求求你，讓我進去看看！」她一隻手緊緊抓住門把不放。

女房東瞅了她一眼，撇撇嘴，用鑰匙打開門，粗魯地說：

「我可沒看見你有什麼值錢的東西！」

門一開，她立刻衝進去關上門，房間裡面黑漆漆的，她亮起天花板上一盞昏黃的燈。

梵谷著名的『星夜』。

「這是我的。」她低聲說。

門後面原本用來掛毛巾的鈎子那兒掛著一幅長十七吋寬十二吋的仿製油畫，是

3

雨停了，她手臂下面夾著那幅『星夜』，拖著那只粉紅色迷彩行李箱，越過馬

路，穿過一條長街，幾步之遙那家星巴克咖啡店的燈光看起來多麼溫暖。

她推開門走進去，一陣咖啡的暖香撲鼻而來，裡面的座位都給人佔住了。她逕直走到報紙架那兒，拿起一份日報，翻到占星欄那一版，就站在那兒讀起來。

凡事總向壞的方向想是雙魚座的通病。

你究竟追求什麼？

別讓多愁善感牽著你的鼻子走，

你會一下子情緒化起來，

月亮今天進入第二宮，

這時，她無意中看到占星欄隔壁那一版有一則廣告。

她讀了那則廣告，悄悄把它撕下來藏在身上那條羊毛裙子的口袋裡。

然後，她把報紙放回去。

經過收款櫃台旁那個亮晶晶的糕餅櫃時，她嚥了嚥口水，拖拉著腳步。

她掏出一張十元鈔票在麵包店裡買了兩個甜麵包，把贖回來的七塊錢五角謹慎

011

地放回去她那個印滿罌粟花圖案的褪色尼龍荷包裡。然後，她坐到附近公園的長椅上開始吃麵包。

她嘴裡塞滿麵包，從身上裙子的口袋裡摸出剛才撕下來的一角報紙。

她撥開了前額遮住眼睛的幾綹髮絲，又讀了一遍那個廣告。

高級酒吧誠聘鋼管舞孃，

樣貌端正，

毋須經驗，

可提供訓練，

工作自由，

薪水優渥。

她很久以前讀過一本星座書，書上說，多情善感又悲觀的雙魚座女孩是絕佳的應召女郎和出色的脫衣舞孃。

早點相信的話，她便不用繞一個大圈子了。這條路不是比較好走嗎？幹嘛要夢

想當舞蹈員？自從一年前她工作的那個小舞團解散之後，她就沒接過什麼好角色。

機會都輪不到她，也許，她根本就不是跳舞的材料。

但是，鋼管舞誰不會跳呢？

她如今已經山窮水盡。荷包裡那七塊錢五角就是她僅有的了。誰會罵她沒有潔身自愛？

要是哥哥有一天回來，認出那個濃妝豔抹，在霓虹燈閃耀的長吧台上抱著一根鋼管賣弄風情的女孩是她，哥哥只會匆匆把自己身上的大衣脫下來替她披上。

「哥哥，我好羞愧啊！你可以原諒我嗎？」

「別傻了，你沒做錯事！」

「哥哥，我好累，我真的累了。」

哥哥會救她離開那個鬼地方。他們兩個人又再生活在一起。

她重又變回乾淨和純潔。

在她的想像裡，哥哥總是會原諒她的錯。

太扯了！她到底在胡思亂想什麼嘛？

她嚥下最後一口麵包，用手指抹了抹嘴唇上的碎屑，咬咬牙，把那個廣告摺

小，塞進去罌粟花荷包裡。

然後，她從長椅上站起來，拖著行李朝公園外面的巴士站走去。

4

下了巴士之後，她在路邊站了一會。黃昏星亮起，她睏倦地走過三個街口，越過一條小馬路。

經過一間教堂時，一個女人派給她一張綠色的傳單。她瞄了一眼上面的兩行大字。

耶和華是我的牧者，

我必不至缺乏。

她把傳單隨手塞進身上的包包裡，抄捷徑穿過一條小巷，來到一幢掛滿霓虹招

牌的大廈。

大廈外面豎著一個長方形的光管招牌，上面寫著：心心撞球室。

她吃力地拖著行李箱走下那條通往地窖的窄樓梯。兩個男人走上來，她側身讓

他們經過。

走到地窖，她推開撞球室的玻璃門進去。

大部分的球桌都給人佔住了，她從兩張球桌之間經過，瞥見左邊一個男人一桿

把紅球入洞。

她朝櫃台那邊走去。櫃台裡那個正在忙著的女孩子看到她，說：

『你頭髮長了很多啊！』

『嗨，小玫！』她疲倦地打了個招呼。

女孩的手腕上有個玫瑰花的刺青，大家都叫她小玫，兩人的年紀差不多。

她逕自拖著行李箱走進櫃台裡，把東西擱到一邊，然後很熟練地抓起一只紙杯

從水機裡倒水喝，骨碌骨碌的一連喝了三杯。

小玫長得黑黑瘦瘦，身材像男孩。

『你旅行回來啊？』小玫問。

『呃？不。我今天晚上可以在這裡睡嗎？』她陷進櫃台一角那張綠色絨面的椅子裡。『我跟我哥吵架了！他呀，老是愛管我幾點回家！所以我索性不回去了！』

她疲憊不堪，趴在櫃台上，臉埋手臂裡睡覺。

『有個男人打電話來找過你好多次。我說你已經沒有在這裡上班了。他問我去哪裡可以找到你，我就說我不知道。我是真的不知道啊！你那時不是說要去當舞員嗎？』

『對呀！我四處演出，好忙啊！』她頭沒抬起來，懶懶的問：

『他有沒有說他是誰？』

『他說是律師行的人，又問我有沒有你的電話號碼。我就把我以前男友的號碼給了他，那個混蛋一直背著我亂搞！』

她趴在櫃台上笑了起來。

小玫拉開櫃台邊一個放滿雜物的抽屜，找了很久，終於找到一張皺巴巴的便條紙。

『他留了電話號碼給你，要你一定找他。你認識律師的嗎？』

她好睏，頭挨在一條手臂上不思不想，沒去理會那張紙。

過了很久，由於好奇心的驅使，她終於抬起臉，一隻手支著頭，看了一眼那張便條紙，上面寫著一個陌生的名字和一個電話號碼。

『現在幾點啦？』她問小玫。

小玫看看錶：『八點啦。』

『律師行這時候下班了麼？』

『我又沒當過律師！』

她揉揉眼睛，伸長手臂把櫃台邊的那台電話機拉過來，拎起話筒，按下了那個號碼。

電話接通了，那一頭傳來一個男人的聲音。

『我想找戴德禮律師。』

『我是。你是哪一位？』

『我是路喜喜，是你找過我嗎？』

『路喜喜？你等一等——』

電話那邊傳來窸窸窣窣好像翻文件的聲音。

她握著電話筒，張大嘴巴打了個呵欠。

『你是路喜喜小姐本人嗎?』對方又再說話。

『我是喔。你找我我有什麼事?』

『是關於乙明芳女士的。你看看明天可不可以找個時間過來律師行一趟?』對方回答。

『那個人怎麼了?』她無意識地把玩著手腕上那條晶瑩的綠橄欖石手鐲。

『她死了。』

她的嘴唇動了動,皺縮著,隨後,她的嘴角又向兩邊延伸,有那麼短短的片刻,她讓人以為她想笑,那卻不是笑,而是發不出任何聲音,也找不到一個可以說的字。

5

天空飄著毛毛細雨,些許雨點濺到她那雙紅色短靴上,她帶著行李,瑟縮在巴士站裡,依舊穿著昨天那身單薄的衣裙。

巴士的班次似乎不多。她跟戴德禮律師約好了早上十一點半。

巴士，快來吧！

車子一輛接一輛駛過。她茫然地想起那張不快樂的臉。那個人已經死了嗎？是

怎麼死的？是自殺麼？那個人似乎一直都活得不順心。她死的時候，是孤零零一個

人嗎？

喜喜想起她第一眼看到那張臉的時候，不是這樣的，那是一張滿懷著希望的圓

臉。

她六歲那年，有一天，姑娘把她領進去院長的辦公室裡，那張充滿希望的臉孔

一看到她，就露出很想討她歡心的燦爛笑容。站在她旁邊那個男人，臉上好像沒有

任何表情。

院長跟她說，這兩位是秦先生和秦太太。

秦太太蹲下來，撫摸她的臉，帶著微笑說：

『噢！喜喜！你看起來好小啊！』

一輛巴士駛進車站，車門嘎嘎響地打開，喜喜拖著行李上車。車上只有幾個

人，她坐到後座去，把肩上的包包和行李箱放在旁邊。

車子緩緩往前走，她扯下頭上的毛線帽，把雨滴甩到地上，然後又戴回去。帽緣下那雙黑眼睛無神地望著車窗上的雨花。

九月初的一個清晨，那個人和她丈夫來孤兒院把她領回家。她捨不得哥哥，哭鬧著不肯上上計程車，他們抱她起來塞進車廂裡。

車子走了很遠的路，停在一幢舊唐樓外面。

她早已經哭累了，那個人抱著她下車。她伏在那個人柔軟的肩膀上，睜開睏倦的眼睛瞄了一眼那幢房子，看見二樓的一個小陽台上爬滿了漂亮的紫色藤蔓。

『這是我們的家！』那個人指給她看。

她的新家是一間有兩個房間的小公寓，長長的屋子，有一排塞滿了書的書櫃。黃色的拼花地磚很舊了，綠色的玻璃窗十分陰鬱。

為她預備的那個房間的床上放滿了新裙子和玩具。

那個人拉著她的手說：

『喜喜，你以後就住在這裡好嗎？』

她淚汪汪的問：

『秦太太，你可不可以也收養我哥哥？』

『要是你乖，我遲些把他接來跟你一起。你以後叫我媽媽，好不好？』

『媽媽。』

那個人好像沒法生孩子，所以只好領養。她丈夫在外面有女人，很少回家。一回家，兩個人就吵架。一吵架，那個男人就會生氣地說：

『阿乙，你這分明是不想我回家！』

他真的乾脆不回來了。

從此以後，那個人不再去照顧她那些藤蔓了，任由它們在陽台上到處攀爬。

每一次，當喜喜跟她提起收養哥哥的事，她總好像沒聽到。終於有一次，她歇斯底里地吼：

『我不會收養你哥哥！我討厭男孩子！我不會再收養，孩子沒啥用處！』

喜喜沒有再提了。

上課的時候，她總是做著白日夢。

在家裡，她雖然試著要感激和可憐那個人，卻不知道為什麼，她就像是報復一

樣，常常千方百計把那個人氣瘋。

那個人怨恨地對她說：

『那天我在孤兒院第一眼看到你時，你看來是那麼楚楚可憐，好像要是我不要你，你就完了。可你看你現在，即使只剩下最後一口氣，你也是會跟我對著幹的。

你把我給騙了！』

到底是誰騙了誰啊？

那個人卻常常跟朋友抱怨：

『她呀是個沒良心的！早知道我就不要她！錢呀我自己花，用不著為別人養孩子！』

那一年，她十四歲，十一月的一天，她放學回家，發現自己的東西全都收拾好放在門邊。那個人臉朝大門，坐在客廳的一把椅子裡，好像一直等著她回來。

『我已經辦好手續了，孤兒院的人很快會來接你回去。我放棄啦！我管不了你。』那個人冷冷地說。

她哭亂了一張臉，苦苦哀求那個人讓她留下來。

那個人久久地望著她，不動心地說：

022

『我不會再相信你！不管我怎麼愛你，你也是不會愛我的！你滾吧！滾回去吧！我決定了的事情，是不會改變的。』

突然之間，一陣輕輕的電鈴聲響起，是她們家的電鈴聲。她眼睛裡頓時浸滿了淚水，禁不住回頭望了一眼那扇緊閉的大門。

那個人坐在椅子裡，幽幽地對她說：

『去開門吧，你自由了！這就是你想要的。』

走了那麼多的路，她又回去了。

可是，哥哥已經不在院裡啊。

巴士到站，她下了車，拖著行李穿過一個街口，轉到下一條路，找到戴德禮律師行所在的那幢小型商廈。

她緩緩抬起目光，瞧了一眼上面那些積塵的棕色窗戶，這時她想起那年那天映入她眼簾的，纏繞著陽台的紫色藤蔓。

離開之後，她再沒有回去過了。

6

戴德禮律師行在七樓。喜喜出了電梯，轉向左邊，在走廊盡頭找到那扇門，門上掛著招牌。

她推門進去，一位胖小姐從接待處裡冒出來，問她要找哪一位。

她報上名字，說：

『我跟戴德禮律師約好了。』

那位胖小姐打了一通內線電話給律師的秘書。不一會兒，穿黑色洋裝、盤著髮髻的女秘書朝她走來，她看上去有二十七、八歲，還是三十歲？

『路小姐，請跟我來。』

她拖著行李跟在她後面，走道上堆滿了文件，她不小心弄跌了其中一些。她想俯身拾起來，女秘書朝後瞥了她一眼，說：

『喔，沒關係，由得它吧！』

面積不大的辦公室裡有幾個職員，每個人面前的文件都疊得高高的，沒有一個

人有閒抬起頭來看她。

她們來到一個房間外面，女秘書敲了敲那個深色的木門，打開門讓她進去，順手把門關上。

一個坐在辦公桌前的男人站了起來迎接她。他差不多有四十歲，還是只有三十五？他有點讓人看不出年紀。

『路小姐，我們找你很久了。』

他伸出手，一隻黝黑的軟綿綿的小手。他戴著厚眼鏡，個頭很小，像個老小孩，輕盈得讓人不可思議。

『請坐……你的東西……隨便放就好了。』

這個房間比外面整潔，書櫃從上到下佔滿了其中一面牆，大部分的書都是硬皮法律書。室內只有一張長條辦公桌，兩把椅子和一張短沙發。朝街的那扇窗戶落下了窗簾。原本可以看到外面辦公室的那個長方形大玻璃，也用百葉窗簾遮著。

『我們一直在報紙上登廣告找你，你沒看到嗎？』

喜喜覺得很尷尬，她看報紙都只看占星欄。她最近唯一留意到的就是昨天那個鋼管舞女郎的廣告。

戴德禮穿一身深灰色的西裝，喜喜禁不住在心裡想：

『這會不會是童裝啊？』

他真的很矮小呀。然而，那副無框厚眼鏡後面流露出來的，卻是精明，而且生氣勃勃。他看起來像一個有很多計謀的聰明小精靈。

小精靈突然把身子朝她探過來，說道：

『路小姐，可以麻煩你給我看看你的身分證嗎？手續上要確認一下。』

喜喜從荷包裡掏出身分證給他。戴德禮迅速瞄了一眼上面的資料，打開門，朝坐在門外的女秘書說：

『茱迪，請你拿去拷貝一份。』

他轉回來，帶上門，動作俐落地坐回去辦公桌後面那張高背椅子裡。

『我們可以開始了。』

那張椅子對他來說有點太高大了，不過，他看起來自信又自在。他從桌上拿起一個檔案夾打開來，裡面附著好幾十頁紙的資料。

『乙明芳女士在十個月前過身了。』

她咬咬嘴唇，等著對方說下去。

026

『據我們所知，乙女士一度是你的養母。』

『一度……是的……』她心裡想。『直到她把我送回去之後。』

『她後來放棄對你的撫養權，所以，你又改回原本的名字。自從回去兒童之家以後，你們雙方再沒有聯絡。』

她微紅著臉點頭，偷瞄了一眼小精靈手上的那個檔案，心裡想：

『那上面是我的過去！路喜喜……秦喜喜……然後又變回路喜喜。兒童之家……那個人的家……然後又回去兒童之家。』

也許那個檔案裡面還寫下了她十八歲離開兒童之家後的生活，譬如這些：

她是一個三流舞蹈員，居無定所，靠著微薄的入息過活。

她愛過幾個人，也被幾個人愛過。金牛座的那個，借了她的錢，一直沒還。雙子座那個太花心，她想用眼淚淹死他，沒成功。山羊座那個長得最帥，對她最好，但她不愛他。水瓶座那個，她以為會長相廝守，但他們幾乎一見面就吵架。

那個屬於她的檔案上面還寫著什麼？

有沒有說她總是很容易愛上別人，卻又很容易失望？有沒有提到她還有一個哥哥？她跟金牛座、雙子座、山羊座，還有水瓶座和獅子座都合不來，唯有天蠍座的

哥哥跟她最好。

那個檔案是不是已經記錄了她二十四年的故事？那些用破碎的夢想與破碎的承諾組成的故事。

『根據我們所知，乙明芳女士並沒有任何親人，她生前在我們律師行立下的遺囑，指定你作為她遺囑的執行人和全部遺產的唯一繼承人。』

喜喜臉上浮起了愕然的神情。

『這份遺囑是什麼時候立的？』她咕噥著問道。

戴德禮回答說：

『是在乙女士死前一年立下的。』

她不知道說什麼好。

那個人明明狠心把她送走，又為什麼要把遺產留給她？

『乙女士的遺產全部是現金。』戴德禮瞥了她一眼，接著說下去。『約數是九百七十萬港幣。』

喜喜望著戴德禮，臉上的表情先是驚愕，然後又變成慌亂。她沒想過是這麼大的一筆錢。

『路小姐，你有沒有問題想要問我？』戴德禮繼續說。

『為什麼？我跟她已經十年沒見了。』她的口氣有點激動，不是因為意外之財而高興，相反，她覺得自己根本沒資格。

戴德禮臉上露出微妙的表情，彷彿想要表明他見過許多像她這樣受寵若驚的遺產繼承人。

『律師行只是負責執行當事人的意願。當事人決定怎樣分配遺產，我們是不會過問的。』

她抿著嘴唇，說不出半句話。

那個曾經是她養母的人，是因為內疚才把所有遺產留給她的吧？

『路小姐，你還有沒有其他問題想知道？』

『她是怎麼死的？』她低聲問道。

『是胰臟癌。』

『她死的時候，有人在她身邊嗎？』

『這個我們不太清楚。不過，乙女士的死訊是她的一位教友通知我們的。』戴

德禮輕輕說道。

他看了她一眼，又說：

「路小姐，辦領遺產的手續可能需要一些時間，你看，要不要我們先行墊支一些錢給你，你說不定會用得著。這筆錢，等你領到遺產之後再還給我們也不遲。」

她臉紅了。小精靈戴德禮是什麼時候看出她的拮据模樣的？是她一進來的時候？還是在她從幾乎空空如也的荷包裡掏出身分證來的時候？但是，她卻渾然不覺他曾經那麼仔細地打量過她。

她想要不太由衷地搖搖頭，她想要微笑拒絕，說她暫時不需要。但她偏偏很想有一張溫暖的床，讓她躺在上面好好睡一覺。

「沒問題的。我們一般都會這樣做。」他誠心誠意說道。

她窘困地點了點頭，微笑以示謝意。

他敏捷地離開椅子，打開門出去跟女秘書低聲說了幾句話。不一會兒，他拿著一個信封回來。

「這裡有八千塊錢，路小姐，你看看夠不夠用。」

「夠了。」她又紅了臉。

他把她的身分證還給她，然後坐回椅子裡，將一份厚厚的文件放到她面前。

『這是辦理遺產確認書的文件，路小姐，請你在有注號的地方簽名，不清楚的話可以問我。』

喜喜抬起她空空的右手，戴德禮適時遞給她一枝筆。

她低下頭，默默地在每一頁簽上她的名字，根本無心去看那些文件上面寫什麼。

她終於全部簽好了，也在律師行墊支八千塊錢的那張收據上簽了名。

她放下筆，對方仔細地檢查一遍她所有的簽名。確定無誤之後，他說：

『行了！』

她鬆了一口氣，站起來，把包包掛在肩上，抓起她放在一邊的行李箱朝門口走去。

走了兩步，她停下來，回過頭去，有點艦尬地問道：

『請問……她葬在哪兒？』

戴德禮看了看她，應了一聲，隨手在桌子上拿起一張空白的便條紙寫下一行字。

喜喜走過去，戴德禮隔著辦公桌交給她那張便條紙。

她站著看了一眼上面寫什麼。

就在這時，桌上的內線通話器傳來女秘書茱迪的聲音。

「戴律師，林克來了。」

戴德禮偏著頭，目光越過喜喜的身側瞥了一眼那個被百葉簾遮掛著的大玻璃。

「你讓他等一等。」他對著通話器說。

喜喜順著他的目光，好奇地轉過頭去看向大玻璃那邊。這時，她隔著百葉窗簾的縫隙看到一張臉，一張年輕的男人的臉。

那張臉的主人也在看她……可是不對，他不是看她，而是無意識地看進房間裡來，而且跟她一樣，眼裡帶著些許好奇。

她的目光穿過百葉窗簾一層一層好像斷層似的縫隙重組了一個模糊的身影。那個叫林克的男人似乎是穿一件深色的夾克在外面有點無聊地踱著。是否她看到他，他卻看不到她？

眼前的場景，為什麼好像似曾相識？

她看到他，就好像看到了另一個人，舊時的關愛與幸福又重回心頭。

「路小姐，有消息我們會通知你。」

戴德禮不知什麼時候已經從辦公桌後面走了出來，朝她伸出一隻手。

她失神地回過頭來握了握那隻軟綿綿的黝黑小手。

對方打開門讓她出去。她拖著行李走出去，卻不見了那個叫林克的人。

她失望地穿過那條狹窄的走道離開。走到盡頭時，她戀戀不捨地轉過頭來想再看一眼。那些疊滿高高的文件的辦公桌之間，這時突然冒出一個形影來。

是他！

小精靈把他叫進去，他緩緩將一把椅子推開來站起身。

當他跟小精靈站在一塊的時候，他看來簡直就像一位儀表堂堂的國王。

那扇門隨後關上了。

他的確是穿著深藍色的夾克，手裡拿著一個文件袋。

他也是天蠍座的嗎？

他身上有她久違了的那種感覺。

她的哥哥，也是這個年紀。

但她已經許多年沒見過哥哥了。

7

從律師行出來，她在幾條街以外找到一家廉價的小旅館。她走進去，租了一個房間，在登記卡上填上路喜喜的名字。

她在櫃台邊的報紙架上拿起一份報紙，讀她的占星欄。

但是，有誰沒有過這種懷疑呢？

你對自己和人生的意義充滿懷疑。

否則，孤寂的感覺會如影隨形。

雙魚座，你需要休息，

她把報紙放回去，取了鑰匙。

等電梯的時候，她用手掩住嘴巴打了個呵欠。

出了電梯，她找到一○三號房，用鑰匙開了門。

房間很小，一張單人床擺在中間，牆上貼著俗氣的間條圖案壁紙。

她丟下身上的包包和行李，脫下毛線帽，匆匆扒去身上的衣服，一絲不掛的走進浴室，扭開蓮蓬頭，嘩啦啦的把自己從頭到腳洗乾淨。

從浴室裡出來的時候，她身上裹著一條毛巾，甩了甩那頭柔軟的黑髮。她現在看起來只有二十歲。

她蹲下來，打開行李箱，挖出她那幅『星夜』。然後，她拿了一張椅子站到上面，把原本掛在牆上那張風景畫丟到一邊，換上『星夜』。

她從椅子上跳下來，坐到床邊，掀開被子，臉枕在一個枕頭上，縮成一個小粉糰似的。

她望著牆上的『星夜』，眨了眨睏倦的眼睛，沒多久就睡著了。

她一直睡到隔天早上。

醒來之後，她洗了個澡，穿好衣服，套上短靴和毛線帽，用床單邊緣擦擦靴子上的灰塵，喝了一大杯水，拎著一個包包，鎖好門出去。

出了旅館，她走到便利店，在櫃台那兒買了一張儲值的流動電話卡，塞進去她

035

那部手機裡，順便買了一份報紙。

她邊走出來邊打開報紙看占星欄，看完之後把整份報紙丟掉。她想起她昨天忘了問戴德禮那個尋她的廣告上面寫什麼。

那些廣告都是怎麼寫的？

她在一家快餐店吃了一份漢堡，離開快餐店，走過一個街口，在一個花檔挑了幾枝鬱金香，抱著花，搭上一輛巴士。

到了墓園，她找到養母那塊小小的白色大理石墓碑。墓碑上，黑白照片裡的女人笑盈盈的，拍照的時候，一定沒想過這張照片有一天會這麼用。

她用衣袖擦拭照片上的塵埃，把花放下，坐在墓前，從包包裡掏出一本《生命中不能承受之輕》，開始讀起來。

八歲的時候，她就用一隻手牽著另一隻手入睡，她想像自己握著的手，屬於她心愛的男人，屬於她託付終身的男人。（註）

她一直看書看到日落。

036

她收好書，站起身，在一行墓碑之間穿過，走出墓園。

她在旅館附近一家小酒吧點了一杯桃子味的伏特加。

坐在對面的一個年輕小夥子靠過來跟她搭訕。

『對不起。』他說。

她沒有反應。

他瞄了她一眼。

『你不會喝醉吧？這酒很烈。』

『所以我每天只喝一杯。』

她把酒一口喝光，丟下那個一臉尷尬的小夥子。

她回到旅館房間，縮在床上，哭了。

半夜裡，霓虹燈光照進來，兩個醉漢在街上大聲說話。半睡半醒之間，她用一隻手牽著自己另一隻手。戴著綠橄欖石手鐲的那一隻手，後來垂在床邊，直到天亮。

第二天，她下午才離開旅館，到地鐵站的補鞋店去替她那雙紅色短靴換過新的

鞋底和鞋跟，這雙靴子的鞋底已經換過好幾次了。

穿著長襪坐在櫃台的高腳圓橙上等候的時候，她打開報紙讀占星欄。

購物會對你有幫助。

振作起精神吧！

這對你沒有什麼好處，

雙魚容易沉醉於悲傷的情緒，

她穿回短靴，一邊走出地鐵站一邊講手機：

『碧碧，我是喜喜，以後有選角打這個電話號碼就好了。』她報上電話。『最近忙不忙？真的嗎？我還好啦，只是家裡有點事，沒什麼耶！』

她掛上電話，在街上晃了一圈，跟一個在樓梯底擺攤子的老婆婆買了一頂手織的白色羊毛帽。羊毛帽上面織著兩隻豎起來的圓耳朵，像熊耳朵。

她隨手丟掉舊的那頂毛線帽。走路的時候，帽子上那兩隻圓耳朵在她頭頂亂顫。

她往東走，經過一列櫥窗之後又退回去，進入其中一家時裝店。

她挑了幾件簡單的衣服到試衣間試穿。

她瞧著鏡子裡的形影，那頂古怪的帽子讓她禁不住發笑，她也發現自己有一雙很黑很亮的眼珠，彷彿是她鑲在臉上的兩顆黑水晶。

她脫掉衣服，她的腰在身上勾勒出美麗的弧度，像兩個英文字母『C』，彼此背對著背，以臍眼為中心，中間隔著一段剛剛好的距離。

她從試衣間出來時，已經套上新的衣服。付了錢之後，她把舊的衣服包好放回去包包裡。

她繼續往西走，在一家藥店裡買了刮鬍刀和桃子味的沐浴精。她內心掙扎了好一會兒，終於決定買一排苦巧克力。

十點鐘，她回去昨天那家小酒吧。

這一天，她點了一球香草冰淇淋和桃子味的伏特加，把整杯伏特加淋在冰淇淋上，用一隻小銀匙一小口一小口的挖來吃。她一邊吃一邊讀《生命中不能承受之輕》。

十一點半鐘，她回到旅館房間，洗了一個桃子味的澡，在浴缸裡用刮鬍刀刮腳

毛。

洗完澡，她爬上床，靠在枕頭上縮成一團。月亮高掛，她夢見哥哥。

『喜喜，快跑！快跑！』哥哥喊著說。

她和哥哥在一家百貨店裡偷東西。他們偷了很多東西，有衣服，有食物，還有鞋子。兩個人想要離開時，兩個警衛追了出來。

她和哥哥拚命逃跑。她一路跑一路跑，跑了很遠之後，發現哥哥不見了。她手裡只剩下一隻很醜的鞋子。

她心跳撲撲睜開眼睛醒來，發現自己躺在旅館陌生的床上，活像一條影子，只有牆壁上那張『星夜』和手邊的一本書陪著她。

第二天，她一大早起來，把幾件舊衣服打包，鎖好門，搭電梯到樓下，在櫃台付了這三天的房租。

她離開旅館，經過戴德禮律師行那幢大廈門口，在對街車站搭上一輛西行的巴士。

她在車上看書，坐在她對面的一個老女人一直盯著她那頂古怪的帽子。喜喜故

意冷著一張臉，很嚴肅的樣子。

車子到站，她下了車，爬上一條斜路，把那包舊衣服送給救世軍。辦事處裡的一個女職員跟她搭訕，不停稱讚她那頂帽子好可愛。

她依依不捨地把帽子脫下來，一併捐給了救世軍。

然後，她在酒吧喝了一杯桃子味的伏特加，讀了報紙的占星欄，很早就回去旅館房間，趴在床上看書。

往後的幾天，她得了感冒，大部分時間都留在旅館房間裡看書，只出去買過報紙和去過酒吧。

手頭上的錢差不多用光的那天早上，她擠眉弄眼在浴室裡刷牙，手機鈴響，她連忙拿起電話，是戴德禮的秘書茱迪打給她，請她隔天上律師行。她吐著泡泡咕噥應著。

喜喜第二天見到戴德禮的時候，他坐在辦公室那張使他顯得渺小的高背椅子裡，身上穿一套深棕色西裝，結一條小花點領帶，看上去依然像穿了童裝大碼。

他真的讓人看不出年紀。

她禁不住在心裡想，他會不會是患了老人症的天才兒童？也許跟她一樣，是個孤兒。

他把一份文件放在她面前，說道：

「路小姐，手續已經辦好了。」

她望著那個數字，那是很大的一筆錢。但是，她為什麼沒有什麼特別的感覺？

就好像這些錢不是真的。

她在那份文件上簽好字，乖乖的，就像一個交功課的學生。

「路小姐，要是你以後有什麼需要，歡迎隨時來找我。」

戴德禮兩手互握著放在桌上，臉上掛著誠懇又聰明的微笑。這一刻，他看來就像一個善良的小精靈，有許多法寶，可以為人實現心中的願望。

她開口問道：

「戴律師……那天我上來這裡的時候……有個人在外面等你……他穿著藍色的

夾克……有這麼高的……』她用手比劃著。『我覺得……他好像很面熟……不知道

我會不會是以前見過他……他叫什麼名字？』

小精靈皺了皺眉頭，一時想不起來她說的是誰。

『我聽到他好像是姓林的……名字好像只有一個單字……』

戴德禮終於想起來了。

『你是說林克？』

『呃……對！他是這裡的職員嗎？』

『不，他是我們僱用的私家偵探社派來的偵探。』

那個人原來是私家偵探嗎？

她不禁想起她看過的電影中那些聰明絕頂又有點落魄模樣的私家偵探，他們好像都有一段不為人知的傷感過去。

難道他真的也是天蠍座，跟她哥哥一樣？

天蠍座都是天生的偵探。

『雖然Google的搜尋網搶走了很多搜集情報和背景調查的工作。』戴德禮笑笑說道。『不過，有些事情Google始終做不來，譬如說，當你要監視或者跟蹤一個

043

人，Google便沒法代替私家偵探。』

『他就是替你做這種工作的嗎？』

『這些只是其中一部分。要看情形，律師行也是替當事人辦事。當然了，當事人的要求，我們也不是全都辦得到，譬如說，假如警務處長的太太懷疑她先生有外遇，我們也不可能叫林克去跟蹤警務處長，除非我們不想活了！』

他說完，得意地笑了笑，正在為自己的幽默感喝采。

『你可以叫他跟蹤我嗎？』她說。

她看到戴德禮臉上露出驚愕的表情，就好像當頭挨了一棍似的，那樣子很滑稽。

他回過神來，問道：

『路小姐，你剛剛說什麼？』

『我想你叫林克跟蹤我。』她說。

她知道這念頭有多傻，但她就是忍不住開了口，就像一個人滿懷希望的對著精靈說出了自己的願望。

戴德禮不再笑了。

『路小姐，我可以知道為什麼嗎？』

跟蹤她有什麼問題啊？她又不是警務處長。

但她還是編了個理由。

『我現在有錢了……可以做我一直想做的事……我一直想寫一本書……一本偵

探小說……和跟蹤有關的……所以……我想找些靈感……』

戴德禮沒有表現出相信或不相信的樣子。

她猜不透他在想什麼，但他好像也猜不透她在想什麼。

『就把我當成是你的當事人吧，說我是幾年前離家出走的少女，我的爸爸媽媽

想知道我的行蹤，想知道我過得好不好……你看這樣行嗎？我會付錢的。』

她感覺戴德禮在猶豫。

她在心裡祈禱……求求你，答應吧！答應吧！

她一臉堅持的望著他。

戴德禮終於說道：

『路小姐，你確定要這樣做？』

她點點頭，問道：

045

『戴律師，你不會告訴偵探社和林克，你的當事人其實是我吧？』

他神情嚴肅地回答：

『我沒有任何理由這樣做。律師是有責任替當事人保密的。』

『那林克什麼時候可以正式開始跟蹤我？』

『我要安排一下。路小姐，這種情況，除了私家偵探社那方面的收費，律師行也是要收取費用的，這並不包括跟蹤你的各項開支在內。』

『沒問題！』

她現在有很多錢！這筆錢終於有點用途了。

『路小姐，你是指定要林克跟蹤你嗎？他們還有其他偵探……』

『不！我要他。』

『你需要一份跟蹤報告嗎？』

『我要一份詳細的報告。』

她本來沒想過這一點，戴德禮倒是提醒了她。她答道：

『你希望林克跟蹤你到什麼時候？』

『我還沒決定。』

戴德禮看了她一眼，說道：

『路小姐，我看這樣吧，你先回去，我做好安排之後會聯絡你。』

她站起身，心裡翻騰著一種興奮的情緒。

戴德禮突然抬起頭問她說：

『路小姐，你身上有照片嗎？』

她從印有罌粟花圖案的尼龍荷包裡掏出一張半身照片。照片中的她當時只有十三歲，用一條絲帶把頭髮全都束起來，身上穿著黑色的緊身舞衣。

拍這張照片的時候，她剛跳完舞，正想要離開那個嵌滿鏡子的排舞室，不知道是誰突然從後面叫她的名字，她回過頭去，紛亂的髮絲在臉龐周圍飛舞，一雙黑眼睛茫然地望著前方。

她一直好喜歡這張照片，照片中的女孩有一種她如今已經失落了的神情。她當時在看什麼？到底是誰喚她的名字？她已經記不起來了。

既然說她是幾年前離家出走的少女，她富有的父母想知道她的行蹤，那麼，這張照片最適合了。

她把照片交給了小精靈戴德禮。

對方接過照片，離開那張高背椅子，從辦公桌後面走出來送她。

兩個人走到門口時，他問她：

『路小姐，你目前是住在……』

喜喜答道：

『我就住在附近的新月旅館，房號是一○三。』

直到三天之後，戴德禮的電話終於打來。他似乎是故意拖延三天，確定這位客戶沒有任何意思改變她那個瘋狂的主意。

他通知她說：

『路小姐，已經安排好了，從明天開始，林克會跟蹤你。報告和帳單要怎麼交給你？』

『你暫時還是送到新月旅館吧。』

喜喜掛掉電話。這時，她正在旅館附近那家小酒吧裡喝光一杯桃子味的伏特加。

她付了錢，把手上看到一半的《生命中不能承受之輕》放回去包包裡。

然後，她站起身，邁著長長的步子，頭也不回地離開酒吧。

從這天起，她再也沒有回頭路了。

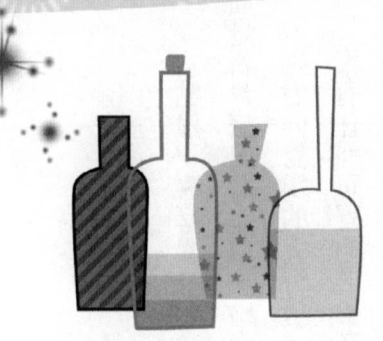

孤寂的愛情

一個人 怎麼 能 夠 跟 自己 戀愛？

1

八點鐘，喜喜醒來，從床上坐起，光著腳走到窗邊，躲在窗簾後面往下看。下面是新月旅館的入口，她看到幾個路人經過，沒有人駐足。

她看向對街的人行道，兩個穿白色校服裙子的女生結伴從便利店走出來。

沒有任何可疑的形影在下面徘徊或者監視。

十一點鐘，她已經穿好衣服，從電梯出來，把鑰匙交給櫃台。

她瞄了一眼大廳的長沙發那邊，一個男人抬起手，打開一份報紙在看，遮住了整張臉，穿棉褲的一雙長腿套上了光鮮的運動鞋。

她心頭一顫，從他身邊走過時，眼角的餘光看向他，但那不是林克，是個頭頂光禿禿的老男人。

她走出旅館，到便利店買了一份報紙，在櫃台付錢的時候，她隔著玻璃門看了看外面。

單憑那張十三歲時拍的照片，林克就能夠一眼把她認出來麼？她覺得自己已經

不是舊時模樣了。從前，舞團裡就有個和她比較投契的女孩不只一次跟她說：

『你的樣子好像每隔一段時間都會變呢！』

糟糕的是，她自己照鏡子的時候也這麼覺得。

是什麼讓一個人的那張臉常常改變？

當時，她微笑把一根手指按在胸口上，對那個女孩說：

『也許是因為，我的心總是在變啊！』

她把報紙塞進包包裡，離開便利店，越過馬路，走到下一個街口，穿過一個露天菜市場，在一個大排檔點了咖啡和雞蛋三明治。

她在路邊的一張桌子坐了下來，一邊喝咖啡一邊讀占星欄。

金星今天進入雙子座，
你的生命將有如被明星照亮，
新的際遇就在面前……

她禁不住從報紙後面偷偷抬起眼睛搜索周圍，卻沒看到她期待的那個身影。

053

隨時留意身邊的人，

你會有一位神秘的守護天使出現。

三點鐘，她在百貨公司買了一支口紅和一對太陽眼鏡，又在飾物櫃那邊看了好一會兒，拿起幾條寶石鑲嵌的項鍊掛到身上研究。

她不時偷瞄鏡子，想看看會不會在鏡子的反映裡發現他。

什麼都沒發現。

她太緊張了，要是林克一直盯梢她，說不定已經發現她似乎一直在尋找一個跟蹤者。

五點鐘的時候，她鼻梁上架著太陽眼鏡，悠閒地坐在公園的綠色長椅上看《生命中不能承受之輕》。

她心不在焉地看了一會，從書上抬起目光，一頭有一張醜陋大扁臉的老虎狗這時掙脫了主人，向她奔來，朝她身後吠叫。

她猛然回頭看了看身後的樹叢，沒看到什麼，只看到一陣風吹過，樹葉抖動。

老虎狗的主人跑上來扯住牠的項圈，喊道：

『多莉，別這樣！』

那頭名字叫多莉的狗被拉走時心生不忿地吠叫了幾聲，兩隻肉肉的前爪朝空中抓了幾下。

喜喜把書丟回去包包裡，從長椅上站起來，悠悠地邁步離開公園。

感謝多莉。

她用手托了托鼻梁上的眼鏡，嘴邊泛起一絲笑意。

2

第二天兩點鐘，喜喜在幾家首飾材料店分別買了一批水晶珠子，仿製寶石和金屬片，其中一家店的老闆娘送她兩卷絲帶。

五點鐘，她在書店買了幾本書。

付錢的時候，她瞥見一個穿深藍色夾克的模糊的側影一閃而逝，手裡好像也拿著書。

八點鐘，她在藥店買了一瓶染髮劑。

八點半鐘，她回去旅館，在櫃台取鑰匙，那個矮胖的門房向她問好。

進了房間，她脫光衣服，拿起剪刀，對著浴室的一面鏡子把長髮剪到齊頸，然後扭開蓮蓬頭洗澡。

當她再次走出旅館的時候，她一把劉海齊頸的頭髮已經變成了紅色。

她一直想要一把紅色的頭髮。

林克會不會認不出她來？

她往西走，到下一條街的酒吧，坐下來喝她的桃子味伏特加，打開一本書看。

她不時悄悄從書裡抬起目光搜尋林克的蹤影。

她看到他了。

他穿著藍色的夾克，坐在離她很遠的吧台一角，隱身在兩個站著喝酒聊天的水手後面。

當你早知道有一個人跟蹤你，你便不難發現他。

林克完全沒有看向她這邊。

當那兩個水手談得興起，偶然移動一下身體，她才看得見他。

他有點寂寞地喝著一杯白蘭地，正在看一本書，不時用筆在上面寫字。

那本書是他的掩護嗎？他壓根兒不像正在監視她。

那兩個高大的水手擋住了她的視線。

以前住在孤兒院裡的時候，院裡有一間圖畫室，她常常去借圖畫書。

她愛用鉛筆在書裡空白的地方寫滿歪歪斜斜的小字。她寫的東西有時是有意思的，也許是從書上抄下來的，有時卻是沒有意思的，亂寫的。

那個負責管理圖書室的懶惰姑娘從來不檢查院童還回去的書。反正那兒許多書都是慈善機構捐來的舊書。

一天，同房的一個院童舉報她，說路喜喜她破壞公物。

舍監認出她的字跡，罰她打掃圖書室。

那天，哥哥偷偷帶了麵包來給她吃，問她為什麼這樣做。

那時候，只有六歲的她，不是要破壞公物，她只是想要佔領那些書。

多年以後，當她想起那些被她塗花過的書，她始終回味著那份幸福的佔領。也許，她當時還不曾明白，她想在她走過的地方留下痕跡，就像小黃狗在街燈下撒一泡尿，留下自己的味道。

十一點鐘，她回去旅館房間。

她開了燈，躲在窗簾後面往下看。

她看到那個穿藍色夾克的背影回去了。

他是回家去嗎？他的家在哪兒？

他沒看上來，於是，她大著膽子探出頭去，盡情地看他。

她用眼睛佔領了那個在夜色裡踽踽獨行的背影。

這天晚上，她沒睡，亮著一盞小黃燈，徹夜坐在房間那張窄木桌前面，用白天買的材料做起首飾來。

3

星期三的這一天，喜喜離開旅館，搭上一輛計程車。

十二點鐘，她在一條有幾家時裝店的小街下了車，走進街角一間小巧時髦的飾物店。

看店的瘦個子女孩看到她，朝她說：

『喜喜？你頭髮什麼時候染成紅色的？你樣子變了耶！』

女孩名叫小綠，店是她自己的，她兩邊耳珠總共掛著五雙耳環，全身上下能掛飾物的地方全都掛滿了飾物。

喜喜望著她，問道：

『你幹嘛？』

『我？』小綠拿起一面鏡子把自己從頭到腳照一遍，說：

『我想看看一個人身上能掛多少飾物。』

『神經病！』

她說完，從包包裡掏出一個小小的黑色的絲絨布袋，把裡面的幾件飾物倒出來，攤開在玻璃櫃上。那兒有三條寶石手鍊，其中一條用了石榴石，兩條金屬項鍊，分別附著十字架墜子和蠍子座墜子，一雙藍水晶耳環。

小綠說：

『好漂亮！你多做幾件嘛！上次做的那些，早就賣出去了，許多客人來問。』

喜喜拿起一只藍水晶耳環比在耳垂上，轉頭看向店外，好像對著外面的空氣說：

059

『我要看看心情好不好……』

小綠把其餘的都往自己身上掛。

『你是在跟我說話嗎？』

喜喜回過頭來，說：

『這裡除了你還有誰啊？』

她沒看到林克，他也許留在路口那兒。

她把那顆藍水晶耳環放回去櫃台上。

小綠馬上拿起來掛在耳垂上，望著喜喜的橄欖石手鐲，問道：

『你這個手鐲什麼時候肯賣？』

『不賣啊！我找了很久才找到十二顆差不多大小的。橄欖石是雙魚座的守護寶石。』

她摸了摸那只手鐲，說：

『這些賣完了告訴我一聲。我電話改了，以後打這個號碼找我吧。』

六點鐘，她在街上晃了一圈，買了一雙襪頭有黃蝴蝶圖案的紫色長襪和一塊蛋糕。

她習慣每年生日這一天送自己一雙長襪。三月十九日,是她的生日。

不管她走過的日子有多拮据,一雙襪子總是她至少能夠負擔的。

要是哪天有人問她生日為什麼要買襪子,她會告訴對方:

『這是我們家鄉的習俗,長襪就是長壽襪嘛!』

這是哪門子習俗呀?

然而,從來就沒有人問起過。

九點鐘,她坐在沙灘看星星,聽海浪,吃了那塊蛋糕。

她看到林克獨個兒坐在海灘酒吧那邊,陪著她吃西北風。

有一天,她和哥哥從孤兒院偷走出來。那時是冬天,他們躲在無人沙灘的瞭望塔裡,白天撿貝殼,晚上看星星,吃乾糧度過了幾天。

後來,她發了燒,比她大五歲的哥哥只得揹著四歲的她走路回去孤兒院。

她趴在哥哥背上,兩隻手抓住滿滿一個膠袋的沉甸甸的貝殼,捨不得丟掉。

她問哥哥⋯

『我們不回去不行嗎?』

哥哥說：

『你病了啊。』

『等我病好了再逃走好嗎？』

哥哥點點頭，把她揹高了一些，吃力地走在黑漆漆的路邊。

『這些貝殼全都是我的嗎？』

『全都是你的。』

『我要找個地方把它們藏起來。』

她抬起頭，看到遠處的星星點點的燈光。

那是孤兒院。這是他們的歸途。

她站起來，邁步走向掛滿暈黃燈泡的海灘酒吧那兒。

酒吧裡坐著幾對喁喁細語的年輕情侶。

她故意朝林克走去。他若無其事地低頭看書，用筆在上面不知道寫些什麼。

她經過他身邊，走到他後面的吧台。

他有一張好看的臉，臉上掛著好看的羞澀的神情。

062

他到底看什麼書？

他也讀占星欄嗎？

他今天晚上會不會偷拍一張她的照片？

她坐在吧台那兒，面對天上點點繁星，喝她二十五歲這一年的第一杯桃子味伏特加。

4

到了三月底，喜喜收到一份戴德禮差人送到旅館櫃台，轉交給她的報告。

她先看照片。

一張是頭一天拍的，她黑髮，走在街上。

另一張照片裡，她已經變成紅髮，剛從旅館出來。

她生日的那天，在沙灘酒吧上也有一張，她呷著伏特加。

小酒館裡有一張，她正在低頭看書。

有一張是在戲院外面拍的，她正在猶豫該看哪一齣戲。那天戲院裡人很少，林克一直坐在遙遠的後排。

他把她的生活列成單子。

其餘大部分都是在街上拍的。林克好像很喜歡拍她走路的樣子。

有一張是她一邊走路一邊打開報紙看占星欄。她記不起那天是哪一天。

有喝伏特加的習慣。（註：指定要桃子味）

每天看報紙占星欄。

住新月旅館一○三號房，每星期結帳一次。

偶然逛展覽會。（計有乾屍藝術展覽，出土木乃伊展覽，歷代刑具展覽）

她趴在旅館那張床上，咯咯地笑了起來。那些展覽會是她故意帶林克去的，就好像一個小孩子偏要證明自己勇敢，一個女人想要證明她的魔性。

她繼續看下去。

似乎沒有工作，

經常一個人在街上亂晃，

收入來源成疑，

沒有朋友，

看不出有男朋友的跡象，

寂寞。

第二天，她把裝著支票的一個信封投到附近的郵筒，寄給戴德禮。

她收起那份報告。

5

星期四的這一天，她離開旅館，帶了前天做的幾條手鍊到飾物店去。

一進門，她看到小綠每邊耳垂掛著一串晃來晃去的綠晶耳墜，染了一頭綠色的

短髮，活像一隻瘦蛤蟆。

「呃！喜喜？」

瘦蛤蟆小綠兩隻手肘撐在櫃台邊，忙著打電腦鍵盤，匆匆抬頭瞥了她一眼。

「這是上次的錢。」小綠伸手到收銀機那兒拿了幾張鈔票給喜喜，眼睛一直望著電腦屏幕說：「有個客人想要一個巨蟹座的墜子……」

喜喜問道：

「是個男的嗎？」

小綠恨恨地敲著鍵盤答道：

「女的，胸很大。女巨蟹的胸都很大！」

喜喜好奇地探頭過去，問：

「你在忙什麼？」

「我要找那個混蛋王八出來！」

「你在打機喔？」

「我哪有心情打機！那個大混蛋死王八龜兒子甩了我，借了我的錢不還，我在搜尋他！你給我死出來！」

喜喜收起鈔票，湊過頭去盯著電腦屏幕看。

三點鐘，她回到旅館，那個矮胖的門房在房間走廊外面探頭探腦地等她，一臉貪婪相對她說：

『路小姐，有個男人向我打聽你……』

『什麼男人？他長什麼樣子？』

『二十幾歲，不到三十，穿藍色夾克，是個高個子，有點不修邊幅，來旅館好幾次了，手裡經常拿著一本《數獨》，我看到他坐在大堂裡盯著你，可能對你有不軌企圖。我什麼也沒說。』

『謝謝你告訴我。』

喜喜說完，飛快進了房間，沒打賞那個門房。他看來一臉失望。

她馬上把所有東西連同那張「星夜」打包，到櫃台辦了退房手續。

6

一個鐘頭之後，喜喜已經住進兔子旅館六〇一號房。

她把牆上那張兩隻小白兔吃紅蘿蔔的水彩畫丟到一旁，掛上『星夜』。

原來林克常常看的是《數獨》。

他不是在書裡做筆記，他是解謎。

六點鐘，她離開旅館，在酒吧喝了一杯桃子味伏特加，然後到電器店買電腦。

八點鐘，她拎著手提電腦回旅館。

她在旅館大廳瞥見林克的背影。

他戴了一頂藍色的鴨嘴帽，坐在大廳的一把沙發椅裡做《數獨》。

她抬起頭，從他身邊走過，無視他的存在。

她進了房間，把電腦從包裝盒裡拿出來，接駁電源。

林克在樓下大廳那兒解決《數獨》。

她在六〇一號房裡，登入Google搜尋網。

她在搜尋一欄輸入林克的名字。

一個畫面跳了出來，總共約有四十八萬七千項符合林克的查詢結果。

有林克華、林克中、林克光、林克炳、林克珠，還有一大堆林克什麼東東。

有四個午夜牛郎林克，三個拳手林克，一部叫《寂寞林克》的悶蛋小說，一個

人類學教授林克（是史前黑猩猩研究領域的權威）……

就是沒有她要找的那個林克。

不，等一下……她找到一個網誌。網主叫朵朵安娜。

7

喜喜打開朵朵安娜的網誌。

一張照片出現在上頭，是一張合照。

十四個約莫十六七歲的男生和女生笑著望向相機。照片是在課室的黑板前面拍的。

她一眼就認出他了。

林克是後排左邊第一個。

他一隻手插在褲子的口袋裡，臉上的微笑顯得靦腆。

一個有一張瓜子臉，留著長直髮，戴頸巾的女孩站在他旁邊。

網主朵朵安娜在文章裡這麼寫：

搬家時無意中找到一張中學時代跟同班同學的合照。

前排右邊第二個，戴著眼鏡的就是我！

後排左邊第一個，長得最帥的那個，是我那時候一直暗戀的男生，名字叫林克。

他是學校推理學會的會長，為了親近他，我那時啃了很多推理小說和電影呢！

偷偷掉過的眼淚，要是加起來的話，至少也可以養一缸金魚吧？

不過，他似乎一直不知道我暗戀他。

我現在的老公也長得有幾分像他。

很久很久沒見過他了。這幾年同學會的聚會他都沒來，也跟大家失去了聯絡。

他到底去了哪？

他做什麼工作？

過得好不好？

有時候，我真的希望他已經變成一個大胖子！

誰叫我得不到啊！

他一定會後悔那時沒選我！

要是誰有他的消息，請告訴我一聲。

那麼，站在林克身旁那個戴頸巾的女孩是誰啊？

朵朵安娜說『他一定會後悔那時候沒選我』，是不是他選了這裡其中一個女孩？

她在網誌裡寫下留言。

朵朵安娜：

我認識他！

他是我一個朋友的朋友，

還是那麼熱愛推理小說，

喜歡喝伏特加。

話很少，但一說起推理小說就會很雀躍，最近一次見面，他還跟我討論松本清張

和福爾摩斯呢！

要是你想知道他的消息，請回覆我或是電郵到我的郵箱。

她署名『泡泡魚』，把留言送出去。

8

朵朵安娜在三個禮拜之後的一個夜晚電郵給她。

親愛的泡泡魚：

對不起，我出門了，剛回來，看到你的留言。

你真的認識林克嗎？

他還好吧？

我以為經過那個打擊，他會變得很消沉。不過，聽你說他雀躍地跟你討論松本清

張和福爾摩斯，我倒是放了心。

他是松本清張迷！

福爾摩斯的柯南‧道爾更是他的偶像！

看來他已經沒事了。

真笨！推理大師還能有哪幾位啊？

林克一定不喜歡笨女孩。

他喝酒會臉紅嗎？

我那時從沒見過他喝酒，而且還是伏特加！

伏特加不是只有酒鬼才喝的嗎？

我現在倒是又有點擔心了。

喜喜回了那封電郵。

親愛的朵朵安娜⋯

他喝酒會臉青，不會臉紅。

他說伏特加是懂得悲傷的人喝的。

想知道多一點他的消息，請打這個電話號碼給我。

她起身到床邊拿手機，焦急地在旅館房間裡踱著步。

十二分鐘之後，手機響起一串鈴聲。

朵朵安娜上鉤了。

一把年輕的女聲問道：

『你是泡泡魚嗎？』

『對。你是朵朵安娜？』

『對不起，好像很冒昧……』

『沒關係啊……』

『你是怎麼認識林克的？』

『他是我一個朋友的朋友，我們只見過幾次面，其實，我跟他不算熟啦。他這人好像挺憂鬱。』

『一定是因為那件事……』

『就是你說的那個打擊嗎？我沒聽我朋友說過，到底什麼事啊？』

『就是他以前老婆啊。』

林克結過婚麼？然後又離婚？

她怔了一會，接著問：

『他跟他以前老婆怎麼了？』

『他老婆是我們同班同學……』

『她也在那張照片裡嗎？』

『對。就是站在他旁邊那個。』

她沒猜錯，果然是那個戴頸巾的女孩。

『他們是初戀情人。讀書時是她主動追求林克的，一畢業就嚷著要結婚。誰知道，結婚不到一年，她就吵著要離婚，說什麼當日結婚是因為好勝。林克對她死心眼得很，自然是不肯離……』

『那怎麼辦？最後還是離了嗎？』

『有一天，他回家發現她不見了，東西全都帶走。他找了她很久，終於查出她

去了英國。他飛去英國找到她，發現她已經跟一個男的同居，還挺著個大肚子。』

她聽了，心中突然覺著一種無以名狀的難過。

『那麼，他一個人孤零零的回來了？』

『他還可以怎樣啊？離婚之後，他變得很消沉，同學會不參加了，也沒有再找我們幾個舊同學，我看他是想避開我們吧！他現在好嗎？』

『他很胖呢，比照片裡那個他至少胖了幾圈，要不是同名同姓，我還真認不出他來！』她低頭摸著腕上的橄欖石手鐲，無心答道。

『天啊！他一定是故意把自己吃成這樣！』

『是啊，人一旦傷心就會放棄自己。』

『想不到我以前暗戀的人變成了大胖子。』雖然這麼說，朵朵安娜的聲音卻似乎有點高興。

喜喜順著朵朵安娜心中的希望說：

『他跟照片比，蒼老了很多耶！看上去至少有三十五、六歲。』

『真的？』朵朵安娜果然中計。『我看他是不會想再見我們的了！請你別跟他說我們通過電話。』

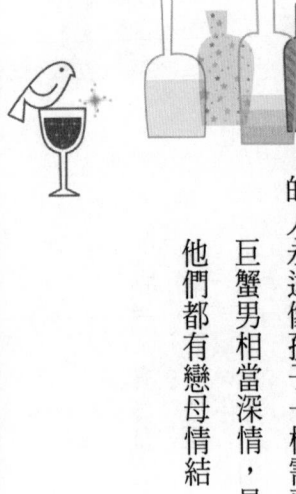

『我不會說。對了，他是天蠍座的嗎？』

『天蠍座？不，林克跟我一樣，是巨蟹座，所以我很記得。』

9

雙魚，巨蟹跟天蠍都是水象星座，性情如水，天生一對。

『你千萬別告訴他網誌的事。他不知道我暗戀過他……』朵朵安娜說。

『今晚的事，我誰也不說。』

喜喜掛掉電話。

巨蟹男對愛情有強烈的自戀自憐，多愁善感，會永遠保護所愛的人，希望心愛的人永遠像孩子一樣需要他照顧。

巨蟹男相當深情，是會躲起來掉眼淚的浪漫螃蟹，無可救藥地依戀往事。

他們都有戀母情結。

九點鐘，喜喜穿上雨衣從旅館出來。

微雨紛飛，她翻起了雨衣後面的帽兜，遮住一頭紅髮。

她孤零零地走在雨中，緊緊抿著雙唇，控制住一股想哭的衝動。

她漫無目的地在夜街上走了一圈，穿著紅色短靴的腳步愈走愈急，彷彿是想要把往事從身上抖落。

往事是碰不得的，一碰眼淚就會嘩啦啦的湧出來。

十點四十七分，她來到酒吧。

林克比她早一步到了。

他坐在吧台一角，背朝著門口，正在做《數獨》。

她走過他身旁時，瞥見他深藍色夾克後面濕了一大片。

酒保這時把一杯白蘭地連同杯墊放到他面前。

她把雨衣脫下來掛在椅背上，坐到靠落地窗的角落看雨。

雨淅淅瀝瀝地下著。這天晚上，她喝了兩杯桃子味伏特加。

在她喝第二杯伏特加的時候，坐在她背後一個三十來歲，帶著醉意的男人靠過來說：

『小姐，你介意我坐過來嗎？』

她瞥了他一眼，望著窗外說：

『不介意。但你得先等我走了之後。』

帶醉意的男人還是把椅子挪了過來坐下，手裡拿著一杯威士忌，逗她說：

『怪不得別人說紅髮女子最無情！』

喜喜嫣然一笑，卻不是對面前這個來搭訕的男人笑。

她憂鬱的目光越過男人的肩膀，望著打在窗上的雨。她是在跟自己笑。

相見爭如不見，

多情卻似無情。

『哥哥，你什麼時候來接我啊？』

剛剛搬到養母家的時候，她寫了很多信給哥哥，每一封都會這麼問。

她相信哥哥有一天會來接她。

她愛搬一張小圓櫈坐到陽台上，隔著陽台上纏滿藤蔓的欄杆看向街上，等哥哥

來。

說不定哪一天，哥哥會突然在街上那片風景裡出現，看上來喊她的名字……

『喜喜！』

她喝光那杯桃子味伏特加，拿起雨衣離開酒吧。

那個帶醉的男人尾隨著她走出來。

她走過三條街，取道熱鬧的酒吧街，經過一條巷子。

那個帶醉的男人不要臉地跟上來纏住她。

『紅髮妹！你很難追啊！』

她壓根兒不理他。

『我們找個地方再喝一杯吧！』他突然抓住她的手臂。

她甩開他。

男人從後面扯住她身上雨衣的帽兜，罵道：

『臭婊子！你不想玩剛剛在酒吧為什麼對我笑！』

她搖晃了幾步，用盡氣力把他推開，看也不看他。

她裹緊雨衣，匆匆走出巷子。

突然之間，她聽到後面傳來一聲慘叫。

她猛然回頭，看見那個男人好像被人推了一把，失去平衡，踉蹌跌倒在溝渠邊，抱著頭痛苦呻吟。

這時，一道閃電映出了一個穿藍色夾克的身影，在巷口那兒轉瞬即逝。

她回身，重新邁步，緩緩往前走。

十分鐘之後，她回到旅館，脫掉雨衣丟到椅子上。

床邊的矮櫃上面放著那本《生命中不能承受之輕》。

她走過去，拉了拉那盞床頭燈的繩子，一隻蚊子給燈光嚇倒了，從燈罩裡飛了出來，伏在天花板上。

她打開書，坐在床邊讀了一段：

愛情故事是在這之後才開始：

她發了燒，而他不能像對待其他女人那樣開車把她送回家。他跪在床頭，心底浮

081

現這樣的想法：

她是被人放在籃子裡順水漂流過來的。（註）

10

第二天十點鐘，喜喜離開兔子旅館。

十點四十分，她坐在公園的長椅上打開報紙讀占星欄，然後打電話給戴德禮，告訴他她換了旅館，請他以後把跟蹤報告和帳單電郵過來。

戴德禮問道：

小說？她壓根兒都忘了。

她回答說：

『路小姐，小說進展順利嗎？』

『我寫得很慢呢……不是太順利……』

十二點鐘，她走進一家書店。

她在書架上拿起一本《數獨》。

她翻到其中一頁讀一個謎題。

玩的人要在一個九宮格的每個格子裡填上一到九的一個數字，每個數字只能出現一次，不得重複。橫的縱的每一行加起來的總數要相同。

她解謎解了半天，連邊兒都沒摸到。她索性偷看書底的答案。喔……原來是這樣……

林克做的是哪一級啊？

這本書把謎題分成四個級別，有極易、容易、困難和極難四級。

書上說，這不是算術，瞎猜也不行，這是推理。玩的人根據線索推敲答案。

數獨大師古德曾經打了一個比方：你是待決的死囚，今天早上行刑，獄卒說要是你及時解得開極難級數獨，你就可以保住小命。

那麼，你死定了。

要是她是那個死囚，那麼，她死定了，除非……是哥哥替她做吧。

不管多困難的謎題，哥哥也一定能夠解開。

她想像行刑的那天，她穿著囚衣。兩名女獄卒把她綁在一張電椅上。

手裡拿著聖經的牧師慈愛地問她：

『路喜喜，你願意悔改嗎？』

她看了牧師一眼，氣定神閒地說：

『不急嘛！』

她瞥了行刑室的大鐘，還剩下五分鐘……三分鐘……最後十五秒……

剩下一秒鐘，行刑室外面，哥哥把謎題解開了。

他們只好放她走。

她把那本《數獨》放下，拿著書去櫃台那兒付錢。

她買了米蘭・昆德拉的《生活在他方》，加西亞・馬奎斯的《異鄉人》和《百年孤寂》。

她先看照片。

到了月底，她收到戴德禮電郵過來的跟蹤報告。

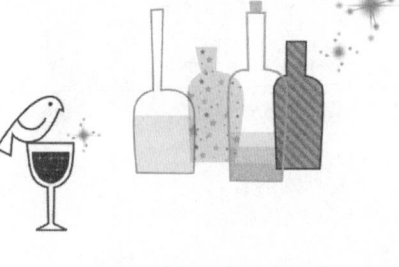

有一張是她在海灘上散步。

那天颱風，她去聽海浪。

一張是她從小綠的首飾店出來。

那天，她賣了幾雙耳環，有一雙她捨不得賣，帶去了又帶回來。離開的時候，她鼻梁上架著太陽眼鏡，遮住了半張臉，耳垂上釘著一顆紅榴石，跟她的紅髮相輝映。

一張是從劇院出來，她去看了『歌聲魅影』。

一張是她從摩天輪上面走下來。

那個夜晚漫天星星，摩天輪攀到半空時，她居高臨下，悄悄尋覓他的身影。

他把她的生活列成單子。

報告上說，她是一位自由的首飾設計師。

她長期住旅館。

她情迷占星欄，除此以外，沒有別的信仰。

她一個人吃飯。

他把她愛吃的東西列成單子，下面加了一行備註（她父母說不定會想知道）。

她把報告存檔，寫了一封信給哥哥，電郵到『雅虎』的一個信箱。

那個電子信箱是她為哥哥開的。

11

到了十月初的一天，喜喜十二點鐘走出旅館，坐在咖啡店裡讀占星欄。

你會有意想不到的收穫。

學習一種技能，

長此下去只會耽誤青春。

別再胡思亂想，

兩點鐘，她從咖啡店出來，把這個月的支票投進郵筒裡寄給戴德禮。

五點半鐘，她在鞋店買了一雙漆皮紅鞋子。

她穿上新鞋子走出鞋店時，無意間抬頭看到對街二樓一列寬廣的落地玻璃窗倒

映著夕陽的餘暉，幾個女孩子在上面上瑜伽課。

她走上去，在櫃台報名。

她每星期來上兩課，學習哈達瑜伽。

導師妮娜是印度西施。

妮娜教她練習時要排除腦海中的一切雜念。

但是她從來就辦不到。當她靜止時，往往有一千個念頭從腦海中掠過。

她愛佔著靠落地窗的位置，不時偷偷往下瞄一眼對街的咖啡館。林克每一次都

隱身在那家咖啡館裡面。

他在那兒總共幹掉多少《數獨》？

他都快成精了。

預備上課。

十二月中的一天，她跟其他人一樣，隨意地在課室的地板上擺著一個攤屍式，

這一天，妮娜沒來。

一雙男人的白皙修長的赤腳走進課室來。

12

喜喜坐起身，兩隻腳掌合攏，雙手伸向前面抓住腳趾。

她好奇地望著男人。他三十來歲，穿白色短袖汗衫和寬鬆的及膝運動褲，有一個寬肩膀，眼睛燦爛地笑著，臉朝他們站在課室前方。

「從今天開始，我會暫時代替妮娜。」他清朗的聲音向大家宣布。「我叫鄭魯，《魯賓遜漂流記》的魯，不是老人家的老。」

班上有些人報以笑聲。

她發覺他渾身上下有一種很特別的氣質，這時明明已經是下午了，他卻彷彿剛剛從清晨的林中散步回來，帶上一身朝陽。他的皮膚上也許還留著樹葉和露水的味兒。

後來有一天，上完課，她捲起墊子站起來，鄭魯走過來問她說：

『你是不是有跳舞底子的？你的身體很柔軟。』

她抬起眼光看他，聳聳肩答道：

『我的舞跳得不好。』

鄭魯饒有興味的說：

『但你的瑜伽做得很好，你有天份。』

她臉紅了，說道：

『哪裡是？妮娜說做瑜伽時要排除腦海中的一切雜念，但我做不到。』

他不以為然地說：

『為什麼要做得到？』

她驚訝地看著他。

他的眼睛清澈如水。

『你坐下來。』鄭魯吩咐她。

她只好重新放下墊子，坐到地板上，兩個腳掌合攏，雙手習慣性地往前伸，抓住十個腳趾頭。

鄭魯早已盤腿而坐，看看她，皺了皺眉說：

089

『你不用這樣抓住你的腳趾，我敢保證，它們是不會跑掉的。』

她笑了，學他那樣，鬆開手，手心朝上擱在兩邊膝蓋上，大拇指跟食指圈起來。

他笑笑說：

『我也有很多雜念。不過，假如你真的想要心無雜念，試試跟我做……』

他說完，微微張開嘴，從身體裡發出一個單調的音節：

『嗡──』

他停下來，說：

『這是一個梵音……』

他說完，閉起眼睛，吸一口氣，繼續唸：

『嗡──』

她緊閉雙眼跟著唸：

『嗡──』

她偷偷睜開一隻眼睛看他。

他合上眼睛，柔軟的頭髮呈深棕色。

她閉上眼，繼續『嗡──』，無暇思想。

他終於停下來了，張開眼睛，問她：

『是不是好了點？有什麼感覺？』

她回答：

『我覺得自己像一隻蚊子。』

他說：

『是一隻心無雜念的蚊子。』

那天，他們一起吃飯。她吃肉，他吃素。她喝桃子味伏特加，他喝氣泡礦泉水。

鄭魯曾經在紐約華爾街上班，然後放棄一切，跟隨多位瑜伽大師學習，回來香港之後，開了這家瑜伽俱樂部。

他單身，獨居，處女座，喜歡大自然。

他有幾個志同道合的朋友，其中一個男的，大學畢業之後跑去當農夫，另一個女的，擁有一家香薰治療所。

他們都是熱愛生命的人。

這些人她都在鄭魯家見過。那位香薰治療所的主人問她住哪裡，她回答道：

『兔子旅館。』

鄭魯住在郊外山腰一幢有三面落地玻璃的大屋裡。

喜喜稱那個地方做『恐怖屋』。

屋裡面養了六隻不住籠子，胖得像隻雞的彩色鸚鵡，在客廳裡自由飛翔散步。這些鸚鵡一見到鄭魯回來，就會飛撲到他身上，撒嬌似的喊：

『鄭魯！鄭魯！』

屋裡還有一條愛睡沙發的黃蜥蜴和一條愛盤踞在客廳那尊巨型佛像頭頂的綠蜥蜴，牠的名字叫無花。

鳥兒常常飛來，在院子裡棲息。夜裡，林中不時傳來貓頭鷹咕咕的叫聲。

一天晚上，喜喜站在客廳那扇落地玻璃前面看向屋外的樹林。

霧深了，夜色迷濛，這附近幾乎沒有可以躲藏的地方。林克他躲在什麼地方？

她一步一步沿著窗邊走，眼睛搜索他的蹤影，這一刻，只有他看得見她，她看不見他。他會不躲在外面台階的柱子後面？

她拿起鄭魯那台用來觀鳥的望遠鏡看向屋外。

鄭魯這時走到她身旁，說：

『晚上看不到鳥。』

她回答：

『我看貓頭鷹啊。』

『貓頭鷹很少會讓人看見。牠們都躲起來。』

『那我看牠們怎麼躲。』

那六隻鸚鵡之一拍拍翅膀朝鄭魯飛去，他伸出一隻手接住牠。

喜喜悄悄挪開一步。

『你不喜歡動物嗎？』鄭魯問。

她拿開望遠鏡，說道：

『我喜歡啊！我一直想養一隻貓，每天晚上用一根繩子牽著牠出去散步。』

鄭魯咯咯地笑了出來。

『只有人遛狗，哪有人遛貓啊？』

她�’噘噘嘴說：

『那我找一隻喜歡被人遛的貓⋯⋯』

鄭魯突然拱起兩個肩膀，用手勢示意她別說話。

『外面有人！』他低聲說道。

他說完，放開手裡的鸚鵡，拿起一根棍子衝出屋外。

她轉身，直直地望著外面院子。

院子裡的燈紛紛點亮了，她心裡撲撲亂跳，重新拿起望遠鏡。

她看到一條人影迅速翻過牆頭。

快跑吧！林克。

隨後鄭魯回來了。

『外面有人嗎？』她顫著聲音問道。

『可能是野豬！』他丟下那根棍子。

他抱著她，安慰她說：

『不用怕。』

她鬆了一口氣。

九點鐘，鄭魯開車送她回去旅館。

他十點鐘回家，上床睡覺。

喜喜十二點鐘在酒吧裡喝她的桃子味伏特加。林克早已經坐在吧台那兒做《數獨》。

這天晚上，他喝了半瓶白蘭地。那苦澀的模樣好像他喝的是醋。

13

鄭魯喜歡叫她住的旅館做『兔子窩』。

他總是說：

『又回你那個兔子窩去了啊？』

那天晚上，他送她回去，參觀她的房間。

他看了一眼她寒傖的窩子，憐惜地說：

『一個女孩子長期住旅館好嗎？』

『挺好啊！自由啊！』

『要是因為錢的緣故……』

『不……』她阻止他說下去。『我和哥哥從小就習慣住旅館。我爸爸是攝影師，帶著媽媽和我們兄妹倆去過很多地方……赫爾辛基、布達佩斯、柏林、新德里，還有西非……太多了……那時我還小，許多都不記得了。』

她走到窗邊，繼續說道：

『我們每次都住旅館，從一間住到另一間……直到一天，我們到了南斯拉夫，爸爸開車載我們出去，車子出了意外，掉到山邊，只有我和哥哥活下來。是哥哥揹著我爬出車廂的。那時我只有七歲。』

她低頭把玩著腕上的橄欖石手鐲，眼裡溢滿淚水。

鄭魯走過去，捉住她一雙手，用眼神安慰她。

她說下去：

『我哥哥也是一直住旅館，他是一位戰地記者，替通訊社工作。我們約定每年在一個地方見面。我哥哥很疼我，他會摸摸我的頭頂，跟我說，我是他的驕傲。』

她手放在頭上，看向窗外。

夜深了，那個穿藍色夾克的身影在對街一盞昏黃的街燈下默默守望。

14

生日那天，喜喜給自己買了一雙長襪。

鄭魯在那幢玻璃屋裡為她慶祝生日，請來他那幾個朋友。香薰治療所的主人送她一束薰衣草，農夫帶來了一籃新鮮雞蛋。

客人離開之後，喜喜趕走那條黃蜥蜴，坐在客廳的布沙發上，喝自己帶來的一瓶桃子味伏特加。

鄭魯坐到她身邊，捉住她拿著酒杯的那隻白皙的手說：

『別喝那麼多酒……至少……別喝伏特加……』

她笑盈盈的眼睛望著他說：

『這酒好喝啊！』

這天晚上，她沒走。

午夜三點鐘，她從床上醒來，轉頭看他。

他睡得很甜，發出平穩的鼻息。

097

她身上裹著一條被單，摸黑溜出客廳。

她險些兒絆倒，連忙抓住身邊一樣東西穩住自己，她摸到一塊滿是疙瘩的皮，嚇了一跳，手一鬆，感到有一條尾巴在她腳背竄過。

她亮起客廳的一盞小燈。

她剛剛抓住的原來是佛像的頭頂。愛盤踞在那個頭頂上的綠蜥蜴無花不見了。

她在廚房冰箱裡找到她那瓶桃子味伏特加。

她站在客廳的落地玻璃窗前面，望著黑漆漆的院子，呷著杯裡的伏特加。林子裡傳來貓頭鷹的叫聲。

那條綠蜥蜴悄悄爬回去佛像的頭頂。

五點鐘，一群鳥兒在院子裡吵個不停。

她喝光了伏特加，回到那張陌生的床上睡覺。

六點半鐘，她睡得很熟。鄭魯醒來，到廚房裡喝小麥草汁，在院子裡做瑜伽。

做完瑜伽，他餵飼那六隻鸚鵡和兩條蜥蜴。

喜喜有時會在他家裡過夜。

她在屋裡時，鄭魯會把鸚鵡拴起來。

那六隻鸚鵡一定很恨她。她也恨牠們。

一天晚上，她和鄭魯坐在院子的紅磚台階上聊天。

他喝氣泡礦泉水。

她喝桃子味伏特加。

他望著她說：

『你把旅館的房間退了，搬來這裡好嗎？我不放心你一個人住在那個兔子窩。』

她看了看他，說：

『不行啊！』

他怔了怔⋯

『為什麼不行？』

她說：

『我有時喜歡一個人。』

他問道：

『你不喜歡跟我一起嗎?』

『留著那個房間,要是有天你討厭我,我可以回去啊。』

『我怎會討厭你?』

她靜靜地望著林子。

『那沒關係……我可以跟自己……』

『一個人怎麼能夠跟自己戀愛?』

她搖晃著杯子說:

『為什麼不可以啊?我跟自己甜言蜜語……我跟自己山盟海誓……我跟自己長

相廝守……我不會背叛我自己……』

『那太孤單了……』他抓住她的手。『我不會讓你這麼做。』

她悲傷地說:

『愛情是一百年的孤寂。』

第二天早上,她離開玻璃屋。

十一點鐘,她買了報紙。

十一點二十分，她在旅館那張床上讀占星欄。

別讓它從身邊溜走。

幸福來的時候，

會遇到美好姻緣。

沒有愛情就過不了日子的雙魚，

夜晚七點鐘，鄭魯在餐廳裡向她求婚。

他把一枚光禿禿的白金戒指放在她面前，柔情蜜意地說：

『你不用現在馬上答應，你準備好再告訴我。』

她抿著嘴唇，黑亮亮的眼睛望著鄭魯，微笑著沒說話。

九點鐘，他們離開餐廳，回去山上的玻璃屋。

半夜三點鐘，她醒來，光著腳到廚房打開冰箱找伏特加。

冰箱裡沒有她要的東西。

她溜回客廳，亮起一盞小燈，凝立在落地玻璃窗前，看著迷茫夜色。

今天晚上沒有星。

她望著手上那枚戒指。

不對，不是這種感覺。

是哪裡出了問題？

籠子裡的一隻鸚鵡拍著翅膀很想出來。

佛像頭頂那條綠蜥蜴無花對她虎視眈眈。

她看了一眼這幢房子，感覺自己像個陌生人

她心中某個東西突然枯萎了。

她把那枚光禿禿的戒指從無名指上扯下來，慢慢走過去，套在蜥蜴『無花』那

根醜陋的尾巴上。

蜥蜴動也不動，彷彿那枚戒指本來就是屬於牠的。

喜喜往後退了幾步，靜靜望著佛像微笑的臉。

如夢幻泡影，

如露亦如電。

她抱著她今天晚上穿來的那雙亮晶晶的紅鞋子，悄悄溜走。

五十分鐘之後，她回到旅館，馬上打包行李，到櫃台退房。

她在機場旅館住了一夜，關掉手機，把頭髮染回黑色。

第二天，她買了一張新的電話卡。

鄭魯再也不會找到她了。

她突然明白，她害怕熱愛生命的人。在這些人面前，她總會覺得羞愧。

十點鐘，她帶著行李和那張『星夜』，搭上往東京的一班飛機。

她在機上發現林克。

他拎著輕便行李，泰然自若地從她身旁走過，在最後一排找到自己的位子坐下。

她低下頭，專心讀報紙占星欄和那本《百年孤寂》。

愛情是一百年的孤寂。

你 遛 我的 影子

愛上 一個人，是不是 都由 沒道理 的 嫉妒 開始的？

1

喜喜住進東京新宿一家便宜的小旅館，把『星夜』掛在房間的牆壁上。

她打了幾通電話，最後一通電話打到對街那家小旅館的櫃台。

她用英語問：

『請問有沒有一位林克先生住這兒？他是從香港來的。』

櫃台的職員回答：

『有的，你需要把這通電話接到房間去嗎？』

她掛掉電話。

終於找到了。原來林克住在那邊。

她走到窗邊，隔著窗簾看向對街那幢有點殘舊的旅館。天已經黑了，旅館的窗戶亮起星星點點的光。

她從機場出來時沒看到他，還以為他跟丟了。

他會奇怪她為什麼一夜之間從鄭魯身邊逃走嗎？還是他跟她一樣，也會在那些

106

熱愛生命的人面前感到寒傖？

她穿上一襲紅色風衣離開旅館，在附近的酒館吃了一碗拉麵。店裡沒有伏特加，她喝了兩杯梅子酒，然後走路回旅館。

她累了，蜷縮在房間的窄床上，望著牆上的『星夜』入眠。

她在夢裡又見到哥哥。

她和哥哥面對面坐在一列北行的火車上。

哥哥不解地問道：

『你為什麼不嫁給那個人？你本來可以幸福的⋯⋯』

『可是⋯⋯可是⋯⋯』她喃喃說道。『我害怕有一天我會變成鸚鵡啊⋯⋯』

哥哥笑了⋯

『那我會變成那條叫無花的蜥蜴。』

三個禮拜之後，喜喜穿著她在東京地下街買的一雙酒紅色的麂皮長靴和深紫色羊毛帽，搭上一列開往長野的新幹線火車。

她拖著行李穿過一個個車廂，最後，她在禁煙的那一節車廂找到一個位子。

她放好行李，把帽子脫下來丟在旁邊的空椅子裡。

車子緩緩離開月台，她打開在車站買的一份英文報紙讀占星欄，也讀一份日本報紙的占星欄。

她試著從占星欄裡的幾個漢字推敲出意思。這時她突然發現，她多麼像是在解開《數獨》的謎題啊？於是，在這一趟旅程中，她都看日本報紙。

窗外下著雨，她揉揉眼睛，靠在椅背上睡著了。

半路中，她動了一下，曨曨曨曨看見她那頂帽子掉到地上。她想伸手去撿起來，但她太睏了。

2

她在椅背上醒來時，看到窗外毛茸茸的飄雪，興奮得把臉貼到車窗上看雪。

看了一會，她轉過頭來，不禁怔住了。

她發現她那頂羊毛帽好端端的躺在旁邊沒人的位子上。

她悄悄探頭出去走道張望，這節車廂裡只有兩個結伴出遊的中年婦人，一個老男人和他年輕的情婦。

她拿起帽子看了看，重新戴回頭上，微微一笑。

這時，坐在走道另一面的其中一個中年婦人看過來，摸摸自己頭頂的白髮，又指指喜喜的頭頂，微笑咕噥了幾句她聽不懂的話。

原來是她不是他嗎？

喜喜臉上浮起失望的神情，笑不出來了。

她在長野站轉搭火車，在第三個站下車。

她拉著行李走出車站。

雪下大了，她伸出一雙手，一朵朵雪花飄落在她掌心裡。

這雪多美啊！哥哥。

她搭計程車到一幢附露天溫泉的民宿，在櫃台辦了住房手續。

她進了房間，換掉牆上的一幅浮世繪織布畫，掛上『星夜』。

然後，她換上旅館提供的日式浴衣，帶了一條小毛巾，踩著日本屐踢踢躂躂的到樓下去泡溫泉。

溫泉裡只有她一個人，她赤身露體走進冒著熱氣的繪木風呂，任由雪落在她白皙的肩膀上。

女子溫泉跟男子溫泉用一面竹牆分隔開，她把眼睛湊上去竹片的縫隙偷看，什麼也沒看見。

後來她發現，林克不住這兒，他住在附近另一幢較便宜的民宿。民宿外面有一個讓遊人泡腳的腳溫泉，她走到那邊泡了幾次腳。

她在長野待了兩個禮拜，每天拿著地圖出遊，在百貨公司買了一雙亮麗的草綠色毛絨手套，吃蕎麥麵吃得很滿足，夜晚泡完溫泉，就睡在榻榻米上。

然後，她一路坐火車北上，在秋田和青森待了幾個禮拜，直走札幌。

林克一路都裝成各樣的人物跟蹤她。

她把他的喬裝列成單子：

在長野時，他是拿著地圖的背囊客和穿著和服的壽司師傅。

110

在秋田時，他是穿著西裝和風衣，拎公事包的上班族和穿制服的餐廳服務生。

在青森時，他是白頭髮、蓄了鬍子的日本中年漢，手提包夾在腋下，走路八字腳。

到了札幌，他又變回穿藍夾克的背囊客。

這一回，她差點兒認不出他來。

離開札幌的前一天夜晚，她到大通公園去看雪祭，人潮摩肩接踵，彩燈映照在雪雕上，如夢似幻。

他跟丟了嗎？

她擠開人群往前走，好幾次故意停下來看雪雕，沒看見林克。

從大通公園出來，漫天飄雪，她哆哆嗦嗦地沿著人行道走向旅館的方向。

她一直往北走，遠離人潮，越過已經關門的商店街，穿過寂靜的車站，走上一條空蕩蕩的街道。

百貨公司打烊了，她食指的指尖在水氣朦朧的櫥窗上一路劃開去，在身後留下了一道綿長的彎彎曲曲的指痕。

走到拐角的那個櫥窗時，她發現走錯了路，猛然掉轉頭。

她瞥了一眼路口的一根圓形石柱，換另一隻手，順著她留在櫥窗上的指痕回頭再劃一遍。

猝然之間，她發現那道彎彎曲曲的指痕變寬了，似乎有另一隻手的指尖在她不覺時，撫過她留下的指痕。

她心頭一顫，沒敢回望。

她沒停步，微笑的幸福的指尖一路在那道變寬了的指痕上緩緩滑過去。

直到它消失在一根柱子前面，她才收回那隻凍僵了的白皙小手，貼到嘴唇上呵氣。

3

第二天，她搭火車從札幌北上釧路。這一回，林克終於跟她坐在同一個車廂。他一頭白髮，穿著樣式落後的西裝，拄著一根枴杖，喬裝成一個駝背的老人，步履蹣跚，在前排找到一個位子坐下來，跟坐在後排的她隔了十二行的距離。

一路上，兩個人走了那麼多的路，喜喜已經不再擔心林克會把她跟丟了。

她低下頭，專心推敲日本報紙上的占星欄，又看了一會書。車廂裡的暖氣和顛簸的車程使人懨懨欲睡。她睡著了。

她睡得不知人間何世，模糊中感覺有一隻手輕輕推了推她的肩膀。她沒理會，那隻手又推了她一下。

她張開眼睛醒來，看到面前一個朦朧的人影漸次清晰，穿制服的車掌對她微笑。他指指窗外，咕噥著日語，原來，火車已經抵達終站，其他人都下了車。

她連忙站起身拿行李。

這時，她看到喬裝成駝背老人的林克拄著枴杖顫巍巍地離開車廂。她走另一邊出口下車。

她拖著行李箱走出車站。

積雪深深，這裡比札幌更冷了。

她終於走到旅程的最後一站，踏足這片蒼茫的雪地。在那個夢裡，她是和哥哥搭上一列往北的火車的。

113

4

許多年以前，她曾經跟哥哥約定，等他們將來有錢，他們要一起流浪天涯。

生命中最早的記憶已然模糊，她依稀記得曾經跟哥哥衣衫襤褸的在街頭行乞度日。

然而，哥哥否定了她這段記憶。

哥哥說，是父母相繼病死之後，他們才被送到孤兒院的。兩個人從來就沒當過什麼小乞丐。

但她不相信哥哥。

她覺得父母不是病死的。她想像爸爸媽媽都是美麗的人兒。爸爸是著名的教授，經常帶著媽媽和他們兄妹倆在世界各地講學。有一天，他們搭的那班飛機在沙漠失事，機上的人全都死了，只有哥哥和她奇蹟地活了下來。

後來，她又改變了想法。

她幻想爸爸是一位足跡遍天下的自由攝影師，媽媽則是一位藝術家。她同哥哥

114

從小就跟著父母遊走世界，見過各式各樣的傳奇人物。他們是幸福的一家四口，直到一天，一場車禍奪走了一切，剩下她和哥哥相依為命。

日復一日，她不斷為這個故事加添許多細微末節，漸漸地，她自己都信以為真了。

她是靠著這個想像的故事來度過無數孤苦漫長的夜晚。

這時，風從她身邊呼嘯而過，雪花如煙雨般落下，就像那些風景玻璃球裡的雪景。她臉頰晶亮，拎著行李，匆匆搭上一輛計程車。

她在一家白雪覆蓋的小旅館落腳。附近一帶並沒有別的旅館，林克尾隨著她住了進來。

他由駝背老人變成了戴近視眼鏡和藍色羊毛帽的年輕遊客。

喜喜住二一一號房，他住二一二。

兩個人的房間只隔著一面空心牆。她把『星夜』掛到那面牆上。林克就睡在她隔壁，在她那幅『星夜』背後。

漫長的旅程中，這是頭一回嗎？林克就睡在她隔壁，在她那幅『星夜』背後。

起初的幾天，她簡直沒法睡好，也沒法專心看書。到了夜裡，她總是忍不住好

幾回把耳朵貼到那面牆上，心跳怦怦的偷聽他在房裡做什麼。

他很安靜。這是偵探的職業本能嗎？

他睡得不好。她聽到他三更半夜在房間裡踱步的聲音，也聽過他在床上輾轉的聲音。有一次，他甚至不小心把頭撞到床背上，發出『砰』的一聲。

他是不是有失眠症？還是他不習慣陌生的床？

他半夜睡不著的時候都做什麼？是做《數獨》？還是在黑暗中想念離他而去的前妻？這時候，他會感到寂寞嗎？

一天午夜，她聽到那面牆背後傳來一聲聲咳嗽。

林克著涼了嗎？

她擱下正在看的書，悄悄下床，躡手躡腳的走過去，頭倚在牆上，傾聽了許久。

他又咳了幾聲。她聽到他擤鼻子的聲音。

都是她不好，把他引來北方這片苦寒的雪地。

她把一張臉都貼了上去偷聽。由於太專心，她頭頂撞到那張『星夜』。畫掉下來的時候，她及時用一雙手接住了，這才沒有發出聲音。

116

她一隻手按在胸口上，驚魂甫定，喘了一口大氣，輕輕把畫掛回去，溜回床上。

他們走了那麼多的路，她想起自己還是頭一回聽到林克的聲音，卻只有咳嗽聲。

後來的一天夜裡，她在床上翻來覆去睡不著，猝然之間，她聽到那面牆後面悠悠盪來一把女人的幽怨微弱的歌聲。

5

她亮起了頭上的一盞小黃燈坐起來，掀開被子下床，裸著腳走過去，背貼牆上。

林克是在聽歌嗎？

歌聲悠悠流轉，如魔似幻，如泣似訴，是『秘密花園』的〈夜曲〉。

她的背依戀著牆，心弦顫動。

她伸出下巴，像貓兒般抬起一條腿，身上穿著單薄的蓋到腳踝的白色睡裙，抱住胳膊，跟自己慢舞。她舞過蒙霜的窗邊，飄過床沿，滑到那張『星夜』底下，驅身在房間裡亂轉。歌聲絲絲縷縷的不曾停歇，依稀可聞。直到她跳累了，摔倒在床上。

這天晚上，她睡得很甜。

第二天上午，她幾乎把所有禦寒的衣服都穿在身上，戴上帽子、圍巾和手套，臃腫地離開旅館。

積雪很深。十一點鐘，她走在渺無邊際、一片蒼茫的濕原上。她在雪中獨步，身後留下一個個足印，馬上又被落雪覆蓋。

人們去看丹頂鶴。她沒去。

她害怕大鳥，害怕胖鸚鵡，也害怕鷹。

哥哥曾經告訴她，鷹會吃腐肉和屍體。從此以後，她看到鷹都會全身起雞皮疙瘩。

雪大塊大塊地落下。

118

這裡好冷啊！哥哥。她裏緊身上的大衣。

跟哥哥一起浪跡天涯的約定，從來就沒有兌現過。

倒是她跟另一個人來了。

哥哥到底跑哪裡去了啊？為什麼一去無蹤？

她哭了，伸手到後面，想要把被風掀開了的、綴著毛邊的大衣帽兜重新拉回來。她笨拙地拉了好幾次，想放棄的時候，終於拉到了。她覺得自己好像曾經碰到另一隻手。

以前每年她生日，哥哥都會送她禮物，唱片、手鍊、書包、書……哥哥常常說：

『你看那麼多的書，不怕將來變成近視妹嗎？』

離開漫原，她在百貨店買了一雙長襪給自己，今年這一雙是魚網襪。

六點鐘，她去吃了海鮮飯，喝了兩瓶清酒。

九點十分，她走進旅館附近的一家酒館。

她脫下帽子、頸巾和臃腫的大衣，拉住手套的指尖把手套扯下來甩在桌子上，

119

坐在窗邊的那一桌。

林克不在這兒，這兒太小了，他沒法藏身。

她估計他是在對街那家彈珠店裡。

她用手抹了抹窗子上濛濛的水氣，偷偷看過去。那兒亮著燈，她看到一排坐在彈珠機前面的背影。

她又抹抹窗子，外面的雪下大了。她眼睛花花的。

她感覺一張臉發燙，眼前的一切開始變得有點朦朧。

她吃了烤魚、牛肉和豆腐，喝了好多杯燒酒。

這酒很烈啊！哥哥。

她雙手撐著桌子，醉茫茫地站起身，穿上大衣，到櫃台付錢。

雪茫茫。

她從酒館出來，蹣跚走在雪地上，走了幾步，腳下一滑，摔了一跤。

她七手八腳爬起來，一雙手凍僵了，這時，她在大衣的口袋裡找到一隻手套，

卻找不到另一隻。

她看看身邊，沒看到那隻手套，說不定忘在酒館裡了。

120

她搖搖晃晃的往回走，又回到酒館去。

她推開酒館那扇木門，看到她那隻草綠色的毛絨手套孤零零地掉在桌子底下。

她果然把它留了在這兒。她微笑著走過去，拉開椅子坐下來，想俯身撿起手套。

但是，那隻手套離她好遠啊！

她的手無奈地縮回來，趴在桌上，臉埋手臂裡，覺得頭很昏，迷迷糊糊睡著了。

當她醒來的時候，她發現自己躺在旅館的床上，蓋著被子，身上依然穿著那身臃腫的衣服。

她那雙綠色手套跟那本《百年孤寂》挨在一起，好好的躺在床頭的矮櫃上，旁邊擱著一杯水。

她坐起來，擰亮頭上的一盞小黃燈，口中乾澀，把杯裡的水喝光。

她覺得熱，脫掉身上的衣服丟到腳邊，拿起手套和書看了看。

林克翻過這本書嗎？他是什麼時候走的？

121

掛著『星夜』的那面牆背後，悄然無聲。

她抱著書，輕柔柔地滑進被窩裡，重又睡著了。

那個夜晚他睡不著，一直在想那個女孩子，心中充滿對她的慾望和憐憫。

他很想去愛她，守護她。

6

四月的時候，喜喜從札幌飛回香港。

她住進蘭花旅館三〇三號房，把牆上那張小蒼蘭的掛像丟到五斗櫃後面，換上《星夜》。

當天晚上，她把在旅途上長出來的頭髮剪成貼頭的劉海，然後染上紫紅色。

她現在看起來像十九歲。

紫色是雙魚座的幸運色。

她在香港機場失去了林克的蹤影。夜晚，她在附近酒吧喝桃子味伏特加的時候

又見到他。

他一個人喝白蘭地，做《數獨》。

第二天，她下午離開旅館時，看到他臉上架著一副太陽眼鏡，身穿藍夾克，混

在對街巴士站等車的隊伍之中，手上拿著筆，低著頭做《數獨》。

他解不開謎題的時候，會不會忍不住偷看書底的答案？

他到底總共有幾件藍夾克啊？

今天早上她打開電腦看戴德禮電郵過來的跟蹤報告。回顧他們剛剛完成的那段

旅程，林克拍的，全是她走路的照片：機場、車站、碼頭、公園、雪地、濕原……

她追趕巴士、轉火車，走在人潮如鯽的熱鬧大街上……

在林克眼中，彷彿她的一雙腳從來不曾停下來。

只有無家的人，才會一直走路吧？

她往東走，在一個報檔停下來，買了報紙，邊走邊讀占星欄。

自從哥哥在她十歲那年送她一本封面印有黃道十二宮圖的占星書，她從此愛上

了占星術。

誰可一窺星辰的奧秘？

凡人只可拈星微笑。

不管哪一天，只要她那天還想要知道今天的占星欄怎麼說，跟昨天又有什麼不同？金星進入雙魚宮會不會有新的際遇？那麼，她就有活下去的力量和好奇心。

心腸太軟只會害苦自己。

凡事要量力而為，

善良的雙魚無法拒絕。

朋友會找你幫忙，

讀完占星欄，她打電話給碧碧。

『碧碧，我是喜喜。我改電話了。』她報上電話。『以後有選角打這個電話找我喔……我還好啦……我跟哥哥一起去旅行了，昨天剛回來……我哥……我哥比我大五歲，我們很親。介紹給你？你失戀了麼？你什麼星座？金牛？那不行啊……我哥是天蠍。蠍子跟金牛這一對，注定有性沒愛……西門慶跟潘金蓮就是著名的蠍子男

配金牛女，沒結果的……況且，我哥已經有女朋友了……』

五點鐘，她帶著在旅途上做的幾件首飾到小綠的店裡。

小綠一看到她，高興得好像遇到救世主似的，嚷著：

『我打電話找你好幾遍了！為什麼你給我的那個號碼找不到你啊？』

『我改電話了喔。』她報上電話，然後從包包裡掏出一個黑色的絲絨布袋，把首飾倒在玻璃櫃上。

『你可以替我看店嗎？』小綠問。

『今天？』

『不是今天，是從這個周末開始，只要三個禮拜。我要去印度旅行，本來有個朋友答應幫忙，臨時又說不行。真是急死我了！』

占星欄裡說的朋友原來是小綠，不是碧碧。

『好喔！』喜喜爽快答應。

『噢！太好了！我買絲巾回來送你喔！』

小綠摸摸喜喜柔軟的紫髮說道。

125

『你就有本事染什麼顏色都好看。』

『你不能只用一種顏色，你得自己調色。』她說著把她做的一顆紫水晶戒指套在手指上看看。

這回林克沒法只拍她走路的樣子吧？他總得拍下她看店的模樣啊。

打那個周末開始，喜喜每天下午離開旅館回首飾店去，在店裡待一整天，有時看書，有時招呼客人，跟客人聊天。遇上三心兩意的客人，她就說老實話，告訴對方，哪一件飾物值得買。

有幾個客人稱讚她的紫色頭髮漂亮，其中一個很時髦的，說她的紫髮可愛得像一根腮紅掃。喜喜把她用的染髮劑品牌告訴她們，又告訴她們是哪個號碼的紫跟哪個號碼的紅調色。結果，客人回家染了紫髮之後常來光顧。

林克一下子看到那麼多紫頭髮的女人進出首飾店，會不會一頭霧水，某天跟蹤錯了另一個人？

每天晚上，喜喜關店之後就去吃飯，喝桃子味伏特加。

林克每天陪她上班下班。他成天待在路口那家茶餐廳裡，守護著她。

126

子，時不時伸手摸摸露在牛仔夾克上的一截頸背。

喜喜好奇地偷瞄了他一眼。他不到三十歲，一臉傲氣，卻又一副心不在焉的樣

他先是在櫥窗外面駐足看了一會，然後直板板的走進來，裝著瀏覽貨架上的首飾。

7

很短，像是在軍營裡似的，約莫五呎十吋，越過馬路朝她走來。

駕駛座上走下來一個男人，穿牛仔夾克、汗衫和棉褲，瘦瘦的肩膀，頭髮剪得

停在對街。

一天，她望著外面發獃的時候，看到一輛黑色跑車駛過之後又慢慢倒車回來，

流和路人。

店裡沒有客人的時候，她坐在櫃台裡，隔著櫥窗玻璃看向外面，看著來往的車

到了五月，天氣回暖，她收起靴子，換上涼鞋和薄衣裳。

一會兒之後，他掉頭過來，走到櫃台前面，帶著些許微笑向喜喜求助：

喜喜問道：

『我想買一份禮物送人，不知道買什麼好⋯⋯』

『是送給女朋友的嗎？』

『不⋯⋯是送給我妹妹的。』

『你妹妹喜歡什麼首飾？』

他摸摸頸背，答道：

『我不是很清楚⋯⋯』

『那她年紀有多大？』

他看看她，說：

『跟你差不多。』

『你知道她是什麼星座的嗎？』她探問。

他好像沒想到她會這麼一問。他假裝思索，然後說：

『呃⋯⋯我不懂星座⋯⋯』

她又問：

『你記不記得她的生日是哪一天？』

他隨意回答：

『十一月……好像是七號，還是八號？』

她盯著他，懶懶地說：

『你根本沒有妹妹……對嗎？』

他被她揭穿時，摸著頸背，露出窘困的樣子。這時，原有的傲氣消失了。他有點尷尬，也有點憂鬱地說：

『我原本有一個小妹子……』他用手在大腿旁邊比了一個高度。『她很小的時候死了，只有三歲，是病死的。』

她心都軟了，同情地望著他。

她幹嘛要揭穿他啊？

『但你還是可以買點什麼給她的。』她溫柔地說。

她以贖罪的心情替他挑了一條綴滿星星的銀手鍊，戴到手腕上比給他看，說：

『你看這些星星做得多漂亮！不管她是哪個星座，都會喜歡。』

『好的，我就要這個。』

他買下那條手鍊。

幾天後的一個夜晚，他又來了，樣子有點累，說他剛剛做完工作，經過這附近，想起她，問她想不想一起吃頓飯。

這時，店裡的音響流轉著一首歌。

看你看我的傻模樣……

牽著你的手，

好想談一場戀愛，

夏日的夜晚，

她關上店門，跟他出去了。

他叫馬林，那天吃飯時打趣說自己是小犬座，實際是雙子座，明年五月二十三日將滿二十九歲。

馬林，跟林克有一個字相同。

喜喜不期然聯想到福爾馬林，一種用來製標本和屍體的防腐劑。

她也想到福爾摩斯。

中學時是推理學會會長，如今當上私家偵探的林克，也一定讀過，甚至迷過福爾摩斯吧？

馬林九年前跟另外三個人組織了一支搖滾樂隊，出過一張不暢銷的唱片，已經沒有太多人記得了。這支失意樂隊在不同的酒吧、俱樂部和派對表演，有一票奇裝異服，看來像離家少女和小怨婦的歌迷跟著他們。

喜喜以前從沒聽過他們的歌。

她不愛搖滾。

他喜歡她，因為她竟然不喜歡搖滾，因為她竟然沒聽過他們的歌，因為她竟然不知道〈苦悶妮可兒〉這首歌。

一天晚上，他陪她走路回旅館。他有點驕傲地提起這首歌。喜喜隨口問：

『是誰唱的？』

他一臉失望：

『你沒聽過？』

喜喜微笑搖頭。

馬林突然就站在人來人往的夜街上，大聲清唱起他寫的這首〈苦悶妮可兒〉。

途人紛紛轉過頭來看他們，有人駐足。

他得意地瞄了喜喜一眼，像個在街頭賣唱的藝人似的，繼續陶醉地高歌。

她抱著手臂欣賞他忘情的演出。

等他唱完，途人陸續散去了，喜喜拍拍手掌，然後從荷包裡掏出一個銅板丟給他。

馬林伸手接住她丟過來的那個銅板，臉上露出一副洩氣的模樣。

她的眼睛淘氣地笑了。

『誰是妮可兒？這首歌是為她而寫的嗎？她是你喜歡過的女人嗎？』喜喜心裡想著，始終沒開口問。

愛上一個人，是不是都由沒道理的嫉妒開始的？

她的目光斜斜地越過馬林的側臉看到那個穿藍夾克的落寞身影。

林克本來跟他們並排走在對面的人行道上，漸漸落後了。

嫉妒是愛情的徒刑。

8

喜喜每天晚上都去聽馬林那支樂隊演唱。到了九月，她已經跟他們跑過不同的

酒吧、夜總會和狂歌熱舞的派對了。

樂隊的另外三個人：喬、韓和小北，她全都熟絡了。他們是夜貓子，都愛喝

酒，沒有一個愛喝伏特加。喬和韓抽菸抽得很凶。小北會趁馬林不在的時候逗她說

話，向她放電。

當她跟他們一起的時候，林克像一頭忠心的大黃狗那樣，總是在附近守護著

她。

她眼看那幾個像離家少女，也像小怨婦的歌迷在喬、韓和小北身上輪流轉手，

今天跟這個，明天跟另一個。

那天晚上，在一個擠滿人的派對上，其他人都溜到舞池上跳舞，他們那一桌只

留下她和馬林。

她呷著桃子味伏特加，把玩著歌迷丟在椅子上的一個鈴鼓。

他喝著啤酒。

她問他：

『你以前也跟歌迷搞嗎？』

他噘噘嘴，好像受了委屈似的：

『我從來不跟歌迷搞。』

他又說：

『我已經警告過喬他們很多次了，別跟歌迷胡搞，他們就是不聽。這些女孩子太小了。』

她望著他：

『要是你妹妹還在，也是跟她們這個年紀嗎？』

馬林略顯傷感，喃喃說：

『比她們大一兩年……』

喜喜搖著手裡的鈴鼓，說：

『要是我死了，我哥哥一定會很傷心。他很疼我。他會摸著我的頭對我說，我是他的驕傲。小時候，我們住在海邊的房子裡，到了夜晚，常常會傳來呼呼的風聲

和蛤蟆的咕咕叫聲。』

鈴鼓哐啷啷的響，她繼續說：

『哥哥的睡房在我的睡房隔壁。我怕黑，他會捲起被舖和枕頭走過來我的房間，睡在我床邊的地毯上，一直陪著我，直到我睡著才離開。他告訴我，那些蛤蟆也是因為怕黑，所以咕咕叫。要是我怕黑，我就是蛤蟆！』

她笑著接下去說：

『他又會把枕頭當成吉他，唱歌給我聽！我都忘了他唱的那些歌，有一首好像是這樣的⋯⋯』

她手在鈴鼓上輕輕打拍子，湊到耳邊傾聽。

馬林的手搭在她的肩膀上，問道：

『你哥哥是做什麼的？』

她說：

『哥哥是開小型運輸飛機的。不過，不是在這裡，是在西非⋯⋯』

馬林臉露一個好奇和讚嘆的表情。

她說：

135

『哥哥的飛機運貨，運人，也運動物。那些坐飛機的動物，要不是鎖在特製的鐵籠裡，就是上機前已經注射了麻醉藥的，免得牠們受驚。有一回，哥哥運過一隻長頸鹿……』

她把鈴鼓放到頭頂上，伸長脖子說：

『由於長頸鹿實在太長了，沒有適合的籠子，只好讓牠捱一劑麻醉藥。一群工作人員七手八腳把牠扛上機艙時，牠簡直就是從機頭睡到機尾，一雙腳一直頂住艙門……』

她收回脖子說：

『哥哥說，長頸鹿睡著時也會夢囈和流口水，但牠真的是太長太長了，牠上機時流出來的一滴口水，到飛機降落時，都還沒流到脖子的一半……』

她笑笑說：

『不過，我知道這個笑話一定是他編出來逗我笑的。哥哥也運過猩猩，他說看到猩猩就想起我，因為我手臂好長……』

她把手伸到馬林面前。

馬林吻了那隻手。

136

『我好喜歡聽哥哥說西非的故事啊！我們約定，每年都會在西非一個地方見面⋯⋯』

她喝光了杯裡的伏特加，望著舞池上方那盞流轉如飛的巨型彩色吊燈，咬著唇，默然無語。

馬林突然說：

『你有沒有發現有個男人好像老是在你出現的地方附近出現？』

她驀然一驚，問道：

『是你嗎？』

馬林撇撇嘴：

『是另一個人！高高的，一副不修邊幅的模樣。我見過他好幾次了，你竟然沒發覺嗎？』他忽然指住喜喜身後的遠處。『你看！』

她心裡微顫，故意慢慢才回頭看去。她身後的遠處是吧台，那兒擠滿了人。

她沒看見林克。

她鎮靜地問：

『你要我看什麼啊？』

馬林醺醺醉意地說：

『我剛剛好像看到他在那邊……』

她說：

『是哪一個啊？』

他的目光找了一會，皺著眉說：

『現在不見了……』

她把頭轉回來，說道：

『你有沒有試過同一天裡，在不同的地方，竟然碰到同一個陌生人兩次？有些人，就是會剛好也去你去的地方……有些人就是會剛好也愛上你愛上的人……』

她醉茫茫地笑笑：

『我的意思是，生命中有很多偶然……雖然世上有千千萬萬的人，時間不斷流轉，你還是會在某天某地跟他相遇……這是命運啊……』

她扯到哪裡去了？彷彿她說了那麼多的話，只是為了拖延時間，給林克機會溜走似的。

夜總會沸騰著人聲和笑聲，她失去了她忠心的大黃狗的蹤影。

138

馬林牽住她握著鈴鼓的那隻手說：

『那個傢伙說不定迷戀上你，所以成天跟蹤你……不知道哪天會突然撲出來……』

喜喜朝馬林吐吐舌頭：

『你別嚇我好不好？』

馬林把她抱在懷裡：

『不用怕！要是他敢對你做什麼，我會宰了他！』

她喃喃說：

『可是……根本就沒那個人。』

到了十月的最後一天，喜喜收到戴德禮電郵過來的跟蹤報告。

這幾個月來，她明明幾乎每天都跟馬林一起，馬林有時候在她旅館的房間裡過夜。可是，這一份報告就跟之前的幾份報告一樣，相片中只有她一個人。

她在酒吧外面踽踽獨行……

她從不同的夜總會走出來……

139

她在人行道上邊走邊讀報紙的占星欄……

她走過燈火闌珊的夜街，一臉落寞……

報告裡，連提都沒提過馬林、喬、韓或小北。

這是哪門子跟蹤報告啊？

她把報告存檔，關掉電腦。

五點鐘，她離開旅館，在便利店買了報紙和一盒『漁夫』原味喉糖。

她早上起來就開始覺得喉嚨不舒服，一定是前一天在酒吧裡吸了太多韓和喬吐出來的二手煙。

她吞了一顆喉糖，邊走邊打開報紙讀占星欄。

深情又時刻渴望愛人關注的巨蟹，

今天將會飽受嫉妒的折磨。

別讓妒忌使你失去理智，

愛一個人，

要懂得給他一點空間，

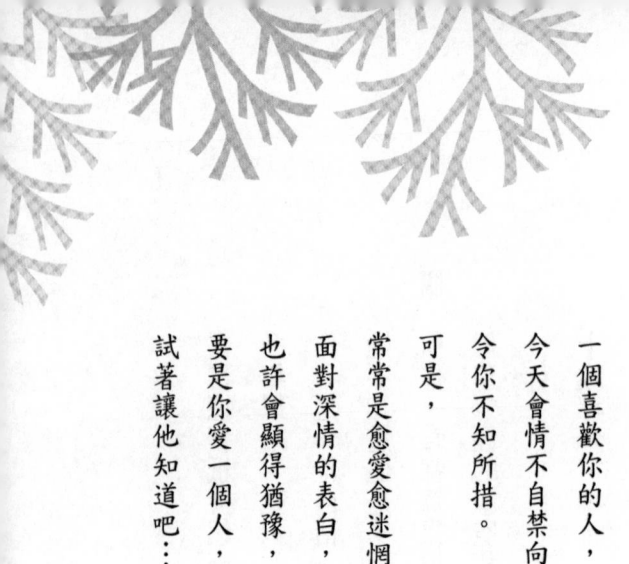

喜喜微微一笑，繼續讀雙魚座那幾行。

別用你的蟹爪子把他抓得太牢⋯⋯

一點自由和一點任性的權利，

一點時間，

可是，

今天會情不自禁向你表白心跡，

一個喜歡你的人，

令你不知所措。

常常是愈愛愈迷惘的雙魚，

面對深情的表白，

也許會顯得猶豫，

要是你愛一個人，

試著讓他知道吧⋯⋯

喜喜把報紙折起來。

多年以來，她只愛讀這個占星欄。

作者是一位自稱『星座小侏儒』的占星家。

她不知道他是男是女，是高是矮，是老的是年輕的，還是果真是個慧黠的小侏儒。但他一直都算得很準。

仰望無涯的星空和神秘不可測的宇宙奧秘時，我們不都只是一個小侏儒麼？

十歲那年，哥哥送她那本封面印有黃道十二宮圖的占星書。她指著圖，問哥哥：

『這是什麼啊哥哥？』

哥哥說：

『這個嘛……是星座圖，我們每個人都屬於其中一顆星……』

哥哥指給她看：

『這是太陽，這是月亮，你是這一顆……我是那一顆……天蠍跟雙魚距離有這

麼遠⋯⋯』

『哥哥，』她抬眼凝望著哥哥，紅了一張臉說。『我好喜歡有你做我的哥哥。』

夜晚十點四十分，星星都已經紛紛出來露臉了。喜喜抵達夜總會外面，看到等著進去的長長的人龍。

守在門口的兩男一女接待員認得她是馬林的朋友，拉開門口圍欄上的一根繩子讓她進去。

那個女的接待員遞給她一張巫婆面具。

9

這一天是洋人的萬聖節。

她戴上面具進去夜總會。

這麼一來，想吃顆喉糖就有點困難了。

音樂吵個不停，到處都是人，她看到一堆吸血鬼，木乃伊、千年古屍、怪臉修女、頭頂上插著一把刀的淌血女鬼、科學怪人、穿黑白間條囚衣，腳踝上拖著鎖鍊和鐵球的囚犯、爛面男鬼和鐘樓駝俠。

那個扮成木乃伊的男人待會要怎麼上廁所啊？

喜喜用手擠開人群，走到吧台那兒，要了杯桃子味伏特加。

她把面具往上掀開些，啜了一口酒。

馬林、喬、韓和小北在台上唱著歌。

有一隻吸血鬼看到她掀開面具，走來跟她搭訕。她想告訴他，女巫好像從沒跟吸血鬼搞過。但她什麼也沒說，吸血鬼很沒趣地找修女去了。

一個鐘頭過去了，馬林他們還在台上。

他們又唱了那首〈苦悶妮可兒〉。

她一度踮高腳尖朝馬林揮揮手，馬林也朝她揮手。

她喝了三杯桃子味伏特加，吞下五顆喉糖，膀胱脹脹的。

她穿過擠滿人的舞池，突然有一隻手不知道從哪裡伸出來抓住她的肩膀。她回

頭一看，那人誤會了她是另一個巫婆，道過歉，走開了。

她穿過長長的走廊，終於來到洗手間。

科學怪人從女洗手間出來。喜喜沒想到她是個女的。

她對著洗手間的鏡子挪了挪那張面具，她現在是個紫髮女巫，有一管可怕的勾

鼻子。

要是她變成這樣，還有誰會愛她啊？

除了哥哥。

她拉開洗手間那扇重甸甸的金屬大門走出去。

走廊上飄著香味的白色霧氣，她咳嗽了幾聲，覺得面具後面有股醉意。

這時，一個戴著木乃伊面具的高大形影從走廊的另一端朝她直直地走來，身上

穿著一件藍夾克。

她悚然一驚。

但她不能停步不前，否則，他會懷疑。

她慢慢往前走，面具背後的那雙眼睛盡量不去看他。

可是，當他走近她，跟她只隔著幾吋的距離時，他突然就停在她跟前。

她沒法不仰頭看他。

他也在看她。

四目交投的一刻，她看到了木乃伊面具背後一雙欲語無言的多情大眼睛。

那雙眼睛猶豫著。

猝然之間，他挪開了腳步，欠身讓她通過。

喜喜點頭表示謝意。

她的一顆心都快跳出來了。

令你不知所措⋯⋯

一個喜歡你的人，

今天會情不自禁向你表白心跡，

她從他身邊走過時，看到那件藍夾克的一邊口袋裡露出一本書的一角

她不用看也知道那本是《數獨》。

她沒回頭，直往前走。

她終於出了舞池，擠開比剛剛更多的人群，擠到吧台那兒，點了一杯桃子味伏特加。

酒保好忙，她兩個手肘支在吧台上等著。

她覺得喉嚨乾澀，禁不住用手掩著嘴巴低頭大聲咳嗽了起來。

一隻大手這時從後面輕輕拍她的背。

她全身一陣震顫，不知所措，沒敢回頭，咳嗽也止不住。

10

那隻手一直在輕拍。

她咳完了，緩緩轉頭過去，看到一張淌血的爛面。

馬林把那張爛面鬼的面具扯下來，笑著說：

「有個男人這樣替你拍背，你也不看看是誰？你怎知道一定是我？」

她沙啞著聲音說：

『我就知道是你，你拍背也跟拍子……』

馬林一臉糊塗：

『我有嗎？我哪有？』

她望著馬林，他臉上淌汗。這雙眼睛比她剛剛在走廊上遇到的那雙眼睛快樂多了。

她的心跳緩下來了。

深情又渴望愛人關注的巨蟹，今天會飽受嫉妒的折磨……

她到底希望剛剛那一隻停留在她背上的是誰的手啊？

『你總共喝了幾杯？』馬林問道。

她酒意醺醺，碎碎唸道：

『我還沒開始喝呢……』

那個酒保壓根兒忘了她那杯伏特加。

『我們去跳舞吧。』馬林把她拉到舞池。

擠擁的舞池上，他們互相纏繞著起舞，馬林兩隻手放在她彎翹的臀上。

她的喉糖已經吃光了。

她又咳嗽了幾聲。

一隻大手輕拍她的背。

她抬起臉，微笑望著馬林：『你又拍我嘍？』

『我沒有啊……』

他的一雙手一直擱在她的臀上。

她驀然摟著他轉過身去，幾張木乃伊面具在她眼前有如幻影般飄過。

她眼花了，把馬林摟得更緊，對他笑。

『我是不是好愛你啊？』她喃喃說道。

她是不是應該結束這一切了？

明天就打給戴德禮。

馬林在她耳邊問：

『你剛剛說什麼來著？』

149

她沒說什麼，剛剛那個是問題。

她臉貼他的臉，輕柔柔地說：

『有一年聖誕節，我在學校的舞會上表演，哥哥來看我。那是我頭一次當主角，有一段獨舞。我太緊張了，一上台就摔了一跤。』

她繼續說：『回去的路上，我一句話也不肯說，只是垂著頭走路，我那顆頭愈垂愈低，差不多貼到肚子去了。哥哥一直陪在我身邊沒說話。直到天黑了，我還不願回家。哥哥突然很認真地說：「喜喜，你一直盯著地上看，要是撿到錢的話，我們要平分喔⋯⋯」那一刻，我們兩個都咯咯大笑出聲來。』

她頭挨在馬林的肩膀上，看向他背後一張張如魔似幻的面具。

這時，她已經打消了明天去找戴德禮的念頭。

一天早上，她在旅館的床上醒來，推開窗，看到一部白色的家庭車在下面緩緩駛過，車頂上綁著一棵褐綠色、胖嘟嘟毛茸茸的聖誕樹，樹幹底部釘著一個木造的腳架，用一張銀色紙裹著。

這一天是聖誕節前兩天。

一年又過去了。

11

喜喜穿上米色風衣和紅色皮短靴，拎著一袋舊衣服出去。

她把舊衣服拿去捐給救世軍。臨近聖誕，送東西來的人比平日多，她排隊等了一會。

終於輪到她時，那個女職員認得她，一味稱讚她的紫紅色頭髮很漂亮。

喜喜摸著頭髮微笑。

她這頭髮沒法捐出來啊！

今天的占星欄寫道：

臨近聖誕，

周遭充滿歡樂，

151

接近神聖的東西會對你有好處……

她瞧了一眼掛在牆上那個耶穌被釘的十字架,把原本打算拿去小綠的店賣的幾件首飾一併捐了出來。

今天不用去小綠的店了。

她在熱鬧的大街上漫步,瀏覽百貨公司的櫥窗。四周擠滿趕著買聖誕禮物的人潮,不斷有人塞給她減價和大抽獎的傳單,她總共見到三個聖誕老人和五棵掛滿飾物的聖誕樹,其中一棵會發光。

她在百貨公司裡買了一雙減價的深紅色絹面高跟鞋,鞋頭上飾著一朵紫紅色的玫瑰花。

從百貨公司出來時,她已經穿上了新的鞋子,不時低頭欣賞腳下的玫瑰。

四點鐘,她坐在酒館裡,蹺起腿,啜著桃子味伏特加,靜靜地讀徐四金的《香水》。

看書時,她喜歡猜書裡的主角是哪個星座的。譬如說,為了追逐香味而謀殺少女的調香師葛奴乙這個人,會是什麼星座的?

會不會是守護神是地獄之王普爾德的天蠍座？

喜歡掌控一切的獅子座？

還是出人意表地，竟是戀家的巨蟹？

喜喜從書裡抬起眼睛溜了一眼周圍，心裡覺得納悶，她好像一整天都沒發現林克。

六點二十分，她走路回去旅館。

旅館大廳中央豎起了一棵瘦巴巴的聖誕樹，上面綴滿一個個閃亮的小燈泡。

她在樹旁走過，搭電梯上三樓。

出了電梯，她停在三〇三號房的門前，掏出一把鑰匙開門。

她開門走進漆黑的房間，覺得腳下好像踢到一樣東西。她伸手在門邊的牆上摸索著，燈亮了起來。她低頭一看，一個白色的信封就在她腳邊。

她放下手裡的東西，關上門後撿起那個信封。

她把信封翻過來看。

那上面用藍色原子筆寫著：『路喜喜小姐』。

她好奇地摸了摸那個信封，裡面裝的似乎是照片。她走到床邊，把信封口撕

153

開，伸手進去。

裡面沒有信，有幾張照片露了出來。

她取出照片。

第一張是馬林在街上親暱地牽著一個女人的手。那個女人約莫三十歲，長得不錯，穿著一襲寬鬆的裙子，肚子凸了出來，至少也有五到六個月的身孕。

第二張是馬林跟同一個有身孕的女人，兩個人中間坐著一個三四歲的小男孩，女人餵孩子吃東西。那男孩長得簡直就像是跟馬林同一個模子倒出來的。三個人正在吃飯，

第三張是在屋外偷拍的。同一個女人，站在窗前，臉露幸福的微笑。馬林從背後摟著她，雙手放在她圓鼓鼓的肚子上，女人的一雙手握著馬林的手。

三張照片裡，那個孕婦右手的手腕上都戴著一串綴滿星星的銀手鍊。這串手鍊是馬林第一天來首飾店時，喜喜替他挑給他口中那個三歲時死去的妹妹的。

最後一張照片，是馬林在他那輛黑色跑車前座，跟一個女孩子親熱。喜喜認得，那個女孩是他們的歌迷。

這些照片全都是最近拍的。

她跌坐在床緣，一張臉痛苦地扭曲成一團。憤怒和悔恨在她胸中有如巨浪般急促起伏，她感到雙腳一陣痙攣，使得鞋頭上的玫瑰也在抖顫。

她咬著嘴唇，鼻翼翕動。

原來，她正在拚命用鼻子呼吸。

這時，一串輕快的鈴聲響起，是她的手機。她乏力地伸手到後面把丟在床尾的包包拉過來，掏出手機。

『喜喜，我到了，你還不下來？』

她站起來，離開床，走到窗邊，看到馬林那輛黑色跑車停在下面。

五分鐘之後，她從旅館出來。

馬林坐在車裡，一雙手擱在方向盤上，眼望前方，輕搖著腦袋。

他在聽音樂，沒看見她。

喜喜直直地走上去。馬林看到她了，朝她笑。

但她沒上車。

她繞到馬林那邊，從風衣的口袋裡掏出那四張照片，夾在擋風玻璃跟雨刷之

155

間。

她沒回看馬林一眼。

交通燈號誌剛剛轉成綠色，車流開始移動，她衝過馬路，後面的車子不停向她

大聲響號。

她大步沿著人行道走，經過一列繽紛的商店櫥窗。

馬林追了上來，生氣地問道：

「你找私家偵探跟蹤我？」

她終於看了他一眼，一臉悲傷。

真好笑！她找私家偵探跟蹤的是她自己。

她繼續往前走，眼裡滾動著憤怒的淚水。

馬林抓住她一條手臂，柔聲說：

「喜喜，我們上車再說。」

她拽開他。

他糾纏著不放手。

她冷冷地說：

『你根本就沒有妹妹，對吧？』

馬林沒回答，想要拉她走。

『走吧！我們上車！』

『放手！』她使勁甩開他。

這時，不知道哪裡走出來一個聖誕老人裝扮的胖子，橫在他們中間，一個勁地攬住馬林。

『先生，聖誕快樂！』

喜喜撇開馬林，頭也不回地往前走。

『你幹嘛！你放開我！喜喜！』

『耶穌愛你！』

『愛你老子！』

她愈走愈遠。高樓大廈外牆的聖誕燈飾紛紛亮了起來，一波波的人潮在她身邊推擠著。她雙手插在身上風衣的兩個口袋裡，垂首走路。

要是哥哥在，一定不會放過任何一個欺負她的人。假使有人欺負她，她會跟那人說：

157

『哼!你去跟我哥哥說!』

街上沸騰著人聲、車聲、笑聲。有人向她問路,她隨手指向身後。一個乞婦向她討錢,她沒看見。有幾個拎著購物袋的人不小心撞倒她,跟她說對不起。她沒理會,因為她在哭。

人聲、車聲、笑聲都遠去了。她走過無人的昏暗長街,聽到歌聲和琴聲。

她抬頭,看到一座尚未關門的教堂,裡面亮著溫柔的燈火。

她踏上幾級台階,走了進去。

這時已經十點半鐘。她在一排長椅上坐下來。教堂裡還有二十幾個人。點著蠟燭的祭壇那兒,十來個披著雪白袍子的詩班成員正在練習聖誕詩歌,伴奏的漂亮修女那雙手在黑白琴鍵上翻飛徘徊。

通往祭壇的走道上,一個高個子的年輕男孩把聖誕的裝飾彩帶掛到天花板去,另外幾個男孩和女孩在下面扶著梯子,仰頭看他,低聲指點點。

一個手裡握著念珠的老婦跪在一排椅子前面喃喃祈禱。

喜喜抬眼望著教堂前方的聖母憐子像。聖母低垂著慈愛的眼睛,望著懷中的嬰兒。嬰兒頭上有一圈光暈,眼睛睜得大大的,透露著亙古的寂寥。

那雙新買的絹面紅鞋把她腳跟的皮都磨破了，正在淌血。喜喜把鞋子從腳上脫下來，擱在腳邊。

她淚眼模糊地讀著一本經書。

後來，她把經書放回去前面的椅背上，起身走出走道。

她看到林克在後面的一排椅子，靠近路口坐著。

他身穿那件藍夾克，手指相扣，閉上眼睛低頭祈禱。

她走過他身邊時，瞥見他腳上穿的是一雙聖誕老人的黑色圓頭膠靴子。

出了教堂，她往右走。

她就知道今天是誰把那個信封塞進她的門縫裡。

林克以為自己是誰啊？她有叫他這麼做嗎？他幹嘛要多管閒事？難道他真的以為她那麼笨，永遠不會發現馬林的秘密？他分明是嘲笑她有眼無珠。他看不起她愛的人。

她心中惱火，好想衝上去狠狠揍他一頓。

她彎過拐角時，陡然煞住腳步，掉轉頭往回走。

林克果然冷不防她在這裡掉頭，他差一點就避不開。就在這時，他突然轉右，

那兒剛好有一幢幾層高的小公寓，他手插褲袋，泰然自若地走進去。

她走過時，看到他背對著她，裝作一個歸來的住客，摸出一把鑰匙，準備開門。

她本來可以走上去，等著看他打不開門的窘態。可是，她突然又不恨他了。

她若無其事，繼續往燈亮的地方走。

她回去教堂，找到她忘在那兒的那雙紅鞋。

她拎著鞋，光著腳走出教堂。

這時，她抬眼看到教堂旁邊立著一幢不起眼的小旅館，門口沒有聖誕裝飾。她幾乎錯過了。

當天晚上，她拎著高跟鞋住進這家荷西旅館四一二號房。

她進了房間，連門都沒鎖，除下身上的風衣，脫掉胸罩，縮在床上，爬進夢鄉。

第二天早上，教堂的六下鐘聲把她從夢裡喚醒。

她回去蘭花旅館，把東西打包搬過來。

160

房間裡沒有掛畫，也沒有掛鉤，那張『星夜』就挨在床頭櫃的一盞小罩燈旁邊。

她染回黑髮，一張臉看來蒼白哀傷。

隨後，她坐到床邊讀報紙上的占星欄。

她無意中看到一段新聞。

聖誕奇聞，

酒廊歌手遭身分不明聖誕老人當街襲擊，

疑人事後逃去無蹤，僅遺下假肚子一個。

歌手輕傷，拒絕追究。

她笑了，不過，不是快樂的笑。

她笑著掉眼淚。

今天是聖誕前夕。

午夜時分，教堂敲響了十二下鐘聲，她在附近的小酒館幹掉了半瓶桃子味伏特加。

她付了錢離開，走路回旅館。

她醉夢昏昏走在空蕩蕩的路上。走了一半，她覺得累，坐到路邊的石階上。

林克在她面前走過時，她說：

『你別再跟著我。』

林克整個人幾乎定住了。

這時，喜喜彎下身去，抱起了腳邊的一條小黃狗。她從酒館出來之後，牠一直可憐兮兮地跟著她。牠鼻子上有一塊傷疤，看來是沒有主人的。

林克繼續往前走。

喜喜站起身，抱起那條狗狗兒，走在林克後頭。

路上只有他們兩個人，街燈下，他長長的影子落在她前方。

她把那條小狗從教堂半掩的圓拱大門放進去，裡面亮著燈。

她走下台階，悠揚的聖誕詩歌在她背後迴盪。

她一直想遛一隻貓。

162

別人以為她愛貓不愛狗。其實，她覺得狗是她的朋友，會忠心耿耿地跟她遊走

天涯，不需要用一根繩子去遛。

一個人不會遛自己的朋友吧？

她搖搖晃晃地走在一盞昏黃的街燈下，回去旅館。

但是，她想到，一個人還是可以遛自己的影子，或是別人的。

就像今天和過去無數個孤寂的夜晚，她遛林克的影子，林克也遛她的。

163

第四章

歸途

愛情是一百年的孤寂。

直到遇上那個矢志不渝守護著你的人……

1

除夕那天，喜喜在書店買了格雷安‧葛林的《愛情的盡頭》。

她反覆讀了幾遍，沉緬於哀傷之中。

有時候，她在旅館的床上一躺就是幾小時。她很少出去了，也不打理自己，看上去有點邋遢。

隔壁教堂的鐘聲已經不再那麼容易在早上把她吵醒，因為她總是在前一晚喝酒喝得太多。

她的漫長夜晚是在酒館裡用桃子味伏特加來度過的，林克用的是《數獨》。

她愈迷糊，他彷彿就愈清醒。

教堂收養了那條小黃狗。

牠一天一天的長大，已經不小了。

她有時會過去看看牠，牠經常在教堂後花園的那尊聖母雕像下面抬起頭，神聖地散步。

166

但是，牠已經不認得喜喜了。

幾個月來，這幢教堂總共舉行過十二場婚禮和四場追思彌撒。她從旅館的窗子看見過幾個穿白色婚紗的新娘和穿黑紗的寡婦。

夜裡，她也從這個窗子偷看過林克歸去的身影。

有天晚上，她看到林克隔著教堂花園的圍籬跟那條黃狗喃喃說著話。他餵牠吃東西。黃狗看來挺喜歡他。

她看著卻覺得妒忌。那條狗兒明明是『屬於』她的呀！

可是，到後來，她又沒那麼妒忌了。看到林克跟那條狗說話的時候。她會想像他們的對話。她認定林克至少有一回是這麼跟狗兒說的：

『那天我幾乎給她嚇死了，原來，她是叫你別跟著她！』

2

到了三月十九日那天，她從宿醉中醒來，已經是傍晚了。

她打開電腦，用哥哥的電子信箱電郵了一張會唱歌的生日卡給自己。卡片上面用粉紅字寫道：

祝你所有願望都能成真。

你又長大一歲了，

生日快樂！

喜喜：

永遠愛你的哥哥

她穿上一襲白色裙子和紅鞋，離開房間，搭電梯到樓下。那個有兩隻皺褶下垂的眼睛和一張長臉，看來像英國獵犬的門房向她問好。這個人總是用奇怪的目光看她。

她今年買給自己的一雙長襪是深綠色的。

今天的占星欄寫道：

168

這個月是你的幸運月，

讓你有機會重新思考事情，

拋開過去，

想想自己的優點吧！

別再沉溺在自憐之中。

她在夜晚去了海灘。

海水沉默無語。

天上沒有星，只有一輪冷冽的月光。

林克坐在海邊的一塊大石上，手裡握著一根魚竿，悠閒地釣魚。他旁邊放著一個塑膠水桶，他把上鉤的魚兒丟進水桶裡去。

喜喜脫掉腳上的鞋子，一步一步走進冰涼的海水裡。

她衣衫盡濕，海水浸泡到她胸前。

她潛入水底，沿著岸邊游了一圈，浮出水面，回到岸上

那塊大石上，只留下一根魚竿和翻倒在一旁的水桶。

她收回目光時，看到林克在她面前跑過。

他在跑步！

他連魚竿和上鉤的魚都不要了，從那塊大石滾到海灘上跑步。

他以為她想自殺嗎？

她淒涼地笑了。

她只是順著星座的指引，想要拋開過去，重新思考事情。

她想起她愛過的一些人，但她不記得她遛過他們的影子。她回憶起鄭魯和馬林時，對他們的印象已經有點模糊了，還有那幾個金牛、山羊、水瓶和雙子……

她只是為自己難過。

林克在海灘的一頭跑到另一頭，又往回跑。

這是個荒謬的夜晚。她突然發現，他是她遛來遛自己的影子的。

那麼，到底是他遛她的時候多，還是她遛他的時候多？

我們在月下遛著別人孤獨的影子。

多年來，他成了唯一跟她形影相隨的人。

她把鞋子穿回腳上。

170

3

這天晚上，為了慶祝生日，她幹掉了一瓶桃子味伏特加。

兩個月過去了。六十篇占星欄，乘以這個倍數的伏特加。

她沉溺在自己的沉溺裡，日子何等的漫長。

她收到的跟蹤報告，都是她來回旅館和酒館的路上。

她總是試著走得優雅，因為她知道有一個鏡頭永遠在某處守候著她。

但是，她沒法每一次都做得到，尤其是酒醉的時候。

不過，林克每一次都拍到一個比較好看的她。

其中一張照片是白天拍的，她在教堂外面猛然回首，雙眼茫然地望著鏡頭。

她不是在看林克。

那天她是在看什麼呀？

是什麼讓她把臉轉過去的？

171

她努力地回想。

是那條黃狗朝她吠叫嗎？

還是教堂在她走過時剛剛敲響了鐘聲？

她酒喝太多，記不起來了。

她默默地望著林克鏡頭下茫然回首的她。她臉上的髮絲紛亂，一雙夢幻的大眼睛看向相機，他把那一刻捕捉下來了。

她在相片裡看到了愛。

但是，那天她回過頭去之後做了什麼？她應該是繼續走她的路。

後來的一天夜晚，她在夢中聽到轟然一聲的巨響。她從旅館的床上驚醒過來，以為是個噩夢。隨後，她聽到玻璃碎裂的聲音，警車由遠而近的警鳴聲，沸騰的人聲和愈來愈多的腳步聲。

她終於亮起了床頭的一盞燈，走下床，拉開門，從門縫探頭出去走廊看看。

她看到一群神色凝重的警察和幾個身穿睡衣、被嚇壞了的住客，這些人把走廊盡頭的一個房間堵住了。

過了一會，她看到兩個警察押著一個穿西裝，沒結領帶的肥胖男人從那個房間裡走出來。

那個男人垂頭喪氣地經過她面前，看上去約莫四十歲，一身酒氣。

那個有一張獵犬臉的門房走來跟她一個人說，那個人是警探，開槍自殺，不過沒轟中自己，倒是轟碎了房間裡的一盞燈。

喜喜聽完，關上門。她漠不關心，溜回床上，醉醺醺的裹在被窩裡，又睡著了。

第二天夜晚，她下樓去買報紙時，讀到那段新聞。

一個債台高築的失意警探昨晚在荷西旅館四樓租了一個房間，準備開槍轟自己的腦袋。最後一刻，他下不了手，槍口挪開了些，結果轟碎了天花板的一盞吊燈。

她丟掉報紙，到酒館去喝她今天的桃子味伏特加。

她選了最孤立的一張桌子坐下來，林克坐在馬蹄形吧台那兒，低頭做著《數獨》。

昨天出事時他也在旅館附近嗎？

當她喝到第五杯伏特加的時候，酒吧已經擠滿了人，酒客們擋住了她的視線，

173

她看不見吧台那邊。

一個穿西裝的大塊頭走過來跟她搭訕。

他喝的是純味伏特加。

他挪開椅子，坐到她面前。

他看上去跟昨天那個沒死的警探差不多年紀。

他開口問道：

『桃子味真的比較好喝嗎？我看你喝了許多杯。』

喜喜拿起酒杯長長啜了一口酒，說：

『有了桃子就甜啊！』

大塊頭望著自己那杯酒：

『那就奇怪了！喝伏特加不是要喝它的苦嗎？』

『有時你會嫌它太苦呀。』

他說：

『你看來有心事。』

『心事誰沒有啊！』

174

『漂亮的女人心事特別多。』他賣口乖。

喜喜由得他說下去。

『有沒有人告訴你，你的眼睛很亮？』

『是嗎？』她微微一笑，把酒喝光。

『亮得像星星。』大塊頭說。

她朝一個侍者招手，想再要一杯。那人沒看到她，一直在忙。

『我去替你拿好了，還是要桃子味嗎？』

她醉醺醺地點頭，看著他起身到吧台走去。

他回來的時候，手裡拿著一杯純味伏特加和一杯桃子味的。

『跟酒談心最好了。』大塊頭說。『酒能守秘密。』

她啜飲著杯裡的酒說：

『我有什麼都跟我哥說。哥哥是汪洋大盜……』她掩著嘴巴笑了起來。『我在說什麼呀！我想說，他是汪洋大海，不管我有多少心事，都可以傾進去……』

她說著說著，覺得她好像看到大塊頭有兩張臉，酒吧裡每個人都有兩張臉。

她再喝一口酒，試圖清醒，卻更模糊。

175

她看到大塊頭那兩張臉朝她笑，他扶她起來。

『我們去哪裡呀？』她笑著問。

『上我的車，我們去一個很好玩的地方。』

『林克呢？』她喃喃說。

她看不見吧台那邊。

大塊頭迅速摟住她走出酒館。

他的車就停在外面。他打開車門，把她推了上車。

她跌坐在車頭，一隻腳騰空了懸在車外，手抓住車門想出來。

『沒有林克，我哪都不去。我要回家。』她手指指向前面的荷西旅館，從皮包裡掏出一把鑰匙晃了晃。『我就住那兒，我不用坐車。』

『那更方便了！但我們還是得開車過去。』大塊頭硬把她那隻腳抬起來塞進車裡，摔上車門。

她覺得頭好昏。他是不是在她那杯酒裡下了藥啊？這個混蛋！

但她無力掙扎。

她想下車，車子飛也似的往前衝，離開了酒館門口。

176

4

這時，她看到林克從酒館裡追出來，拚命想追上她。

可是，太遲了。

大塊頭把車拐進荷西旅館旁邊停下。

他摟著喜喜下車，手裡拿著她的門匙。

她身不由己地跟他走。

他們搭電梯上了四樓。

他用鑰匙進了房間，摔上門，把她扔到床邊去。

他脫掉西裝，解開皮帶扣，露出一口白牙，笑著說：

『我會很溫柔的！包你爽死！』

他剩剩褲子，走過去扯住她的頭髮，把她拉到床頭，壓在她身上。她用手推開他，他抓住她兩個骨碌碌的手腕，她手腕上那只橄欖石手鐲斷成兩截。她用腳踢

177

他，沒踢到。

『哥哥！救我！』她喃喃說。

房間的門這時突然從外面打開來。大塊頭轉身看向後面。

喜喜看到有兩張臉的林克衝進來，看到守住門口的獵犬臉門房那張臉變得好長好長。

林克把那個大塊頭從她身上扯下來，朝他的臉轟了一拳，然後又一拳。

她聽到打架的聲音和倒地的聲音。

她看到一個人躺在地上給另一個人拖了出去。

房間裡的一切又回復平靜。

她好像看到林克蹲在她床前，握著她的一雙手，問她：

『你怎麼了？』

『哥哥，你為什麼現在才來啊？我想睡覺了。』她閉上眼睛低聲回答，轉過頭去，摟住一條被子，臉埋枕頭裡，沉沉地睡著了。

她一直睡到第二天下午。

她醒來時，隱隱約約地聽到隔壁教堂敲響了黃昏鐘。

她頭痛欲裂，爬起身，用一杯水吞了四顆頭痛藥，又回到床上去，靠著床背坐著。

夕陽從窗縫細細地流進來，她身上依然穿著昨夜那身衣服，手腕上佈滿瘀青和抓痕。房間裡的一切平靜如故。那張『星夜』依然挨在床邊的矮櫃上。那條斷成兩截的橄欖石手鐲躺在『星夜』前面，十二顆橄欖石完好無缺。

她心中一陣酸楚和羞恥的感覺，嘴角皺縮著，哭了。先是啜泣，終於放聲大哭。

她哭著拉開床邊的抽屜，找到一把剪刀。

她手裡握著剪刀，赤腳從床的另一邊下床，走進浴室，對著鏡子梳她糾結的長髮，然後剪到齊肩。碎髮如雨絲般紛紛飄落她臉龐上。

剪完頭髮，她踏進浴缸裡，扭開蓮蓬頭，把自己從頭到腳洗一遍。

要嘛死了算，要嘛就好好活下去。

何況，她很有錢啊！她銀行戶頭裡還有養母留給她的一大筆遺產。

她洗了很久很久，像魚兒回到大海裡似的。

她開始快樂地唱起歌來。

洗完澡，她用一條大浴巾抹乾頭髮，又用那條浴巾裹著身體。

踏出浴缸時，她看上去像二十四歲。

她甩甩頭髮上的水珠，坐到床邊，打開電腦。

喜喜：

你近來好嗎？

我很好。

哥哥不在身邊的時候，

你要好好照顧自己啊！

雖然外表看起來不像，但我知道你是個堅強的好女孩。

哥哥永遠都會以你為榮。

你是我的驕傲。

　　　　　　　　愛你的哥哥

她寫好了信，把信從哥哥的電子郵箱寄到自己的郵箱。

收到信後，她又讀了一遍。

六點二十分，她修好了那只橄欖石手鐲，重新戴到手腕上。隨後，她把頭髮吹乾，穿好衣服離開房間，搭電梯到樓下。

她在大廳見到那個獵犬臉門房。

她朝他微笑。

他看到她的改變時，略顯驚訝，但是儘量不表現出來。他的獵犬臉是他最好的掩護，不容易看出表情。

喜喜終於明白，林克收買了這個門房。警探開槍的那個夜晚，林克也在她附近。

她走出旅館。

經過教堂時，她看到那條黃狗在後花園的聖母雕像下面沉思默想。

她朝黃狗笑，覺得黃狗好像也對她笑。

她在便利店買了報紙，讀她今天這篇遲來的占星欄。

上面寫道：

181

雙魚座的人往往擁有哲學家的思想，

能在困境中找到出路。

覺悟是你今天的主題。

魚兒，善用新的一天吧！

她在百貨公司買了幾件新衣服。

走出百貨公司時，飄雨了。

她想起現在是梅雨季節。

她穿上新買的草綠色雨衣，瀟瀟灑灑地走在大街上。

她在一家擠滿客人的西班牙餐館找到一個位子，坐下來吃了墨魚、油浸鱔苗、

火腿、炒蘑菇和一大盤海鮮飯。

她向侍者招手要帳單時，一個年紀很小的女侍走過來跟她說：

『小姐，剛剛有一位先生已經替你付帳了。』

她狐疑地看了一眼四周，沒看到什麼人正在看她。

『他人呢？』她問道。

『那位先生已經走了。』女侍回答。

『他長什麼樣子？』

『那位先生喔？他有六十幾歲，白頭髮，矮矮胖胖的……』

『他有沒有留下姓名？』

『沒有喔。他付現鈔的。』

她有點納悶地站起身，拎著東西從西班牙餐館出來。

她在餐館裡根本沒見到什麼老頭。她知道那個女侍對她撒謊。是有人教她撒謊的。

雨停了。

她帶著微笑，大步走路回去。

5

第二天，喜喜把剪短了的頭髮染成褐色，她的一張臉看起來有點蒼白。

隨後的日子，她每天都離開旅館去散步，吸收陽光和新鮮的空氣，臉上的蒼白漸漸褪盡。

她什麼都知道了。

每次在樓下大廳見到那個獵犬臉門房時，她表現得不冷也不熱，免得對方懷疑。

她又開始做首飾。她做了一套十二個星座的墜子。

一天，她約了碧碧喝下午茶。

碧碧比她大兩歲，是她以前那個小舞團的經理。小舞團解散之後，碧碧轉到藝廊工作，她認識很多行內人，一直有介紹喜喜去參加選角。

碧碧拎著一個提包走進咖啡館來，一看到喜喜就說：

『很久沒你的消息了！你失蹤了啊？』

『沒有啦！我哥哥在德國工作，我去跟他住了幾個月。』

碧碧點了一杯牛奶咖啡，問道：

『西門慶跟潘金蓮真的是天蠍男配金牛女嗎？《水滸傳》裡面有這麼寫嗎？』

喜喜把口裡的咖啡吞下去……

184

『你說什麼？』

『你上次說的！你說天蠍跟金牛注定有性沒愛。』

喜喜想起來了。那天，碧碧要她把哥哥介紹給她，她只好胡扯一番。

『喔！是占星家根據野史推算出來的。』

『我最近認識了一個天蠍男呢。』碧碧自顧自說下去。『我把這事告訴他。他

說，他才不是西門慶！』

碧碧說完，咯咯地笑了起來。

『我有禮物送你。』喜喜從包包裡掏出一個黑色絲絨布袋，把裡面的一雙仿祖

母綠耳墜倒在掌心裡。

『送你的，祖母綠是金牛的守護寶石。』

『噢！好漂亮！是你做的嗎？』

碧碧把耳墜釘到耳垂上，問喜喜⋯

『我好看嗎？』

喜喜笑著點頭。

『你應該去當珠寶設計師啊。你有天份。』碧碧說。

185

『我喜歡跳舞啊。什麼時候有選角你找我吧。』

『你多久沒跳舞了？』碧碧突然問她。

喜喜啞了。

在夜總會裡跳的那些不算數啊。

她的舞都荒廢很久了。

『我待會去跳舞，那個老師很好，你要不要來？』碧碧問道。

於是，她跟著碧碧去學佛蘭明哥舞。

那個女老師是從西班牙來的，只會在香港停留半年。喜喜在那個鋪上木地板的教室裡跳得汗流浹背。

不跳舞的日子，她到海灘去。

她穿著比基尼游泳衣在海裡潛泳，躺在太陽傘下面讀書。她讀了娥蘇拉‧勒瑰恩的《地海孤雛》，褚威格的《夜色朦朧》和徐林克的《我願意為你朗讀》。

徐林克跟林克只差一個字，但那是從德文譯過來的。

到了夜晚，她用一杯桃子味伏特加獎勵自己。

喜喜：

你真是個讓人意想不到的女孩子！

我的好妹妹，看來我不用再擔心你了。

愛你的哥哥

這封信，喜喜看了兩遍，才從哥哥的郵箱電郵給自己。

那個月底的跟蹤報告，有幾張照片是她穿著比基尼走在海灘上的。

她在照片中是個快樂的女孩，享受著年輕的光陰。

6

十一月的一天，喜喜終於有一個參加選角的機會。

她一大清早把舞衣和舞鞋塞進大如郵袋的包包裡，搭電梯下樓。

她心情愉快，朝那個獵犬臉門房嫣然一笑。門房有點受寵若驚。他似乎想以笑回應，不過，他臉那麼長，嘴巴又小，等到他兩邊嘴角向上延伸，露出靦腆的微笑來，也許要等上好幾秒鐘。

喜喜等不及了。她焦急想看看今天的占星欄怎麼說。

她在報攤買了報紙，邊走邊讀。

可是，這天的雙魚座占星沒有透露任何玄機，沒有『今天是你的幸運日！』或是『今天你會心想事成！』之類的打氣話。

她轉而讀巨蟹座。有時候，你身邊那個人就是你的一面鏡子，可以照出你的模樣來。

要是林克幸運，她也會幸運啊。

然而，巨蟹的占星並沒有『身邊的人今天會令你刮目相看，令你更欣賞他！』之類的說話。

她再讀下去，讀哥哥的天蠍座，卻又再失望一次。天蠍的星座占卜沒有『你的家人今天令你感到自豪！』這類說話。

她收起報紙，走過教堂門口時，又退了回去。

她把兩張百元鈔票投進教堂的捐獻箱裡，捐給窮人，也祈求好運。

她走下教堂外面的台階時，心中充滿了希望。

不過，這一次的選角，一下子就結束了。

這是一齣大型舞劇，會演出一年。她抵達劇院的時候，才發現高手雲集。許多來參加選角的舞蹈員都是十多二十歲的，比她年輕多了。

她在更衣室裡換上舞衣和舞鞋，戰戰兢兢地等在觀眾席上。前面幾排座位上坐著舞劇的導演、副導演和工作人員，每個人都帶著一張嚴肅的臉。他們要從超過一百個舞蹈員中挑出不足十個人。

舞蹈員零零散散地坐在劇院周圍聊天。

喜喜偷偷轉頭，瞧見林克。他頭戴鴨嘴帽，佔著最後排一個陰暗的角落，混在其他幾個來試鏡的男舞蹈員中間。

可是，林克沒機會看到她上台跳舞。

上午的選角結束，還沒輪到她。

189

下午的選角開始了沒多久，副導演就宣布，已經找到適合的人選，其他人可以離開。

喜喜根本沒機會上台。即使可以上台，她也知道輪不到自己。整個上午，她看到的都是身手不凡的年輕對手。她在觀眾席上看得膽戰心驚。

她卸下舞衣換回衣服，垂頭喪氣走出劇院。

午後的陽光明媚，她瞥見頭戴鴨舌帽的林克混在對街巴士站等車的人群裡。

喜喜越過馬路，直直地朝巴士站走去，嚇得林克馬上掉頭走進巴士站旁邊的一個公園。

他幹嘛躲開啊？她只是沮喪得很想要一個懷抱。

但她知道那是不可能的。

一輛巴士剛剛駛來，她搭上那輛巴士。

她隔著窗玻璃，瞄到林克從公園裡跑出來，悵然望著車子遠去。

當她回到旅館房間，從窗簾縫往下看的時候，林克早已經在樓下守護著。

他隔著教堂花園的圍籬，跟那條黃狗喃喃說著話。

她想像他是在說：

190

『我不知道怎樣安慰她。』

她離開窗，爬上床，打開電腦。

她的電腦裡有一張林克在這下面看上來的照片，是某天她用她的相機從房間的窗縫裡偷拍得來的。

她輕撫著電腦裡的他的那張俊臉，手指在屏幕上留下了一個個指印。

這就是她的懷抱。

哥哥看她時也是這樣的。

她住在養母家時，哥哥有時會來看她。

每一次，哥哥走的時候，她都會跑到爬滿紫色藤蔓的陽台上目送著他離去。

哥哥會看上來，揮手叫她回去。

7

漫長的兩年過去了。兩個生日，兩雙長襪，七百三十篇占星欄，二十次參加選

角落選，還是三十次？

其中的一次選角，喜喜窺見了命運精靈悄然留下的足跡。

那天，選角結束之後，她到劇院旁邊的咖啡店買了一杯咖啡站著喝。一個女孩走進店裡，看到她時，朝她微笑，走過去跟她打招呼。

喜喜覺得女孩有點面熟。她看來也是參加完選角出來的，外套裡面的黑色緊身舞衣未脫。但是，剛剛劇院裡有一大票人，喜喜對她沒什麼印象。

『你是路喜喜嗎？很久沒見了！』穿舞衣的女孩熱情地說。

喜喜努力回想，女孩叫什麼名字來著？貝蒂？瑪麗？瓊安？

幸好，女孩很快就自己報上名來。

『我是小夏！我很久以前在那個解散了的小舞團待過一陣子，你不記得啦？』

喜喜好像有些三頭緒，但女孩那張臉太普通了。

『那齣舞劇，你為什麼不演啊？』小夏又問。

喜喜聽得一頭霧水。

『哪一齣？』

『不就是「惡魔的花園」囉！』

她沒忘記，好多年前的那一天上午，她去了參加『惡魔的花園』裡其中一朵吃人花的選角。她沒什麼信心。下午的時候，她心情忐忑地回劇院後台去看告示板上張貼出來的入選名單。名單上沒有她的名字。

『他們沒要我啊。』喜喜說。

小夏笑了……

『唉！那一次，我本來也以為我落選了。名單上沒有我的名字。我就是不甘心，伸手摸摸那張名單是不是只有一頁，誰知道後面原來真的還有另一頁，我的名字在上面！你的名字這麼特別，我不會忘記。但你沒來啊……』

那張名單總共有兩頁嗎？

那天要不是落選了，她不會到撞球室去過夜，因此也不會知道戴德禮找過她。

那麼，到了第二天，她不會在律師行見到林克。

戴德禮也許早晚會找到她，她還是會繼承養母的遺產，但是，她不會剛好在那天遇見林克。

要是沒有遇見林克，而是去演那齣舞劇，她的故事便是另一個版本了，一個她永遠不知道的版本。

命運的精靈引她走上另一條路。

她隔著咖啡店的落地窗看向外面，那個穿藍夾克的暗影在對街的商店外面徘徊。

每一次她落選，他都陪她歸去。

她轉頭問那個叫小夏的女孩：

『你今天也落選了？』

小夏一臉尷尬地說：

『不。我來買杯咖啡就回去。今天馬上要開始彩排呢。』

小夏有點抱歉的轉身走到櫃台那邊買咖啡。

喜喜拿著咖啡走了出去，越過馬路，取道公園往東，幽幽地走在熱鬧的大街上。

她把空空的咖啡杯丟進垃圾桶裡去，在書店買了一本雨果的《鐘樓怪人》。

十一月的晚風吹起了，林克在她身後的某處溜著她失意的影子。

她到底比較喜歡命運的哪一個版本？

8

為了揮去那股惆悵，為了揮去心裡的失落，她在書店買了一本米蘭·昆德拉的

《不朽》。

書裡其中一段讓她深深著迷。

（註）

術（請把占星理解為生命的隱喻）說的是更細緻的東西；你無法逃脫你生命的主題！

占星術似乎教我們要相信宿命——你無法逃脫你的命運！但是在我看來，占星

生命的主題！

要是她仍舊選擇那一天走上戴德禮的律師行，卻是早一步，或是遲一步，她和

林克就永永遠遠不會相見。但她偏偏在她的命盤上跨出了那決定性的一步；或者

說，她偏偏在那一刻停下了腳步，轉身看向他。

195

於是，經過了這麼多年，她那天回眸時看到的身影，始終守候在她百米之外。

這是她星座的命盤！

十二月初的一天，命運的頑皮精靈又再一次踮高腳尖在她身邊掠過。

那天，她在一間舞蹈室參加選角。

她落選了。

她收拾東西，離開排舞室，走在冬日斜陽裡。一個高個兒的男人緊隨其後，從舞蹈室出來。他有三十來歲，一頭略呈波浪的天然柔軟鬈髮，夾雜著些許白髮，一張臉輪廓分明，鼻梁上架著一副無框眼鏡，肩上掛著一個背包，看來像藝術家。

他帶著微笑，直率的問喜喜：

『落選了喔？』

喜喜剛剛在舞蹈室裡見過他，但沒見到他跳舞，不知道他是不是比她早到，已經跳完了。

她聳聳肩，問他說：

『你也是？』

196

他臉露尷尬的神情……

『我不是舞蹈員。我是拍電影的。我想拍一個舞蹈員的故事，那位編舞家是我的朋友，讓我來看看選角的情況。』

她應了一聲，繼續往前走。

他趕上她，說……

『你願意跟我談一談嗎？我正在搜集資料。』

喜喜答道……

『你該去找剛剛那些入選的舞蹈員啊。』

他托了托鼻梁上的眼鏡……

『我想拍一個失意舞蹈員的故事……』

她瞥了他一眼，不知道好氣還是好笑。

終於，她說……

『你這人頂坦白。』

對方笑笑……

『這個算是我的優點。』

197

喜喜繼續往前走：

『今天又不是只有我一個人落選，你去找其他人吧。』

『但你的舞姿很奇特。』

她瞧他：

『奇特？這個我可以當作是讚美嗎？可是，要是你說一頭鵝走路奇特，鵝不會覺得你是在讚美牠。』

『你不是鵝。你像歌德風格的畫家畫裡的女人，小腹是微微鼓起的，仰望天空，頭俯向地面，眼睛望著塵土。』

他挑起了她的好奇心。她禁不住摸摸自己的小腹，原來她有個小肚子嗎？怪不得她每次參加選角都落選。

她對這個說她的小腹仰望天空的男人油然生出了一份好感。當他問她是否可以請她喝一杯咖啡時，她欣然答應。

兩個人去了幾步之外的一家小小的音樂咖啡館。

喜喜看到音樂咖啡館的角落放著一座自動機器。

那是一部像點唱機的機器，裡面旋轉著一個電燈泡。她從荷包裡找出一個五塊

198

錢，投入那座機器，一張粉紅色的小卡片吐出來…『這是你的個性』。

喜喜唸道：

『你樂觀的性格感染身邊的人，經常為別人帶來歡笑。人生中美好和幸福的事情都有你的一份。但是愛熱鬧的你，有時難免缺乏深思熟慮。』

她望著那張小卡片皺眉：

『不準！不準呀！』

她轉頭問他：

『你要不要投幣試試看？』

他笑了：

『你不是說不準嗎？我不相信這種隨機的偶然。』

『那你相信什麼？』

『我相信自己的意志。』

他們在咖啡館裡從偶然談到意志，從意志談到命運，又從命運談到占星術和生命的主題，談得很投契。

他是列文，一個美籍華人，居於羅省，在美國拍小成本電影，來香港探望朋

友。

他是天秤座。

天秤都愛美：美麗的人和美麗的東西。

他深深為她著迷。兩個人連當天的晚飯都在咖啡館裡吃。

『黃道十二宮圖的形狀，剛好就是一個時鐘的鐘面……』喜喜用指尖在木桌上畫了一個鐘面比劃著說道：『我們都在這個鐘面上。一個人出生的一刻，星球之間會形成獨特的位形，這個位形就是你一生永恆的主題……』

列文雖然不見得認同，還是饒有興味地聽她說。

後來，他離開一會上洗手間。

就在那短短的幾分鐘，她突然覺得空虛，渴望他快點回來。

愛情是從這一刻開始的。

她一直望著他將會回來的方向。幾分鐘之後，列文回來了，他邁著大步，朝她微笑。空虛的感覺一掃而空。

不過，這段戀情非常短暫，時針只是在她人生的鐘面上走了七個鐘。

七個鐘頭之後，列文要搭飛機回羅省去了。

兩個人在咖啡館外面道別。列文答應會寫信給她。

七個鐘頭了，林克一直在咖啡館附近等著。她目送列文的計程車一路遠去時瞥見他在前方。

她朝那輛車子揮揮手。有兩個人同時向她揮手。

一個是坐在車廂裡的列文，他隔著車子的後窗回應她。

另一個是林克，她好像看到他在前方怯怯地對她揮手。

因為喝了太多咖啡，那個夜晚她睡不著，一度憧憬美國的生活。

隨後的三個月，列文的信從未間斷。

二月底的一天，喜喜收到列文寄來的一張往羅省的單程機票。

這時，她正在溫暖的旅館房間內。

她走到窗邊，從窗簾縫朝外望，看到林克在下面。他雙手插在褲子的兩個口袋裡，隔著教堂花園的圍籬喃喃跟那條黃狗說著話。

他身上藍夾克的衣領翻了起來，外面颳著二月冷冽的風，他哆嗦著。

她把那張機票退了回去。

201

9

三十歲生日的那天，她給自己買了一雙襪頭縫了蕾絲花邊的黑色長襪。

哥哥的生日卡也是這天電郵到她的郵箱。

喜喜：

你又大一歲了！

在哥哥的心中，你永遠年輕！

還記得那年的壽包子嗎？

下一年生日，

哥哥再做給你吃好嗎？

生日快樂。

愛你的哥哥

下午，她搭車去了哥哥以前工作的那家小餐館。

小餐館不見了，附近的商店也面目全非。他們在那兒蓋起了高樓大廈。

她繞著大廈走，以前那家小餐館的後巷如今變成了露天廣場。

她曾在這兒留下了時間永遠洗刷不掉的記憶。

十六歲離開孤兒院後，哥哥在這家小餐館當廚師學徒。那時候，她住在養母家。

放學後，她常常來看哥哥。

哥哥會偷偷拿東西出來給她吃。兩個人坐在餐館後門的台階上聊天。

十一歲那年的生日，哥哥在這裡做了壽包子給她，每一個都像桃子般漂亮。

哥哥說：

『是師父教我做的。好吃嗎？』

她坐在台階上點頭，吃得滋滋有味。

『你師父對你好不好？』她問哥哥。

哥哥笑笑說：

『當然好！他說我有做菜的天份，他教我的特別多。』

『哥哥，你也吃！』

哥哥拿起一個包子塞進嘴裡。她看到他那雙手因為常常泡在水裡，變得紅腫龜裂。

『哥哥，我不想住在那個人家裡，我可以搬來跟你住嗎？』

『餐館宿舍裡住的全是男人，你一個女孩子怎能住這兒？』

『我們可以搬出去啊！你現在出來工作，不是有錢了嗎？』

『我的薪水哪裡夠我們兩個人生活？而且，你還要讀書呢。』

她噘著嘴…

『我實在沒法再忍受那個人多一天！』

為了跟哥哥一起，她常常誇大其詞，把養母說得很差勁。

『等我賺到錢，我再來接你走好嗎？』哥哥說。

一顆眼淚從她臉上掉了下來，她低聲說…

『那要等到哪一天啊？』

10

她的轉捩點也是三十歲這一年發生的。

九月的一天，她到劇場參加一次選角。那齣舞是講一個豔舞團的故事。

她在台上跳了一段獨舞，冒出一身汗。

她回到台下，用一條小毛巾抹去額上的汗水。

當她從導演和他那個助手身後走過時，他們沒看到她。她聽見那個男導演跟他的助手說：

『這個有點老了吧？我們要的是一群小舞女。』

事情就是在她猝不及防的時候，這麼殘酷地發生了。

她從劇院出來，打著傘在雨中徘徊。路上行人的傘好幾次粗魯地把她的傘撞開了，雨水濺到她臉上和頭髮上。

那天是她最後一次參加選角。

她以後再也沒有回去那座劇院或是任何一間舞蹈室了。

205

有一陣子，她加入了一家俱樂部。

那家俱樂部只招待女性。

她每天在俱樂部裡做三個鐘頭的運動，然後到蒸氣浴室裡把自己烤一烤，讓身上多餘的脂肪跟著汗水一起揮別。

一天，她赤裸裸的坐在蒸氣浴室裡，一條毛巾遮住私處。

另一個女人走了進來，跟她面對面坐著。女人有一對大胸脯，顏色深而大片的乳暈和圓滾滾的大腿，把毛巾鋪在蒸氣浴室的一排板條椅上之後，光溜溜地坐了下去。

女人看她看了很久，看得她開始有點不自在。

對方突然開口說：

『你是路小姐嗎？』

她不記得什麼時候見過這個女人。

『我是戴德禮的秘書茱迪。』

喜喜想起這張臉了。她好像只見過茱迪兩次，她兩次都有穿衣服。

茱迪主動說：

『我沒在戴德禮那兒上班了。』

喜喜露出好奇的神色。

茱迪抹了抹肚子上的汗水，好像有滿腹牢騷想要傾吐似的。

『我受不了長期當他其中一個情婦！』

喜喜吃了一驚。雖然有幾年沒見過戴德禮，只跟他用電郵和電話聯繫，但是，記憶中這個小精靈是那麼的小，像個老小孩……

茱迪好像猜到喜喜心裡在想什麼。她恨恨地說：

『你別看他這樣……他挺勇猛……』

喜喜忍住不笑。

茱迪又說：

『你小心他！我早就想跟你說了！他一直騙你的錢。那些帳單都是經我手電郵給你的。他收的錢比私家偵探社還要多，而且，所有的開支他都加大了數目。你別看他一副誠懇的模樣，他這人壞透了！你都沒懷疑過那些帳單嗎？那麼大的一筆錢！』

喜喜只關心一件事。

『林克知道嗎？我是說我僱他跟蹤我的事⋯⋯』

茱迪抹了抹頸上的汗珠答道：

『他不知道，偵探社那邊也不知道，他樂得有一個長期顧客。戴德禮雖然壞，倒是個守口如瓶的律師。陰沉又自私的人通常嘴巴都很緊的呀！這幾年，他生意愈做愈大，辦公室也愈搬愈大，但我連他一共有幾個銀行戶頭，一共有多少身家都不知道。我敢肯定，連他老婆也不知道！』

喜喜鬆了一口氣。她很少去注意戴德禮給她的那些帳單上的細節。她只知道，只要按時繳付那些帳單，她每天打開窗子的時候，便會看到那個穿藍夾克的形影。

他跟她哥哥看來是同年的，他們幾乎擁有一樣的孤獨眼神。

要是時光倒流，也許她當天不會僱林克跟蹤她，而是走上去認識他。

然而，過了那麼多年，已經回不去了。

茱迪說：

『你到底為什麼找人跟蹤自己呢？僱一個保鑣還比較划算啊？』

喜喜不想回答這個問題。

『這裡熱死了！』她拎著毛巾赤條條地站起來，好像是說：

『你都這樣看到我的身體了，還要看我的心嗎？』

她走出蒸氣浴室去淋浴。

淋完浴，她收拾東西悄悄溜走了，以後再沒有回去那家俱樂部。

11

十月的時候，喜喜逮到一個跟蹤者。

那個戴一頂拉得很低的白色鴨嘴帽，穿短夾克和牛仔褲的傢伙，幾乎是一開始就給她發覺了。

喜喜按兵不動，等了兩星期才出手。

她暗暗替那個身材瘦削的傢伙起了名字叫鴨嘴獸。鴨嘴獸每次出現都戴著耳機，手臂下夾著一份報紙來掩飾。

喜喜在旅館外面和酒館附近見過他。她在街上漫步時也看見他。有幾個夜晚，

她在房間的窗簾縫往下看時，見到那顆戴著白色鴨嘴帽的腦袋在街燈下面輕搖著。

有一天，鴨嘴獸甚至大著膽子在她四樓房間外面的走廊出現。喜喜從門後面的孔眼看到他，鴨嘴獸好像想找出她住哪個房間。

喜喜想看看鴨嘴獸長什麼樣子。但鴨嘴獸的一張臉藏在帽子的暗影裡，她看不清楚。

後來，隔壁的住客回來，把他嚇跑了。

鴨嘴獸跟蹤她的時候跟得笨手笨腳，從來就不懂得留在安全的距離之外。林克比起他高明多了。

她只好自己來。

可是，喜喜不明白，林克為什麼不出手。

她不怕那傢伙。鴨嘴獸笨成那個樣子，也許從來就不知道，他跟蹤她時，還有另一個人在後頭。

那天晚上九點二十分，喜喜從旅館出來，假裝沒看到鴨嘴獸。

她沿著人行道往北走，引他走上一條僻靜的長街。

轉到一個拐角時，她躲在拐角的暗影裡，站著不動，在那兒等著鴨嘴獸自己走

210

進籠子來。

鴨嘴獸果然上當。他走到拐角時還以為跟丟了喜喜，慌張地看了一下四周。這時，喜喜突然撲出來抓住他一條手臂，吼道：

『你是誰？』

鴨嘴獸嚇了一跳，想掙開來逃跑。喜喜不讓他跑，兩個人糾纏的時候，她把他頭上的鴨嘴帽扯了下來。

帽子下面的一把長髮披散了開來。

她做夢也沒想到鴨嘴獸竟然是個女的。

這個女鴨嘴獸看上去只有二十歲，一張有點蒼白的臉和一雙驚慌的大眼睛，身材瘦小。她剛剛抓住她那條瘦巴巴的手臂時就已經覺得奇怪。

『你幹嘛跟蹤我？』她沒放手。

她以為女鴨嘴獸會否認。

鴨嘴獸卻直直地說：

『我喜歡你……』

喜喜一時啞了，紅著臉放開那隻手。

怪不得林克一直不出手。他這時一定是躲在附近大笑呢！

鴨嘴獸沒逃跑，整了整歪到一邊的衣領，重新戴上帽子，把一頭長髮藏了進去，說：

『我那天在酒館外面見到你之後就一直跟著你，沒有任何目的⋯⋯我以前從沒做過這種事。你不喜歡，我不跟就是了。』

喜喜把掉在地上的報紙撿起來還給鴨嘴獸，指了指對方甩在肩膀上的一邊耳塞，問她說⋯

『你聽的是什麼？』

鴨嘴獸把那個耳塞遞給她。

喜喜將耳塞湊到耳邊去聽。

原來，鴨嘴獸是在聽歌。她還曾經以為是什麼通訊器材。

『這歌好聽！』喜喜搖著頭說。

鴨嘴獸摸著扁扁的肚子朝她覥覥地笑。

喜喜問道⋯

『我剛剛是不是弄傷了你的肚子？』

『不……不是……我肚子餓……我等你等了一晚……』

『走吧！我們去吃飯！我請客！』喜喜說。

兩個人在一家印度館子吃了烤雞、咖哩蝦、咖哩魚、羊肉炒飯、馬鈴薯沙拉、印度麵包和冰淇淋。鴨嘴獸餓得好像可以吞下一頭牛。

鴨嘴獸也是一個雙魚座，還在唸書，逃學來跟蹤她。

又是一個只要做夢就能過活的雙魚座！

有那麼一刻，喜喜覺得好像從鴨嘴獸身上看到了自己。

她問鴨嘴獸：

『你跟蹤我的時候，心裡都在想什麼？』

鴨嘴獸用一隻小銀匙挖了一口冰淇淋，塞進她那個櫻桃小嘴裡，說道：

『就是覺得很幸福啊！雖然大部分時間都只可以看到你的背影。』

喜喜明白了，原來是這個感覺。

後來，她們在餐館外面道別。

喜喜微笑說：

213

『對不起，我還是喜歡男生。』

鴨嘴獸失望地噘噘嘴。

臨別的時候，她突然問喜喜：

『我可以摸摸你的頭髮嗎？一直跟在你後面的時候，我最想做的就是這件事。』

喜喜禁不住伸手摸摸自己的栗色長直髮。她羞澀地笑笑，點頭表示允許。

鴨嘴獸伸出一隻瘦骨嶙峋的手摸了摸她的頭頂，快樂地說：

『跟我想的一樣⋯⋯』

『呃？』

『很厚，很柔軟⋯⋯』

鴨嘴獸摸完，滿足地縮回她那隻手。

『再見啦！』喜喜說。

她雙手插在身上風衣的兩個口袋裡，沿著人行道走，越過一個十字路口。

幾部夜車在她身後駛過。

夜已闌珊。

214

她是不是已經老得只有女孩子才會愛上她啊？

這些年來，林克是不是也想過伸出手去摸摸她的頭髮？

前幾天，她在浴室照鏡時，無意中發現頭頂上長出了幾根白髮。

她驚駭憂愁了許久，想起以前負責管理孤兒院圖書館那個懶惰姑娘。那個姑娘常常拿著一面小鏡子，把頭上的白髮一根根拔掉。

喜喜動手將那幾根白髮塞進她的黑髮裡，自欺地把它們藏在底下看不見的地方。

但她以後再也不能不染頭髮了。

她想起她從來就沒有摸過林克的頭髮。要是可以，她想摸摸他頸背上那短短的、像胎兒毛似的髮腳。有時候，她從房間的窗簾縫看下去，他剛好背對著她，低垂著頭跟教堂那條黃狗說著話，或是逗牠玩，她看到的就是這個地方，軟綿綿的、看上去好可愛。假使能夠用手摸摸的話，她會覺得很幸福。

215

12

這一年的聖誕，喜喜買了一雙皮手套寄給哥哥。

她在郵包裡附上一張聖誕卡。

親愛的哥哥：

天氣冷啊！

我好想你。你什麼時候回來？

你要多添衣服，小心保重。

　　　　　　　　　永遠愛你的喜喜

她在郵包上寫著：

芬蘭聖誕老人村

路明先生收

然後，她把郵包投進郵箱裡。

聖誕前夕，她去看了歌劇『孤星淚』。

聖誕那天，她中午離開旅館，帶著一束鬱金香到墓園去看養母。

她放下手裡的花，坐在墳頭讀托爾斯泰的《復活》，一直讀到夕陽西下。

夜晚，她在酒館裡幹掉了三杯桃子味伏特加。林克在吧台那邊喝白蘭地，做《數獨》。

這天的占星欄寫道：

節日的氣氛熱鬧，

這是個與親人和朋友歡聚的日子，

你卻倍感孤單。

十一歲那年的聖誕，她去餐館找哥哥，她在後巷裡等著。哥哥偷偷拿了雞腿和排骨出來給她。

她坐在後門的台階上，沒胃口地吃著，又再一次催促哥哥：

『你什麼時候才接我走啊？你知道嗎？那個人成天恐嚇說她不要我了！她要把我送回去孤兒院！我死也不要回去！』

她說著說著嗚嗚地哭了。

哥哥默言無話，雙手絞在一起。

哥哥是愛她的，終有一天會回來接她。

她年紀愈大，愈是這麼相信。

13

寄給哥哥的那個郵包在第二年的聖誕退了回來。

天殺的！

一年後才退回來？他們把她的郵包送去環遊世界麼？

她在旅館房間的床上拆開郵包。

那雙送給哥哥的皮手套和附在郵包裡的聖誕卡安然無恙。

她在『永遠愛你的喜喜』後面，加上了兩行字。

又一年的聖誕了，

哥哥，永遠想你。

她在郵包上面又清清楚楚地寫著：

路明先生收

北緯六十六度三十三分，芬蘭羅瓦涅米聖誕老人村

她把郵包投進郵箱裡，沒寫回郵地址。

然而，即使她寫上了回郵地址，也是退不回來的。因為，她住的荷西旅館在聖

誕夜起火了。

那天晚上十二點鐘，她在酒館裡續一杯一杯，總共幹掉了七杯桃子味伏特加。

林克幹掉了四杯白蘭地。孤獨的日子過得太久了，她發覺酒是她最好的朋友。

她離開酒館，一路搖晃地回去。教堂裡亮著燈，在她經過時盪來悠揚的聖誕詩歌。

那條黃狗趴坐在教堂外面的台階上。

牠認得她，朝她搖尾巴，卻又不失莊重。

她回到旅館房間，衣服沒脫，醉醺醺的倒在床上。

午夜三點鐘，隔壁房間起火的時候，她昏睡在醉鄉裡，渾然不知。直到濃煙一瞬間從門縫裡蔓延進她的房間，把她燻醒。

她張開眼睛，看到房間裡到處都是煙。她用手掩住嘴巴不停嗆咳，瑟縮在床頭哭泣，眼睛漸漸睜不開來。

哥哥，林克，占星欄，伏特加，『星夜』，再見了！

猝然之間，一個人撞開門衝進來，用一條濕毛巾蓋在她鼻子和嘴巴上，捲起被子把她裹著抱起來奔出走廊，穿過黑濛濛的濃煙，沿著樓梯拚命往下跑。她滿臉淚

220

水，頭靠他的胸膛裡，雙手勾住他的脖子，摸到他頸背上軟綿綿的流著滾燙汗水的髮腳。

她臉露慘淡的微笑，抓住那個地方不放手。

她終於摸到他了，模模糊糊看到他那張被煙燻黑了的臉流露出焦急緊張的神情，好像害怕她會死。

她醒來的時候，發現自己躺在醫院病房的一張床上。

梵谷的『星夜』挨在床邊的白色矮櫃上，完好無缺。花瓶裡插著一束新鮮的紅玫瑰。她的粉紅迷彩行李箱和那個像郵袋般大的包包就擱在床邊。

她緩緩坐起身，拉開床邊的抽屜。她的手提電腦也在這兒，幸好她上了密碼，沒有人能夠打開來看到裡面的東西。

她咳嗽了幾聲，覺得喉嚨疼痛乾澀。

護士看到她，微笑說：

『路喜喜，你醒了啊？』

對方倒了一杯水給她，又給了她幾顆藥丸。

喜喜用水把藥吞了。

『你已經睡了兩天。』醫生吩咐讓你睡。』護士說。

『這束花是誰送來的？』她沙啞著聲音問道。

『是個男的。』

『他長什麼樣子？』

『是個高個子，穿一件藍夾克，挺帥的。昨天早上你睡著的時候來過，今天早上又來過。我還以為是你哥哥或者男朋友呢。』

當天下午，喜喜帶著那束紅玫瑰、『星夜』和行李離開醫院，搭上一輛計程車。

她住進橡樹旅館五一一號房。

門僮替她把行李拿到房間，她打賞他小費，跟他要了一只花瓶，把玫瑰插在花瓶裡，放到床邊。

她丟開牆上那張橡樹掛畫，把『星夜』掛上去，溜上床，不一會就倦倦地睡著了。

222

林克在第二天找到她。

14

她下午兩點鐘離開旅館時看到他，他坐在旅館大廳的一張沙發上，打開一份報紙遮住臉。那雙長腿交疊著擱在地上。

她假裝沒看見，邁著輕快的步子從他身旁走過。

她去買了做首飾的材料。

夜晚，她在附近的酒館喝桃子味伏特加。

酒館裡有一部古老的點唱機，她每晚都投幣點唱。

這段日子，總共有四個男人跟她搭訕，她沒理會他們。

她在橡樹旅館只住了短短的兩個月。

一天早上，她接到銀行職員打來的一通電話。

對方在那一頭說：

『路小姐，你有一張票子轉不過來，你今天之內可以把錢存進你的戶頭嗎？』

她說道：

『我戶頭裡有錢啊。』

『路小姐，我想你有點誤會了。目前你戶頭裡只有港幣五千二百一十元零七角。』

她怔住了。

她去了銀行，結果證明銀行沒錯，她的戶頭裡只剩下那個數目。

她想起戴德禮的秘書情婦茱迪告訴她，戴德禮一直在騙她的錢。

這個惡毒的小精靈！

但那是她自己甘心情願的。

這些年來，她度過了許多無所悔恨的時光。

她在第二天退了房，拎著行李搬到一家名字叫小巴黎的廉價旅館。

房間裡只有一張窄床和一個五斗櫃。

她把『星夜』掛在門背後的鉤子上，然後坐到床邊打電話給戴德禮。

224

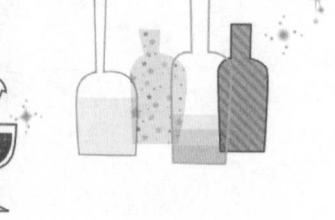

『戴律師，我是路喜喜……』

『路小姐，找我有事嗎？』

『我沒錢了……』

對方沒說話。

喜喜繼續說：

他無情地試探：

『我的意思是，我付不起請私家偵探的錢了。』

『那是不是要林克停止跟蹤你？』

她好不容易才答道：

『是的。』

『那我明天通知私家偵探社。』他一副公事公辦的語氣。

『就這樣辦吧。』她低聲說。

掛線前，這個惡精靈假惺惺地說：

『路小姐，以後你有什麼需要的話，隨時找我。』

『我沒有其他需要了。』她掛斷電話。

225

這天晚上，她在附近那間嘈吵的酒館幹掉了半瓶桃子味伏特加，一直坐到打烊。

林克在吧台那邊喝白蘭地，做《數獨》。

她害怕以後再也見不到他了。

她一頭醺醺醉意地走路回去旅館。

凌晨四點鐘，無人的漫漫長街上，她知道林克走在她後頭，最後一晚遛她的影子。

她回到旅館的房間，抵住窗邊，隔著窗簾縫偷看他獨自歸去的背影。

她想起許多年前，他頭一天開始跟蹤她的那個夜晚，她也是這樣目送著他離去，用她的眼睛佔領了他的背影。

她想起在北海道釧路茫茫無邊際的雪地上，她哭著伸手去後面想把被風吹開了的大衣帽兜拉回頭上去。她拉了好幾次都拉不到。最後一次，她覺得她好像碰到了一隻手，那隻手幫她提了提帽子。

她想起荷西旅館起火的那個聖誕夜，他抱著她拚命奔跑下樓梯，她抓住他的頸背，張開眼睛，看到他臉上淌滿汗水。

226

他們一起走過了萬水千山，腳下茫茫……她一度以為他是能夠結束淒苦無依和

漫漫長夜的那個人。

她從來就沒有認清一個事實：他畢竟是她用錢僱來的。床頭金盡的一天，她終

歸要失去他。

再見了，林克，再見。

她痴笑醉倒在床上，潰不成軍。

15

六個鐘頭之後她醒來。

她的一顆心翻騰著走下床，從窗簾縫偷偷看出去，目光所能抵達之處，再也沒

有他的蹤影。

她枯站在窗邊，不知道今天和以後的日子要怎麼過。

她又打回原形了。

227

孤寂永隨，這是她的星座命盤，生命永恆的主題！

她溜回床上，一整天都沒出去，喝光了房間裡的那幾瓶小小的樣品酒，其中一瓶是純味伏特加，一瓶嗆喉的白蘭地，一瓶難喝的威士忌和一瓶味道怪怪的薄荷酒。

第二天，她醉茫茫地醒來，拖拉著腳步回到窗邊，推開窗看下去，赫然發現他。

她慌忙縮回來關上窗，隔著窗簾縫再看一遍。

是他。

他穿著一樣的藍夾克，在對街徘徊，沒發現她看他。

她看他看了很久。

他是來跟她道別的嗎？

她換好衣服，離開房間，走出旅館，在街上晃了一圈。

林克就像過去每一天一樣，在她百米之外，不曾離開。

第三天、第五天、第七天，他照樣每天來。

他們一起穿過漸漸深的暮色，走過夜色朦朧的寂寞長街。她在酒館裡喝桃子味伏

特加，他喝白蘭地。她又開始重讀《生命中不能承受之輕》，書已經有些破爛捲角。他繼續做《數獨》。

他離去的背影在昏黃的街燈下漸漸消逝，天亮的時候又重回她眼前，不曾跟她說話，也不曾道別。

第八天，她打電話給戴德禮，問道：

『戴律師，我是路喜喜……你是不是已經通知偵探社那邊不要再派林克跟蹤我？』

『我已經通知了。他們這幾天都找不到林克，他沒去上班。他是不是還在跟蹤你？』

『沒有。』她掛掉電話，心中感到無限平靜。

這一天，她手頭的錢也用光了。

她一大早離開旅館去找小綠，想取回寄賣首飾的錢。

然而，當她抵達首飾店的時候，發現那兒已經變成了一家二手皮包店。她問店面那個臉生的女孩以前那家首飾店怎麼了。女孩回她說，聽說首飾店生意不好，三個月前就倒閉了。

229

怪不得小綠的手機停用了。現在還可以到哪裡去找她啊？

喜喜徬徨地從店裡走出來。

那筆小小的錢原本是她最後的希望，如今卻沒有了。

旅館沒法再住下去，她回去打包行李離開。

她拖著行李到墓園去，坐在養母的墳頭上讀那本《生命中不能承受之輕》。

暮色深沉，她從墓園出來，走了一大段路，吃了兩個甜麵包，到公園的水機喝水。

喝完水，她坐到公園的長椅上，在一盞街燈下面看書。

夜深深，公園關門了，她拎著行李出來，沿人行道走。

這時，她抬眼看到一間二十四小時營業的麥當勞。

16

喜喜用行李佔住角落的一個位子，買了一杯咖啡，繼續看書。

她瞥見林克坐在遙遠的另一個角落，背著她，應該正在做《數獨》。他面前有一排鏡子。

半夜三點鐘的麥當勞，零零散散地坐著一群不願回家的男孩和女孩，嘰嘰咯咯笑著，大聲說著話。有幾個流浪漢趴在桌上睡覺，甚至還打鼾，沒人理會。

她累垮了，把包包緊緊抱在懷裡，挨在手臂上打盹。

她不知不覺睡著了。

醒來的時候，她發覺自己頭埋桌子上，臉龐下面好像壓著一樣東西。

她抬起頭。那是一個麥當勞的紙袋。

她不記得她睡著之前桌上有個紙袋。

紙袋裡頭鼓鼓的，她好奇地打開來看，裡面有一疊鈔票。她數了數，總共有一萬塊錢。

她看向林克那邊，他背對著她，但是，牆上那一排鏡子照出他的形影。他正低著頭喝咖啡。

他給她錢！這個傻瓜！笨蛋！

她拿著他給的錢離開麥當勞，住進一家廉價旅館。

不過，她在那兒只住了一夜。

她一大早趁著林克還沒回來就打包行李退了房，搬到老遠鄰近紅燈區一家簡陋的日租小旅店，用一個假名登記。

她不想負累他。

她也不想他看著她凋零。

再見，林克，再見了。

也許這是她今生唯一一次做到了。她在最好的時候轉身離開，在對方心中留下時間永遠刮不落的身影。

她在侷促的房間裡翻開了行李，只留下《生命中不能承受之輕》和《百年孤寂》兩本書，把其他的書裝進行李箱裡，拿去捐給救世軍。

那個認得她的女職員說救世軍不要書。

她想問，為什麼衣服和家具是必需品，書卻不是。

但她沒問。

那個女職員愛書，要了她的書。

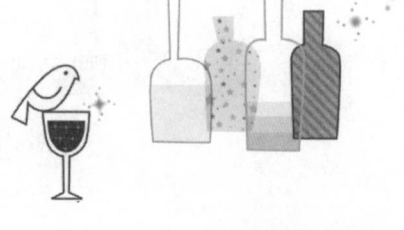

她把書從行李箱搬出來的時候，一角發黃的報紙從其中一本書裡掉了出來。

她彎身撿起那一角報紙。

薪水優渥。

工作自由，

可提供訓練，

毋須經驗，

樣貌端正，

高級酒吧誠聘鋼管舞孃，

她悲愴地笑了。

多年前的那天，她山窮水盡，撕下了報紙上的這則廣告。

如今她又山窮水盡了。

233

17

喜喜搖身一變成了美豔的鋼管舞孃。

她染了一頭劉海齊頸的紅髮，把身子塞進去那套分成兩截綴著流蘇的性感舞衣裡，露出一大片白皙的胸口和纖細的腰肢。

她的臍眼有如小花蕾，穿著黑色魚網吊襪帶的長腿，套上一雙酒紅色的麂皮高跟長靴。

她夜夜在那個鑲滿彩色燈泡、一直發亮延伸到吧台的長方形舞台上，纏繞著一根冰涼的鋼管起舞，賣弄著成熟卻又天真的風情。

她在酒吧裡的藝名叫珊兒，是來應徵的那天隨便想到的。

應徵的那天，那個女領班要她跳一段獨舞看看。

這一次『選角』，她終於『入選』了。

那個大家都叫她『媽媽』的女領班瞄了一眼她身分證上的年齡，對她說：

『三十二歲是大了些，不過，你身段好，會跳舞，那幾個臭丫頭沒有一個真的

會跳舞！而且，你勝在有一雙脆弱的大眼睛，男人看了會心軟！你的嘴唇卻很叛逆！』

然後，媽媽說：

『這裡沒有舞孃會用真名，你打算叫什麼名字？』

於是，她變成了珊兒。

年逾六十的胖媽媽一身過時的風情。她臉上的化妝永遠煞停在她年輕美麗的那個時代，太厚太白，胭脂塗得太紅，兩條粗黑的眼線直插鬢角。這雙火辣的眼睛好像已經飽覽過人世間一切情愛，心底再也起不了波紋。

因此，她反而擅長古老的伎倆，教導喜喜如何用舞步挑起害羞男人的激情，滿足性狂熱男人的窺私欲，安撫孤寂的男人，也用她那雙脆弱大眼睛鼓舞沒有愛情的人。

喜喜跟著媽媽的話去做，而且做得出色，客人都為這個新來的舞孃著迷。她曾在另一個舞台上飽嚐被冷落的滋味，如今卻在這間酒吧裡贏得了無數仰慕的目光。

媽媽喜歡她，替她擋開了一干給她迷得神魂顛倒的仰慕者，為她省了不少麻

235

煩。

她開始存錢。

沒輪到她出台的時候，她在後台那個盪著廉價香水味的化妝間裡讀書。

多年以後，她又再讀《百年孤寂》。

媽媽說，她是第一個會讀書的鋼管舞孃，問她家裡有什麼人。

她告訴媽媽，她只有一個哥哥，在西非開的小型運輸機。

她又說了那個長頸鹿流口水的故事。牠橫躺在機艙裡，腳頂住艙門，一滴口水

從飛機起飛到降落都還沒有流到脖子去。

媽媽笑得花枝亂顫，全身的五花肉起了一陣波動。

「哥哥和我每年都會相約在一個地方見面。」她說。

時光是否會永遠失落？永難喚回？

她一直惦記著林克，回首遠去的日子，心裡油然興起絕望的哀愁。

18

林克在失去她十四天之後終於找到她。

她出台的時候沒發現他。

那個駐場的中菲混血歌女就像過去每個晚上一樣,唱著蒼涼的情歌。

喜喜抱住那根亮晶晶的冰涼鋼管,把絕望的哀愁和永無止盡的思念化成靈魂深處的舞步。她的乳房仰望天空,眼睛俯視塵土,那雙在燈影下閃著炫人亮光的長腿一腳踏在愛情的荒漠上。

她美得驚人,這份美是歲月打造出來的。

她一根鋼管換一根鋼管,一直舞到吧台前方。吧台兩旁數十雙欲望的眼睛貪婪地仰視她。她痴笑輕狂,回首顧盼,猝然看到了他。

她失神了一下,抓住鋼管,以一個輕笑掩飾過去。

林克找到她了。

他是怎麼找到的?

天啊！她難道忘了他嗎？他是偵探。

也許她一直都在等他。

她把他一路引來這裡，就像一個人向一隻貓拋出一個好玩的毛線球，明知道那隻貓終歸會受不住誘惑跟來。

季節變換，時光荏苒，她從來就沒有停止過把這個男人綑綁起來作為愛的對象。

如今他們兩個人都老了。

她舞到他跟前，抓住鋼管，朝他對面那個男人抬起一條腿。那人想伸手摸摸她的靴子，她揚起頭嗔笑，用鞋尖輕輕踩了踩他的肩膀，引來一陣笑聲。

這時，她雙手抓住一根鋼管，朝林克轉過身來。往日天涯，而今咫尺。她俯視他，他仰望她，兩個人之間只隔著幾吋的距離。他今夜喝的是桃子味伏特加。她的眼睛試探著他的目光。他那雙多情的眼睛曾經透露著亙古的孤寂，如今卻因為尋找她又多了一份失落，也因為嫉妒而發紅。

她看得心都碎了，傾身在他一人面前起舞。

她不是說過了嗎？嫉妒是愛情的徒刑。

238

她對他舞得太久，身後的人都開始鼓噪。

她把自己拋向另一根鋼管，跳著銷魂傷心的舞步，心中始終帶著他的影子。

那個歌女唱著每天晚上都會唱的一首歌：

那個長夜，

漫天星宿，

得睹芳容，

魂摧魄折，

想認識你，

想愛你，

想守護你，

換幾聲歡笑，

一場熱淚，

告別飄搖無根的生活。

我不是暗影，

239

我，終究是愛你的。

我是歸人，

她扭動身子舞回去，抓住一根鋼管在他眼前滑開來，俯身跟他面對面，凝望他的眼睛。

的眼睛。

要是再有人敢因為她獨獨看他一人而鼓噪，她是有可能放一把火把這裡燒掉的。

她拿起他面前那杯伏特加，貼著唇邊，輕輕啜了一口酒，眼睛從酒杯上看他。

『先生，我們見過面的嗎？』她的聲音微顫，她的氣息在他臉上低語。

沒等他回答，她放下酒杯，抓住那根鋼管，轉了一圈。其他人紛紛朝她遞起酒杯，想她也喝一口。她沒喝，嘴角一咧笑了。

她迴轉到他跟前，繼續問道：

『你是不是常來的？我們在這裡見過嗎？』

多年以來，兩個人第一次對話。他眼裡憂鬱的神情消散了些，低聲說道：

『我第一次來……我找這裡找很久了。』

240

她一笑嫣然，抓住一根鋼管，如蝴蝶般對他展翅盤旋，喃喃說：

『那麼，我們會不會以前在什麼地方見過？東京？北海道？下雪的夜晚？還是火車上？』

她屈曲一條腿，與他等高。她的眼睛亮得像星星，在他眼裡輝映著光芒。

她看他竟看出了鄉愁來。

這一生，她只愛過一個人，後無來者。

她朝他伸出一隻修長的手，溫柔地用手指劃過他頸背上軟綿綿的髮腳，然後微笑舞著起來，收回那隻手。

其他人嚷著也要她摸摸。她淡淡一笑，傲然揚起粉撲撲的下巴，一路舞回去舞台的另一端。

我，終究是愛你的。

我是歸人，

我不是暗影，

長方形舞台上的燈在她身後一盞盞熄滅，送她翩然歸去。

她滿臉汗水，垂首不語。

愛情是一百年的孤寂，直到遇上那個矢志不渝守護著你的人，那一刻，所有苦

澀的孤獨，都有了歸途。

19

喜喜走回去後台，媽媽在走廊上一直追著她，好奇地打聽：

『剛剛那個男人是不是你男朋友？』

她沒回答。

『是舊情人？』

她沒回答，閃身進化妝間，把門從裡面關上，笑著從門縫說：

『媽媽，我要換衣服！』

她聽到媽媽在外面咕噥了幾聲。

她坐到一把椅子裡，脫掉腳上的長靴，用一張手巾紙抹掉臉上淋漓的汗水。

這時，外面有人敲門。

她看向門那邊大聲說：

『媽媽，我不想說呀！』

敲門聲依然繼續。

她不情願地站起身去開門。

『我說了不想說……』

她打開門，站在門外的不是媽媽，是一個陌生男人，約莫四十歲，一張方形臉，身上穿著米色的風衣，目光炯炯。

『你找誰？』她隨手抓起一件外套披在身上。

『你是不是路喜喜小姐？』

她怔了怔，答道：

『是的，請問你是誰？』

那人亮出證件。

『我是北區重案組的陳雲治督察。』

『你找我什麼事？』

『路明是你哥哥嗎？』

她微顫點頭。

『我們找到了他的骸骨。』

她忍不住悚然寒慄，淚水盈眶。

『你說什麼？我不明白。』她的聲音發抖。

對方拿出一本記事簿來，翻到其中一頁：

『你哥哥二十年前失蹤的時候，你報了警？』

她點點頭。

對方繼續說下去：

『警方一直找不到他，只知道他失蹤前跟一群童黨來往密切。童黨的首領十八年前因為殺害另外兩個人被捕。他在獄中一直否認殺人。最近，他信了教，誠心悔改，不但承認他殺死兩個人，更供出他二十年前殺了另一個人，那個人就是你哥哥路明。他們本來打算綁架一個富商的小兒子，路明不肯。他怕他揭發他們，把他殺了，埋在一個山頭。我們最近把骸骨挖了出來。』

她全身簌簌發抖。

『不可能，那不是我哥哥。』

『我們對比過遺傳基因，你哥哥的遺傳基因跟骸骨的遺傳基因非常吻合。』

她搖著頭，嘴唇在哆嗦……

『不可能……我哥哥不是壞人……』

那個警探從懷中掏出一條已經氧化了的銀鍊子，鍊子的末端附著一個天蠍座的墜子。

『你認不認得這條鍊子是不是你哥哥的？我們是在那堆骸骨裡找到的。』

她伸出抖顫的手接過那條已經變色的銀鍊子，看了看，一口咬定說：

『我沒見過。』

那人同情地看了她一眼，說：

『路小姐，什麼時候你方便來警局一趟？』

『我哥哥沒死！你弄錯了！』她把門從裡面關上，挨在門背上，緊緊抓住那個天蠍座的墜子，指甲掐陷入掌心。

這個墜子是她親手做給哥哥的。

她的一顆心曾經抵擋過現實生活中最無情的打擊，卻受不了往事的折磨。

這是她一生中最辛酸的部分，夾雜著悔恨和罪疚。

哥哥是她害的。她永遠不會原諒自己，是她一再用眼淚和謊言來逼哥哥的，結果把他一步一步逼上了黃泉路。

那個悽苦的星期三，哥哥來看她，她又一次掛著滿臉淚痕催逼哥哥：

『你快點接我走吧！那個人真的會送我回孤兒院去！我聽到她打電話給院長，我寧願死也不回去！我苦死了！那個人還打我！』

哥哥用手指幫她擦著眼淚說：

『我就是來告訴你，哥哥很快會有錢接你走，我們以後一起生活！誰也不離開誰。』

『真的？』她抽著鼻子哭泣。

哥哥下樓去的時候，她走出去陽台看他。

哥哥以前都是一個人搭車回去的。然而，那天，她看到一部黑色小汽車在下面等他。三個叼著煙的小混混，站在車邊大聲說著粗話聊天。

哥哥上了那輛車。

246

那天之後，他再也沒有回來了。

十八年前，她在報紙上看到一宗童黨殺人的新聞，她認得那個被捕的首領就是那天其中的一個人。兩個死者的照片登了出來，不是哥哥。

哥哥要不是已經遭遇不測，決不會丟下她。可是，她不相信命運，她一直想念他，深信他會回來。

那天，是她最後一次見到哥哥。

她撥開陽台的欄杆上一束遮住她視線的紫色藤蔓，跟哥哥揮手。

哥哥穿著一件藍夾克，轉頭看上來，微笑揮手叫她回去。

她多麼想念那天揮別的陽台。這是她一生中最悲傷的往事。

要是時光可以重來，她會叫哥哥別上車。

20

她換好衣服，穿回長靴，把那條銀鍊子放到身上米色風衣的口袋裡。

她打開門，從化妝間出來。

那個警探已經走了。

她蹣跚地穿過後台昏暗的長廊，朝後門晃去。

藉著死亡，

我們直抵天上星辰。

她推開那扇沉甸甸的後門，抬頭看到無雲的夜空上亮著幾顆晚星。哥哥在星星裡，這是她生命永恆的主題。她又快樂了起來。

她看過去，看到對街那個穿藍夾克的身影。

他一直在等她。

她走在柏油路面的邊邊上，走在回去的路上。

林克朝她走了過來。他不是走在她百米之遙，而是走在她的身邊。

兩個人默默而幸福地走著。

她對他說⋯

248

　『要是你明天來這兒，就見不到我了。』

　他訝然問她：

　『你要去哪裡？』

　『我明天要結婚了！』

　他臉上的表情凝住了，酸楚地問：

　『你跟誰結婚？』

　『我跟會跟我結婚的那個人結婚啊！』她離開他身邊，悠悠地走在前方。

　走了幾步，她臉朝他轉過來，倒退著走，那雙黑亮脆弱的大眼睛望著他，輕柔

地問：

　『你知道這個人在什麼地方嗎？』

（二○○五年‧光文社）暢銷系列‧單著……《十字》

（二○○四年‧光文社）暢銷系列‧單著……《十字屋敷的小丑》

（柏）引用本文著作目

長夜裡擁抱

張小嫻

長夜裡，當這個出了口，總的你突然覺得鼻子酸酸「酸酸的」，總覺有些溫潤，可以擁抱一下嗎？那種熟悉的感覺，難以言喻……

張小嫻長篇小說溫暖力作！

長夜裡擁抱

長夜裡，星星都出來了，
她卻突然覺得鼻子酸酸的，眼裡有些濕潤，
可以擁抱一下嗎？
那種熟悉的感覺，難以言喻……

不管是滿天的星星，還是飄過的雪花，
時光隧道的哪一端，
他們曾有過甜蜜的時光，

只要珍美能夠醒來，她不認得我也沒關係，忘記我也好。
我答應，我什麼也不會說，除非她有一天自己記起來。

但是為何他們的相遇彷彿都在重演這一幕，
他一直在等待，而她卻永遠都不可能認得他。
在不知不覺中，
把他的身影從生活中抖落了……

任何東西都能買，
也能賣，
那……愛情呢？

紅顏露水

邢露，有一張如花般亮麗的容顏、一雙如水般深邃的眸子。因為留戀繁華過往的窮畫家父親，邢露從小便了解自己的骨子裡，有著嚮往奢華的天性；因為視錢如命的勢利母親，她也有一顆不滿於貧窮現實的好勝心。

當徐承勳出現時，邢露很快就讓他落入了『愛的陷阱』。她一步步算計著他的反應，卻也在不知不覺中，逐漸失去內心的防線！

徐承勳是真的愛著她的。這個有著繪畫天分的大男孩，不僅畫出了她心中的夢，願意為她擺攤賣畫，甚至，想與她生一個孩子。

但是，她也可以愛上他嗎？對一個曾經受過傷，如今選擇出賣自己愛情的女人來說，真的可以得到幸福嗎？……

張小嫻10年有愛
散文精選典藏版 1

重量級情話

網路流傳最廣，張小嫻的經典情話：
世上最遙遠的距離，不是生與死的距離，
不是天各一方，
而是我就站在你面前，你卻不知道我愛你！
想愛，就看張小嫻！

重量級的愛情天后張小嫻，十年來不斷的綻放出獨一
無二的愛情思索，一語道破我們面對愛情的甜蜜和孤
單，輕透明晰的情話每每牽動著我們的心。

在小嫻的散文裡有體貼，讓我們總能放下不安的心去
面對愛情。在小嫻的情話裡有坦然，讓我們不論何時
何地都能在其中找到慰藉。因為小嫻，讓我們終會明
白，自己的愛情、自己的心情……

張小嫻10年有愛
散文精選典藏版 2

男人要的三份禮物

愛一個世界大一點的男人,你也會變得海闊天空。
愛一個小世界的小男人,你只會退步。
想了解男人,就看張小嫻!

女人最完美的戀愛生活:
永遠被十來歲的男孩子思慕,
被二十來歲的男人仰慕,
跟三十來歲的男人戀愛,
被四十來歲的男人深情地愛著,
與五十來歲的男人討論人生……

在小嫻的散文裡有透徹,因此我們開始瞭解,男人是
用『耳朵傾聽』來發出愛的信號。在小嫻的情話裡有
了悟,所以我們開始明白,女人只有在愛情裡才能成
長。因為小嫻,我們終於開始知道,該如何談一場
『聰明』的戀愛……

張小嫻10年有愛
散文精選典藏版 3

你微笑，我說謊

美好的愛情，不是讓我們變得自私，
而是使我們變得善良和寬容……
戀愛旅途再出發，必讀張小嫻！

對男人，妳可以撒這些謊話：
『你很幽默！』（即使他的笑話令妳打呵欠。）
『你看起來很年輕啊！』
（即使他的皺紋可以夾死一隻螞蟻。）

對女人，你不妨說這些謊話：
『妳今天很漂亮。』
（即使你認為她那一身衣著很沒品味。）
『妳看起來很年輕啊！』
（雖然她比上一次跟你見面時老了一些。）
『單身很好啊！』
（既然她已經很久沒有談戀愛。）

小時候撒謊，撒的是不必要的謊言，純粹為了逃避責
罰。長大了，我們才明白，人生，總有需要撒謊的時
候，為的只是對方一個微笑……

國家圖書館出版品預行編目資料

我終究是愛你的 / 張小嫻 著.--初版.--臺北市：
皇冠文化. 2008.07
面；公分（皇冠叢書；第3754種）
（張小嫻作品；39）
ISBN 978-957-33-2432-4 （平裝）

857.7   97009676

皇冠叢書第3754種
張小嫻作品 39

我終究是愛你的

作　　者—張小嫻
發 行 人—平雲
出版發行—皇冠文化出版有限公司
　　　　　台北市敦化北路120巷50號
　　　　　電話◎02-2716-8888
　　　　　郵撥帳號◎15261516號
出版統籌—盧春旭
責任編輯—沈書萱
美術設計—王瓊瑤
行銷企劃—周慧真
印　　務—林佳燕
校　　對—鮑秀珍‧沈書萱
著作完成日期—2007年
初版一刷日期—2008年7月

法律顧問—王惠光律師
有著作權‧翻印必究
如有破損或裝訂錯誤，請寄回本社更換
讀者服務傳真專線◎02-27150507
電腦編號◎379039
ISBN◎978-957-33-2432-4
Printed in Taiwan
本書僅限台澎金馬地區銷售
本書定價◎新台幣240元

● 皇冠文化集團網址：
  www.crown.com.tw
● 皇冠讀樂Club：
  blog.roodo.com/crown_blog1954
● 皇冠青春部落格：
  www.wretch.cc/blog/CrownBlog
● 皇冠影音部落格：
  www.youtube.com/user/CrownBookClub
● 張小嫻愛情channel官網：
  www.crown.com.tw/book/amy
● 張小嫻官方部落格：
  www.amymagazine.com/amyblog/siuhan
● 張小嫻udn部落格：
  blog.udn.com/AmyChannel

S0-BBD-415

George O'Brien was brought
He left Ireland in 1965, after
and was educated at Ruskin College, Oxford
and Ph.D. at the University of Warwick, where he lectured in
English from 1976 to 1980. He was then appointed assistant
professor of English at Vassar College in New York and in
1984 took up a similar position at Georgetown University,
Washington, DC, where he is now an associate professor. He
was awarded a Hennessy/New Irish Writing Prize in 1973, and
the 1988 Irish Book Awards Silver Medal for Literature for *The
Village of Longing*, the first volume of his autobiography; the
second volume, *Dancehall Days*, was published the same year.
Both volumes have recently been reissued by Blackstaff Press.

CHICAGO PUBLIC LIBRARY
BEVERLY BRANCH
1962 W. 95th STREET
CHICAGO, IL   60643

OUT OF OUR MINDS

George O'Brien

THE
BLACKSTAFF
PRESS

BELFAST

● A BLACKSTAFF PAPERBACK ORIGINAL ●

Blackstaff Paperback Originals present new writing, previously
unpublished in Britain and Ireland, at an affordable price.

ACKNOWLEDGEMENTS

A short section of *Out of Our Minds* was first published in *Soho Square 6*
(ed. Colm Tóibín, Bloomsbury, London, 1993)

First published in 1994 by
The Blackstaff Press Limited
3 Galway Park, Dundonald, Belfast BT16 0AN, Northern Ireland
with the assistance of
The Arts Council of Northern Ireland

© George O'Brien, 1994
All rights reserved

Typeset by Paragon Typesetters, Queensferry, Clwyd

Printed in Ireland by ColourBooks Limited

A CIP catalogue record for this book
is available from the British Library
ISBN 0-85640-541-8

R07125 99818

BEVERLY BRANCH
2121 W. 95th STREET
CHICAGO, ILLINOIS 60642

for Pam,
Ben and Nick

'Fortis imaginatio generat casum,' disent les clercs.
From Montaigne, 'De la force de l'imagination'

Walk right in. Sit right down.
Daddy let your mind roll on.
The Rooftop Singers

CONTENTS

WHAT THE BUTLER SAW

'Wuzzis, wuzzis?' they cried, and ''Ere, 'ere' deafly, clamouring for a hearing, all pissed out of their minds except little Jack Worrell. And when I'd served him another few light ales he too would be weeping and shouting for snob drinks with the rest. Because this was the day Sir Winston Churchill was being buried, and this was the belated wake put on for him by the regulars of the public bar of my new home, the Jolly Gardeners, Black Prince Road, by Lambeth Walk, behind Decca on the Embankment.

If wake was the word. I needed the notional stability of proper naming. But for all I knew both word and practice were foreign to Jack and Co. I didn't like to ask. I'd got strange looks in my three weeks here because I couldn't pahlivoo Cockney proply. I still felt false saying 'Wotcher', and 'Ta-ta'.

Opening my mouth now, though, would only cause more estrangement. I didn't know their Churchill. The dinner time ideologues of my childhood had acquainted me with a wrong 'un, the scourge of Erin, bully, boaster, and bather in brandy, not the victor and chrysostom in whose name this epic booze-up was being staged.

Jack's wife, Betty, four foot eleven to his five-one, was as plain and thin as a length of sticking plaster, a material whose effect on the short hairs her manner imitated with uncanny tenacity. She usually sat facing the street door against the partition, her back as erect as a rifle. Gavel of brown ale to hand, she surveyed all who passed, vetted whoever entered, laid down the law, tore off the frequent strip. 'She knows her own mind, ole Bett does,' the men'd mutter, cowering, giggling, in the silence following a tirade. Now she swayed at pub-floor centre sloshing back whisky macs, orating on the times she'd seen. Trundling with the nippers over to the Elephant to sleep down the tube. Old Mrs Freeman jumping out her bedroom window, an obscene firework in a burning nightie. Powdered eggs, how they repeated. Snoek, a Boer delicacy, contradiction in terms. Betty shook her head, and tears inched down her candle-yellow, candle-narrow face. All looked at her in stupor, aware of her great stature. Mother Lambeth, the Madonna of the Buildings, shedding tears of milk and pearls.

'Boove's gin!' roared George. He meant the dear stuff. The real thing today, and ice and lemon too, ordered in a tone which said, I know my rights! George nodded vehemently, as though insisting that he was definitely going first class and the whole hog. His face was a plate of rare roast beef, with a wattle of scrag end beneath the chin, which continually trembled, as mute and as expressive as a weather vane. 'Where are they now, then?' he demanded, attempting to lean far enough over the counter to see the telly, screened off from the pub by partition of the Jug and Bottle for the patrons of the saloon only.

De Gaulle, that other Dev, was entering St Paul's. Kaunda, too, and other leaders of those other Irelands.

Si monumentum requiris, circumspice.

George still couldn't see, so I called the roll to him.

'Nig-nogs, eh?' George sunk his snout into best bitter's froth. He worked as a ticket-taker at the head of the escalator down Trafalgar Square tube and came into his own when trains departed. He ordered pork scratchings, also Smith's crisps, the special ones that came with the little blue bag of salt. Dripped into the dregs of his pint, the salt made a seething, short-lived half-life, the way the world at large worked on the man himself.

And, 'Waaaw!' went Terry. 'My guvnor's dead.'

Terry had turned up unwashed from some ungodly shift in greasy jerkin and slime-shiny boiler suit. A skull that was a bucket, and starting from it a brush of crewcut hair, a night worker's dirty-linen coloured face. Bottle-end specs and turned eyes, head tilted as though he was looking for fight, but he was only looking for focus, half seas over on Lemon Hart. Tattoos blotted doughy biceps, signatures of service and palmier occasions. 'My guvnor's dead. Waaw!' leaking sweat, snot and tears on neighbours' mufflers new this Christmas.

I sidled over to the saloon, where telly and decorum held the hour. Telly England I could handle. It was contained, containable, a nation of uniforms, a club for formidable brass bands. Life proceeded like a Churchill speech, with measured tread and brazen summons, soused in righteousness. The medieval dramaturgy of death acted out its protagonist's vocabulary – herald and postilion, horse and drum, catafalque and eulogy. Bearskin followed beefeater's primeval plaid, and Garters joined forces with Black Rod. It was all that in Ireland seemed unhappily enigmatic or idiotically farfetched. All that the landscape had been forcefed and disgorged as ruin: it was the imperial annals of my childhood – *Wizard*, *Hotspur*, *Champion*, *Lion*: names of a daring, power and whiteness that was not ours – steadfastly upheld in panels so neat and final they might have been telly's avatars, more than adequate. Foremost of the escorts were the Royal Irish Hussars.

History was the loyal onlooker's colourful reward, not a *via dolorosa*. I couldn't tear myself away. I might have been a small boy again on Sunday after second mass in the front

4

room of Swiss Cottage, waiting for lunch while *Family Favourites* flooded in, and wolfed down its litany of novelties – the Ox and Bucks, signalmen and sappers, groups with names like comic-book tools: Wrens, WRACS, WRVS. All domesticated and dissembling – 'With a Song in My Heart' (and a particularly syrupy version at that). This was the forces' disarming theme, not with a round in my breech, which I understood was how they visited Cyprus and Malaya and those alleged beasts, the Mau Mau.

Akrotíri spoke in static. The announcer's voice was speaking (I could see) from a shack on the windy side of a mountain. There were 'terrorists' perched on rocks outside the window, dreaming of 'freedom', absentmindedly picking burrs from their sheepskin vests. I recognised them easily. They were Apache braves. Jeff Chandler would be along in a while to point the way to them. They had just cycled in from Ballysaggart. EOKA was Greek for Sinn Féin, IRA. Grivas, loosely translated, was Griffith with a gun, and Makarios, Mannix (more Irish than the Irish themselves).

Yet, even though the air was crackling and the voice of the outpost raised, everything was fine. Black Watch could pale into insignificance and Green Howard wilt and Sherwood Foresters might yet be cut down root and branch. Still would sweet Jean in London and sound Bill Crozier in Cologne spin the hits. Here's one a lot of you have asked for, it's The Platters and 'The Great Pretender'.

My grandmother and major parent, Mam, did try to change my tune every so often by reminding me, 'Huh: they used to call it *Forces' Favourites*.' But her vaguely remonstrative, implicitly ironic tone was lost on me. I'd heard her sound that way about a lot of things. It only meant the times they were a-changin'. All I cared to hear was this stamp collection of the air, with liveries, denominations and arcane values to please the most fastidious (yours truly). And here, too, though Mam never heard it, and I could hardly bear to, my reality was named in requests to be remembered from afar, the triteness of undying love protested, the fond hope of being together again: 'counting the days, darling'; 'missing you'. Soon. Love. Naïve candour and estrangement's verblessness. All putting me in mind of Dublin and my daddy. And Dickie Valentine doing 'Finger of Suspicion' did seem to say it all.

Yet, despite tuning out Mam's remark, I knew radio couldn't have the last word either on forces or on favourites. For one thing, there was that photo in the parlour. It showed the head and shoulders of a clean-cut young man. He wore a peaked cap that kinned him closer to Colbert the stationmaster than to Cooney the cattle-drover, and there were bright but indecipherable insigniae on the shoulders of his jerkinish jacket. This was one of the Alexanders, a British soldier, son of Captain Alexander, a gruff old party with a white moustache and a spread the size of his gratuity out the Mayfield Road. We lived where old imperial retainers could manage to retain. Was it not as natural a fate for one of these old hands' handsome, bored, under-educated sons to serve the crown as it was for the neighbours, labourers, to shoulder pick and shovel for McAlpine? It was the photo that was strange. And in the best room, too, where only priests and high insurance men sat for very long.

'Why?' I pointed to the picture.

'He was killed in Korea,' came the snappish reply.

I didn't understand. (I made a memory instead.)

Then, for another thing, there was my Aunt Lizzie, who joined the Royal Army Medical Corps after years of nursing in dull Colchester. It was as if there was nothing for it but to declare herself English through and through. I thought what she'd done was against our religion. And she seemed to show a convert's zeal by being posted first to Glasgow, where Catholics, I knew, were dog food. But she sent a snap. Her unrecognisably broad smile and her rather regal blue-and-crimson cloak made everything all right. She looked no more compromised than if she had joined the Good Shepherds. It was hard not to smile back at her novice-happy eyes. Soon afterwards she shipped out for the foreign missions, first stop Kuala Lumpur, later Lagos, where she met a man – more than a man, indeed; an English Protestant banker – and married in style. So then she'd volunteered for the well-to-do as well? It was strange, as unlikely a story in its way as the non-story of young Alexander, a fairytale of love and wealth and warm weather. And, like the reader of a fairytale, I thought I was being told something about who I was, and felt exposed.

Being motherless little me in oversafe Swiss Cottage in somnolent Lismore, County Waterford, was complicated enough, what with having three parents, and a mammy dead since before I could remember, and a daddy up in Dublin. I was his son during the school holidays. The rest of the time I had his mother, Mam, his brother George and sister Chrissy to protect and pamper me, more parental than parents themselves, yet unreal by being three, by being compensation. Orthodoxy was what I wanted, not complications. I loved being Catholic, belonging to a holy family, and knowing I could be good to the last drop if I tried. I loved being Irish and having as meal-time guests de Valera, Nehru and the Boers. Given half a chance, Mam would cry, *Jambo, Jomo!* But now she had a daughter who was all God-save-the-Queen, with a husband who said 'church' not 'chapel', and was happy: one of us, yet not; different, but related; as intimate a stranger as my father, and as difficult for me to ask about. I pondered timorously the moral of the fairytale. Families are a front for leaving home, marriages mask disloyalty, life betrays itself in a confusion of raised voices and slammed doors. And at the same time, Lizzie was living a version of my story, only hers wasn't called Lismore, but England.

And here I was – Terry, on Martell now, bawled an order I automatically served – discovering an England of my own with memory alone to guide me, confused that there seemed neither right nor wrong to where I was, no scheme, no pattern, no consistency. Not for the first time since my boat came in I felt I'd left but hadn't yet arrived. I was

7

cold. I was waiting. I stood in an official anteroom, all vibes and echo, guilty of departure but wanting to feel innocent.

Alone, behind the bar, I tried to console myself by imagining the confusion of other. Mightn't Terry's mouth-organising 'Waaw' bewail his changing times? He was a family favourite, but dim as a Toc H lamp, to whom national service had seemed salvation. He took its bollickings in his stride, found compensation in the boyish closeness of platoon and squad, saluting to a Heron of the Queen's Flight, in conjugating the fabulous verb 'to man'. He was born again a bulldog, and once, in Aden, went with a bint who turned his blood to sand. Demobbed, he headed to the palais down in Streatham, all hair oil and hormones. This time he'd *defny* look those Judies in the eye. He twisted his neck around in its unfamiliarly tie-bound collar, feeling a momentary rush of confidence, as of blood to the head. But Carol and Heather continued to pass by on the other side, on parade to 'The March of the Mods'. They were forming a big strong line for Joe Loss. ''Ere, wuzzis Madison, then?' It's the dance sensation that's sweeping the nation, thassall. He should've gone down the pub instead, his future all at once a cold-shouldering present.

Imagining Terry's past, of trying to match myself to it, did not allay the present. I was too aware of difference, and its protection, to get beyond it. But at least Terry's rum-fired, crass, delirium of the brave was more engaging than the nothing that was doing in the saloon. That was another Lismore parlour, packed with dazed stillness. Ernie and Dave and Beryl and Connie all called for their brown ales and milk stouts with surplus hush and extra ta's, then self-effacingly slunk back to where family, neighbours and old mates kept on the qui vive, as rapt and unflinching as an honour guard, heads thrust slightly up and forward at the Pye.

As had so many of his live shows, Sir Winston's positively last appearance commanded a captive audience. Once again – it was a gift he had – all were on the edge of their seats to witness this canonisation of the commoner, this last word in compensation for the mythological failure whose name sometimes flashed around the disputatious pub, the Juka Winza.

They barely moved. They barely spoke. They waited, vague, expectant. Solemnity might yet produce a formula (as so often previously). At Ludgate the skies should still resound in brazen fanfare with one of his punchlines (*Now this is not the end. It is not even the beginning of the end . . .*) and their beloved prisoner break the bonds of death, rise up and bid them stand at ease, stand easy. No surrender! That was what he had preached (and his father before him). No better time than now to practise it.

The saloon's tense attentiveness might have been a mute call for a miracle. But it also conveyed that there was no use pretending. The onlookers knew they were at a funeral, not a wake. Theirs was a duty, not a booze-up. Their hero'd bought it. He had surrendered. Somehow they had to find it in themselves to wrestle with the concept, pin it down. This was it. Everlasting Coventry. Eternal jug. He who had delighted them by speaking their minds for them, now cruelly asked them to think of him. The shroud. The silence. To think was as dumbfounding as to lose.

All things considered, then, the telly was a godsend. It was a way of not talking. It made things surprisingly bearable, resembling recent Christmases. The confident chronicling that dimblebied along so imperturbably was the sound of surfeit. But sobering realisation that public life was not all coronations and Grace Kelly weddings rendered them inert, immobilised as much by the medium as by the event. They were a mute, unwaking escort, indoctrinated with a cultural Novocaine which stiffened upper lips to the uttermost and made of the soul a bowler hat. They sat like the guards on horseback up in Whitehall. Like gulls gripping a wire.

And then, out of nowhere it seemed (out of my mind?),

there came a row and a ruction. I forget which stage it was in the proceedings. The launch had arrived at the South Bank. The coffin had been entrained for Bladon. The Charon-class locomotive had already crossed over from Waterloo. There was a thunder of footsteps in the pub, and shouts of semi-recognition and other sounds of eagerness and scrambling. Jack and George and Jack's son, Pete, and Terry, and everyone, were standing on the benches under the windows, straining to look out. I don't know if they could see that South Bank wharf — I doubt it. And if the train did come our way (there was a railway bridge over Black Prince Road) would it be visible from the public bar? Perhaps it was the inverted blitz of HM fighters screaming by above that roused them so. I may even be imagining all this.

In any case, the scurry to the windows is one of the clearest images that day has left me with, as strong as the groundless memory, or fabrication, that as the coffin was being shouldered down the steps of St Paul's one of the able-bodied pallbearers almost lost his footing. I don't know if I saw that slip, or if, either then or at some later time (though oddly, not now, actively recalling), it struck me that there should have been one. And all I can say about the public bar uprising is that I must need something like it to be true, something unexpected, vaguely anarchic, dis-respectful of property, bad form, some would-be collective shout of Cheers, an intolerable raspberry bestowed upon the grim saloon. I want the pub folk to have seen something that the telly couldn't show. I want them to have imagined themselves an escort also, their mufflers and moleskins no more out of place than any other of the day's uniforms.

Soon after the clatter and rush, the show ended, the telly darkened, it was time. The sky all day was iron. Through the open door I saw the black light slide off the concrete flats and grey brick fronts, the gifts of reconstruction, bequest of peace and Labour. The regulars took hands and walked into the valley of darkness. Home.

I watch them slip away from me, needing to remember that for five indecorous minutes they had their finest hour. Otherwise, it seems like I wasn't there at all.

THE DUMB WAITER

I

The shortest way to Lambeth was via Kilburn High Road. That was where the Emerald Staff Agency was, fount of life. I'd seen its ads in the *Irish Independent* when I was sacked in Dublin and in dire need of agency. Getting the looking for work done for me seemed a brilliant, ultramodern, totally non-Irish idea. The very thought converted dislocation and disorientation into fantasies of self-sufficiency and ready money – all from just a rub of the Emerald green! And any minute now, this best-foot-forward day, I'd make fantasy come true.

I didn't trust London buses, though. Apart from their cocknified, vowel-swallowing destinations – Hammersmith Bdwy, Wandsworth Bdg – they often indicated they were bound for different places even when they had the same number and the same direction. They were streetcars named desire, for their ports of call were all seduction and their route numbers mighty high. When my geographical sea-legs were less rubbery we'd rove out together. Me and London. Me and the new life. The good life.

Meanwhile, I stuck to the supposedly foolproof tube. But here it had fetched me up at Kilburn Park, with neither sight nor light to be seen of Emerald, famed emblem of remuneration and of ease. I had to walk. That was fine, at first. I enjoyed imagining myself free. From newsagents' racks the *Kilkenny People* and the *Connaught Tribune*, the *Anglo-Celt*, the *Kerryman* waved to me, limp semaphores. Cork crooning and the West's flat vowels floated towards me during lulls in traffic. I gave them a deaf ear. If that lad ducking into the Fox and Grapes, gumboots, split and dried plaster holding together caubeen and gansey, turned out to be Kip Tobin of Botany, or Andy Ahearne of Church Lane, Lismore, I'd have jumped on a bus to avoid him. He could have even been my Uncle George himself, who years before had vanished into England. I would have run without a second thought to his disappearing act, wanting only that he leave me to mine. Transported beyond the let-down that was Ireland, I could at last reject the roles that had failed me there. Now I could begin. With nothing, as nothing. Agency would fill my vacancy. My mind was a blank cheque.

By Quex Road I wondered why I couldn't smell the ocean. I'd been walking all morning, but still no beacon of green did me beguile. Pangs of smallness, tiredness, began to play on me. Passers-by were making the sign of the cross. Quex Road, where the chapel was! There my pal in boarding school, Johnny, prayed with his people. They were from Kilmallock. They had a flat nearby: Salisbury Road. John had a father and a mother. Brothers. John brought back pictures. His brothers looked big and strong. One worked in the underground, the other in a bank. Now they had a house, lived together. A family.

I stood at the traffic lights. The light was green. I couldn't cross. I felt unwanted, erased, disembodied. It was kind of numbing, a kind of clouding over. London and I dissolved into a dream that somebody (maybe even me) had then forgot. Fitter by far for me a visit to the Blessed Sacrament. Leave the cash nexus, foreign ways. Confess, repent,

amend. God will provide. But I could no more go down that
road than I could use the phonebox opposite, reverse the
charges and ring home. I had no reason to believe anyone
would answer me. I went into an ABC for a coffee. A black
woman with a faraway look created steam, made change,
said, 'Thank you.' The thing in the cup tasted like an idiot
child of Horlicks, but warmed me. The woman was humming though her eyes were sad. I dreamt of a rosy-cheeked,
roly-poly countrywoman at the Emerald door, calling to me
gaily, 'Wisha, come in; you must be famished. Would you
down a pullet? I've the kettle on.'

It was a glass door that met me, at the head of thinly
carpeted stairs above a confectioner–tobacconist's, and a
girl with a jet-black crow's nest of a beehive hairdo. Could
she help me? 'Please' came into what I said a lot, and I
smiled till my face felt tortured. 'Fenkew,' the girl kept
replying, variously pitching the second syllable. She'd see
what she could do. I took a seat. She gave me a form, and
teetered off on her stilettos to quell a screaming kettle.

The form impressed me. Up to now the blanks had all occurred when least expected, unofficially, in the family, in
Dublin's lack of promise. These London blanks, so simple
by comparison, seemed to say I was expected. Somebody
like me, anyhow. I felt encouraged. Age: nineteen. Name:
Seoirse, styling himself George. Should I put that? I gnawed
the end of the Biro, gazing blankly at the certainty of things,
the grey filing cabinets, dull flooring, the shriek of colour
from the apple-green telephone, the *Mirror* folded by the
Royal typewriter, the box of Guards. Education? Roaring
priests and stinking cabbage. Futile Irish, steady Latin. The
confessional of state exams. Gold Flake. Radio Luxembourg.
And in my experience nothing worked. Not I, fired twice.
Not family, who offered no alternative to the boat and
recollection. Not father, who'd remarried, as I thought,
rather than take me to himself in fabulous Dublin, where I'd
never feel loneliness or longing any more.

There was no room for any of that. There wouldn't be

enough room in a book for it. Miss Emerald would hardly want my life story. And I certainly didn't want it. For me, the fresh start, the clean sheet, the new leaf. Name, rank, serial number, and nothing but. Being someone else was all I could think of. I had no idea that fleeing only kept alive what was left behind.

'This way, please. Fenkew.'

It seemed a long time later, but the man behind the desk was only just finishing his elevenses and crushing out a Peter Stuyvesant in an ashtray overflowing from the morning's inactivity. He was a thin man and his face was lined and lifeless, a beaten track the colour of dust or of old ice. He took in myself and my form with a single offhand look. Then he hung his head and spoke into the phone. I was reminded of confessing and confessors, duty and dire straits.

He had a Dublin accent. Not the paper-tearing sound of the inner city (Gair'ner Strhee, Deh Que-omb) but too-round vowels and sibilance bespeaking elocution and the better areas. It, too, seemed inappropriate. Or rather, it was the right sound but the wrong manner. And there was his appearance as well, not old but withered. The smoky room, the ratty lobby. The work that hardly represented energy. Everything about where I was suddenly seemed anomalous, much less clean-cut than the free me contemplating it. Those elocution lessons had cost money, and here now their tired, smoke-coloured beneficiary wasn't even on the wireless. Was it an image of my future that I was looking at?

It also appeared that I was not expected. But the reason for that was clear – describing me as 'very intelligent . . . quite presentable'! Who was he trying to fool? If half the things he said of me were true, I wouldn't be depending on the likes of him for work, I'd be at least a commercial traveller with a car. When I caught his eye with a sceptical smirk, however, he only gripped the bridge of his nose and squirmed, as if I had intensified his private appreciation of my uselessness and the difficulty of things at present.

'Filled? . . . I see,' he said. 'Thanking you', ringing off.

There was a pause, or sigh, the lighting of yet one more cigarette. Then, unnerving in its own way, a burst of energy, desk drawers rattling and banging, tin boxes of index cards clattering. For the first time, the thin man looked at me directly, virtually smiling. And he had the very thing. Even as we spoke, I could be a technician for the Automobile Association. He stood up. I should hurry. Here was the number. 'Say technician – that's what they call them. It's basically answering the phone, and I believe there's a bit of walkie-talkie work as well. You'll be trained. Plenty of overtime. Double time at weekends.'

There – he was a decent skin after all. Of course he had to put on a bit of a show before becoming my daddy of the day. I imagined that like a lot of older people he preferred the oblique approach to shots in the arm and pats on the back. But it was clear now that he liked the cut of my jib. Why else would he have invited me to adopt his own stock in trade, the personal touch and act the agent in your own right? Just dial TRAfalgar and a sparkling future. AA, eh? Ah, indeed, he really was a decent, genuine Irishman, deep down, after all.

'Putting you through.'

It was exciting. I accepted manfully that motorbike and sidecar would not be for me, nor yet the dried-cowdung brown uniform with yellow trim and insigniae vesting in me power to salute. But maybe one day I'd be worthy of the association's enigmatic emblem (an arrangement of spikes and circles, an apotheosis of tyres and the foes of tyres). A future of trunk roads and lanes o'erhung with hollyhocks could be mine. At school Pig O'Hara bade us open our poetry books and learn off by heart, 'Would I were in Grantchester, in Grantchester.' Tea then seemed such milk-and-watery desiring. Now I foresaw with keen anticipation evenings when, rump raw from rainy riding, I would Englishly bleat for a cuppa. And in other ways besides would be made new, if once allowed to be an acolyte in the

church of the motorbike militant. And on windy nights I'd
be a voice in the darkness, an almoner for ailing Austins,
condoling on battery failure and kindred cardiology, bewail-
ing the A3's emptiness after midnight, master of all the
inflections of 'Sir', the greatest word in the language.

There is a tame colonial boy, technician is his name.

So then lanky streak of Dublin misery said, 'Ever considered the catering trade at all?'

There were no technicians, or they were not technically
technicians, or there were no vacancies at present, or since
I didn't really know what I was talking about, the gruff customer at the other end saw no reason to waste his valuable
time with me. 'Sorry, can't help you, I'm afraid.' Click.

'Don't be so stupid!' I yelled at the drone and the silence.
'You *won't* help. That's what you mean. Talk straight,
English hypocrite. *I'm afraid . . .*' I smarted anew from the
old familiars, self-pity and rejection. And now I was bucket-
ing on the Bakerloo in the direction of the Elephant and
Castle.

Catering! That zone of sweat and stoicism. That was supposed to be the making of me. Wardsmaids, waitresses,
charwomen, usherettes, sad black lady urn-keepers at the
ABC. I was one of them. Not a man, though that was no
news. I'd learned at home I was no sex. What ailed me was
the thought of being a servant, a drawer of water, mere
Irish, someone not to be trusted with machines. It was as if
the thin man had conferred his own impersonality on me,
I felt so empty, so remote, so obedient, so resigned. The
train rocked on through the interminable tunnel. I slunk
along the streets from Lambeth North, estates of cold brick
on either side of me, and locals hurrying, heads down.

There, in the failing light, was the Jolly Gardeners. Its
three stories were too tall for their surroundings, making
that west end of Lambeth Walk look like an impasse. A lone
bare bulb burned on the top floor. The sign creaked in a chill
breeze from the river. Little folk in primrose breeks and
scarlet jerkins played hide-and-seek amidst the olde worlde

lettering of the faded forest green nameboard. I felt too far
gone to believe in them.

I did what I was told and rang the side-door bell. The door
at once shot open, and a square figure with a bullet head
and thick specs appeared. It was Himself. Big Tom of Tuam.
Saviour. Boss. First, though, he looked energetically up the
street, then down, as if some youngsters had just played the
ring-and-run prank. Then quite intently looked me up and
down, face shortsightedly close to mine, breath of Branston
Pickle. There was a pause. 'Come in, so,' said he, somewhat
longsufferingly.

Mid-afternoon. The pub was an aftermath of smells, stale
smoke, beer spills, piss. It was dark, too, though, which I
was glad of. I didn't want to be seen cringing. Big Tom
held up the counter flap. 'Through here.' We went into the
office, as airless as Emerald-land and bare but for a calendar
showing cleavage. He went to the safe and took a form from
it. 'Sign this.' I looked at the blank space and put my
name there.

Ten quid a week all found. *Yes, grand, whatever you say: I
accept and submit, and a ten-fold blessing on you and yours.* Good
money. Tom's face came close again. I'd be working weekends. So no chance to spend, see I'd save. I'd be making
more than I was earning, like. I made some sort of noise to
signify I did indeed appreciate the beauty of the system,
designed, so thoughtfully, with me in mind, and the point
regarding savings, with its piquant implications of a life
hereafter, was subtlety itself. And all found, three square
meals daily and bed by night. *Talk about luck!* Already I was
most eternally grateful. 'I'm the guvnor, by the way. Call
me Guv.' Oh, I will, your honour, sir, I'll address you by
the ninety-nine names of Allah, by Christ, sure you've only
to whisper your desire for same. 'Don't forget it, now,'
intoned Big solemn Tom, eyes narrowing to a squint to see
how I was really taking it. I'd have all day Wednesday off
and Thursday morning.

We climbed dark stairs to the first floor family quarters,

18

where hefty Tess with lantern jaw and pullet-choking forearms posed in a gloomy forest of front room mahogany. The kids were still in school, Brendan and Siobhán, two dotey things . . . Said Tess to Tom, 'Let him be sure, whatever he does, to put the run on Brendan if he as much as shows his nose inside even the saloon.' Ah yes, child-minding: would that be extra?

We climbed another flight, up to the low-ceilinged servants' room. A frozen pond of colourless lino, a gas fire, sofa, chest, hospitalish iron beds . . . *Oh no, another fucking first, room-sharing!* But Big Tom was eyeing me again . . . *In fact, dear guv of mine, these arrangements suit me down to the ground. It isn't only their tastefulness and heartwarming homeliness . . . The walls, distempered ice blue, exactly the colour of my poor mother's eyes, and if you want to know the truth, Tom — may I call you Tom? — I feel so close to you and your great work, with which, need I add, it is an honour to be associated — it takes me back, that's what I really like about it, really.*

'I may as well tell you,' Tom said then. 'I'm taking you on on two conditions. The first is that you have a batt once a week. And the second is that you're a practising Cat'lic. I'm a Knight of Columbanus meself.'

Cleanliness, godliness, anything, everything. Take me, I'm yours. You've paid Emerald, haven't you? By the way, did you hear the one about the whore and the huckster? Brought her down to his own level.

I could have laughed, could have cried, could have screamed. But instead I said, mildly, yes. It was colder outside than in. And I was colder inside than out, from uncertainty and fear. I could only imagine for myself compliance, surrender, desirelessness.

But, as though to soothe my gutlessness and make no choice seem best choice, the rest went quickly, and I felt nothing. In no time I was an ad for service in a starched white jacket, staring like an idiot at my first customer as he went, 'Forced bran.' He kept repeating this with quiet authority, and why not? He knew much more about it than

I did. But, beyond looking for poultry feed, I had no idea how to help him. Eventually, red-faced, he just shut up and pointed. Oh – Forest Brown!

I uncapped the bottle of ale and began to pour. Bubbles of muddy suds belched genteelly into the glass. I watched it all the way, as though watching would convince me that I'd begun at last and that all my English firsts were now behind me.

I've often seen that brown ale since in my mind's reliable eye. It was at the time, holding and pouring, that I couldn't quite acknowledge the reality of it.

II

There may once have been jolly gardeners like those on the nameboard, kicking up their heels though far from being all found, their worldly goods hanging in a hankie from a stick. When all Lambeth was a polder, they were king. When old Blake was round the corner, they piped and piped for joy, and the poet imagined them true heirs of Albion. Green and pleasant land. All as far away as home, now. I was not in the business of horticultural hilarity.

Still, there were the Breton onion peddlers, Charles and Yves. I thought their names were Shirl and Eve at first. I thought of boarding school and boys called Betty Phelan, Susie Hamilton. But these didn't seem like men who'd stand being nicknamed. Yves, the older, looked as stony as the coast he came from, face the colour of limestone, canny eyes like slits in battlements. And though nothing like as craggy – he was oafish, ponderous, yokeloid; his people had cameo roles in *Madame Bovary* while Rodolphe shot the shit with Emma – Charles's sheer bulk was formidable. They rolled their own cigarettes with Boar's Head tobacco, which was seaweed steeped in creosote (nothing would please me but to try it, like a man – when in Lambeth do as the Bretons do).

By day they pedalled through Brixton on to Putney, left Lavender Hill, wound up at Dulwich, their wares hung over the handlebars in loops, the golden apples of the sun, suburban-style. I heard them roaring out their presence where commerce had to be discreet or not at all, in those Penges which are the acme of privacy, those states of semi-detachment which are anathema to earthiness, the Plumsteads and the Mitchams mapped out in gardens, walks, villas, ways, and countless other prettified, sought-after confinements. Feel their firmness and silky skin, lady. Speak with maharajahs bearing pomegranates. I looked on jealously from the privet.

By night they drank and fought. They drank to fight. That was a way of being together that they understood. Intimates, they knew language was their most wounding weapon, and everything in their language sounded like the cruellest barracking. Fired by cider, first, then brandy, then bottles of Flowers' Brewmaster, they heaped upon each other's heads what sounded like the slops and dregs of all that was Bretonically derogatory. We all drew back a pace and smiled, pretending we knew how it was when it came to Frogs and passion. Beloved infidels, their lumpy ganseys, the kind of homespun I remembered from childhood as being to the outer man what stirabout (which the material resembled) was to the inner. And when, no matter how crushing their argy-bargy sounded, they linked arms and stumbled off to their onion-rancid room, tolerant head-shaking followed them as though they were a tableau vivant of 'My Old Dutch'. For they were regulars, after all, 'They're *owroigh*', ole Eve and Shirl.'

I tried to translate *owroigh*'. Joe Nagy, the Mackenson fiend, was defny *owroigh*', even though he'd tried to poison Jack, George and the gang. He was a Hungarian refugee, with black glittering eyes and a quiff that had the blue-black sheen of a crow. I'd come across Joe before too. He was a bonier, more lined edition of the face on my old Yugoslav stamps. Jack loved to tell the poisoning story, and when he did, Joe slowly let a great vulpine grin spread over his face, so by the time the story ended it seemed that his high Hungarian cheekbones had been pushed painfully upwards, glueing his eyes shut and crinkling his low brow, so that he looked like a gargoyle of delight. Joe's first had just arrived, see, so he was down the pub calling for cigars and brandy and Gawd knows what, a regular bleeding Winston Churchill (stone me, I think yore guvnor even stood a round that night, and we wuz drinking in here an' all, not – Jack jerked a dismissive thumb towards the saloon). So anyhow, it's midnight, and we're all turfed out. But ole Joe 'ere says 'ere come on back to my place. Wool, his wife's still in the yospitle, so we get a few quart bottles and right. And Joe has this proper spread laid on. There's aim sandwiches, crisps, pickles, jellied ills, we've never had it so bleeding good, eh? Wool, I mean, he's a daddy, any? Still, fair do's. I remember when our Pete came along we had nuffink: ask her. (Betty's face of stone corroborated). So, there we are, scoffing away. George takes a real fancy to these dainty little chicken legs. I had a few meself, an' all. Some Ungarian nosh: had this red stuff on: dead tasty. There was ole George, smacking his lips and going, ''Ere Joe, got'ny more of that chicken?' – scoffed the lot, had George! *Chicken?* Joe goes, most upset. That's no chicken – it's pigeon! Blimey; I thought George's going to faint dead away. And so should I've done an' all. And of course we've all had some, so we're standing there looking at each other and coming over all queer, and pretty sharpish it's nothing only, ta-ta, Joe, thanks for a lovely time, mate, then back indoors double quick, into the carzey chop-chop, and finger down the frow'.

Jack looked at me expectantly, but I didn't get it. 'Faacking pigeons,' he explained. 'TB.' So I went, 'Oh', miming comprehension, thinking it must be some kind of folktale. Pigeons must be these Cockneys' idea of child-stealers, milk-turners, fly-by-nights, carriers of the indefensible, inexplicable great white plague. How quaint. Cryptococcosis never crossed my mind. I thought instead, sentimentally, of Joe scouring the borough for paprika, trying to remember how they used to do things in Tiszakécske from which he had always thought wild horses couldn't drag him. Now here he was a daddy, devoted to milk stout. Accepted. Settled. If that was what *owroigh'* meant, I was lost.

'Ha-ha! You'll never go back now . . .'

I cringed. I winced. It was Gort the mocker, and he was not at all *owroigh'*. I called him Gort to myself, not knowing his real name or anything else about him, except that he had a Galway accent and the go of a tinker and the regulars talked of him as a bleeder who was bad news. He only dropped in on us when temporarily barred from the Feathers, the other Whitbread house up Lambeth Walk. But his irregularity added menace to his much-repeated greeting, catch phrase, gibe, prophecy, warning, judgement, insult and everything else I insecurely made of it. Worse than not knowing how to answer him was not knowing when. He was as bad as a boss.

'Tell me, now; did you do Latin at school? How would you say, a pint of light and bitter, *más é do thoil é?'* His laugh was the sound of a bucket scraping an empty well. 'You're an educated-looking gorsoon, so listen: if a centipede a pint how much would a precipice?'

Go 'way, God blast you. Leave me alone. Leave me to the loneness that at least I can call my own. Let me be foreign and amongst the foreigners. But it unnerved me that this was just what he had in mind. Was there more, something I couldn't face? His tramp's bold glare and shoulder-swaying gait made him seem so knowing. Had he just taken one look at me and seen nothing new? That was the thought that hurt. There was no visible me. I'd happened a million times before in all those lads and lassies from all those Lismores, all those suitcases hauled through Euston secured with binder twine, all those unavailing Pioneer pins and scapulars and miraculous medals, all gone for good and nothing to show for it.

And maybe he felt he had a right to heckle me, being one

of them, one of us. He wore one of the uniforms: muddy
wellingtons and the stuffing seeping from the oxters of an
addled jacket, grimy denims and greasy hat. His country
now was Charing Cross; his countrymen, Embankment's
poor. Don't fool yourself, said his appearance. The likes of
us are not the romantic egotists of exile. We lack even the
drama of the refugee, some newsworthy curse of history to
make us tolerable, pitiable, credible. European. We're just
banal immigrants, boy. In it for the money.

If Gort had been a regular I might have learned more from
him, or about him, like his right name (his was the only one
I didn't know), or he might have seen how well I understood him. (*Father!*) But I doubt it. Big Tom wouldn't have
stood for it. He hated Gort. It was easy enough to see why.
Any self-respecting Knight of Columbanus must have been
inclined, either by the camber of his own small soul or by his
peers in the lodge, to look askance at a compatriot who
didn't observe the weekly ablutions rule. Besides, Big Tom
wouldn't have me talking to Gort because he couldn't bear
me talking to anyone. I was to work and nothing but. Words
were not pleasures but activities. Scrape, scrub, haul, sweep,
wipe, were the roots of Big Tom's vocabulary, and I, learning them as though for the first time, was slow, dumb.

A char came to dust, and a whistling window cleaner paid
a weekly call. I bristled at his chirrup. But it was live-in colleague Joe and I who did the rough stuff. We started at eight
sharp. Then, after a stale taste of the night before, porridge
and red tea, and back to the detritus of others' pleasure,
crumpled papers full of treble chance, filter tips with lipstick
traces. Wash all the ashtrays in the one sink, put out fresh
place mats. Sort out the empties. Worthington bottles
couldn't go with Whitbreads, but they could go with Bass
and Guinness. That was important. Fill up the shelves.
Winch full crates from cellar to bar on the dumb waiter
(agent of my nemesis). Don't watch the ceremony of the
addage, in which a place was found for the slops collected
in beer engines' bedpans. Added to what? Joe officiated,

carrying the white plastic bucket. But he wouldn't say. His sole concern, contracted from his guvnor, was that everything looked as if it was bathed once a week, as if it was as much a victim of neatness as, say, a misfit in a starched white jacket.

And all for nothing. Slow mornings with old dears in for their remedial Guinness, and Ernie, the saloon's solo fixture thanks to the thirst put on him delving in the Decca boiler room. Occasionally at lunch time a natty gent breezed in, surprising us by the wan but pretty girl on his arm and a blustery manner. Scotch and dry was the order for his ruddy jowlship, and for the lady, Babycham. She ensconced herself in a corner, crossing her long thin legs, exhaling the smoke of her Benson and Hedges as if smoking were the acme of the voluptuary's art. Her escort — blazer, foulard with amoeba pattern, slacks of cavalry twill, temporarily between positions in the motor trade — loudly called for shepherd's pie, needing to impress.

Most evenings there were only a sprinkling of regulars. Pete Worrell's wife, lost, lonely, pretty Linda, sitting by Betty, saying little, drinking splits of bitter lemon, her purse in her lap. The gay couple in their powder and paint dropped by and mingled, acting for an hour as if they felt right at home with the salt of the proletarian earth, each one of whom made sure I knew he, she, personally detested pooftahs, but well this couple's neighbours, see, and *owroigh'* really. Some nights it would have paid to call time at nine, but Big Tom kept us at it. It was his job. And there was always tomorrow to prepare for — so, wash and sweep, fill up, fill up. He hung out in the even emptier saloon, pretending that he and joviality were old mates, guffawing when he thought he should, accepting cigarettes although he didn't smoke. Ash peppered his unchanging blue serge suit. Smoke dribbled out of the side of his mouth and made his eyes run. And all the time I felt him watching me, his vigilance making me a skiver. I so often left the dumb waiter down — in the basement to be loaded, rather than safely full and flush with the bar floor − that it must have seemed deliberate. A booby trap for Brendan. After all the times he'd told me . . . I must have been looking for trouble.

That's the reason, I see now, that I feel I must call that guv Big Tom. Not because of his bulk: wife Tess was twice his size. But he cast a bulky shadow. He was authority's inescapable oppressiveness, made yet more weighty by the Irishly small space in which we worked. Although he was only doing to me what was being done to him by his fear of others. The Inspectors. Agents far more powerful than those of Columbanus and his unmerry men.

There were two types of inspector. One came from the brewery, the other from the borough. They were either in the great unwashed pocket of the ratepayer or folded into the pukka wallet of big business. Men from outer space (the world), who'd have no cause for quarter. And you knew not the day nor the hour when either might descend, smiting the unready with penalties, fines and dire publicity, costing him his licence, throwing wife and little ones on to the damp, dirty streets of the labyrinthine, pestilential, unGalwayfied Smoke (God between us and all harm). If they see the slightest hair astray on you, they'll have your guts for garters. Therefore, underlings do not smoke behind the bar. If you're offered a drink, just take the price of it. Abandon props conducive to being social.

Because if there was one thing it was necessary to be in this life it was to be *sure*. All the more so with clowns around who didn't take proper care of the dumb waiter, so that the child could run down unbeknownst to everyone and plunge headlong into the black cellar hole and break his skull, crack his neck, die roaring with the blood pumping out of him, everyone, but especially himself and Tess doomed and helpless, watching the nightmare of their emigrant lives. There was no imagining that wasn't terroristic, no future conceivable without dread. Therefore, he had to sack me for leaving the dumb waiter down and purposely putting the child in danger. Or so he said.

I had never seen Brendan inside the bar, and never ever near the wretched winch. But by the time Big Tom gave me the boot – damp, dirty streets, et cetera – things were too far gone between us to be influenced by facts or actualities. We both knew that a hole in the floor was my mark and seal. I was the uncertainty and recalcitrance everyone sensibly fends off with paranoia.

I remember never being asked who or what I was, or if I don't exactly remember, no twinge of interest presents itself to be embellished, no echo returns of a laugh shared or a back slapped, there's nothing that imagination might inflate, imitating the roundness and the resonance of the fullness of time. Life was the dreadfulness of simplicity itself.

There were the consolations of cleanliness, of course. Wednesday night was bath night, and when I emerged from my scorching purgation Tess was usually in the offing. Would I like to watch a bit of television? She'd put the kettle on. Pristine me was ushered into the mahogany museum. The kids, glowing in their nighties, regarded me with wide kids' eyes. They couldn't stay, though. The news was on: adult time had officially begun. Then *Play for Today*, with strong tea and a couple of figrolls. I watched the broken jigsaw on the screen attempt to unscramble itself, registering its intensities and withdrawals, the unfamiliar angles and rare fisticuffs, the evasions and abruptnesses. '*Dul*ling,' the mistress sultrily intoned. Later a man said in a tense, stern voice, 'For God's sake, Moira –' Tess sighed: 'I dunno how you can watch that old rubbish', she was away to her bed – to say the rosary, I supposed. But watch I did those elliptical, storyless entities, fascinated by their opacity and thinking that I now knew why Jack Worrell called telly the haunted fishtank. (If Ken Loach did not exist, it would have been necessary to invent him.)

I watched because I thought I'd learn something. I watched because the channels were not mine to change. I stayed to the end because I thought the cost of hospitality must be paid. They knew where I was and what I was doing, which meant I wasn't above in the bed wanking the night away, a banned book (I was trying to read *Lie Down in Darkness*) beside me on the pillow, seizing my chance, if that's the word, the one time the room was unshared. No. I was clean. I was innocent.

As for godliness, uncannily precise inversion of self-abuse though it was in theory, in practice it turned out to be less restorative than cleanliness. Not that Sunday mass was entirely without pleasure. It felt fine and manly to step out to it with Joe those early Sunday mornings. The air was hoary, the cold enough to snap the bridge of a nose. But as soon as the church hove into view out of the mist all pleasure ceased. The very appearance of the place put me right off. It was hardly more than a glorified shed, tucked into a niche on the side of a side street, its frontage a lot narrower than the Jolly Gardeners', no steps to stop and gossip on, no neighbouring graveyard giving worship point. It was no grander than the Methodists' down the road, for God's sake. Stables were all very well in warm climates. And as well as being cold, the place was empty, therefore colder still, just a handful of strangers, mostly spindly women, none of the next-door faces that used to make religion tolerable.

The priest's voice was thin, unctious, impersonal, more a function of training than conviction. He addressed us briefly. His theme was charity. He condemned not, neither did he rouse. Kindness was uncontroversially enjoined. His overamplified sing-song went by metallic leaps and bounds over the heads of the scanty faithful. 'Let us pray.' But there was no us. Ah, where was the old harangue that used to have us shaking in our shoes, the fierce ukase and the thunderous riot act under whose fiat we sinners, knowing no better, thrilled to the unity that came from being given hell? I tried with Joe to find words for what I never thought I'd miss as we walked back. He thought I was mocking.

At least, though, Sundays were also when regulars

strolled in promptly at noon, rested, smooth shaven (how fascinating and delightful to see 'in the pink' literally translated), sated by footer coverage and gossip about swell and starlet. There was a band in the saloon. Just piano and drums, but thanks to the music, for once the present was enough. 'Knocked 'em, bonked 'em, thumped 'em, bashed 'em, right down in the Old Kent Road,' went Tony's fingers. He swung 'The White Cliffs of Dover' *à la* Acker Bilk. It was trad. It was mod. It was whatever you're having yourself. *Fings ain't what they used to be.* The feints and squeezes, fly-by-night airs and cocky graces tipped a knowing wink not only to the ivories' essential ticklesomeness but the world's. I was the only one trying to listen, my efforts costing Whitbread a fortune in wrong change. But I could no more pretend I was an employee than could the customers. The aroma of our mutton dinner wafted down the stairs. Tony tinkled through 'These Foolish Things'.

When it was all over I climbed up to the room, a song still in my heart and a half-stone of mash in my gizzard. I saw the long afternoon stretch out ahead full of possibilities. Maybe I'd write home today (maybe I'd decide I had a home to write to). Maybe I'd sink into a long read of the Styron and mercifully lose sight of myself. Joe turned the gas fire up full and kicked off his shoes. He was for sleep. Outside, it was beginning to rain.

Joe slept quietly, just the odd fitful snore, not a bother on him, slain by the weight of lunch, and thankful. But then he was on his sober way, knew where he was going, accepted apprenticeship now as the just price of mastery of his own house later. Upward and onward in the trade: Jolly Gardener begets Green Man begets Lord Nelson begets Kings Arms. That way certainty lay. Joe, son of Big Tom, was no daw. And at long last, after ten or fifteen years living clean and saving everything, he'd go home, paint on a lintel notice of a seven-day licence, have a little bed and breakfast too besides. He's married now, help is living in, all found. Later, the children reared, he feels drawn to politics, stands for Fianna Fáil, which is still in power.

I looked out the window. There was the unglistening ocean of London brick: grey, damp, dull red. My future. Somewhere out there, the lunch-time melody has its echo. I hate its inaudibility. I'd imagined I was on freedom's road, but here I was as if I hadn't budged, my fears of rejection, uselessness and isolation confirmed rather than relieved. I should be led by silent Joe, count my savings and think them blessings. Go back. Lismore . . .

I went out the Ballyduff road, and over to Tallowbridge, then round the Sweep. I saw a hundred townlands and the name of every one of them was welcome. I went down by Camphire. The River Bride nuzzled through bright abundant fields and cows stood in the oozy shallows, cooling. At Curraheen a girl with red hair waved. But a'ready I was passing Janeville. I was flying down Spillar_'s Hill. I was going the wrong way, had no direction. But I couldn't stop.

I woke with a dry mouth. The letters home remained unwritten. I put aside *Lie Down in Darkness*. It was black night all over London. Joe stirred. Time for another stint downstairs. I turned off the suffocating fire. The room reeked of sweaty socks. That was the end of Sunday.

III

That Styron novel came from Cecil Court, and I knew Cecil Court because I lived for Wednesday, my day of rest, my day of mounting restlessness. Even if all the day amounted to was walking from pillar to post, being out gave me the grand illusion of latitude and capitalicity. Pacing the unvarying round behind the bars lacked such a sense, somehow. And to escape was human; to forget, divine.

The first or second Wednesday, as I set out, Big Tom asked where I was going so early. 'Up West,' I breezily replied. Whether it was my cheeky cockney chappie affectation, or that he saw something even more objectionable in my awareness of how free my day might be, this answer drew one of his withering, cockeyed looks. Impudent brat, rolling into God gimme patience. Who did I think I was, exactly, that I couldn't be content to stay close by, sip a leisurely morning Guinness with the racing page for grand company, address my wit to picking out a cushy cross double and amble up to the Joe Coral.

To do otherwise was to heed the tocsin, 'London calling'. It was obscurely but inescapably to betray, to risk a bad end. Maybe Big Tom meant merely to be fatherly, his glare a stern statement for my own good, because he knew me for a weakling. *There is no other life, fooleen! Run the race you're drawn in, and stop pretending. Stick to inn and village, idiot child.* Up West was passionate neon and bad company and all his Columbanic knighthood should oppose. But I just said, 'I'll ring if I'll be out to dinner.'

A damp wind billowed in from Gravesend, chill, invigorating, spurring me well beyond workaday dawdle. I was so alive I felt virtually businesslike. The damp smelled fresh and vaguely earthen, uncommercial; now was I in truth a jolly gardener, about my cultivation. At this hour, tenish, the city was rising in earnest, towers and bridges stretching out from thin blankets of grizzled haze. Earth has not anything to show more fair, eh? There it all was, now, strange words like minster and palace, cloister and chapterhouse, made real as stone. In comparison Dublin was an architectural deserted village. Dull would he be – yes, yes, quite so. But why couldn't I warm to being upon Westminster Bridge?

Wordsworth had had summer on his side, of course, but weather had nothing to do with it. And neither had loyalty to Dublin. (I'd never go back now.) It wasn't even the reflexes conditioned long ago by the mere mention of the mother of parliaments that created my standoffishness. The Royal Festival Hall made me feel the same way, although I knew it was an entirely different kind of place, a civic rather than an imperial palace, a peace offering (though that peace's character was more ably conveyed by the sense of bouncers' shoulders given by Shell House, opposite). I froze up as well at the dome of St Paul's, and Somerset House, the National Gallery, County Hall, Saint Thomas à Cobley and all. The surfeit of fake Vaticans overwhelmed me. I was confused by the absence of ruins. These weren't simply buildings, they were monuments to being significant. They were all much too finished, too final, too full of themselves, too much at odds with my transience and insubstantiality. Give me Cecil Court, not Lord Cecil B. De Mille.

It was hardly a street at all, too narrow for cars or even to admit much sun, no more than a hens' race between St Martin's Lane and Charing Cross Road, a thoroughfare the image of insignificant me. I can pretend now that this was why I was drawn to it. I wasn't drawn. There was no reason. It happened. That was all I wanted, for my free day to ratify my freedom.

I see a jeweller's, also a shoe-repair place, and I'm sure there was a newsagent's kiosk, with a frosty miss in charge, her hands red raw with cold. There were some other fronts as well, windows whitened and only one of their tall double doors ajar. Sometimes men in hats went in. Cardboard brokers, shareholders in Chinese peppermint mines, out-takes of Dickens. In back rooms they wet thumb and index finger, turned ream after ream of yellowing invoices (c.i.f., Macao), brushing aside cobwebs, unknotting and reknotting red tape, green-eyed like little yellow gods. But what I really enjoyed was no imagining but how pleasantly unhurried the pavement was, and how I felt that this was London on a scale that I could live with. This place was a bridge between the narrow pub and the wide other. And then there was the bookshop.

Books were what had brought me to this part of London in the first place. It wasn't temper, language, work or outlook that England and I had in common, but that small superfluous good, the paperback. So, to Foyle's I came, my first day off. A papal yellow banner hung outside, much larger than any flag on my way in and much more uplifting. This was my kind of country. But inside, though, it was more like Euston, with departments as numerous as platforms, and trainees shunting busily to and fro. Instead of the city smells that gave intoxicating greeting as I left the boat train, there was the heady plumage of what seemed more like parasols, awnings and the seaside of life than mere dust jackets. I was carried away. And there in the midst of all, my very own lost baggage, *banned books!* Lady Con and Henry Schlong were eating naked lunch. Artilleryman Mailer blasted and bombardiered all around him. Baldwin, Heller, Roth sprang to the eye in the livery of Corgi. Calder Willingham, how do you do? Ye're me mates, right? Great crack we'll have together from here on. But say: who's this Malamud published by unfamiliar Ace? What do you think of David Karp? How to survive England: read American fiction.

Labelling didn't necessarily entail direction, however. I made this discovery at the Mayfair theatre. There was to be a conversation between Malcolm Muggeridge and Norman Mailer about *An American Dream.* Tynan would be there, and all those other big names in print from the quality Sundays. It didn't matter that I couldn't tell one from the other. I'd breathe their cultured honeyed air. I'd be legit.

The host enquired (I hear his sibyline sibilance), 'Are you suggesting, Norman, that the penis is a gun symbol, or that the gun is a penis symbol?' The guest's face crinkled into a virtual tantrum of charm and he hunched up his shoulders then spoke in a series of short, breathy clusters, for all the world resembling combinations of jabs and crosses thrown at a target which moved only because he made it. His breath was audible, a light rasp, as of plimsoll on canvas. I have no idea what he said or what happened next. I remember smug laughter in the audience. I remember an air of confidence so overwhelming as to feel reckless. And I remember wondering, What is all this? and being only able to reply, Don't ask me, I only work here.

Perhaps some of those present had already begun stream-lining the various bandwagons of abandon on which we all went out of our minds a few years later. In their midst that evening, however, I felt more or less dead than alive, laid out in the suffocating, indomitable corduroy of my hipless-ness, a foreign fiction, but hopelessly banal. Me thinking that I was somehow liberated, unbanned, when I was quite incapable of even rendering to penis the things that were penis's, much less to gun those that were gun's.

Foyle's was for spending, but I quickly found my day out was not a money matter. There had to be mystique, too, at-mosphere, personality, specialness. To these the hot pink of Foyle's florescent ambiance was not conducive. So I tried Collet's. But there were always too many bearded men con-versing earnestly with the staff, and more off-puttingly with each other, making me feel alone.

The Cecil Court bookshop made being alone feel right. It was a small shop, but had few customers, so felt big. In memory it seems a dim place, perhaps because the floor space was bisected by a floor-to-ceiling bank of shelves, and I liked the cavelike dimness. Or like the idea of it now. It adds a surreptitious air, a rumour of defiance, to my free time. And there were books! – tiers upon tiers of them, shelved horizontally in narrow black compartments and lots of paperbacks to fuel the dominant fantasy of the would-be man of property, bulk buying. Books on ballet launched faerie queens through encellophaned air. Evergreen, Grove Press and City Lights beguiled me. They didn't fit in pockets. They looked new and difficult. They had unheard-of authors – Radiguet, Ionesco, Ferlinghetti . . . Everything about the place expressed the dreamy fetishism that was my love of books: the turning over of new leaves, the inky freshness, the talismanic colophons, the innocence of the unappropriating look and touch, and of commerce made tolerable through sublimation.

I could go on. The week's work had been purged, and not through the confessional, but by its precise opposite. I had committed the sin of self, had been left alone with my appetites. I knew the criminality of it, heard the charges of treachery, betrayal and sacrilege. But on I briskly went, up St Martin's Lane or along William IV Street, high, buoyed by the ebb and flow of naïveté and need, the pitch and toss played by aspiring sophisticate against belated altar boy. *Il se promène, au lisant le livre interdit de lui-même!* Or, if not exactly reading it, hoping to be judged by its cover. Boldly I ventured where no tubes ran, dusty Seven Dials, Mayfair of the mews and MG Midgets, Soho.

Babylon, Babylon! Lascar seamen, Turkish coffee, Jewish delis, Cinerama, Chinese papers, Yorkshire puds. The world was a sordid rainbow, and the pavements seemed perpetually wet, as though constantly scoured. There was the 2 I's. I'd heard of that: someone had dreamed up Tommy Steele there. It looked ordinary, all formica and fanless, and smaller than I remembered from pictures in *New Musical Express*. That's how it goes, city-wise. Guitars and coffee bars, the mud and wattle of the pop age, were ancient history (over five years old), so passé that boutiques were being invented to replace them. Ronnie Scott's looked the part, more, being dark, awaiting the wee small hours and night's subversive pulses, when the crooning, moaning, fretting locomotion of the reeds came into their own. Ben Webster, Stan Getz. For adults only. Tubby Hayes. I wistfully walked on. Leafless limbs in Soho Square, office blocks ashen-faced in late January light. Kettner's. The Establishment Club. I passed by. Aubergine, moussaka, goulash, cappucino, lox, Balkan Sobranie. This finite place's inexhaustible inventory. Each new word named pleasure and desire. Each new word was an act of learning, teaching me reasons for being here.

And there was sex, foreignest of all, as pervasive as alleged in childhood pulpits, its clergy shady characters in black shirts and jackets with lapels like traffic islands. They prowled the dark electric doorways singing hell's praises, the verse of which went, 'The show's just starting', and the response, 'Twelve exciting girls'. At three in the afternoon? They must take me for a proper mug, I knew as well as they did that nobody was exciting until after dark. Even their sunglasses said as much. Behind those shades gyrates the night-time of your mind. 'A dozen gorgeous lovelies!'

I passed by on the other side, pretending indifference to the unholy grottoes in case the Greek Street Godivas made me have an accident, then paused a few yards further on for an un-full frontal. I'd have preferred it if the pictures were life-sized. But since everything else about these figures was beyond me – their spread-leg stance, the hair just long enough to veil and unveil breasts, the zone from waist to thigh girdled with encomia – their larger-than-life presence seemed unreally right. I was just glad to see what I had never seen (had hardly hoped to see), nipples like sore thumbs, implication of v, fleshpots front and rear, and the body unbanned.

Maybe because my erection was so mechanical and in-voluntary, or because traipsing from club hoarding to adult bookshop window as chill dusk fell could feel, at length, as cold as charity, I began to concentrate on what might lie ahead. I tried to read the pinups' expressions. But terms like sultry, kittenish, brazen, Jesus-Mary-and-Joseph-lookadah, got me no further than the sexsational clichés covering their cardboard crotches. And even if I did make it to her bed-room, I'd have to be President Kennedy and she Marilyn Monroe to make the encounter credible. Brother Murphy and Mother Benignus. No incongruity could match the reality. Which was only natural. This was the city where nature was artifice and the body was merely a medium, a currency; where to strip was to tease and the world became flesh became devil. Even my small stand insisted that the show go on, even though the stand made me feel like a combination of Noddy in Toyland and a spare prick at a wedding.

I never did meet Maureen with the large chest for sale or Pat the French polisher. I never had the good time promised, would hardly have known what to do with one. A nice time would have done me fine. So I dreamt of what kind of time that might be, as before long, my walks grew longer and I was able to cruise through Soho as a matter of course and on through Fitzrovia, over as far as Marylebone. Here I felt safer. Here, one of these days, I'd meet, on the tube, in a bus, inevitably, a mature sixth-former bursting out of her gymslip, Jenny, given to angst and Mars Bars. And I'd fall, deliberately, heavily, happily and for ever.

Not that her charms mattered to disembodied me. I was firm on that. (Charms they certainly were, needless to say. Pop's suburban doubletalk would be our lingua franca. I smiled, imagining us tiffing playfully over her unfortunate attachment to Cliff Richard.) Much more important than bumps fore and aft were ears. She'd be all ears, but hours later, if I stopped talking, she might kiss me, maybe even on the mouth. Her lips would taste of chocolate. I'd experience chaste meltdown. Everything between us would be riskless, costless. I'd understand that absence was a synonym for desire. I'd be in love, plain and simple.

Till that happy day, then, Maureen and Pat, if it's all the same to you, I'll go on dating myself on Wednesday afternoons – at the Cameo-Poly watching Anna Karina, who at least was enigmatic, at the Globe on the corner of Baker Street and Marylebone Road, dining early on a pork pie and a pint of Truman's, pulled by slack-jawed, watery-eyed Jimmy, whose accent placed him in the parish of Kilmac, a million miles away in County Waterford. He turned to the racing page. I ignored him as well. It had possibilities as endless as the Wednesday city and the gymslip girl for company. I'd seen one of her mothers step briskly out of a shinily plaqued doorway in Harley Street. Another in bedroom slippers and a choker of pearls made haste for an Express Dairy, carrying a poodle. The real thing was probably that invisible but debonair someone for whom a taxi waited, purring throatily, outside a block of ample old apartments in sleepy Seymour Place. They'd just love to have me for the holidays. Would I like an apéritif? No fanks, I'd quip ever so wittily; brough' me own pair-o'-teef, ta. Oh, how they'd adore me! And sitting on my seat-edge with the schooner of sherry, I'd be, at last, a long way from Lismore and Lambeth. And never would go back.

Big Tom caught my drift, too. The dumb waiter always fatally down. 'The child will break his shagging neck!' Let him, I glowered.

I stopped dancing attendance on the all-important regulars in the saloon. I mixed up the empties and failed to fill up. How could I bother my head with the rubbish of earning a living with Balcombe Street beckoning and *The Peach Thief* (Bulgaria) at the Academy? I swept up and dried up and declined to shut up, as brazen as bedamned.

I didn't have to wait long for walking papers.

'In the office. *Now.*' The last harangue, its theme the old familiar of my unfitness (how I embraced it). Its irresistible connection to my open-floor assassination plot against young Brendan was the 'real' reason I was being 'let go'.

I tapped my foot. I shook my head. No, I had nothing to say.

Big Tom got very mad. Fight denied, his face turned crimson. 'Sign that!'

Coolly, I complied, delightedly depriving myself of dole, though I didn't realise that till Big Tom, with a snide smile, let me know. Ah, stuff your scrap of paper. I pocketed the tenner 'in lieu of notice; but I want you out of here within the hour'.

It would be dark . . . I spoke then – I hope my voice was steady. 'I want to call a taxi.'

Big Tom flung the phone across the desk at me: 'Call yer fecking granny. But get out!'

I ran upstairs and threw my duds into the bag. Leaving again. Another uninspiring boss, another unfulfilling home. Lismore, Dublin, Lambeth . . . It wasn't the repetitiveness that now came to mind, however, but the novelty that I'd felt every change presaging. Each closed-behind-me door had left me freer than before. Now more than ever. The wide world of the city would sustain me, no strings attached. Its pattern, too, was based on repetition, street by impersonal street, wage by dulling wage. At least, though, I could make my own of it, and live, somehow, improvising, learning, myself alone. Here might be one whose name is writ in gutter. But let me start, at least. I stood on the kerb, impatient for the cab, shivering a little in the mist from the river, but with never a backward look, telling myself that it was time indeed for starting. I'd be twenty in a week.

THE CHAIRS

I

That night I slept in Highbury, in my own room, as proud
a possessor of my own keys as if the estate agent had given
them to me for free. By noon next day I'd landed a sales
invoiceship at Calor Gas (Distributing), Great Portland
Street – in the heart of London's West End! Posher yet, it
was at the (Holding) company's Cavendish Square palace
that I was taken on. Passing the stern commissionaire, his
pseudomilitary finery a rehearsal for the sleeve of *Sergeant
Pepper*, I dismissed him as a fancy-dress guvnor and crossed
the cathedraloid lobby, pretending not to notice his sus-
picious glare. And to rise in the world, I carried no hod. I
ascended to the twelfth floor. I sank to my calves in carpet.
There was a door of frosted glass marked potently, Person-
nel. This was style. Thrice I blessed the name of Alfred
Marks, the genuine article, a real man, neither afraid nor
ashamed to put his name to his work, not like old, faded
Emerald.

Miss Languid Edwards would see me now. She clearly
was an Officer, a Director, a Chief or Head, because there

was no typewriter in her office and she was a woman. She tilted her head from side to side appraising me, trying to find a favourable light, perhaps, or maybe needing to rid herself of a pain in the neck. With slow, delicate gestures she arranged and rearranged my paper life on her bare desk. It seemed to be accepted that I bathed. And she was obviously too well bred to let religion come between us. She knows me, I thought, happily.

Ten quid a week? Done. A week in hand? Certainly, certainly – worth two in the bush, ha-ha (but what did it mean?). But I was too high on unfamiliar glee to be practical – besides, to admit not knowing would be too embarrassing. The sympathetic look Miss Edwards gave me once I'd signed on, however, made me wonder if I'd done something wrong. Maybe I owed it to myself to rise above the Big Tom scale. Still, word that I was to be paid partly in the new currency – luncheon vouchers – sweetened the deal. Novelty meant more to me than cash. And now she was giving me her long, cool hand.

'Did you know,' she said, 'our managing director is a cousin of the Queen?'

Ah, this is class all right, I told myself, and I felt as smug as a butler.

As I made my way knightwise across the chess-quiet grid of streets to Great Portland Street and Sales Invoicing B, I began to see what that royal remark was getting at. There was a Cavendish, then a New Cavendish, and next door, a cluster of Devonshires. For a moment I couldn't believe it: I'd apparently found anchorage in the urban manor of the lords of Chatsworth and Lismore. What Miss Edwards meant, and I now understood, was that I'd just been taken on at Lismore Castle. Or rather, more amazingly, it was not the castle itself whose staff I'd joined, but its modern-day transformation.

I was in a higher Lismore, a Lismore transfigured. This parkland of cut stone had so much more poise and pith than the unpaved groves at home (*home!*). I paused to view its stately progress west through Wigmore and Welbeck. Mother Nature, ivied turrets, the Blackwater valley itself – all such picturesqueness was mere sentimentality compared to this irresistible will-to-townhouse and an architect's plan. Here was history making sense, making progress. Things had gone places and had made places things. And I could see with pride that all the Lismore rents, paid by my people and the people of lads I grew up with and poor people up in Botany and down Church Lane, and all our people before them, down the generations, had not been coughed up in vain. They'd found apotheosis in a tower block and a job for me. They'd made good my escape. This precinct of composed façades must be the home I've always longed for, I said to myself, where there never was a hint of ruination and where polite ladies-in-waiting told me how I could be of service to them – oh, sweet antidote to Greek Street! – and would pay me to believe them. And Mrs Ross, greeting me with hand outstretched, was going to be Miss Edwards's sister, sweet mother of Jenny Gym, and my mother also . . .

But Mrs Ross, invoicing boss, was no Lady Languid of Castle Cavendish. Even her appearance said so. She was hefty – and it the reign of Jean Shrimpton. Her hair was strawberry blonde, short and waved, nothing like Joan Baez's. Some of the strawberryifying potion seemed to have spilled onto her puffy cheeks, and around her little eyes she was albino pink – the very opposite of being pale from dope and trying to look natural. She was even unwith it enough to wear lipstick.

And her manner was not aristocratic but English. That meant strict, impersonal, stroppy, sergeant-majorish, efficient. Rude, as well: calling me mister to my face, a thing that had never happened to me, making me blush. (Miss Edwards had called me nothing, and I'd felt very comfortable with that.) Is she out to get me, I began to wonder, to show me up somehow? I was afraid again. But, deep down, it turned out she did care. Underlining the clerkship's intellectual challenge, her voice dropped to a confidential purr and I was graced with a commercialised extract of tenderness: 'This is a good opening for a bright boy.' Then briskly on. *This* piece of paper goes *there*, see, and D & C Notes with T 22s, 'and you check the codes, see,' and bring them *all*, even the cancellations, to the machine room. Most important of all, everything had to be signed. 'For example, you would put' – she checked Miss Edwards's note of introduction to tell me my initials – 'Oh well, we can't have that. GOB – looks ridiculous. Let's have GB instead, shall we?'

Oh, go ahead, don't mind me. Squelch that O' for the sake of the company's good name. Sure it's a thing of nothing anyhow. And the flagship enterprise of HM's cousin can hardly employ clerks whose initials might excite provincial dealers to derision. Lucky my name wasn't Gerry O'Dwyer! But then, what was in a name? (I had to have this job!) As little as there'd been in blood or family or nation, to my mind. Wasn't Mrs Ross my mentor thanks to such empty heritages for which that very O' had stood? It was only a hole which had provided no foundation. Without it I might be more myself, could live untied in the fluid present, concrete my nourishment.

Besides there was no time to brood. Mrs Ross was smartly parading me along a corridor to see my chair and meet my supervisor. 'This is Noel' – Mr No—L, as I would hear him cry in desperation down the phone to depot managers at Ellesmere Port and Neath. Definitely a mister. Obviously the real thing. He wore a suit, his shoes were highly polished, his tie had narrow alternating bands of clashing colours. He had had his name changed, and then some. But I could tell that when Nimal Abeywardena was translated into Calorese he didn't feel the whole of his native Ceylon contract into a solitary teardrop. No sentimental islander he, but Head of Sales Invoicing B, foreign but unfazed, relaxed, perhaps even relieved, to be here. I felt better already. Maybe third world solidarity would rule OK (as we had not yet learned to say). And, decent man, he at once produced a large Player's and lit us up with a gas-charged Ronson the bulk and tone of a hip flask, then with a charming drawl invited me to meet 'these other good-for-nothings'.

People! Colleagues! Oh, brave new world! Peter, whom I was replacing, had vivid yellow pimples. Lawrie completed the B team. He wore motorcycle leggings and was a Jehovah's Witness. Tricia whispered that last piece of information to me, and her olive-black, olive-sized mobile eyes flashed a friendly smile. She worked for Mrs Dundas in Section D. D dealt in cannisters, B with the gas in them. From Contracts (Section C, bulk gas), kindly, doddering Mr Mogg and impossible Nellie Hodges, five feet of misanthropy in pink stockingette . . . Greetings all, my new kin, no stranger and mercifully much less permanent than actual family. And I'd see them Monday. Noel and I shook hands with a warmth that felt almost brotherly. He was *owroigh'*, ole Nole.

Now evenings stretched invitingly ahead. I could start *Under the Volcano*. The Classic, Dalston, had on *A Kind of Loving*: I wouldn't mind seeing it again, the uncut, un-Dublin version. I might even write, now that I had my single room. Take that Biro and knock down the walls! Let the mind roam, let the world in! The pen is mightier than the sword! Page mounted upon page. Ideas coupled, procreated. *I'm free*, I thought, feeling as complete in myself as an abstraction. And I was a commuter. I couldn't get more modern than that.

I wrote. At some point later I even thought enough of the thing to type it – on Liz's Baby Hermes, it looks like (its e's were going blind, I remember). A touching tale it was, as well, without a doubt, all hundred and sixty-three quarto sheets of it, rankly stale from years of bottom drawers and basements, top copy long since lost, a dog-eared thing in ghostly carbon. I try to look away from it. Instead, I read. The paper rustles, out come unquiet, supposedly outgrown, selves. I called it 'Shadows and a Traveller' but, though I've just reread it, I can't say whether the title refers to a condition, or all the characters together, or some of the characters and not others, or whether the title is a signpost for the reader (unlikely: I never imagined readers) or what.

The protagonist and narrator is Philip, a delicate youth, and an orphan by any other name. His mother's dead, his father crippled in body and twisted in mind. Under those circumstances – bearing in mind that the time is the present, the scene Ireland – there's nothing for it, evidently, but Philip must turn priest. But first, before attaining an unexplained and inexplicable apotheosis of his losses by studying in Rome, he is invited up to Dublin for a holiday by his Auntie Maggie. This holiday is The Test. Will our hero to his own self be true? Will he survive the cynicism of cousin Tom ('very witty in an acidic kind of way')? And how will he fare with Kay, who only wanted to be kind? '"Women are creatures with a conceptual mechanism, and are instruments of incidental pleasure." These were the Rector's own words.'

Dublin is Gotham and Phil's Gethsemane. He almost succumbs to a dancehall daze. But the call of the non-life proves stronger. The Test is passed. He departs for Rome and black clothes, transcending with all the smugness of his calling 'these foothills, Tom and Kay, on which I was content to graze so inconclusively . . .' A tale of irony, a tale of poverty, a tale of the powerful, yet, thank God, ultimately powerless tides that surge hungrily around the soul of youth. And so on.

Not that I'm particularly embarrassed by the writing, however embarrassing it is ('I look out into the dim velvet tones of an ailing summer and I see beacons that beckon me along. I see manifested in my silent mind the flesh of faith, the blood of self-generation.'). There was worse to come, in Earls Court short stories the following year, in a thriller, 'Ice', written the year after that (1967) in Mrs Spiegel's, above Lloyd's Bank on the Finchley Road, near Frognal. What gets to me now, in ways for which irony is no defence, is the sign of time spent, and memories of futility. That fact and that feeling are what the carbon represents. It's less a copy than a photo album, less that than an uncanny replication of the emptiness that is both the writing's impetus and theme. The pile of shabby paper is a shadow the traveller hasn't shaken.

I remember seeing nothing between me and nullity but a blank sheet of paper and feeling my heart an ice floe of intractable language. I remember the voices raised in argument from the landlady's basement flat flying up the drainpipe as I damned them for distracting me while at the same time doing my utmost to gather every scrap, envying them the energy of their animus. Doorsteps of Greek bread stood like stanchions in my midriff and the chop lay singed and bloody, discarded in disgust and, with a kind of shame, going dinnerless because of hastening to my higher calling, my art, to which meat and bread meant nothing (its only fit accessories were cigarettes and coffee). If I am embarrassed now, it's not on account of what I was writing but of what writing was, an office which I'd ordained for myself as a substitute for living. As Philip could have told me, the prig, the prick, the loser. My freedom, of which I was so proud, turned out to be more end than means. I became stuck with it.

A time or two on Saturday I took a nineteen to the Angel, aiming for the undiscovered City, but up and down the City Road, in and out of Old Street, I felt discouraged. The king had left his counting house. Warehouse, emporium, clerkery and mongery were in hiatus, shells standing in the dock of time, abashed and unfrequented. Skinner Street and Shepherdess Walk had seen better days. The winter air was dark and brackish, the exhalations of a freighter's hold. There was an atmosphere of tide at ebb and low cloud cover. On my right, Clerkenwell of the bombings and Pentonville of the hangings. My glum mood felt them overshadowing the streets' gloom. The bomb was these thoroughfares' nightmare, but the rope made it bearable. That was history. When will you pay me? my self-pity tolled, attempting in childish desperation to dun the moribund streets. When I grow rich? . . . Their nullity mocked my own. So quickly home, then, head down, skirting Shoreditch and back to Highbury via Ball's Pond Road, hoping at least for tiredness but fixing instead Nescafé for something to do, and so to wank.

Academys and Classics became my seats of learning, larger than bedsitters with larger windows, vast improvements on the increasing pile of unread paperbacks on the chest against my room's broadest, blindest wall (books I'd bought as urgently, and displayed as proudly, as if they were my past's missing photographs). Would I have time to get from the early house of *The Devil at Four O'Clock* at the Tolmer, off the Euston Road, to the five ten screening of *From Russia With Love* at the Astoria, Finsbury Park, and be able to have dinner at a Wimpy as well? Life was plausible when, after lunch and throughout the evening, it became susceptible to scheduling, organisation, form, a facsimile of story, like Philip in the city.

Calling a Wimpy 'dinner' showed as much sense of occasion as thinking the Astoria a mere cinema. To say the very least, it was a picture palace, one of those rare venues fully entitled to more grandiose soubriquets, such as Regal, Ritz, Palladium or even Empire itself. An imperial court, indeed, was what its interior apparently intended to evoke. It was 'Isis Unveiled' as an admass serial, projected in endless instalments of terrazzo. To approach the auditorium through the echoing hallways was to experience in an exalted, intransitive, more permanent form the alleged attractions of the main feature now playing. Plus, it had a fountain.

Unfortunately, however, it only showed ordinary movies, chases and clinches, clinches and chases, time-killers which did my killing for me very well, but which were the Wimpy's ocular equivalent. I wanted the atmosphere and jeopardy of the unusual, the unforeseen angle and the enigmatic event, a foreignness which would compensate for weekend London's undramatic emptiness. I wanted my movies to be in the genre of one, the way I'd hoped to see myself. *Accattone*. *The Sargasso Manuscript*. *The Criminal Life of Archibaldo de la Cruz*. I sat with half a dozen others doing solitary in the Everyman at the first house of *Il Mare* by Giuseppi Patroni Griffi, a name I lingered over like a sauce, its shots of the heaving motion of the mindless sea the very nausea of loneliness itself. And afterwards, in the half-light of four o'clock, there was needling, unIrish rain.

What I was doing seems so pitifully obvious to me now. Without knowing it, I was trying to be my father, with his artsy metropolitanism and his taste for the international. These were the only features of his life, or rather, what I knew of it, which I embraced without reserve, with many a silent tribute. If I'd left behind the man, I had, with inculpable attachment to the superficial (the very stuff of memory), retained the manner. He bought books and loved the cinema. So would I. And I'm struck, too, by the bald fact of his life that, once a widower, he took up with film, as though it was especially helpful in alleviating the mourner's darkness. Out of some frustrated sense of self-dramatisation, or some presumptuous yen for fitness and cohesion which only permit the story to be told rather than the truth, I wonder now if I was mourning too, twitching like an emotional amputee for losses that could only be expressed by means of geography.

Dear Daddy, Everything is fine here. I saw *Through a Glass Darkly*. What do you understand by the word 'home', tell me? Your obedient son, Seoirse.

There were many, many letters that I didn't write.

Dear Aunt Chrissy, I don't even have your address. Dear Granny Royce, and all in Enniscorthy, you lost my mother, you lost everything, now you're losing me. I've mislaid the words to 'The Boys of Wexford' (who fought with heart and hand) and so must fill my mind with Fellini and Godard. Your loving grandchild, guilty heir...

Dear Mam, I've done a few of the things you predicted. The Bless me father for I have sinned and Oh my God I am heartily sorry? I tried them once, but – may I speak freely?

– to hell with them. They're as implausible as a monk's manicure. Especially amongst strangers. As for the mass, Saint Joan of Arc's on Blackstock Road was no better company than freezing Kennington, just a little less cold, bigger crowds, later in the day. There was something I did warm to that last time I was there, though. In my umpteenth scan of the congregation I thought I saw Packy Foley from Round Hill. I jumped, delighted. But when mass ended, I lost sight of him, or more probably (I prefer not to remember) hung back because he wasn't by himself. There was a wife in a white mantilla, a crowd of lads. Or he was alone, but in a suit, signifying seriousness. As well as being himself, you see, he might equally have been a miracle, an hallucination, a film clip, an honest mistake. Fiction is at least as real as faith. I must bear conceivable perspective in mind, I've found. In other words, it's been hard to know what to trust. And as you know, Mam, there's no *who* in the trust department any more, otherwise I wouldn't be here with all this rejection and rejecting writhing unwritten around inside me, would I?

Such whines and wails were never vented, though. My wounds have made me what I am, I thought. Perhaps I was lost in them, hiding in their depths, but I surely would be lost without them. And it was vital that I not give anyone a chance to make me better. They'd had their chances. To the world I would be dead to sentiment; to myself, alive to nothing but. So, not a word, especially not to Granny Royce, who had never done anything but love me.

Later that year, there was a black-bordered envelope, her sister, Auntie Gret, saying, peacefully in her sleep. Lucky at last. I looked out the bedsit window, watching the human glow that once was Enniscorthy dwindle to a cinder. Funeral private. The air felt full of all the things I never said to her, whisperings and bleatings, the homing sonar of a blind bat.

For real contact I addressed myself to my bedclothes. To sleep, perhaps to rub; aye, there's the dream . . . I needed no sweet-tasting girls in gymslips to spur me on. I stormed the sheets as though they were an emotional map of the mean streets down which a man must go. (The penis, mightier than the sword . . .) And the energy of my engrossment compensated for the enervating Saturday excursions to the shabby City. The pillow proved highly huggable. It was almost enjoyable, after a while, to lie of an evening holding it close and confiding in it all the longing, all the hope of love. I took its warmth for solace and its unjudging silence was acceptance. Little tunnels, little mounds gave it an anatomy that I could enter and caress. As the moment inched to crisis on the fraying, frictionless muslin I could forget my mind. Afterwards I could tolerate this stain that was myself, this projection of unorthodox tears. Before the night was out, the blot would be indistinguishable from its tatty screen, as though to prove how really fictional I felt.

II

The first sign of wanking-induced madness is hairs on the palm of your hand. The second's looking for them. We feared this at school, Johnny and I. But that wasn't why I rang him. It was because I found myself becoming brighter, due perhaps to lengthening evenings and blooming forsythia in Holloway, near the prison, but also due to Calor Gas, the human place. Forty hours' exposure weekly to others, to their essential yet — for all my feigned detachment, my uncontrollable defensiveness, my theory of 'the English', my shyness — endearing strangeness, had its effect. Slowly, and with no memory of having put my mind to it, I began to change.

It took time, though. Early on in invoicing I was quieter than the chair I sat on. The workplace substituted rules for personality. That was 'typically English'; a military style perfected for a regimented race. But then church aisles sported battle standards and redcoats paced night and day outside the Royal Butlin's and doormen's greatcoats were adorned with what looked like liquorice allsorts commemorating England, home and beauty. It seemed only natural that all occasions of rank and power took their organisational cue from the armed forces. In moments of lubberliness, I may have imagined that fate had press-ganged me into service. More and more, though, now I was able to pretend I'd enlisted. Accept as earnest of survival the Queen's cousin's shilling, and hope not to be invalided out.

It was impossible to remain rigidly at attention, however. The work was child's play. H. Hobbs Wilson, Wood Green: C 0104J. Code on docket tallied with code in book. I GB'd the docket. Dealers' names and whereabouts gradually became more a diversion than a duty. Tordoff's of Heckmondwike was a wonderful mouthful of foreignness to me, a dish of onomastical tripe and onions. With surprising ease, all those Beckett-echoing Hams and Wicks loaned themselves to list-making just like the ones I used to know. I fashioned a chaplet of favourites from each Calor region, and each name rivalled, as a fantasy of knowing and belonging, the mantra I'd made as a small boy of Ballymurphy, Borris, Gowran, Goresbridge on the bus from Granny Royce's farm outside Enniscorthy to Kilkenny where there was a Woolworth's. Stringing together Taunton, Tiverton, Barnstaple, Bude, I could imagine all over again that I was getting somewhere and there'd be treats in store.

Not that I needed to go that far, or take a bus. All I had to do for novelty was grab a piece of likely looking paper, call 'query' to my indifferent colleagues and roam the hallways for half an hour. As long as my desk top was littered I could do as I please. Leaving my desk chair was evidence of my diligence as conclusive as sitting there all day. I went down to Dealer Accounts, where Raffiq of Peshawar and Sylvia Lugano had chat and, better yet, had accents. Time and again the Dublin woman in Filing reassured me, and herself, that Eamon Andrews was a very saintly man. She'd

met him at a do in Chiswick once. I had to laugh at Mrs
Dundas, all the way from Epsom, blaspheming Southern
Region ('Ye gods!'), striding in at ten o'clock as tense as a
sentry, terms like West Indian, unions, Pakistani, rearing up
in her dire mutterings like glints of weaponry.

Lawrie tried to proselytise. Nobody listened. Lawrie left in
May. Noel tried a Doug Smith treble at Folkestone, fancied
Scobie at York. Nobody cared. Michel from Mauritius got
the typist from Drimnagh into trouble. Peter Banks from
Palmers Green and Sales Invoicing A came by to blow my
mind with talk of Buxtehude. Tricia's ex-boyfriend, Reggie,
had his own group now, the Action. Lawrie scowled at her
and said she was a Mod, she ought to watch it. Departing
colleagues provided cake for all for our last tea together.
Birthdays were celebrated with lunch-time piss-ups at the
Lord Nelson, Carburton Street, scotch eggs and shepherd's
pie, chased by two pints of Red Barrel and 'Cheers, love;
cheers, love', all the way. Who'd have thought it? I was
sitting pretty in Empire City.

Bobby came.

Nellie Hodges had a tantrum, dashed D & C notes to the
floor, swore Mr Mogg was trying to grope her, wasn't
taking any more, was shown the door. Bobby was her
dramatic replacement. Bobby had hair the colour of honey
and a throaty contralto, a voice of smoke and vermouth. I
gawked across the office at her, fixated. Her every move
possessed surpassing grace and beauty – oh God, look:
she's lighting another Benson and Hedges . . . She flounced
around uttering sighs erotic in their impatience at the sliding
scale for NAAFI, Middle Wallop. 'Blahst!' And when, if Noel
teased her, she flapped her wrist and groaned like Frankie
Howerd ('*No!*'), it made me weak.

Struck, I gawked on, a bullock ogling a field of clover.
Her very domicile, Stanmore, described my sense of her
precisely. She was the living end, and further than her my
little tube could not conceive of going. She told me her
parents came from Donegal (oh my love, my love! the race

has fated us), invited me and pal Johnny to a party at her place, opined that I might like her younger sister, broke the news first to me – 'I think of you as a friend' (well, bugger you) – then to the office at large that she was engaged and flashed around the diamond (may your honeymoon be a swamp of Spanish tummy). My insides swooned and soughed like a bullock's colicky bawling, the beast in me distrait, disgusted. She sent me a wedding invitation. I tore it up. But I was sorry then.

And so, slowly, the boy on the burning deck was turning, was being turned, not just into a clerk but a colleague, a one-among-many instead of a solo act. It was like boarding school. The desks, the chairs, the being in one's place, the time-cheating, the flappy overlords, the foreign comrades (Ballyhaunis then, Columbo now) – all reminded me that once upon a time I had been tethered plausibly to a common life. Others' rituals, quirks and gestures once more intrigued and charmed. These might be instruments of freedom more persuasive, for all their imperceptibility, than either pen or penis. Greatly as I was inclined to call myself a creature of circumstance – fated only to the anonymous reality of class, my name castrated, my history unlovely, my body unloved – there could be something round about me which belied bereftness, of which I might, on a good day, even shyly approve.

I felt I was ready to ring Johnny. The station nearest him was Alperton, a grand, long, one-and-elevenpenny ride from Arsenal. Pleasant it was of a Sunday afternoon early to rattle by the blossoming window boxes of the cliff-high rooming houses in Barons Court, to glimpse green Chiswick space under watery sun on the long run into Acton. UnHighburyish overground travel – an excursion into light. Dogs, prams, kites, footer: it was Sunday all afternoon. And tea was its sacrament, white cloth and water, gleaming vessels and Mother ministering in a smock apron, the kitchen chasuble.

'Butter and eggs and a pound of cheese.' The line our

English teacher, Pig, was fond of Chesterbellocally declaiming when in what we naïvely termed 'good form' – after 'lunch' – always came back to me at Johnny's tea times. Not because of our happy memories, but because of my swinish lust for all before me: the brawn, the hazlett, the sweet home-grown tomatoes, the home-made scones, the second helpings of steaming apple cake. I cleared my plate as though I were the best child in the world, trying to eat my way into house and home, as though sooner or later during my orgy the family would as one cry, Stop! We'll have you if only you'll eat natural!

Delicious as the food itself was, what gave it extra savour was that I was not just eating. I was at a meal. It was a meal because Johnny and his elder brother, Joe, kept sniping at each other. And Joe's pal Ned, from Rathkeale or Abbeyfeale or maybe Pallaskenry (any place would please me; it only had to be, like every other thing in the room, like home) would be on hand reporting in virtually vindictive detail on the old neighbourhood in Kilburn, where he still lived, and the doings there of well-known, woeful gobshites and cute hoors, 'saving your presence, ma'am'. 'Cute Kerry hoors.' There was a suspicion in Ned's tone that intercounty interaction was a species of miscegenation, one of the Great Wen's secondary infections, the primary one being that there was nothing for it now but roul up the sleeves, lads, and work like fucking niggers. Ample, ruddy Ned, with a laugh as abrupt as a window smashing.

'Oh sure I know, Ned, boy: wisha don't be talking.'

And Tony, Johnny's oldest brother, would wheel by, parched from an afternoon under the feckin' oul Cortina.

'You smelled the tea.'

'I did, I did.' Tony rubbed his hands together briskly, laughing, glad to be at home.

To deserve tea, and because it was Sunday in springtime, Johnny and I felt we had to avail of the open air, though I would have much preferred to stay indoors, where there were people and Limerick accents. But Johnny seemed keen

to be off out, the house perhaps feeling smaller with everyone at home than it did on workdays, when time together
was limited and tiredness made of silence a more pleasing
art than conversation. But lest a stroll as far as the little park
by the tube seem too middle-aged, Johnny rummaged in the
stairs cupboard for hurleys and a ball. With these props we
could claim Sunday as our own by attempting to replay
what often used to be the best part of the day, going up to
the field for a few pucks. Ten minutes of bending, lifting
and striking more than sufficed, however. We signalled to
each other helplessly that we were out of puff. Johnny mud-
died his good shoes and went, respectably, 'Well, flip it,
anyhow!' We donated generously to the London Transport
pool of lost balls. We had to have a smoke.

No, we hadn't heard from anyone at school. We wondered
what Muldoon was doing. There was a brief flurry of other
names and memories. But we were far from all our former
classmates. We'd never be National School teachers or sit the
Junior Ex., would never have land or livestock. Nor, thank
God, was there a fear of our turning into apprentice priests
either, shut away from life as former pals now were in the
seminary at Ballyboden. We were the difference that was
England. Johnny would explain to me what that was.

But Johnny wasn't interested. With his family as prophylactic against change, he needed only taking *Juke Box Jury*
and Jimmy Greaves in to guide him, was in no danger of
Me's mighty questions – who was I? what was I? where
was I going? And he made our dissimilarity more obvious
by sometimes tossing the hurley to one side after one per-
functory puck, saying he was shagged. He'd been out till
the last tube (the Central ran to Hanger Lane till after midnight). He'd picked up a bit of stuff at the Grotto Club, a
Marylebone rendezvous for Catholic youth (no palais slags
allowed).

'What did you do?' he'd ask.

I'd go, off-handedly, 'Oh, I'm reading Dostoevsky at the
moment.' But I had murder in mind. I saw the dim sheen

of the dancefloor, and girls' covert glances raking him. Tall, slender, brown-eyed, confident. He had the cut of a grey-hound, the air of a thoroughbred. A fast mover. His shirts were ironed, his trousers pressed, he was probably pulling in fifteen a week clerking in the Midland Bank, Harrow Road.

'This bird at work asked me to a party in Shepherd's Bush last night' – he paused, something about bush seemed to amuse him – 'I nearly missed twelve mass!' He had the knack.

Sometimes I laughed along with him – 'Oho, there; the hard man. A bird in the Bush is worth two in the hand.' His complacency demanded my cliché as tribute. But I cringed and squirmed inside. First family. Now girls. It wasn't fair. Boo-hoo. I wound myself up with the greatest of ease into a small, unuttered whine. I'd come all this way by tube to meet the self I thought I couldn't be. Change? Some sick joke, that. And friend? This lanky drip beside me? Don't make me laugh. What good's a common past if can't make up present differences. I wished it was tea time.

Sated at last and talk desultory, we smoked Gold Leaf and dried the dishes. Dusk gathered in the tiny window above the sink. Imperceptibly, as the day drew to a close, the family drew into itself, all in now for the night, work tomorrow. They had their tasks to be about, and in an hour it would be *Sunday Night at the London Palladium*. I had to go. 'Ah, no; stay.' I couldn't. Ah well, sure it was a long way home, and trains were scarce.

The long wait at Alperton reintroduced distance. By the time the train came I was anxious to get back to my Biro, to my Penguin classic. The virtually empty carriages dawdled at Acton, dawdled at Hammersmith, ghosted through the early evening back to the chilly room. I sat oblivious with the tattered Fontana of *The Leopard* in my lap, my eyes glued to it, not reading, letting my mind be lullabied, transfixed at Don Fabrizio's telescope, by the tensionless suspense that was the empty vault of night.

Leaving Johnny was a lot less easy, though, when his flame of the moment extinguished ('Ah, she was getting too serious'), he invited me to hit the Saturday night high spots with him. Not that I wanted to leave, at least not at first. It was like old times to shave and put the clean shirt on in hope of hugs. I liberally applied my best face-saving discovery yet, the septic pencil (mightier than the Wilkinson Sword). And hotfoot off with me, surprised by my own enthusiasm, to Baker Street, all change for the Grotto Club, or Victoria, where there was a similar establishment. Soft drinks minus fizz, a Hammond organ in the doldrums, the bland leading the bland. Urban Catholic fun. The unSoho.

Still, these venues were much more desirable, uptown, or commonsensically safer than the All-Ireland Pat and Biddy shindigs that had Cricklewood crawling with police vans. There, the tube stations stayed open past the last train so that 'suspects' could be taken down the stairs 'for questioning'. Their tiled passageways were easily washed down. Kilmallock Ned told a silent Sunday tea time all about it. And whether it was fear, experience or some other kind of truth that spoke through him, the effect was to remind Johnny and I that we were sober Friary boys who'd passed the Leaving Cert. Clubable, in the non-police sense, should be our middle name.

I may have stopped believing in miracles, but still I saw no reason why one shouldn't happen. But I might as well have tried twisting the night away at the Polar Icecap, Spitzbergen, for all that befell me in any of the clubs. No girl materialised, all smiles, from anywhere I knew. (I'd never go back now.) As the evening ground towards midnight and my partners kept saying, 'Do what?', even if I'd only asked them where they were from, I'd withdraw into the atheism that is non-romance. I'd look around for Johnny. But by then, his bird pulled, he'd be outside. If I made a move, though, I'd make the last tube, I could hug the gas fire and ask Julien Sorel how he'd handle this fake Massabielle, three streets from the Edgware Road.

We went to parties, too. Semis in Ealing – four quantity surveyors sharing – shook to their foundations. Damp White City basement flats overflowed onto the street. Minis growled late into the night, and puke welcomed Sunday. Vaguely offstage, where all the interesting things happened, a Cindy or a Clive collapsed.

By the time Johnny and I found wherever the action was, everyone knew everyone and nobody knew the hosts, though the harried girl in the kitchen who relieved us of our Party Four or flagon of Strongbow had all the appearance of a crashed gate, bristling but flattened. Come one, come all. Open house in W11. Bring a bottle and grab a chick. The whole joint was jumping to the music of the libidos (not so much a pop group, more a way of life).

Parties were darker than clubs. The Walker Brothers emoted, 'Sun Ain't Gonna Shine Any More', and a fucking good thing an' all, mate, everyone agreed, two-stepping somnabulistically. Dark brought out a myriad Marianne Faithfulls, convents of Cathy McGowans. There were microskirts, and fishnet stockings, and even no stockings. There was leather. Leather seemed to be working its way up, not on feet, but covering bums, riding Nortons, turning into waistcoats.

I usually ended up wedged against the arm of a sofa with a couple passionately prone beside me, out of cigarettes and half seas over from stannoid beer. But that was all right as long as my end was near the record-player. Sandy Shaw, Unit Four Plus Two, Peter and Gordon, Radio Luxembourg redux, here in somebody's unliving room, grooved plastic was the night's major personality, confirming like a visit from the paraclete a proper sense of self. Where had I been without it?

With it I by God was, and (I remembered) always had been. Wasn't being thus one of the first bonds between Johnny and me at school, trying to tune in Jack Jackson's seven o'clock Sunday show on the St Declan's houseroom wireless? The power of the hipster was with me then. I dug

Hank Ballard and the Midnighters the most, I flipped over Maxine Brown's 'It's All in My Mind'. Lads sidled into earshot, as though I were the Duke in the forest of Arden whom we met on our Intermediate course: 'Now my co-mates and brothers in exile,' I could go, 'the hottest thing on the American charts this week is by Little Anthony and the Imperials.' (The motifs were epic, the mood expansive. It was the hour of Sam the Sham and the Pharoahs.) I had been touched by some sort of electronic pentecost, and warbled in tongues. The Marcels, 'Blue Moon', the Fleetwoods, 'Come Softly to Me', the Crystals (thunderous as a teenager's heartbeat), 'Da Doo Ron Ron'. Pop gave me a pleasure that was as strong as knowledge. Thanks to it, I felt, I could dream of inventing a life of my own, with a self as safe as soy bean, and a mind that was all the colours of a Wurlitzer. Sandy Nelson tom-tommed 'Let There Be Drums'. Yeah, yeah, yeah! And there were drums. Also sweet lips, and arms to go with charms. Let there be falling in love. Let there be 'Our Day Will Come' by Ruby and the Romantics.

Johnny offered me a radio. The thought of one had never crossed my mind. Radios were well outside the price range of my pleasures. The two-pounds-ten I spent on a pair of itchy, ill-fitting trousers for Bobby's party meant having to choose later the same week between food and tube fare. And I had to get to work for Friday's omnipotent brown envelope. The only way to live was not to mind. I couldn't have everything, even though that was all I ever wanted. I tried being realistic.

'Thirty bob,' said Johnny, pulling the life buoy out of his jacket pocket. My heart leapt up. It was the endearing size of a paperback and, like myself (I made the link at once), had been in the wars. Its body was nondescript, its name was missing, its on–off/volume control – or speaking voice, as I would fraternally have it – was a sometime thing, often drowned in static (an unwelcome accent). With a mild pang in my lower intestine at the hill of baked beans the deal was costing, I forked out. I'd never eaten poorly for a better reason. Besides, I needed some sort of pick-me-up after the affair of the trousers.

III

Johnny thought it was the party that caused our falling out. It was all my fault that there were no good women at it or something. But, to me, the chill set in over the trousers. Not that Bobby's was anything to write home about. It was crawling with chartered accountants, sales reps, mohair suits. The words 'golf club' (both meanings) were uttered frequently. People at least two years on the wrong side of twenty-five excited themselves by putting Helen Shapiro on the radiogram. Some of them were *wives*. Johnny whined. All this was less than he was due, somehow. I called him a moody shagger.

There was one marvellous moment, early on, when Bobby introduced me to her younger sister, Catherine, all soft hair and scent of sandalwood. We danced to Herman's Hermits' 'Silhouettes'. But all that led to was a virtually day-long trip on a thirty-six to her flat in Catford, and her asking me, 'Are you timid?' We were walking near the crematorium at Hither Green. 'I am, all right, like,' I said.

And Johnny and I made a woeful flag of the trousers. I must admit, however, that in the first place, those trousers, as articles of clothing, were the end (being inconceivable as any other part of a line). They happened this way. Johnny thought, on account of the night that was in it, and the fierce crush I had on Bobby, that I should definitely spruce myself up. And right enough, he had a point. It wasn't every day I was asked out to Stanmore. I pictured myself looking at the flesh of her in snaps of Benidorm, using her immaculate bathroom, perhaps even seeing where she slept. I should be dressed for such intimacies as these. Bobby deserved it. And worldly me knew that girls were peculiar about clothes, got a kick out of a nicely polished stretch of winklepicker. Moreover, Johnny knew a drapery ostensibly within my means, Mick's of Paddington, outfitters to a hundred thousand Shanagolden Neds. In this dark, dusty and depressing huckster's off the Harrow Road I inserted myself into the hairy, squirmiferous trews.

There was too much electric light. Bobby was too busy to sit beside me for the long-awaited soul mates' colloquy which she seemed so superbly well-equipped to give (the golden syrup of that vibrato!). There were too many bouffants, chiffon, bitten-off phrases. There was too much suburbanity, Englishness, things on crackers. I topped drink with drink, then, in one fell swoop, took all our feeling out of place out on the one thing I felt free to detest, the trousers.

The fry that was my weekend brunch came up, the apple cake we had at Johnny's, coffee, tea and hostess's Mateus Rosé all, all at once, all of a puddle in my shaggy lap.

'Into the kitchen, quick,' Johnny ordered, and there I swabbed myself with a week-old *Sketch*. But the smell was dreadful, and had to be at all costs smothered, because, as sure as vindictive God, Bobby will walk in that door this minute . . . That was why Johnny dived into the cupboard under the sink, produced a flagon of something practical and slung some on me. Bleach.

The party dissolved, and fifty bob was down the drain. Never as much as a touch of Bobby's hand. And a head that was all barbed wire and jagged glass.

Still, although it showed that friendship could be unexpectedly expensive, nothing would have come of that fiasco, probably, if there hadn't been another one soon afterwards. Despite the Calor paper-chase and its fine social life, I wasn't able to let go of all my self-pity and self-doubt. I still needed to believe that nobody knew the trouble I'd seen, that my true initials were JOB. I probably also wanted to get on Johnny's nerves because he was so obviously better off than me. And because I began to see that we were not alike, which I resented. And because I wanted sympathy, as well as tea.

I brought up money, or rather not having it. Being broke became the synecdoche of need. Yeah boy, two-ten and the bloody trousers gone. You should have given me the shagging oul wireless. Not that I mentioned radio or trousers out loud. My footing in another person's world was too precious to be compromised by demands or confrontations. I sang as dumb about what bothered me as any cowed family member. The money-whine only came out as generalised spleen. Life was not worthy of my actually living it, a rank flowering of an adolescence that would not go away, and don't stop me if you've heard this ...

And so it was I came to London Transport. At first I thought Johnny had made a simply brilliant suggestion. I'd seen the ads. There wasn't any trouble seeing myself. The basic rate was excellent, and then there would be weekend work and double time and overtime, free travel and canteen facilities, no time for anything but work (I heard Big Tom applauding from afar). I might even be turned into a happy chappy smiling from a poster. Why not? I was white.

The recruiting office was at the far west end of Marylebone Road, but how far a cry it was from Cavendish Square. Metal window frames, walls matt-finished in muddy cream, stone stairs smelling of Jeyes Fluid. My heart sank. Hospital, I thought vaguely, or maybe army. Before the interview there was a test, some sort of adding the halfpence to the pence. My naïve heart sank further, sickened not only by the sterile place or its ditto rituals but by myself for supposing I was meant to be at their disposal. Down with uniforms! I will not serve! So when the interviewer asked what Johnny had informed me was the all-important question – 'You're planning a career with London Transport, are you, then?' – I found myself offensively laconic.

'Naw. I'll stick it six months, maybe, for the money.'

Appalled to hear money substituting for career, the portly party in blue serge on the other side of the desk said grimly, 'Well, I think that's all. We'll let you know, Mr – ', and looked down at his notes not, I knew, to find my name, but to erase it.

Johnny shook his head. I'd just produced another discouraging page in the annals of my Moody Shaggerhood. He'd be giving me up as a bad job . . .

I knew he didn't mean it, but of course, Do give me up! I said to myself, always on the alert for possible rejection. When it came down to it he was no help. All he had to offer was a mock-up of me as emigrant and prole. First, in déclassé trousers. Now, slaving night, noon and weekends on the buses. No talk of joining him in banking, though. No fear. No introduction to County Hall, where, in virtually the same parish as the Jolly Gardeners, his clerking life had started. I saw it all. He was saying we were not a bit alike. He was trying to get rid of me. I was poor and hapless and a sponger. I was no class. I was so far out on my own – Highbury, for God's sake – as to be no better than a lapsed Irishman.

Well, he could stick his Sunday tea, I thought. It was just a cosy lie, anyhow, its orderliness and lack of drama sure signs of self-deception. And the company was only an excuse for sentimental neighbourliness, a mock-up of shelter and campfire against unfaceable stone and iron London. But I would face it. If my pants offend me, why I would cast them off. I didn't care. *Not* timid. Not me. And another thing. I didn't want to shift birds from dancefloor to doorway and stand ankle deep in crisp bags and chip-shop wrapping, groping and groaning till there was nothing for it but to get the last train home to Ma and Da. So look, I couldn't care less for any of it. I had something else in mind altogether. Here's yer oul thirty pieces of silver and gimme the wireless.

It was as though I'd been so attuned to being played false over the years that, given the choice, I'd sooner have a radio than a friend.

Yet, rather than gathering the momentum I've tried to impart to it here, as if there were a drama, my resistance to Johnny was almost imperceptible, involuntary. The seething embarrassment, the class consciousness, the unfulfilling Irishness, or whatever other strain of moody-shaggerness that ailed me was, as usual, well suppressed. I began staying in, with my radio. Now the room was tolerable. That, suddenly, was all I thought I wanted. Johnny rang me at the office with the weekly word on clubs and parties. But at just the time we'd be setting off down windswept Goldhawk Road towards the Animals and living rooms' red crepe paper light shades, the Leipzig Gewandhaus under Vaclav Neumann was due to do Schubert's great C Major. I didn't want the small beer and anticlimax and the sun of a pallid Sunday any more. The Third's confident continuity crew were steering me beyond all that. Big music would never let me down.

That crew oozed class. If cummerbunds could speak, this was how they'd sound, this is what they'd say. They could come trippingly out with Concertgebouw and Gennady Rozhdestvensky, Janáček, Kodály, *allegro assai*. They were so assured that the number of times they had to say 'We return you now' didn't embarrass them one bit (I loved that 'we'). If anything, they seemed to have a sly relish for repetition, for intoning with extra, laughable seriousness, whenever Beethoven's Seventh Symphony was up, for instance, that Wagner thought its scherzo, 'the apotheosis of the dahnce'. Endearing masks of unreal imperturbability, ushers of otherness, their accent another one of England's countless uniforms. Gas tickets altogether.

No Who, no Kinks, and no Small Faces. Beatles? Mouth organs. Bullshit. Ditto Dylan. Rosko on Caroline knew me not. Blackburn, TW ('*Hell*-o'), Everett and every other pirate's patter fell on my deaf ears. Pearls and dicky bows played music, not records. Records had Moody Blues and Honeycombs on them, were paeans to lost causes, hymns from the white suburban ghetto of chastity, were only about wank-long. (LP's didn't count. They were still just about for adults only.) *Music*, though, had to be listened to. Anyone going to the trouble to create such a noise had to be serious. I tuned in religiously to Anthony Hopkins, *Talking about Music*. To this day I can hardly tell ostinato from andante, but I loved the hazy general idea of great complexity manageable in the right hands – myself to a tee . . .

I looked out the window and saw Highbury turn to winter, saw my first year in England end, and at my shoulder the Swan of Tuonela, uplifting, enigmatic, crackling. There was only the symphonic mode. The world seemed wide. I felt restored to my favourite, most deceptive, most powerful vision of myself – the wide-eyed, silent, impressionable, feather-brained, harmless child. I took up the Biro which, in a former life, was a phial of Philip's life's blood, and I swung it with abandon in my 60-watt auditorium, digging everything from Bach to Bax and back again, my increasingly long, increasingly greasy, increasingly artistic hair flopping to the tempi. And soon it was spring, season of temporaries. Real shadows. Proper travellers.

I'd noticed these children of Conduit and Brook Street the previous year. But then I'd found them more threatening than attractive. They were freer, they were better paid, they came from places such as university, Australia, the stage. Explaining how to use the code book or why it was vitally important to retain cancelled D & C notes evinced from them temperamental sighs and prolonged visits to the bathroom. I wasn't being taken seriously. Desk chairs were for permanence and the likes of me. As for proper young people, the more they acted just like a rolling stone the more plausible they were.

Perhaps, though, it wasn't only that I was better able to see the temporaries for what they were. What they were for was becoming clearer independently of my being a little more broken-in. Red was becoming the colour of tourism, not the blood of empire. Military clobber was in at weekends. Side streets led fashion trends. Swinging suggested impermanence but meant good. The world was temptation, not discipline, a clitoris, not a swagger stick. Already, 'man' was replacing 'mate', and 'fuzz' supplanting 'the lawr'. Rumours of war would come from way east of Suez, while bank-holiday battles made a madhouse out of Margate. New faiths abounded with the promise of macrobiotic eternal life and saffron hope and glory. Wafers of rainbow would soon be sacramentally dispensed in the Church of the Joyful Chemical. The Troggs were doing 'Wild Thing'. Love was in. Even I might change my tune.

Quite what this smiley-face, long-haired, bell-bottomed spiritual flea market amounted to I had no idea. I didn't want an idea. I just wanted to go on being glad that youth looked like official policy. The stage was ours. Whatever came out of our minds would do just fine. I even thought that maybe I was young, though perhaps it was a bit early to say for sure. All I knew was that when Barnet Maureen from E.R. Reed paraded up to Filing ahead of me, the length of her skirt and the length of her legs and the sheen of her long black hair combined to make a mind-altering substance. In March I was listening to Webern. Tears such as stars might shed in their enormous silence. Ice jewellery. By May I was caught up in the irresistible rise of Dave Dee, Dozy, Beaky, Mick and Titch.

Nicki was a student. She had class. She had a POPesgrove number. I rang it as soon as I dared, about six-thirty on the day she gave it to me. A crusty Dad hacked off his message with a military bark, 'Frayed sheezite!' And she left at the end of the week.

Sarah was an actress. Resting. I asked what she'd been in. She waved elaborately, covering multitudes. 'You wouldn't have heard of them.' Being Irish, I supposed she supposed. So I decided to dislike her. She did most of her resting against filing cabinets, speaking hollowly of her frightful scene at home. 'You'll never guess what he's done now . . .' – the drunk she lived with in South Ken. Sarah wore black flowing things and broad belts with big buckles tight around her waist. Her face was pinched and tense. I saw a cluttered room, overflowing ashtrays. There was a smell, which I thought I could see too, but that was just the vivid impact of the wallpaper yellowing in the top floor bathroom (sharing). So I decided not to dislike her any more, and tried to seem kind. Damsel in distress, I'll comfort you (I mean myself). But I didn't know how to, didn't count that she thanked me for listening. Anyhow, she must have been all of twenty-four. Too old for romance, too used to life, too far from gymslips, too long in London. And she wore glasses. Difficult as dislike was, it was easier.

Hilary at least was young, more fledgeling than chick, the way her short hair spikily stuck out. She was an actress too, though neither resting nor working. She just never stopped being relentlessly bright, chipper, gung-ho and a thorough pain in the neck. So we started lunching together. She went on about how dead good life in Earls Court was. I ought to move there. Her father, 'a great guy', was a writer, lived in St John's Wood. 'Mum's shacking up with Simon at the moment. He's a photographer. Quite brilliant, actually.' She seemed somewhat distracted, perhaps a bit daft. So we dated.

We went to the Hammersmith Odeon to see a *Carry On* (she and Jim Dale were like *that*). *Up Shit Creek*, I thought uncharitably, shelling out for Maltesers. It was just like Hilary to want something when asked. Jim Dale was bursting out all over. I sat in a limbo of unlaughing as Hilary clutched my hand, put her hand on the inside of my knee. Her convulsions of merriment were strong enough to have her committed. When I squirmed she tried to tickle me, and afterwards nothing would satisfy her but to walk home to her 'pad' in Earls Court Road. She asked me if I liked hot chocolate at all. She definitely is daft, I thought. She took my hand, but not to shake it, as I was trying to do.

My heart pounded and my innards turned to lukewarm liquid. We tiptoed up the narrow lino'd stairs to the gas ring, the no photos, the cupboard that was bookshelf, fridge and safe. We were members of the same institution. I never expected to know someone – someone English, at that – who seemed as orphaned as I thought I was.

'Take a pew,' she said gamely.

I sat on the edge of the trunk at the foot of the bed. And she wasn't joking. She made the watery hot chocolate, chattering. I thought I was the one supposed to talk. Not timid, *not* timid, I told myself. Just frigid. Unmoved. Immovable. She gave me a soulful look. I kissed her cheek, perhaps we hugged. She asked if I'd like some music. After another pause, I said, no, I'd never read Katherine Mansfield, and was that the time.

'Shh,' she hissed down the stairs after me. 'Don't run.'

Carmel took Quantas Flight 103 back to Kalgoorlie. Also Dave and Kev, all sober handshakes. I brought the radio round to Dunedin Don's damp Fulham shoe box. Don really liked classical music, he said. The concert opened with the *Siegfried Idyll* and when it ended Don went, 'Ah, that was loike a muneloight noight.' Fiona left to have her baby. Tom Proctor put the seal on his two weeks in Central Records with a bottle of Appleton rum. We toured the corridors the Friday afternoon he left, each swig making us feel we really knew each other.

But I was permanent. My office chair said so. Its angular frame, arthritic castors and thin padding seemed a rhetoric of foreverness, expressing lack of mobility, being imposed on from above, having little cushion against the future. I was one of the duty-bound and steady, Mrs Duffy, Ruby Ramasinghe, Mrs Ross, the new clerk in Invoicing D, Malik, late of Rawalpindi. He trekked in from Stoke Newington on a seventy-three, shirt an Omo dazzle and pinstripes pressed, sense of self and purpose conveyed completely in his incessant, 'Yes, moddom. Yes, yes, moddom.' His lonely eyes hunted the boss's every move and nuance, flinched from her power, as though she were as worthy of his devoted service as the mother of parliaments herself. Noel kept on backing horses.

I fell for Helga. As soon as she mentioned the epigraph of *Darkness at Noon*, I was hers. 'Man, man, one cannot live quite without pity.' I knew exactly what she meant. And she'd know I knew. She was very intelligent. She was reading politics at Edinburgh university. Her father was a soldier. One Saturday we went as far as lunch, scotch eggs and halves of Double Diamond, at the Antelope, Eaton Terrace. She lived nearby. I rode the nineteen down to Sloane Square, agog with expectation. A student, mind. To begin with, however, we made heavy weather of *La Nausée*. Then we moved on to Orwell. *Down and Out in Paris and London* – yes! *Homage to Catalonia* – oh yes, yes! Our minds moved together. We were smiling. I felt so good. This was the first time I'd actually *talked* to anybody, I told myself, and talk was the kind of coming I'd dreamt it would be, way beyond the gymslip and hot chocolate. *'Faute de mieux,'* Helga liked to say. *'La Peste. Force des choses.'* I liked her doing that. Afterwards I read that there was a sexual revolution going on at the time. I'm not quite vain enough to believe that I must have been having a run of bad luck.

Colin Bulawayo spoke of exile, dressed in khaki. Becky Kessler left for Kibbutz Ma'an Zvi, via Hendon. Wanstead Tricia Wright went off to harvest grapes in the Mâcon country with her French boyfriend.

'Why not come along? He won't mind.'

Very funny, Tric.

'Oh *do*.' Her tone all coy and Bobbyish.

Sunshine, wine, France, fatigue from fresh air – chords of an anthem I suddenly yearned to sing. 'Ah, I can't . . .' I was too embarrassed to explain that there could be no going forward. I had nothing to fall back on, see. The little job, the little room which was its private replica, were my life. I was permanent. I must have wanted it that way. And I certainly did not.

PLAY

I

Pat pecked me on the cheek. 'Cheer up!' she said with a confident laugh. She'd lost her heart to a jazz drummer currently gigging in Ostend, she said, and 'I don't want to get involved'. I played drums too, I'd have her know. But I behaved like a gentleman, accepting bare cheek, if that was all there was, unaffected – meaning disaffected – and in (I thought) control, as proud of myself as if I'd invented the Pill. Which I had, in a way. For myself. Since sex wasn't possible, let's pretend it wasn't necessary. Pat's train home to Chislehurst came and went. I went back to my room.

All that was necessary was difference. That was what one could be that spring, different, just as twelve months later, 1967, being stoned was where it would be at, and militancy all the rage the year after that. Difference was the sense I got from all those Rita Tushinghams and colonial boys, from their hair and legginess, cheesecloth shirts, denim jackets, socklessness and sandals, from Fraser and the back room at Better Books. The novelty of surfaces once more tapped into some familiar childish depth in me. I was different too.

Not the way they were, maybe. I hadn't class or suburb, church or country. I didn't have a body, much. But none of that mattered. My hair was getting really long. I felt like I had something of the spirit.

Fraser was definitely different. He was a woman. Or so girls made out, pointing to his suede shoes, his pink shirts, his high Ayr whine, their wrists limp, going 'Ooh' and pouting. All because he called himself an artist, thought I, disappointed in them. But then when he brought his paintings into work, I didn't know how to take it. He'd struggled through the morning tube with something like a roll of carpeting wrapped in grubby brown paper. It seemed a lot of trouble to go to, and for what I wasn't sure. It didn't occur to me that maybe he wanted to talk, or to cause talk.

One picture was of a flesh-coloured football very much out on its own on a field of hallucinatory green with, in the background, a flattened border. The ball was growing. It seemed to pulse. The grass was chemical.

A second canvas showed a large unhanded clock, its face flecked with red paint (blood?), its numbers defaced by what might be bullet holes. It dangled at an oblique angle from a derrick made of bones, the victim of a seizure of some kind, expiring against ominous mauve sky. Was I looking at the alienation of modern man, the riddle of time, the political football? I couldn't tell, so naturally I said, 'These are very good', knowing that way that he'd leave his remaining three surrealistic flags unfurled. 'Aye, well,' said Fraser, 'I've still got a lot to learn', and gave a little squirm. I'd made a friend.

Therefore, he imagined he could go on embarrassing me. He kept firing questions across the office at me whenever he felt like it, that's to say, all day. 'Ghelderode? Huysmans? Radiguet? Rilke?' At least I thought at first that these were questions, and his catechism made me feel ignorant and uncomfortable. I concentrated on the unknown fate of several Sievert cylinders, which comprised an Initial Delivery from the Saxham depot to somewhere in Felixstowe, not easy with 'Arrabal, Arrabal' resounding in my ears.

But questions were not what Fraser meant at all. He was uttering anathemas on the awful office, on all offices, on the species office, especially the impossibly cretinous Glasgow art school he'd just quit. He was intoning salutes to soul mates, mantras and mating calls from his real life.

'I know exactly what you mean,' I said (Fraser was discoursing on Nietzsche and truth), feeling vague but enjoying the vehemence.

'I must rejoice beyond the bounds of time . . . though the world may shudder at my joy, and in its coarseness know not what I mean,' he'd go, having been reproved for slipping up on the Air Products bulk rate. Strange psychic tocsins could fall upon the air at any time, reckless splashes of Dayglo paint, stabs at an unfinished self-portrait, graffiti advertising the main event, which was life after deadly work, at Better Books. *Quand le front de l'enfant, plein de rouges tourmentes,/Implore l'essaim blanc des rêves indistincts* . . . And, *o, der Wohnsinn der grossen Stadt.* Even to hear him pronounce Rimbaud and Trakl was an education in fierce sonorities, music of the rictus and the bedevilled mien.

'Charrring Crrross Rrroad!' Fraser squawked, appalled. Imagine someone of my sophistication, erudition and general man-about-townery (his friend, that is) not knowing where 'the finest bookshop in the British Isles, in my daifnitely unhumble opinion' was. Fraser was shouting over rush-hour traffic, a capercaillie russet rising in his face, his small blue eyes as hard and glistening as glass marbles, swaggering along, to all appearances dying to *épater* some unsuspecting bourgeois, some lookalike of his stingy, disapproving stockbroker da in Ayr. Every inch the artist, mad, bad and dangerous to know. Cars slewed to a standstill for him, fuming. His sight is poor, maybe, I thought, Astairing my way round bikes and buses. (Could that explain the paintings?) But whatever he was, and notwithstanding a strong desire to be spared the embarrassment of accidental death in Oxford Street, never mind my unaccountable lapse in bibliopoly, I happily hastened to keep up with him.

'Shop' hardly seemed the word for Better Books. There were books in the window, granted, but they were displayed at knee level, or lower, as though it was beneath the management to window-dress. The inside was deceptive too. There seemed to be as many tables as shelves, and no counters, and staff without ties or retail affectations of any kind. And then there was the totally unexpected back room, with its machine for Hilary-strength beverages and Roneo'd magazines, all opacity and staples, a room with all the incongruousness and pleasing plausibility of a select bar in the back of a fishmonger's. There was *Ambit* and *Gambit*. *Priapus. Solstice. Poor. Old. Tired. Horse. New. Departures.* This was where the man who claimed to have built an orgone box hung out, preaching the second coming of Wilhelm Reich. The man with the streaky beard who made poetry with tape recorders became familiar. I overheard him talking theory. No better place, in fact, for Brian to hold court, with me and Fraser his prime pages, and sometimes a chap who called himself Domenico.

Fraser swore Brian was an absolute genius. Just one look was all I needed to be convinced. He was thin, seemed highly strung or in any case was young to have so little hair, even if its scarcity showed his domed forehead to advantage, dome true sign of giftedness, as my lack of one, discovered when I was fourteen, informed me. On top of which, he was impatient and quite pale, and in his face the monk fought with the fop. I was jealous. Fraser said, enviously, that Brian also possessed the necessary dedication. He traipsed in on a twenty-nine every afternoon from Turnpike Lane, as regular as any worker, having spent the morning in bed execrating the indispensable *Daily Mail* and memorising the works of T.S. Eliot. 'My nerves are bad tonight,' he'd go, out of the blue, whinnying for added authenticity. Or he'd do the 'Ta ta' tattoo from 'A Game of Chess'. He relished stalemate. He was the real thing. He dressed in black as much as he could, and hated his father. Tales of prodigal filiality up Tottenham way came across with flair, patternings of I said and he said, cascades of phrases followed by pools of silence. The rage, the coldness, the drama! Brian's green eyes glinted with the pleasure of being audienced. Fraser, appetite whetted and quite excited, would beg for more. They both greatly enjoyed the protracted nagging and pleading for Brian's poetry. I could see how fond of each other they were. Eventually Brian went, in a Kenneth-Williamsy snarl of pleasure, 'Oh all right!' His most memorable poem was 'The Ring of the Telephone'. 'No hope. Drop dead. Get lost. Go 'way.' It was the voice of alienation. It was the no communication. The jangling phone doth to the world complain ('my nerves are bad tonight'). It was man without Browning or Wagner, said Fraser. Language is just a machine now. It can't really *speak*. 'That poem says it all,' said Fraser. 'That poem has got mental discipline,' Fraser said, making discipline sound like the lash of Knox.

I preferred it when Brian snittishly refused to do his own stuff and instead did, brilliantly, 'The Last to Go' from the hit review *Pieces of Eight*. His Mum had taken him to it for his birthday. I was being superficial. It worried me. But even now I think it was better to eat at Jimmy's than punctuate at Better Books. Mostly, anyhow.

We hated the cavalry at St James's Palace. We spat at poodles and pekes. Aldermaston marchers were okay, if obviously the idiot children of a misalliance between Canon Collins and Bertrand Russell. Mr God and Lord Mammon. Even the titles were the wrong way around. But the movement's capacity for chaos through inertia (declare your principles, sit on the road) was endearing. We were the ones, really, who should be arrested. We were the real danger, for we thought decadent thoughts. Domenico should definitely have been taken in charge for standing on a park bench, uprooted nasturtium in hand, and reciting that poem of his which ended, 'And fucked till dawn spawned on the windowpane'. The old firm of Muggeridge Tynan should hear this. But lyric had been fucked in the Great War, *hirten begruben die Sonne im kahlen Wald*, and all that (Fraser).

Therefore, nothing would do me but to call myself a writer once again. I produced prose poems, affectations of aftermath, declaring life to be as good as over because it wasn't romance. They had 'tintinnabulation' and 'the residue of wonderful' in them. 'Over the bridge the people flowed, under the bridge the water crawled.' Brian said with a sneer that he liked that, while Fraser strongly suspected mental discipline. The circle of my silent listeners was a pool in which it pleased me to see depth.

We pondered the irrationality of the system. Speech wasn't effectively free until you were arrested for it. Oh for fifteen minutes in the dock at Bow Street! It told against us, imagine, that we didn't wear a uniform, like Mods, Rockers and all the other *Untermenschen* whose existence gave the very idea of an élite, and our self-image, a bad name. Yet if the militant modishness of Muswell Hill vamped by, or the sun was suddenly eclipsed by a detachment of hairy, helmet-bearing greasers, we rapidly bethought ourselves and made for Hyde Park to hark at good old Soper.

But at Speakers' Corner we were no different from any tourist. Why didn't we shit in the Serpentine? Why didn't we choke a royal duck? That certainly would have spawned a fine cacophonous lyric, provided 'fuck' with rhyme and reason. It never occurred to us. Actions could not speak louder than our words. Action was dumb. We cited Sartre's Daniel. Far from entering the lions' den, he was having trouble with kittens. How well we understood. How feelingly we saw ourselves as satires perpetrated by the age of reason, meaningful (a favourite term) only by being dropouts from careers in commerce and the arts (the world that peace made). We glad superfluous men, happy surplus values, proud mice in the race of rats, children bearing Godot's message, the rough beast's stable boys. We walked up the Bayswater Road. Then we walked down the Bayswater Road, had tea at the Marble Arch Golden Egg.

But I wasn't getting to rejoice beyond the bounds of time.

Anarchist as adjective and boheming around could, despite appearances, be tiresome. There didn't seem that much to Speakers' Corner, to Better Books' back room, the splintered cups, the coffee spills, the sodden wads of *Peace News*. And I felt severer pangs about who we thought we were when I heard about the readings. While Fraser and I scoffed chips and 'fasowlya' (that was Greek), poets were performing. Was that what I wanted?

Not that I would have missed Jimmy's. It was only six bob (two luncheon vouchers) for the platter of meat and beans and rounds of fresh Greek bread as thick as tractor tyres. And the man himself was worth the price of admission. Jimmy did nothing, a nothing that was so complete that it seemed to contain multitudes. He stood by the cash register, the smouldering cigar eternally in his mouth a totem to his immobility. A short round figure, in shape and stature a vertical version of the cross-section of tunnel which was the dining area. A tube tunnel, of course, everyone agreed, glancing nervously around, trying not to think of the other common, subterranean, urban freeway. The waiters roared at all and sundry, plopped plates down with a clatter. The kitchen help was Bakerloo brown, with red eyes. He capered by the quaking clientele with buckets of offal and a wild grin. Jimmy stood unperturbed and imperturbable. His heavy daughter took the cash and thanked us grumpily, hoping her mother would come soon to escort her back to Kentish Town.

A couple of hundred yards away, the tape-recorder man was serving syntax salad. Yes, I wanted it too, and whatever else was going, outrage and loudness, voices from roof tops, bards spilling beans, lay Redemptorists giving the world hell. But Fraser and Brian demurred. None of the poets were dead. How could we tell that they were men of vision? Some even were American. That seemed poor taste. They were hip. They were often full of hop. Archbishop Eliot would not have been amused. Wholly Communion indeed! ... So we didn't lend a hand to levitate the Albert

Hall. 'Dear old thing,' said Brian in a finicky falsetto, 'whyn't they leave it alone, then?'

Long after it took place, however, Wholly Communion lingered. Its poster, all night and ectoplasm, haunted me, the last word in black and white, like a photo of a dream dawning. The title zigzagged cross my mind like the irregular verb, graffito. I tingled as it told me it *was* possible to make such jokes, out loud, in public, no French or German needed. They could be posted up on the walls of banks and galleries, could make these square institutions underwrite something other than themselves. Poetry, world of underminings and alternatives! Possibilities of resistance and retaliation leapt to my mind like drugs, like weapons. I foresaw blazing tar barrels in Green Park, choirs of saxes honking out the Whitehall stomp, young prophets prophesying more youth, an end to Eleanor Rigbyhood and Highbury; cold hideaway. More, more! Let all things that happen be Happening things! Poetry, making of God a pun!

My powerful, vague desire to be a dedicated follower of fashion did not arise because I felt the scene was there for me assiduously to dig it. It was true that I was nothing without novelty. But I also needed some way to resist my friends' resistance to groovy verse. Even if I didn't have a reason to resist them, though, boredom would eventually have made me. This was the way I went, going on by breaking off. I hated how diurnal pettiness tarnished the visionary gleam of new, improved self-acceptance. The minuteness of actual life could debunk the grandeur of the turning point, the pseudo-sacramental thrill of the epiphany, and all the other mere phrases invented to make life seem noteworthy. Novelty was wearing off, while the whine wore on, despite Fraser trying to teach me to salute it as 'crrutteek' (a term for which superficial me could only think the Scottish voice box had been expressly designed). 'Critique' was a great word, right enough, but now it crystallised a dour mood of what I no longer found intriguing. I was tired of playing poor scholar, numbed by their knowledge and their affectations. Now that I was used to them, they seemed just as limited as myself. Being different made no difference. How about whining like Dylan, or even a Jaggerish pout? How about a wheel to which we might put our, let's say, problematic shoulders? It was time for a change.

I moved to Earls Court.

A pretty philistine thing to do, mused Brian and Fraser. Earls Court was death. It was a warren. It was where Australians came to puke. But I liked the caravanserai, Philbeach Gardens. (I mean one of the four flat-infested houses at the corner of the Warwick Road.) The whole area was chock-a-block with caravanserais, a festival of temporary Land's Ends stretching from Brompton to Ladbroke Grove. There were colonial boys both mild and wild, and next door, cool-looking French girls over for the summer to improve something or other, plus a big Mac Fisheries and a crowd perpetually around the tube. The whole world was a Calor Gas.

The fifty-seven-and-sixpenny wardrobe Mrs Rees called a room was saving me a half-dollar a week, and it was in the front of the house as well. So there was a hum of traffic all around me. For once I felt on the same plane as my transience. This was city enough, and life. I no longer had to pilgrimage up Charing Cross Road all the time. Some evenings it seemed plenty okay just to raise the window and survey the scene. Some Sunday afternoons I took my ease by forsaking pals and Green Park for Alan Freeman going, like a speaking sunray lamp, 'Greetings, Pop-pickers!' I ate Express Dairy banana-flavoured yoghurt. It tasted as exotic as Jimmy's baklava.

I wondered why I didn't miss the two playmates and *la vie bohème*. Then I wondered why I should. I knew as little of their story as I did those of 'Le Bateau Ivre' and *Ecce Homo*, whose stupefying pages I turned in hopes that Brian and Fraser would become my guardians, agents, mentors, siblings, family. But in the end, I only knew that Nietzsche said

78

it all, whatever it was, and that *avant garde* was French for beatnik. And what I felt was stronger. I felt again what seemed to come most naturally to me, a safe solitariness, an absenting which I could rationalise as autonomy, resistance and dissent.

The sun inclined towards Hounslow and my mouth was parched from cigarettes. I tossed the butt down to the gutter with an autographer's flourish, put on the saucepan for yet more instant coffee, turned to the card table, which was all the room I had to work and eat on, and began again. 'Yet Larry, although he decided there and then to move from Willesden, found it difficult to do so. He owed quite a lot to Auntie Maisie . . .' A story to paper over absence. This was all I knew on earth.

And it turned out the same way for Brian and Fraser. They, too, had their story, had their ending. Fraser vanished into thin Ayr, Brian told me over a beaker of Better Books sludge. Parents came into it, also ticket of leave, and cancellation, which Brian pronounced as though it were a disease. 'Come in, Number One, yer time's up!' he went, with a hollow bark. I thought at first that perhaps he was bestowing one of his verses on me, not realising that why Fraser left was too banal for straightforward telling, and that, in the face of it, Brian could only try being clever.

It took me unawares that he and Fraser might be people, not book ends. It had never occurred to me that all their talk might well have been beside the point, an unwitting but unavoidable conferring of a mistaken identity on their trial marriage of true minds. I never thought how their themes of unfulfilment, abandon, crisis, disgust, repression, all the solitary soul-outpourings of the existentially love-lorn, might have been passionately repeated to escape what ended up being inescapably accentuated, the fears that make flesh mute. But the notion that philosophising was bred of loneliness was a big anticlimax. That kind of carry-on was for the like of me and Helga, where sex was impossible. I expected more of overmen. But they too had been appalled by irrational unreasoning need, how it upstaged, debagged, unmasked, embarrassed them, filled them with humiliation and vague dread, left them looking at themselves and contemplating the human that was all too human.

II

One last look over my shoulder showed Brian still in the back room and Fraser flogging his foaming hobbyhorses down the long road to the *ailes*. And there I left them. I was smoking Kent now, and was reading the *Guardian*, drinking too much at lunch time and indiscriminately saying 'stupid twatface'. I'd met Bill. And there was no doubt in my mind that compared to everybody else I'd met, permanent or temporary, Hibernian, Antipodean, Colonial, sub-, neo-, or failed Brit, Bill was the real thing.

It was the beard. That great brown mat of his, flecked with grey, with odd streaks of ginger, stretched from lapel to lapel and as far down as the second button of his jacket. It was a brazen flag, a uniform of the universal antisoldier, a naked acre of the self's soil, a portrait of the artist. Beside it, Fraser's acrid marmalade of madras shirts and puke-yellow cravats paled into the stuff of kirk-going. I'd never seen such a flagrant image, and fell for it at once.

He was a wordsman of Clan Dedalus who didn't give a toss for money (the same as myself, the same as myself!). He read of 'pataphysics' – the science of imaginary solutions – in the *Evergreen Review*, and *Ubu Roi*, fresh out from New Directions (quite possibly he'd been to Cecil Court!). Dazed and delighted, he turned Absurd. His second play, *The Stamp Collection*, was set in a front room and featured a clerk with a fetish, ended with the roof falling in, a downpour of debris onto the stage and our hero half-drowned in it, groping for his hinges.

Bill was married. I'd never known a married man, not

properly. She was an American. I'd never known one of them either. Carly. She sported Bill's beard's counterpart, a splendid swathe of corn-yellow hair that swung loose and free down to her waist. They met at The Pike Theatre, Dublin. That was where his first play was put on. I loved his fame. It was called *The Kip, Dossers, A Doss House* (Ibsen was finally being buried at the time), something along those lines, drawing on his experiences. I saw the cuttings from the Dublin papers, the intrigued, mildly ironic greetings of 'a slice of life in the raw' set in London far away among 'the emigrant class'. But that was Dublin, as complacent as a pig in shit. At least there was The Pike, a wooden handkerchief in Baggot Mews, everything about it saying, 'Fuck yer plush!' It was Theatre Festival time. Bill's play ran a week. Carly was in Dublin doing Europe. I loved the romance of them.

This was the real thing. This was a man in cinemascope. A travelled man, an artist. A survivor of wastes. A resister. A hard man. He wasn't afraid to say, 'Fuck Dublin.' In him, I could see, it was one thing to leave, and another to mean it. I'd only left. He'd taken his unassuming Calor chair, too, like a man, and plied the right dramatic pen in the evenings after meatloaf in the draughty flat. Like me, permanent. He lived in Wimbledon. It was as remote as Highbury had been. (He was like me!). Background, status, avocation, domicile. He was the image of myself, the Johnny I'd been looking for. A married man. Well, let him let me be his first-born son.

We never called it adoption, of course. They were my friends, not my parents. I was just coming to dinner. I thought adoption because I wanted dinner to last my whole life long, a season ticket to belonging. Happiness was a roast chicken.

As in the days of Johnny, it was a delight to potter in the daylight through unfamiliar stations, to glimpse the river from on high at Putney, to unfurl my *Guardian* as though it was an advertisement for myself. A couple of four-packs of

Long Life from the Peter Dominic's near the station, and I felt stateside smart, strutting on agog to my alternative, and therefore realer, home off Worple Road. Bill stuck the four-packs in the fridge and ran through his repertoire of deft, fastidious kitchen gestures. He diced and spiced, sliced cabbage for his own coleslaw, would take an egg and with one wrist-flick and crack, the yolk slid free. An artist to his fingertips. I loved his style.

The fizzing Long Life was broached without ceremony. We talked *Guardian*. Bill was bitter about Labour. There was no sense in the world of Harold Wilson, sidekick of psychopathic L.B.J. Then on to Richard Roud, the Friday film critic. He kept us up to date with Losey. We liked Losey, because Dirk Bogarde always smoked Kent in his films and the Pinter-scripted ones often had an Irish character. Brian Phelan played a pub Paddy in *The Servant*. He got to say, 'I had a bit of good luck today.' But none of the customers was listening. We laughed ourselves silly at that. The good luck was the nobody listening. Was that the Absurd? I asked. Bill laughed like mad again then. That was at the Classic, King's Road. The evening ended up in a Finch's, I think, or some place at World's End in honour of Beckett and his son Murphy. Or was that the night we closed the Henekey's at Notting Hill Gate?

Talk, talk! Terry Coleman. He was not too bad. But Stanley Reynolds was a prick. How good it was to have one's say out loud. And knocking back the limitless drink was just as liberating. We raised our voices, struck the table, modulated in next to no time from the civility of 'But surely . . .' to the more familiar 'Arra, for fuck sake! . . .' The room steamed up and stank of cauliflower. We let the chicken singe. 'Jeez,' went Carly in mock-shock at our excesses, bored already, having heard so much of it before, seeing the long night ahead and all those halves of lager. Peter Lennon, however, was just plain strange. Every now and then his Thursday piece was about Dublin or some other Irish rubbish. In a quality paper . . . From a writer

based in Paris (the Dublin that died and went to heaven)!
Imagine having such a frayed string to your bow, we said,
and trying to squeeze a number or two from it still. Who
gave a shit for Ireland? We shook our disenfranchised
heads, bewildered and amazed. Carly should put on her
coat. We were going to the pub.

The Fox and Grapes was our home from home, a Courage
house braying with horse brasses up by the common.
The suburbs' weekend squirearchy, all blazers and blus-
ter, threw challenging looks our way, trying to place us.
We didn't seem like chaps whose spiritual bailiwick was
Richmond RFC. We took no notice, were too busy getting
seriouser and seriouser, racing round the libraries of ourselves, standing rounds to old acquaintances. White wine to
Oscar Wilde, pink gin for Raymond Chandler. A bowl of
plámás for Sean O'Casey. 'Tha' fella,' said Bill acidly,
'making himself out to be a fucking humanist – self-
deception!' And a dozen stout for Beckett, because Sam was
the last word and the sooner I got that into my head the
better off I'd be.

We promised each other, swaying home with midnight
striking, that we were staggering on to the Transfiguration,
laughing like drains. We drank to exile, the only way, the
way of lonesomeness and worldlessness, the way of the in-
consolable, vaguely rabid mind. Let commitment rejoice in
the committed! No such delusions of grandeur for us. No
words could change our world. We drank to pataphysics, to
its recognition that difference made no difference, to its proof
by dot and tangent that God did not exist (nothing new there
except method, but, Jesus, _quelle méthode!_). Nihilism could
be fun! We drank to Antonin Artaud, mad and damned in
Dublin, blessed cause of consternation to the Brothers of St
John of God. Deportee, naturally, the same as ourselves, in
his way. I loved thinking 'exile'. Bill made it seem true
domicile. My man, Bill, inventor of a life for me.

It was too early to say what shape this life would ultimately
take, of course. But in the meantime, I could love it for being

latent, for the twinges of hope that it unexpectedly sent through me, like phonecalls from the future. There would be something left after Adamov and Albee, wouldn't there? – when we'd done with Arthur Kopit, *The Connection*, Ugo Beti, and Slawomir Mrozek. And it wouldn't be Carly's sober silence, either, which I kept hearing as vividly as if it were a warning or a threat. But what? Postures, gestures, notions, tones waved and wavered in my mind, like faraway magnolias agitated by a Maytime zephyr, like anarchists on an Acapulco honeymoon.

Whatever. I'd make no demands. I was charmed just to be able to play good doggie. Just as long as I belonged to someone. I already owed Bill for being shown that life, liberty and the pursuit of happiness was all a matter of what came into the head and out of the mind – I loved his philosophising. He'd given me more than any girl. Sometimes he'd even listen to me. Need spoke a lot louder than sense in me. Guru, boyfriend, brother, spouse ... I loved the idea of him.

Then Merrick turned up.

I knew the name. Bill had often spoken wistfully of him. But I considered him a wraith, a might-have-been. He was an actor, Bill had known him since The Pike, he'd been a child star, Anna Neagle had patted him on the head, he'd made money, and had known hotels. But all there was to show for fame and fortune now, Bill said with a kind of gloomy satisfaction, was that Merrick's face refused to age. He was ASMing. Bill laughed, unamused at the obvious absurdity called career, meteor of cruel life. Worse, the previous summer playing Butlin's in wet Pwlheli, Merrick had landed himself a silly wife and lived now in a silly flat in Highgate which he couldn't afford. That was why he hadn't been around, said Bill, and his small brown eyes grew hard and bright, pitying and unpitying lost Merrick, the romantic, as though to say, Poor fool, going down the same unhappy road as the whole world and thinking that there's never been the like of it, just because it's your brush and her gluepot. 'Still, though, Merrick's a great guy,' said Bill, wistfully.

I pretended to be glad to hear it, but I couldn't stand the sound of him. He had a name. He had a reputation. His star was only in eclipse (and sure enough, Merrick did go on to shine as a stupid pupil in *Please, Sir*). Bill spoke as if he missed him, and that made me worry that I was not a good enough replacement. He had a larger claim on Bill, through seniority. He was a proper orphan. I could only style myself one. His looks easily outdid mine in waifishness. Plus, it was threatening that he worked in the theatre. Every night and twice on Saturday, he handed Richard Burton the crown without which he was nothing, in *Camelot*, at the Theatre Royal, Drury Lane, and every so often, with a little circumspection, had a slash in the Queen's own lavatory, abutting the royal box. He wasn't permanent. He seemed happy. And he insisted that we sing. But for Bill's sake I'd put up with him, I thought, not daring to have a sake of my own.

The singing was a kind of autobiography, a calculated shout of 'Why not?' Bad luck to respectable Courts and Gardens! was our cry. Our souls were hellish black, and black our cackling minds. Attend to their live loose ends and poor connections, you who dare sleep. Receive our static in the name of song.

> Oh had he dyad by Pearse's syad, or in the GPO,
> Or shout and roar and screech and bawl the something
> of the foe
> Or forcibly fed while Ashe lay dead in the dungeon of
> Mountjoy
> I'd roar and screech and shout and bawl me own dear
> Laughing Boy.

Black night, be idiom and medium!

Swaggering as best we could around the Crooked Billet, we effed out the 'forcibly fed', and laughed like lunatics at the bogus poetry, the absurdity of language trying to sing the cemetery of history. We were rebels. We were tinkers. We were miniature Brendan Behans, never more ourselves than when howling at the empty dark, showering the laurel and arbutus with the vocal equivalent of broken bottles. And Wimbledon slept, oblivious, indifferent, benighted, complacent. Our unquiet *quêtes* went through the darkness more innocently than storybook spooks who overnight sour the milk.

Not that we minded going unnoticed. It was kind of true to life. And, somehow, traipsing past midnight all along the Ridgway, roaring seemed to have its own integrity, a theatre for three and a perfect audience. Solidarity, fraternity, untouchability! It was as though we'd at last discovered who we really were. And when my head didn't feel like a bucket of water in someone else's wobbly hand, or when I wasn't hanging on to gate, pillar box, or bonnet of Morgan, heaving, I believed our brackish owlhooting was the best of fun. I even gathered from Merrick and Bill, waiting up ahead, pointing at me, doubled over laughing, that puking and lightheadedness made a welcome sideshow, my own landmarks on our road to God-knows-where, my personal echoes of our night's great No! – as expressive, in their way, of imaginary solutions as mindless eructations of chaotic song.

But it turned out that I was really on the road to nowhere with them. Soon, at closing time, it was fear, not fun, I felt. Sensations of exposure, more powerful than drink, surged through me. I found myself looking back on the pub fire, locked away and dying, and shivering. I felt a wind off the black common flapping with the sting of a wet teatowel in my face. Our acting out wasn't left on the street where it belonged. We didn't just have one last laugh and put the kettle on, make tea and have a final smoke before abandoning ourselves to our hard-earned comas. Instead, all that delirium of the brave, which had given us safe conduct back to Bill's flat, degenerated frighteningly into the original shit of things. Simply, it wasn't me Bill loved, but Merrick.

86

I suppose their games were staged simply as new proofs of absurdity. Bill said, 'C'mere till I grope you', and Merrick, with a pretty simper, did. But by doing so he made all previous lonelinesses preferable to the one that hit me. Hilary's hideous chocolate suddenly tasted sweet and warming. Mrs Ross's unmanning of my initials was a kind of mothering. More than my good name was being taken from me now. My whole idea of belonging, and of feeling safe, of thinking that I'd made myself at home, was being scoffed to crap.

Bill's hands made menacing advances, swooped, appeared to pluck, like something preying, but without touching. But it wasn't the gesture that made me feel so vulnerable. At least not just it. What hurt was realising that if there had to be a grope, I was the one who needed what it meant and wasn't getting it. There never was a grope, though. They weren't serious. Bill thrust his beard into my face and said, 'Ah sure we love you, don't you know that, you stupid twatface?' and he and Merrick collapsed in laughter. They were making fun of need, the one thing that I could put my name to. I still hear them laughing at me. I still feel the recoil of my sulky rejection.

Sometimes it felt like a kind of falling, this rejection, a swift, sickening lurch and plunge through dark bitter night. Then, at other times, back in my room, it was as though it paralysed me, and all there was for me now, by way of feeling, was glacial cold and dread. This was the void, the terror, that the Absurd mirrored and defied. I stayed inside my claustrophobic Earls Court closet, dreaming of interrogation rooms, sadistic laughter, the mind beyond midnight and the quaking body, places that were anything but home.

III

'*Styu*-pidt!' Liz went, banging the machine with small fierce fists.

She was all by herself in a cubicle off Central Records, typing dealers' names on to metal plates. When they were done, I'd be redundant. The machine was very modern, very temperamental, very rented, and Dave, her ratty Section Head, kept roaring at her that time was money. We had to laugh. The English-speaking people's ancient chant . . . '*So* bourgeois,' said Liz. She preferred to dilate on the pleasures of 'Get Away', by Georgie Fame.

'Yeah,' my insincere grin agreed. She was just another Calor temp. Still . . .

Self as adoptee had foundered and I'd been low. But the past twenty months had shown me London as one enormous *Dalton's Weekly* or *Exchange and Mart* of personalities. Selves were just so many buses, belated, uncomfortable, slow to get going. But there would be another one along eventually, perhaps even one going all the way.

Besides, sliding from one self to another seemed part of the swing of things. Life as advertised appeared to be mainly a matter of subverting and supplanting, drifting and floating. Dropping out was in. Did leaving Ireland count? How about not praying to Holy God? They could count, if I wanted them to. It could be fun being where there was real opium and real masses, where the secular sacrament of the Sunday joint meant both more and less than hitherto. (In the new year Liz and I were to consider the pun seriously as a name for our group.) Even empire seemed a little dodgy, a flag on a carrier bag. Upstart Mintoff was a riot, having his say, having his day, looking as if he'd get his way. FA seemed to have more bottle than in FO. Jules Rimet ruled OK, and knowing his subjects, loved all animals except Argentinians. Jules found himself a regent, Pickles, who ran to ground in Beckenham the golden, stolen trophy. Lawrence's Corner was doing a bomb in fab old military gear, drag for the First World to ponce about in, while the Third World slouched towards Westminster (or was that Havana?) to be born, winds of change and a big stink, later encountered as Enoch. It was the pontificate of John and

Paul. '(I Can't Get No) Satisfaction' was released. I dug it the most.

This is me, smiling as though hard of hearing at incessant tales of Nobby Stiles destroying the Portuguese. There I go, cheating the tube, as brazen as a native. I make for Dillon's and my faithful Friday book-buy, eeling my swift way through lower Fitzrovia, the image of a citier who knows his way around. Here I am, thinking of Liz as more mere office mindlessness.

It took a thunderstorm to change my mind about her.

Black rain shot with unEnglish vehemence from a livid sky, a treat on a tiresome Thursday. Old dears of all kinds round the office muttered darkly that they should never have put that Post Office Tower up near us, too much electric. But the offices of the Nigerian trade delegation, two floors down, came out on to the catwalk in their superb robes and grinned with delight at the show of force, appreciating its lack of inhibition. I remember because in the middle of it all, Liz rang me. Would I come over right away? She was scared. I thought . . . I didn't think. I was needed. I had to go. And she was all smiles. 'Thanks,' she said, and called me by name. It had been sweet of me, she said. '*Sweeeet.*'

It was the sound that did for me. Its soft swoon was more of a siren to me than her sincerity. Letting my avid eyes rest on her unrevealing neckline was impossible. I was not a body. I was not for love. But oh – intangibles of voice, infatuate me! Sometimes I heard a rich quaver in it, a throb, tense and molten, when with passionate promptness, 'Yes!' she went, stabbing a finger at her machine, 'that piece of shit.' Sometimes, there was a trill to it, when she was surprised, or when, grinning, she flipped two fingers at Dave's departing back. Some kind of woman! I'd never known one to say or do the like. Some kind of bell and cello, some kind of fabulous tonsils. By the following month I liked her short curly hair, as well, liked it being unwillowy, untrendy. I looked with pleasure on how full her lips were, how green those eyes, how baby-smooth her face. And how her legs did not seem cemented together at the top.

I told myself to be realistic. There definitely had to be a boyfriend. She'd certainly be leaving soon her summer sublet in some smart postal district. A fortnight in Greece first, then back to university. She'd turn into another person once the scarf of special colours was put on again and books I'd never heard of opened and mind once more came into its unmechanical own. But, as usual, realism brought no relief. And there came evenings full of the Wimbledon blues. I'd fling my Pelican – *The Western Intellectual Tradition* – from me across the wretched room. I'd say the word 'sex', hoping that utterance would prove prophylactic, as the couch-doctors vouchsafed.

Once named, however, the thing – knot, block, impasse – grew more inescapable. Its long, inhibiting shadow of a self unseen, some gothic monstrosity. Its gloom made all too evident areas where no self of mine had ever settled comfortably or for long, deserts and salt mines with names like inner, feeling, intimate, personal, need. Now, *not timid*, I wanted to cross those parched places and enter the valley. Spill milk. Ooze honey. Yes! I groaned, gravid with the appetite of the whole hog. I was a beast, if not at heart, deep – or at least further – down. It was such a relief, after being so certain that I was nothing but the nicest, bestest little adoptee in the whole wide world, the mouse-quiet manchild who had never a need. All sex had ever been was a sore thumb sticking out, an ugly head, reared, the yardstick of my unloved, unloving life, as *non grata* as an Irish accent. After unfond farewells to the Pats and Helgas, the turned cheeks and cold shoulders, and Bill with his allure that turned to threat, suddenly there was a frank smile, a show of interest, a call on the internal phone because she was bored and did I have a minute. I had more than that. Absurd as a one-way pendulum the drive may be. But it had me. It made a sense that might satisfy. Life, life . . . it seemed I wanted it. There I stood, anyhow. I could do no other.

There was a boyfriend, John, and the room they shared was where, a year before, in the long ago, I had imagined thin divorcées, poodles, and amontillado from cut-glass decanters. Gloucester Place, a large, two-windowed room, twice the size of any I had lived in, with walls some impossible-landlord-paint-sale colour (teal blue springs to mind).

I was jealous. They had space. They had location. But what I really hated was that both of them lived here. They *shared!* John, who was no older than me, had his side of bed and dressing table, slung strands of spaghetti against the wall behind the sink to see if it was done (it was if it stuck) while his beloved braised the meatballs on the hotplate. He was more at home here than with his disapproving parents out in Hanwell, and didn't mind when Liz called him 'puss'. Indeed, it seemed as effortless as Italian cooking for him to say 'puss' back. These must be the high old ways of love, I thought, having never been around cohabitation, much less a pair of lovers.

Much as 'puss' impressed me (it seemed vaguely disloyal to be embarrassed by it) I told myself that it wasn't a patch on *sweeeet*. Or on *witty*, either, which was what I was as well – '*sooo* witty' – the evening of our one and only drink *à trois*. I wanted to take them to the Globe, where I would greet the barman familiarly and impress, by God, the pair of them to within an inch of their domesticated lives. Jimmy would remember me from when I was travelling solo from the Jolly Gardeners, and would act accordingly, favouring me with the shy smile of an old, sincere, retainer. But John didn't drink, really, didn't seem to want to go out, much less walk beyond a hundred yards, which of course was fine, 'No, the Volunteer is grand, honest.' My compliance only made his unmoving eyes more dark.

I knocked back two manly pints while he sipped a half of shandy and held his horrid peace. I was intent on sparkling, relied heavily on *Beyond Our Ken*, Ricky Livid, Jules and Sandy, Rambling Sid Rumphole, Seamus Android, and the character with the loose false teeth. Oh, the wit of it. John's looks got blacker and more incredulous, but as long as I kept my patter going, I could ignore his moody-shagger act. It wasn't till I was on the seventy-four going home that I saw with a start what a caution he'd obviously meant the evening to be.

He didn't want Liz not to have her laugh, if she was sure that was what she really wanted, but he didn't want me giving it to her. He was there with her, not me, making sure that neither of them came to any harm, while by the same token providing upstart me with an emphatic, menacingly understated, letdown. I grinned. Acting the poacher was exciting. But what if John began to warn me off properly, had mates, big fists, loud voices. I blanched. I'm innocent, s'help me, guv, yer Englishness, sor. I'm as harmless a forelock-tugging Paddy as you'd hope to meet in a day's walk, a dazzled rabbit, not a threat to property. I'd more than likely walk, or run away, fall back on the known world of passivity and others' power.

But Liz didn't want that. She said that John was black and dumb because he had had it. For once, I had nothing to say, struck dumb not only by being confided in, but by the passion of it. It wasn't just John. Life was a drag, generally, basically. The room was grotty, the job was shitty. Typing, I mean, *really* . . . She wasn't some seventeen-year-old with two CSEs. As for the so-called freedom in temping, it wasn't what she understood by freedom. The whole system – and it really was a system too – just stank, was so *unreal*, these sirs and suits and pensionable positions. The whole Bit was prehistoric, irrelevant. John hated it too, the collar and tie, the ready-reckoner. And now they were hating each other hating it, and there was no money. 'Bad scene, man,' said Liz. She had to go to her mother's in Hampstead when she wanted to play the piano.

There was no university. There was guilt instead. Not that there was anything to feel guilty about, guilt was bourgeois, just parents on a God trip trying to stop you doing your own thing. (I solemnly reassured her that she never said a truer word.) Basically, all that had happened was that she and John had dropped out. 'Big deal'. She'd shocked me again. I'd thought, half-longingly, that the higher-level learning must be as sweet as a drug, a detergent that beats as it sweeps as it cleans. But my vision of edifices all in glass and everything modern came to nothing more, if I understood her, than a row of Biros in some so-called superior's top pocket. Strawberry Hill had actually been as boring as a long committee meeting of the Labour Party, all statistics and no delight, everyone 'so fucking *keen*', uptight. And anyway, training, being trained, was an insult to anyone's intelligence. The whole system was basically just one great big falsies' factory. And her voice seemed to writhe with refusal. I got the idea that Liz was almost as familiar with anticlimax as myself. Dare I think we were alike? . . .

We were, we were! Her father was French. I'm foreign, too, I said (at last a label that fits, classier than immigrant, less paranoid than exile). Two Aquarians, our names inscribed in the stars. Way out! But *in* as well. I began to have a feeling like arrival. My ship was coming in. This was the dawning . . .

Then Liz left.

Mind? Me? I just went out and bought another Penguin Classic, *Rameau's Nephew*, I remember ('*mes pensées ce sont mes catins*'). Trying not to think French, trying very hard instead to concentrate on humming 'Paint It Black . . .' French meant insincerity, deception. French bed. French leave. French letter. Frenchip. My father used to holiday in France, thinking that his life was his own, and not mine. Frogs. Slippery. Cold-bellied. Hard to know which way they'd jump. Themselves and their *l'amour toujours*, allure too pure, and all the rest of the great fake that is foreign, other people, sex, the whole wide world which declined either to womb or woo me. I knew that Liz all right.

The phone rang.

In Philbeach Gardens it was in a booth in the hall with a

buzzer next to it on which whoever took the call croaked out the room number of the callee, four for the blond Rhodesian and his Indian girlfriend in the room below me, nine for the non-stop New Zealand rodeo overhead. I was six. She'd said she'd ring, but breaknecking it down the stairs, every iota of me in a fine frenzy rolling, I bore in mind what that meant. It was no different from agreeing to have a drink and then say, Know your place, keep your distance, Perfidious Albion.

She said my name, said she missed me. She and John had split, and she was living in Swiss Cottage. She'd written me a letter, had I had it yet? Ah, a letter, of course . . . That would be the way, very English. She was wondering if I might be free for lunch on Sunday, some friends of hers would like to meet me, and all of a sudden there was nothing wrong, back up the stairs with me, singing the praises of FRObisher, whose patron saint was undoubtedly Sir Martin, the explorer. Only he and I knew how it felt to be in Baffin Island with hopes of seeing Cathay.

The letter came next day, for this was a magic time, posted in Bristol, where Liz had indeed said she was going to visit old friends (it was a time of truth). My vagueness now about the letter's contents is a perfect replica of my first blurred reading of it. She spoke of knowing intuitively. There was a lot of 'you', meaning me, in it. With love. And it was just brilliant. I remember that. But the superficial fact of pen and ink was as important as any sentiment. Writing's permanence guaranteed words' truth. I hadn't had a letter in months, not since the one addressed in my own hand, from *Encounter*, unaccountably sending back, with compliments, my prose poems.

Lunch was in a Balcombe Street basement with Louise and Bas Double-Barrelled, brother and sister sharing. Bas had been to China and was musical, which was how Liz had come to know them. Louise had a husband with bad nerves. He would not be joining us. Carlos was there with his violin, though, a small man from South America, with whom, I surmised, Louise was doing something French and classy, befitting NW1.

The flat was dark, a little dowdy, no 'best things' on show, I was relieved to see, but plenty of cushions and pouffes and armchairs and sofas offering ampleness and warmth. I sat sipping a thimbleful of Dry Sack, thinking garlic, artichoke, aubergine, wine, savouring the air of *luxe*. I imagined myself as in the *Alexandria Quartet*. I see a print of Matisse's *Pianist and Draught Players* on the living-room wall before me, over the piano. It was probably some friend's perspective of the Downs, but there was a picture, I remember, and it seemed to glow. Two men exchanged showbiz gossip from the classical music scene. Delighted sallies from the women spilled over from the kitchen. Rich aromas. Decanters chinking. Rafäel Frühbeck de Burgos. It was another world. I remember sitting and staring, not entirely conscious, as befuddled and pleased as if I'd just alighted from the right red bus.

That day I had a lot of firsts – brie on hot French bread, olive oil on salad, olives themselves as big and black as does' eyes, corned beef from the Bloom's in Baker Street. The men plumped for a hearty Burgundy, a trifle on the naïve side, but I'd be amused by its pretension (though not half so amused as drinking it on an empty stomach made me). And for the ladies, a Chablis from the fridge. We all said, 'Mmmm', appreciatively and a little furtively, like children alert to adults in the offing who might spoil the sport if, as seemed likely, we began to giggle. So this is England, I thought, broad-mindedly, primed by the delightful foreignness, the place where supposedly there were no plain people, just palaces and titles, big nobs and oompah, no life only correctness. Begod I'll go home for Christmas, look all and sundry in the eye and say, as casually as bedamned, Oh, it's not so bad, y'know, once you get to know it. Home? Why, this was it. Thank you, yes, a touch more wine.

After uninstant coffee, the musicians did some dizzy thing by probably Prokofiev. All applauded, then at four took tea

– strange stuff (Earl Grey, another first), and unaccompanied, to my surprise, by bun or bicky. Suddenly, was that the time? Good Lord. Goodbye, goodbye, we'd be in touch, the girlfriends hugged and kissed, like French people. Bas shook my hand and vaguely said, 'So nice', which pleased me no end because I knew for sure now he was class, and he had no need in the wide earthly world to say a word to me. No doubt about it, I'd arrived.

Marylebone Road in thin September light. There'd been a shower, and grey was the colour of London, in the puddles, in the shop fronts, in the low clouds, in my muddled head. The psychic hangover which always seeped in when stimulus withdrew was beginning to congeal, the familiar anticlimax of emerging from the movie to see the ever-present, unoriginal world still there. Back to gentleman escorting lady to her bus. Back to fool who would never go further.

But when the 113 came, Liz smiled. I got on. She opened the front door and then her door. The land of my abandoned dreams stood before me, a girl's room, full of unwanted old furniture, just like my own (we were alike).

We were alone. I sat on an uneasy chair, lit a cigarette. Liz made tea. Our lips touched. Our tongues touched. It was half-six of a September Sunday afternoon in Lancaster Grove, Swiss Cottage, NW3, centre of the universe. I was over twenty-one-and-a-half years old. I didn't know what time it was, or who, what or where I was. Everyone may have gone to the moon. Now Jupiter had just aligned with Mars. I was all of a tingle. At long last I was entering the promised land.

ONE-WAY PENDULUM

I

Evening after evening, following something hot and hasty from the Vesta range in Philbeach Gardens, I skipped as though on honeydew had fed to Warwick Road and a thirty-one to spirit me to Swiss Cottage. Buses could be trusted now. They helped me gear up for the greater wonderment. I examined my reflection in the twilit upstairs window, squared my shoulders, straightened my back, swept my hair around and behind my ears. Voices representing all the single rooms I'd ever lived in chorused indecipherable encouragements. My nerves crackled like static. I knew where I was going, I thought. I had a damsel with a dulcimer.

We snaked by little shops and empty side streets and doors of tall houses on which bells and nameplates were inscribed like Braille graffiti. This was North Kensington, this was Rachmanstown, where the whores holed up from Friday to Friday waiting for the lads from Lismore to be paid. Whatever else, I wasn't confined to the Harrow Road. I turned up the volume on the inner voices, feeling their rush more than their meaning, high on the superstition called hope.

And the way from Chepstow Road to Kilburn fascinated me like a sore or a deformity, the streets hospital wards of homes that were casualties of something more peremptory than time and weather, though just as invisible and insidious. Something cruel and familiar, such as profit. I looked eagerly, anxiously, down at these ruined neighbourhoods, feeling some sort of tug from the black kids playing in the gutter, the burly topers in their donkey jackets, the wiry wideboys foraging through overflowing skips for the makings of a few antiques. It was as if I wanted to have something to do with them. They were where the action was. Where they lived was news, and to be notorious was trendy. I kept on the lookout for a bust, a roach, a commune, Caroline Coon, anything connected with the voguish offences that were standard now on 'Home News' pages. Pad begat squat begat fuzz. Dangerous. Fascinating. Life! I felt almost up to it.

At Westbourne Grove the caravanserais of Earls Court seemed finally to yield their promise and become bazaars, bright awnings, Indians, Africans. Someone on the fourth floor played a flute, the couple in the basement changed their lives with comfrey. Mild dusk was spiked with cardamon, turmeric, all the perfumes of Arabia suffusing lotusland takeaways. There was an after-hours feel, boxes were being unpacked on the pavement, nothing was running to schedule, there was no time like the present. Even furniture seemed vaguely restless. There were always men moving it around, into vans, into shops, into basements, young men in denims with ponytails, pale, thin, older types, whose soiled white shirts resembled their sad, wrinkled faces, smarter gents in leather jackets disappearing briskly through shadowy doorways with items of bamboo, wicker, rattan, porcelain, cloisonné, cartons, crates, carryalls of pewter and brass. This was the moon the song said everyone'd gone to, nocturnal reflection of the daily round, a roaring trade in rejects, a nation of Portobello shopkeepers, most without shops. This wasn't England at all. This was all out on the street. This was the world, amorphous, improvised, protean, coloured, a theory of possibility, not a settled state, an Oz of postures, conjuring *Oz* up, a giant joss stick, a colourdrome. Turn on!

Liz's room was in a fine pile on a corner of Lancaster Grove, presided over by Mrs Kenny from Ballinrobe, who whenever the fancy took her dropped by to see how we were getting on at all. She kept an eye on Liz, whose mother, herself a *rentière*, knew Mrs Kenny's mistress. Such connections made it only prudent, Mrs Kenny seemed to think, that Liz be looked after. Mind you, as she was fond of telling us, she liked the youth, the go that do be in them these times. She herself had taken to mini dresses, sure didn't she have a fine pair of spawgs under her, even if she did say so herself, not them kippeens of things you see on some of them, that Twiggy, 'Mother *of* God . . .' Mrs Kenny's husband, Joe, a porter at the Royal Free Hospital, disapproved. Minis were nothing more than 'pussy pelmets', he said. 'Dirty scut,' said Mrs Kenny proudly, wiggling her bum, and sidled out with a sly, how's-she-cutting? look to me.

There was no cutting. There were fond friends' swift embraces when we met (vivifying clean scent of skin, tantalising touch of hair, instant of transient warmth . . .). And there were sibling intimacies. But by and large, we strolled and chatted. Liz showed me another new London, where no buses ran, Belsize and shortcuts to Primrose Hill past Yeats's house (Liz spoke in awe of Sylvia Plath), Gospel Oak and Frognal on the overground. We sat for ages over capuccino and a strudel in Conrad's Bistro, Belsize Village. The burly mein host scowled at us for taking so long and spending so little. But we couldn't help it. Our tongues wagged without wearying, rigged pendulums, incapable of slowing down or stopping or of going back for just a tick, as I often wistfully wanted, to the other kind of tonguing of that opening Sunday of ours, the feast of the arrival.

But talk meant more to Liz. Maybe she was lonely (we

were alike). Her voice made my timbers shiver, anyway: Blossom Dearie's knowing doll shot through with Nina Simone's smoulder. It made me half afraid, the power of it. I only knew intensity as family displays of arctic moods and flaring tempers. In Liz it spoke in ways that could transform that unutterable desert, the single room, into an endearing hothouse, where a hundred flowers would bloom. Let it change me. I would be Haight to her Ashberry. I saw myself risen in the world, imagined myself taller, felt high, doped by difference. I washed my hair more often.

When last-bus time came, we hugged again, we kissed some sweet, dry, chaste, brief kisses on the lips. Five times a week this happened. Standby, surrogate, sidekick, somehow, anyhow, I was wanted. Liz called me 'Silly Billy', and I went, 'Meh-heh-heh', as tame as any puss. It was the dawning of the age of relationships. It was the revolution.

Besides, I didn't know the first thing about it!

I don't remember what I must have said. I remember that it was the first time she shouted. I knew that we were being serious about sex. We were fighting.

Nature was a rapist. Nature drew blood. Think about the sweaty palms, the headaches. I shied away. My virginity and her martyrdom did not make up my idea of heaven. She lowered her voice eventually.

'Les anglaises ont débarquées,' she said, and tried to laugh, unaccustomed to my silence.

'Aye, aye,' said I. 'The Redcoats.'

Mother Ireland's curse. I had a lot to learn. Far from ST belts I'd been reared, only sopranos had diaphragms. Durex, Playtex, Tampax, constituted a kind of x-rated liturgy, to be approached cautiously, considered critically, only acknowledged with maximum ambivalence, if at all. And Liz had her mind set on being a real woman. Down with falsies, fashion lines, cosmetic counters! The Pill was a conspiracy. Just because men were swine, did women have to be guinea pigs? 'Those things are lethal, man!' She was bored with sex, anyhow. It was no big deal. She was glad that we could be friends. I said I supposed I agreed. I lurked round Liz's sense of outrage and watched the D-cups and elastic of men's egos shrivel from the heat of her contempt into black rubbery smoke. Burn, baby, burn! I affected being cool.

In two minds and united, we did our best to abjure the mutinous body. Evening dissolved into night. The last bus was long gone. Radio London had closed down. But still we talked, nearing the inevitable by pretending to be indifferent to it. Head would avert heart. That was the mature way, signature of mutual respect, commitment, seriousness, freedom (we knew all the names of sublimation). A marriage of true minds for us, not furtive hand in fetid glove, not that insipid nexus of lodgement and withdrawal. Liz told me of Nicole, who stroked her hair and held her close, motheringly, but better because there was delicious strangeness too. Getting away with it. Nobody knowing. Rebellion. This was way back when Liz was eighteen. She missed Nicole, she said. So do I, I thought.

The air in the room grew viscous, heavy. Our voices softly plied, weaving intimacy's supple wrap, beyond criticism, beyond narrative, working toward the very sex of talk. We lay Molly-Poldy fashion on the bed and felt each other smiling in the darkness. At times like that Liz said, 'We're making love.'

My trousers told me differently, though. That was the trouble. I had my rage, too, but it was different to Liz's, all ache and pressure, unspeakable (we were not alike). A time or two I lunged at her, reverting to type since self dared not declare. But that only knocked the ashtray over or spilled tea. I bought a packet of three, then thought, Hope they don't die before I get old. I had to keep remembering, Better a role than a nature. Better to be self-denying and have company. Liz was too old to have sex. I was too old not to. It all seemed quite sardonically lifelike.

But then, sometimes, after long silence and a last goodnight, she'd take my hand and we'd exchange a furious few minutes. My tongue and finger would be told where to go. I tried to make the most of the hasty trip, tasted with gusto the salts and soils of the invisible, virtually spectral, country, though never going all the way. My finger was turned into a one-way pendulum, absurd, mechanical, relentless. Liz shuddered, yelped, and slept. I called it love.

Pop was much better. I discovered this in bed as well, in Balcombe Street. Louise had asked Liz if she'd mind awfully watering the plants while she and Carlos weekended in Bournemouth. We'd have no Mrs Kenny, no landing bathroom queue, all mod. cons., including conjugality. A bigger place, a better time. It stood to reason. I stretched out on the bed and felt as manly as a proprietor. But Liz jumped up and danced. It was 'You Keep Me Hanging On', I suppose (never was shagger-moodier than I, suddenly). She shook her hips tremendously, and I saw the drive of her, the abandon, and how oblivious she was to vibrant breasts and legs which suddenly seemed beautifully long.

Lovin' Spoonful's 'Summer in the City' came on, its beat an agitation that couldn't easily be danced to, *very* innovative we agreed, intelligent (those car horns), without knowing it on the verge of saying 'progressive'. But it was the guitar break in the Hollies' 'Bus Stop', and the string figures in 'Eleanor Rigby' that really turned Liz on. They were first class, she claimed, wouldn't listen when I called them bloodless, lacking the seam of dirt and danger in which Stones and Animals and I delighted. If there had to be Beatles' numbers, let them be 'Got to Get You into My Life', cranked up the chart by groups with halfway proper, no-pun names like Cliff Bennett and the Rebel Rousers. Let there not be pretty things, just Pretty Things.

Liz had heard of Elvis, Bill Haley, 'Michelle, Ma Belle,' and had perhaps a hazy recollection of, say, Shane Fenton and the Fentones ('I'm a Moody Guy'). But she basically wasn't with it. She couldn't tell Cliff from Little Richard, the Impalas were to her a road not taken, Phil Spector not something understood. She was a virgin. My mind was a

Hot 100. This was a heat that I could stand. I knew Duane
Eddy was on the Jamie label and that he had Jim Horn on
sax. I knew the Everly Brothers' hits were written by Felix
and Boudleaux Bryant and issued in the States on Cadence.
I tossed around the names of Pomus and Schumann, Goffin
and King, Lieber and Stoller, which felt now more familiar
to me than parents. I felt glad recalling how they'd nursed
my teenage aches with pleasure, felt proud as I revelled in
baby autodidacts' first words, that they now conferred
authority on me. I called to mind a garage in Lubbock, a
shack in Tupelo, stoops in Flatbush, in South Philly. All
those tracks the Italian kids, black kids, kids from small
places let me cross. All the lonely people. For once remembering was good. Sam Cooke was good. Eddie Cochran was
good. It felt so good to say so.

I was a hit. Liz loved my lore. Now this was real togetherness. And the world was looking good as well. Already
there were English labels with meaningful names, Immediate, Deram, Reaction. Soon Duffy Power and Dickie Pride
would cease being cynosures, and it would be as though
such hits as Heinz's 'Just Like Eddie' never existed. No
more death. All we needed was love. Chris Montez sang
'The More I See You'. Liz and I made sheep's eyes at each
other. Something told me I was into something good. I
called it happiness (easier, normaler, than love), thanked
my lucky stars.

Every Thursday we rushed to the paper stand at Finchley
Road tube for our weekly fix of first *MM*, then *NME*, *Disc*,
Record World. We read what Chris Welch wrote about
Hendrix at the Speakeasy in *Melody Maker* and gasped.
We had to know which major waxing was being rush-
released on Friday, who had partied at Robert Stigwood's,
Stanmore, when would Lulu's current tour take her to
Huddersfield, who'd be playing the Marquee. Above all, we
needed to peruse the thaumaturgical charts, the week's
definer, substantiater of images, astrologer of sales. 'Reach
Out I'll Be There'; its first week in at eighteen, the following

week shot straight to the top. That was our kind of action, its directness the record's very being, simple in style, other-worldly in aura, immediate in impact, travelling at the speed of youth. Levi Stubbs went 'Hah!' and 'Hah!' we echoed histrionically. Liz kicked up her legs.

And Liz was liberating me as well. I could pretend to be sick, she said, and take three days off without a doctor's cert. We hid in plain view in a booth in the HMV shop, Oxford Street, and listened to the dawn of our creation. Dylan, Donovan, *Turn! Turn! Turn!*, everything, anything, *Pet Sounds* over and over. Liz was insatiable for 'God Only Knows'. And if, feeling a bit stale, we wanted our minds well and truly blown, there was Coltrane ('Softly as in a Morning Sunrise'). There was Cathy Berberian. The booth was our room from room, could with the unnerving promptness of a chord change undergo at mid-afternoon in the West End the soft apocalypse of our late night talk. Listening to whole albums was, like our intimacy, a sketch of excess, a cartoon of going all the way. No words, no touching. We would simply look at each other and know we were one, know something was carrying us away, our minds still climactically vibrating with 'My Back Pages'.

O rave new world! We swaggered through streets where earlier I'd shrivelled from all kinds of cold, to the Flamingo, to Tiles, to the Whiskey-A-Go-Go. Down Wardour Street to the Marquee. Don Chinn electrified Liz with his enormous Hammond, dishing out licks as sizzling as Jimmy Smith's, driving the thing as though it were fuelled by great balls of fire. Alley walls shouted bright messages of peace. Parks and thoroughfares cried against imperial might. Ill-lit door-ways held smack off-sales. Bert Jansch did 'The Needle of Death'. The Creation performed 'Painter Man' at the Flam-ingo. While the lead guitar took its break and made sweet moan, the singer sloshed dollops of Dulux on a screen to make a primal-looking posy. Art was graffiti. Flowers were power. Girls wore Donovan caps.

The million children of Alexis Korner turned up at the

Marquee, also the Action. The Move in unison slung forward in a line, withdrew, then up again and back, pointing the necks of their guitars out at the crowd and leering. Something dramatic was intended. They wore pinstripe suits with wide-lapelled jackets, like thirties hitmen. Later they signed with Deram, then after that with Regal Zonophone. We saw the Herd, unthundering and exotic in shirt of shocking pink, lime green, mauve, tight white trousers, hair *en bouffant*. They performed goofy antics with arch seriousness. Did we see them sacrifice a rubber chicken (shrieking organ and tumultuous tom-toms)? I must be imagining that, which may mean, because of how life was then, that it certainly happened (after all, Liz and I formed a group). We saw everybody who was nobody, and some before they were somebody.

Brit rock. Brittle stuff, like its seaside namesake. Too much of it would probably cause teeth to fall out. But it was a treat, no doubt about it. And it persuaded Liz and me that we could do it too, would, in point of actual fact, we said, make a far, far better job of infinitely superior material.

We saw Cream. It was their first London gig, fresh from their triumphant début or something at the Windsor Jazz Festival. They came on dressed as convicts, broad arrows on grey, canvas-looking uniforms, and they opened with 'I Feel Free'. Our anthem. Liz and I knew we had no real alternative.

Yes!

II

Mrs Kenny knocked on the door and yodelled, 'Special delivery.' John was downstairs with Liz's amp and organ. A Farfisa. In a van.

Perhaps I shouldn't have been quite so surprised. Fortified by our diet of pop, Liz had determined that her trouble

all along, 'of *course!*', was that she was, in fact, creative.
She'd been stifled. She named the usual suspects, family,
school, the system. (I said I didn't doubt her.) Forming a
group, therefore, was obvious, natural, inevitable. She
would play organ, and I agreed at once that they certainly
seemed made for each other, a most impassioned instrument it was, to be sure, and that's where it was at, basically.
Letting feeling speak, that's what imagination did. She
would play it as a lead and not a rhythm instrument, the
way it was in Johnny and the Hurricanes, from whom, I
suggested, much could be learned. And she would do
her own material. And she would sing. And since there
weren't really very many women instrumentalists–vocalists,
and because to everything there was a season, she would
definitely hit, and hit big. Why, she'd out-Cilla Cilla! And
I'd play drums. 'D'you know?' said Liz, smiling her most
benevolent smile. 'I had a *feeling* you were going to say
that.'

So I became a drummer (name me to know me). It was her
intuitions, Liz said. She had had one the day of the
thunderstorm. And she'd been right. Now another one
sparked the organ. Our verbal love made intuitions ping
and pulse in her, she said, little thrills of homage to aura and
suggestion, emotions transformed into a private zodiac
potent as a dream in Shakespeare. We weren't far from
India and joss sticks.

I wanted to drum. The group was a future, being in it
would be as good as a pay raise. I fancied myself rocking
around the clock to a single beat, the pulse of things to
come. It was my ideal role, to be in the background adding
essential and not entirely unobtrusive fill-ins, while up front
the organ heaved and squealed, a seeming human thing.
Every so often I'd erupt into a solo, the sound of large things
falling, of me losing my temper and drumming out the
old order. Grinning as maniacally as Ginger Baker. Master
of time.

I thought back to where my drumming came from, Aunt

Chrissy at the piano, the Marino danceband, Lismore, at their weekly rehearsal in our house, me beating a box, up late with big people and feeling loved. I was a flower then in the eyes of my fond aunt. Now the little drummer boy had every chance of growing up to be Mr Tambourine Man. And to be loved as once I was, even, possibly, perhaps . . .

Liz and I felt closer together than ever. Talk was more fervent, talk was more real. We realised, rejoicing, all a group could be, a proper family, a small firm, a friendly building society, a non-stop car ride to some coast or other. I'd write lyrics to Liz's music (they'd be about love, I knew now why songs always were), and the music would be kind of black, only progressive as well. We'd get a manager, an A & R man, a plugger. We'd cut an acetate first, and tour America, and Tony Hall would return our call. And all would be well. Liz could feel it. *Yes!* And I could almost feel her feel it, the drive of her mind in her eyes' brightness, the lust to appear, as one of the newer categories of specialness had it, 'live'.

I did worry that, while talk was certainly one of the best things in life that were free, as Bern Elliott and the Fenmen reminded us years ago, such things were strictly for the birds and bees. Money. Rock machines would be our salvation and ultimately we'd make millions; but without a sprazzi between us, how could we land one of those fine coiners? All would be well. Here I was lugging a large Marshall amp up three flights of stairs. John was our road manager, we should not want, was that it? Did Liz say let there be cash and there was cash? What kind of extraordinary person, sibyl, demiurge, potentate, was I dealing with exactly, creative beyond my timid mind to plumb? Organ, van, John, group. No links, only results. And for her next trick, Liz enlisted Michelangelo Antonioni.

John Gee, emcee of the Marquee, made the public announcement that they were looking for us, they being an all-hair-and-boots kind of girl taking names on the way out, and us being anybody young and groovy-looking. Report in fabbest gear to Borehamwood Studios by eight the following Monday morning, we were told.

Long tube out to Edgware, Green Line bus, mist rising off the green and pleasant, pulse pumping like an accelerating pendulum. Warehouses filled with magic loomed through the filmy air. But before very long the first day, the place turned into Bore'em-good. Girls with stark white faces and turquoise eye-shadow crossed and uncrossed their long thin legs and lit up Bensons. Girls dressed like Matisse interiors lolled disconsolately, turned their backs on their hairy menfolk. There were Regency bucks, the odd codpiece, some Beardsley out-takes, me in a splendid tunic from Wardrobe. Everybody wished for some shit (it should have been laid on), but we hadn't a roach between us. Nobody knew what we'd been called for, or even that the film was *Blow Up*. When a few names floated to the fore, we tore into them hungrily.

Dishy David Hemmings, he was good, what's this we'd seen him in? Who's this he was married to? He was a star, but more important he was a bloke too, someone like ourselves, a mascot of classlessness, really, was what he was, created by the happy times. Vanessa Redgrave was much less interesting (her name spelled establishment), but she did put us in mind of *Morgan*. How true that film was, we all wistfully agreed. The talk fluttered away.

Next morning, though, it was all 'Quiet, please' and lining up in rows. We were in a club and the Yardbirds were on stage, all plugged in and ready to mime. Jeff Beck was grinding the frame of his guitar into his amp, producing what sounded like yawns of cosmic boredom. We were not to move. We were to stay with eyes fixed dead ahead. We were in a trance, not at a dance. But by then I'd heard that Antonioni was our host and feared not. If anyone had a purpose regimenting us, he had. 'And turnover.' For perhaps the eighth time, the tape came on, the band flailed mutely, Keith Relf stepped up to the mike and mouthed, his hair, face, and shirt as sleek as silk, and as fluorescent. 'Cut!'

The maestro himself made this interruption. He was carrying out a tour of inspection, rearranging people. A fine figure of a *signor* he was too, I noted, as he worked his preoccupied way down our row. Aristocratic in bearing, artistic in mien, vaguely papal but reassuringly secular, fine fingers joined at fine mouth in thought, fine in his dove-grey polo-neck and forest-green velvet jacket, olive complexion sickly and intriguing. The most famous man I'd ever stood this close to, more exciting to behold than Jeff Beck! His *L'Avventura* and *L'Eclisse* had stirred my father in his soul, confusingly, excitingly, making him talk. Should I tell His Eminence that (chance of a lifetime)? Should I tell him that I didn't mind the waiting, really? In return, he might tell me what he thought of Richard Harris (Limerick, Ireland, *The Red Desert*). *Sancta Charisma*, we had lots in common!

'Follow me, would you?' Basil said, peremptorily. I swear to this day he was pointing at me, and Liz whispered, smilingly, 'You're in!' But he was only pointing at my tunic. Not that I blame him. It was a wonderful number, nacreous grey with yellow cuffs and facings, tight-fitting, high-necked *à la* Nehru, more artifact than clothing, the kind of thing a subaltern would have died in during Antietam, Little Big Horn, or some much movie. But what about my un-shaven intensity, the riveting and demented stare I donned as Jeff Beck bashed and bashed his Fender till it was time to throw its pre-severed neck to us freaks in the front row? Heart hammering, I queued up at the Pavilion, Piccadilly Circus. But the dive we'd all been ordered to take to get that grail of a guitar neck had overwhelmed and buried me. The sole sign of my presence is the blur of a yellow cuff as I'm buried under hundredweights of artificial hippies.

But we were paid. Twenty-three quid apiece. That was the point, Liz and I agreed. Making imaginary climax from anti-climactic life was second nature to us by now. 'Hi Ho, Silver Lining.' Before the week was out, a stocky tough two flights up in Greek Street had me signing a maze of dotted lines.

I was all of a sudden the owner of a bass, a big tom-tom, a pair of little tom-toms, all Premier, a high-hat, a Ludwig snare, a Zildjian crash, and a bad case of the jitters. It felt strange to be responsible for this private property of mine, and the drums appeared to reciprocate the strangeness, clustered in the middle of Liz's floor like a miniature Easter Island. I took the sticks and hit them a few flogs. The skins made brackish, ominous answer, not sounding a bit like fun.

Loyalty to our dreams meant that we didn't talk about bad vibes, however. We just readily agreed with Mrs Kenny that we couldn't possibly rehearse in the room and stowed the drums on top of the wardrobe. Besides, we said, there were rather more important matters to attend to. Material, for one thing. What was the point of rehearsing when we hadn't written anything?

And there was the matter of a name. I had a million of them, and knew name to be lifeblood of image. Ours should put an audience on the same plane of pleasure as the Impalas, the Elgins, the Crystals had put me. It should be a song of youth, a jingle with an ethos, a catchy byword which seemed so effortless, so natural, that its being commercial would seem beside the point. The Miracles, the Ventures, the Coasters, the Drifters. Jimmy, Jackie, Johnny and the Leopards, Cheetahs, Jaguars. It was a jungle out there, as who better than we two knew, dog eat dog (not bad), the rat race (*hein?*).

The trouble was, names were changing. We heard, in awe, John Peel play Moby Grape and Jefferson Airplane. We were freaked out by the Mothers of Invention, drugged by the million airs flooding in from millenarian America. There was an album called *Electric Music for the Mind and Body* by Country Joe and the Fish. The Velvet Underground had on drums Maureen Tucker, a woman! Who were all these people ('My Generation')? And what exactly was this stuff they were playing? Not pop, not fun, guitars cutting and slashing, deep detonating crump of drums. This was rock, utopian counterpart of the military-industrial complex, its infantry the hippies. This was the revolution. We lay on the Swiss Cottage bed, turned up Big L and let *The Perfumed Garden* waft the night away, with blues from Paul Butterfield, and all the colours of the rainbow in the fey flutings of Charles Lloyd, the two of us speechless supplicants of mind-fondling California, mind-blown and happily bodiless. The Crocodiles, the Hyenas, Joey and the Jackals...

I had to give it up. We discovered another urgency. The new wave forcefully bore down on us. We had to conceive a sound – if, that is, we ever wanted to get out of this room and face the public, which was the whole point, basically: to break out, to take the world and shake it. And at least a sound was something we could verbalise. We knew well what we wanted. Something black, but not blue. The blues were traditional, rural, hick. We were city cats, cool, hot, hip. Aggressive. Progressive. 'Wild Thing.' ('Born Free.')

We wrote. I whistled up melody lines as tube wheels drummed me down to Warren Street. I invented lyrics to make love to Liz's music. Now world was all rhyme. Hair, care and everywhere harmonised with ironic wistfulness, I think, in our 'Laughter in the Dark'. Tame went well with shame in the upbeat 'Phone Call'. We experimented. We created cunning pop hooks only to subvert them with extravagant, if unplayed, improvisations. Soon our repertoire included an unforgettable, but forgotten, satire on the protest-song fad, 'I'm Fine (The Fifty-Nicker Song)'. There was 'The Hump,' a hunchback's hateful chant – 'Away, away, down in the dark' – all wheezing organ, tom-toms and bad taste, our first single, our first Number One.

The Farfisa crooned late into the night, amp humming humidly along. Liz leaned into the keyboard, pretending to give it everything she'd got. The organ gave a sexy little scream. Liz writhed langourously, modulating. The weight of all my earlier evenings in that frustrating room was lifted from my mind by those throbbing chords of hers. It felt so right, this miracle of music...Oh, food of love! And look how it had even transformed me into a real writer.

When I think of certain occasions like this
I'm reminded of all the things that I miss
[Motown *Dum-DUMma-Dum* of drums here]
Like your hair
[Hot squawk of organ]
And our laughter in the dark
[Hollies-tight harmonies]

'Then you go,' I said *'hum, hum, hum, hum, hum, hmmmmm.'* Liz frowned. 'What – E E F♯ G B C? Wow! *Yesss!*' Glowing. ('Funny How Love Can Be.') 'By the way, puss: what key was that in?' 'Give me excess of it,' cried I (and long may the drums stay silent . . .).

Being sensible, however, we agreed that it would not be till we were actually on stage before a sell-out crowd that we could be properly excessive, with me robotically dancing while I banged a tambourine against my head and our unrecruited bassist drumming, preferably with the neck of his guitar. The unknown lead guitarist would introspectively, lasciviously, Hendrixly stoke his Stratocaster. Liz, front and centre, would with intense abandon Piaf through the night, a fire siren, and solo as self-indulgently as any San Franciscan. Oh, we'd be beside ourselves, stoned out of our minds on the adrenalin of outrageousness. Chanting, possibly. Or possibly just grunting. The whole crowd one collective grunt as well. Sole accompaniment a cowbell. Yes, that was how we'd do 'The Hump', with a refrain of 'Unclean! Unclean!' No words but grunts on 'The Hump'! Oh, inspiration! On the night, it'd be a riot. We laughed and laughed foreseeing such fun, and the crowd would be over the moon.

Knowing we were sitting on a Royal Doultonery of hot platters and gold discs, Liz insisted that we copyright our songs at Stationers' Hall. She was so savvy, so mature . . . To Ludgate Hill we made our way, as confident as people with rights. I felt so sophisticated. Footfalls volleyed off terrazzo to the hall's high-vaulted ceiling. We spoke in whispers, filled in forms, tendered words and music, paid in fivers, with a pang, for the eight years' guaranteed protection. The little clerk smirked. But we revelled in the paranoia that made us businesslike and our dreams real. Hand almost in hand we walked along the Strand to celebratory elevenses at the Corner House opposite Charing Cross. It was Valentine's Day. Our birthday. Over Lyons's grey fluid we admired our golden child, the future. We had come true. We smiled smugly. The Turtles. Peace and love. 'Happy Together.'

The Riot Act! Liz was not amused. 'But we mean it,' I protested, feeling ever so clever, so she did concede that she supposed something along those lines was what she had in mind, vaguely. I was getting nervous. We would have to have a name to give the aspirants, droves of whom, even as we spoke, were headed our way, ad in hand. Light Up An Embassy? Mnnn: something like that . . . Excited, I saw that I'd identified a concept (another of the brave new words that were in the air then). Puns – of course! I'd been imagining wildness, understandably, but hadn't I rather overlooked the subversive substance of our musical revolution? Forget The Lynx, make it The Missing Lynx. Or Gorilla Warfare, with suits to match. The pun was mightier than the word.

'The Sunday Joint,' said Liz, decisively. I gasped – how brilliant! She was light years ahead, true daughter of Aquarius. I looked at her moonily, overawed all over again. She had the gift, she had the gifted's daring. Person of culture. My Queen!

'Except,' I said, tentatively, a couple of days later, laughter and congratulations ebbing, 'we don't do dope.'

Liz gave me a pitying look. That was the whole point. Our music should be the dope that people did. 'Silly Billy.'

Ah, I was no match for her, brainbox of mine and guiding light . . . Once more she'd offered me identity. I couldn't wait to see my glad surrender to her on the faces of the newcomers who'd happily complete our fab foursome.

The bell shrilled four times. It shrilled for us. We looked at each other with straight faces and tense stares. Liz lit the good Indica joss sticks, drew the blinds, plugged in the bedside lamp and draped the shot silk, electric blue blouse over the shade. Her boots fitted me pretty well, and wearing the outsize pink shirt borrowed from John outside my trousers neatly told the world that we hung loose. I checked that the Indian bedspread was thumb-tacked securely to the wardrobe door and kicked the *International Times* into an eye-catching crumple by the bed. The door bell went again. Liz hastily back-combed my hair. We were in business.

The only trouble was we didn't know that to form a progressive band it was necessary to be in art school. Our poor wannabes shivered unfeelingly through 'Shakin' All Over'. All rictus and spasm, they picked apart 'Be-Bop-A-Lula' as if it was a particularly stubborn-embarrassing pimple. Black soulmen from south London sang more tunefully, but why had they all lost those loving feelings? Oh, do something, I screamed in the pained silence that, once they'd performed, swallowed up the room. Surprise us. Surprise yourselves. But I knew that silence was the truth, the sound of inhibition, the still, sad music of reality. They could only function in their own small rooms, not here in NW3 in semidarkness, before strangers. I heard them loud and clear. Their silence sang the hollow song of Highbury.

They banged their old guitar cases against the banisters as they left and always closed the front door with a crash.

'Incredible,' Liz said in a small voice. 'Not one of them reads music.'

I put on the kettle, drew back the curtains, raised the stiff window for a breath of air. The empathy with which the auditions left me were strong reminders of doubts and vulnerabilities of mine that were supposed to be all bygones. But tea helped. And afterwards we went for a walk, laughing, in the dark, alone together and ourselves again. After all, we said, there weren't many like us, so naturally it would be difficult to find them. But we would. Hadn't we found each other?

And Clive banished all misgivings. He was eighteen and starting to write his own stuff. He hated soul. Our own Clive. No kitsch of sincerity for him. Liz and I looked at each other, proud parents. Our first. Happy Clive whipped out the twelve-string from its napless bed and in a trice had all Swiss Cottage shuddering with his heavy-handed *chunka-chunk, chunka-chunk*. The name of his song was 'What's the Name of My Uncle Bill?' It was a cryptic saga of common-law marriage and illegitimacy. It was the voice of housing estates. It was prole life speaking to us of our very selves, all identity crisis and adult ignorance. It was easily the equal of the closet-buster currently sweeping up the charts, Pink Floyd's 'Arnold Layne', very clever, certainly, but obviously west London with its *ching-ching-ching-ching* (to the power of two)/*bad-a-dang*. It was going to sell a million. Clive had a toothy grin and a penduluming pelvis. He was perfect. And as though to convince us he was really ours, he asked us if we had a name.

To this day, I don't know why I blurted, 'Blood.' I wanted something pinker than the Floyd, I suppose, or maybe I wanted to act inspired. At any rate, I couldn't stop. We'd come out in lab coats, I said, butcher's aprons, nurse's uniforms, battledress, all wrinkled and smeared red, and we'd have a big heart painted on the bass drum, pounding, and I'd change my name to O Positive. O for Outrageous, see? Liz was laughing, eyes all agog, and put an arm around each of us. All that was required now for everlasting happiness a bass player.

Suddenly it was Easter, sunshine and mild air, winter and discontent all gone, for ever ('Be sure to wear flowers in your hair'). A friend of Liz's, François, came over from Paris, sat stripped to the waist in a Cromwell Road pad play-ing a bamboo flute, eyes closed, beating the bare floor with a bare, brown foot. Every so often he paused to shred some shit into a disembowelled Embassy for himself and Liz and me. We sprawled on the floor against large cushions with Indian cotton print covers, all simple smiles and world enough and time. The sun shone in the French windows all evening long. François glistened in his playing. All evening long his raga rambled, the aimless cooing of the peace-and-love bird. It was easy to believe that Krishna was in his heaven, all was right with the world.

'A Whiter Shade of Pale' came out. Liz heard the organ in it as the sound of all her intuitions coming true. John Peel broke into the Pete Drummond show with acetates of some of *Sergeant Pepper*. It had a sound called phasing. That was the sound of blowing minds ('the answer, my friend . . . '). It was the year we'd all been waiting for. 1967. 'Lucy in the Sky with Diamonds.'

III

'Aw, rel*aaax*, man,' Robin the bass-player went, one more time, passing the joint back to me. We were in the belfry of Holy Trinity, Haverstock Hill, waiting for Clive. As usual. I took another two or three deep, rapid tokes, but what I needed was a snifter of Aspros. This was much worse than waiting for *Blow Up*. It was rehearsal Saturday again, and my mind was splitting with embarrassment and dread.

Robin outcooled the lot of us, was so laid back that he could have been laid out. Naturally, I found him to be the real thing. He'd been involved with the re-formation of Them, details of which were as fuzzy as an Afro, but the point was, he might have shaken the hand of Van! And it wasn't only that I envied the names he dropped. I liked his style, his sandals, his grass, his sheepskin jacket (original version – sleeveless, buttonless, peasanty, with soiled wool unrespectably, suede-lessly, on the outside). His tanned face grinned unflinch-ingly at thirty. There was a cottage he was renting down Dorking way, and it was fucking beautiful man. Hedgerows, birdsong, sweetness and light. Woods to grow your own shit in. With luck, in time, a yoghurt-yielding goat.

He produced a pouch. It had a hieroglyphic on it, which he explained to me slowly, soft-voiced and insistent, had something to do with the Mother. Earth. Conjunction. Symbiosis. Moon. Applied at the right angle it would stop the rain in Kerry. And the cosmos was ballad and benison. The pouch itself had come from a friend (that was important), had been fashioned from a panda's scrotum by some green-eyed, yellow idler to the north of Katmandu. 'You *must* read Casteneda.' But I wasn't listening. I heard instead Liz's carrying voice complaining, and neither doxology or dope could save me from that sound. Robin shrugged and smiled. He took no notice of her. But I was scared. She was all I had. Or all I didn't have.

She was downstairs in the chill church hall shrilly bitching to John about such realities as the non-existent thirty bob the place cost to rent, Clive's hopeless time-keeping, me. The thought of being among life's trials was too real for me. Did I not love her in my fashion? Was I not her drummer? But staunch John was the one who listened now. His dark eyes drank all in, and it was useless my denying the thirst that was in them. His heart, I knew, was always pulsing, 'Puss-puss, Puss-puss', the sexy shimmer of a high-hat opening and closing. With John, things were what they seemed. He'd not played false. He'd come back into his own with the van, the only thing we had that was going well.

Clive was turning into a dead loss.

'He seems to have forgotten we discovered him,' Liz complained. He was our Number One, and we had rights, like parents, like owners.

But he preferred to act the bastard, spitting 'Soul!' at a figure of Robin's, sneering at my boring, stompy beat. 'Is that all you can do?'

I couldn't drum. And however much Liz resented Clive the prima donna as a musician (not as a friend), she agreed with his assessment of my hit-and-miss stickwork. But, I tried to explain, I'm only a musician because I'm a friend, I'm beating these bloody old skins because you want me to, because I want you to want me to, because I love you, surely to God I don't have to be good at it as well (how real do you expect me to be?). I said she was bourgeois. She said that was just a lie. She was nothing but a stiff bitch, snapping all the time. And you ain't no friend of mine.

That morning, semistoned with Robin – my last rehearsal, probably – I saw that life as I'd imagined it was coming to an end, again. I gazed forlornly on London of the venues all spread out below me, toys on a playroom floor abandoned. The Roundhouse, UFO, our erstwhile bower of bliss the Marquee, the right royal Albert Hall, my Vatican, where in a recurring dream I'd drummed with the New Vaudeville Band and, to acclaim usually reserved for 'Jerusalem', we'd done our latest biggie, 'Finchley Central' . . . How insubstantial they all seemed, suddenly. I was not Van Morrison nor was meant to be. Image no longer offered sanctuary. That lucifer of fantasy scratching the stone surface of need, that itch called imagination which had caused drums to be bought, and had persuaded me that I must play them, had shown itself to be no more than a bad dream. The getting on with things, which we'd so brilliantly inaugurated at the HMV shop, had boringly become stuck, just as in real life. The one-way pendulum – the beat that bore my name, my desire to be nothing only Liz's instrument (the way I thought of love) – couldn't keep it up. I feared I was falling, a plunge from a belfry into black, agitated emptiness, a kind of rehearsal for acid-vertigo later on that summer. In the night I heard heavy, hollow things falling. It was the sound of my drums being repossessed (we couldn't pay, we wouldn't pay).

Liz bought a goose-necked mike, thought she'd take over vocals, changed the group's name to Limousine. Clive left. Calor Gas left for Slough. Liz found a singer, Derek, from Ceylon. We went to audition him at a restaurant on Earls Court Road. He perched on a bar stool by the cash register and lilted with a lisp 'The Green, Green Grass of Home'. Liz loved him. I told her she was daft. The world had only just

118

recovered from Frank Ifield, and she wanted to front a band with a guy whose notion of material made Matt Monro progressive. But Derek was *sooo* sexy, Liz said. He could writhe, he could shimmy, in his voice was the quiet storm of passion, Liz said. He was black and knew about such things, wasn't hung up, had rhythm, Liz said. She had a feeling about him.

I moved to Finchley Road, by Frognal. John slung the suitcase and the Sainsbury bags into the van and smiled. My new landlady, Mrs Spiegel, sat in front of the TV and cheered on Israel in the Six Day War. I lay on the bed and brooded, wanked and brooded. What did this Derek have that I didn't? White teeth. Plus he was a genuine Third Worlder. I was just a weird West Briton, fake Yankee mongrel. And my good name was gone, one more emasculation. Limousine. What kind of a name was that? It was a bourgeois name. A fucking French name. I sat staring at the reflector of the one-bar electric fire, *Steppenwolf* unopened on my lap, seeing nothing. It had looked like I'd come so far. I'd smoked dope, got in debt, felt a clitoris. But each of these was its own reward, apparently, not a down payment on security. *Plus ça* bleeding *change*, innit, eh? Once more my life amounted to a single room. My heart went out to me.

But this room was the biggest I'd lived in, and there was morning sun. I began *A House for Mr Biswas*. Perhaps Liz wouldn't stay long infatuated with the green, green grass of Trincomalee (before the summer was out, Derek had left Limousine to be an ape man in *2001*). But whether or not wasn't as important as acknowledging the old nag to go on. I'd never go back. There was no doubt about it. And if I couldn't make the musical grade, I could make the scene.

Thanks to Calor Gas I was redundant, a condition more plausible and a designation more resonant than any I had yet imagined, a grand sound, with the rumble of a drum in it. I was officially a victim of progress, and to prove it, was officially being paid. That was the law. When news of the

move first came out, 'Slough!' was slung about as synonym
for insult. Worse yet, all this was because of The Computer,
that cocky pirate radio of the brain cells, whose rock-'n'-roll
was hard arithmetic. The Computer wasn't quite so shocking as Arthur Brown with his hair ablaze at UFO, but they
did seem two of a kind. But when the day of reckoning
arrived, it was all fond goodbyes to the alleged pooftahs and
suspected secret drinkers, to Rose and Maureen in the
kitchen, to Noel who never bossed. Goodnight ladies.
Goodnight sweet ladies. I took the money and made for the
King's Road to meet Liz.

She'd rung. Was I in a huff, or something, feeling down?
I'd been so quiet she'd worried. Silly Billy, of course, we
were still friends. And she had a feeling everything was
going to be all right. Had I heard 'Light My Fire', by the
way? Wasn't it just fabulous? I could not tell a lie.

'Better than "A Whiter Shade of Pale",' I declared, essaying independence.

'Yes!' Liz went, and I knew nothing had changed. I had
to be around her. A little later she said she was so pleased
that I was coming into money. I understood with pleasure
that I might still be useful.

We had a second honeymoon cruising the boutiques. It
wasn't as exuberant as our HMV one, but had a similar
proleptic thrill. Spending was a much better drug than
earning. And strolling down King's Road, it was clear that
spending was definitely in. Spending was what the stars
did, after all, and who amongst us cruisers didn't think we
could be stars? We were made to feel important. Girls with
faces framed by inverted commas of bottle-blonde hair
simpered unreally as Liz fingered the flimsy wares, ushered
us as delightedly as bridesmaids to the makeshift little
dressing rooms in dusty, dingy backs. Liz giggled like a
young girl with a doll as she did me up. I tried to kiss her,
but she was too busy deciding for me.

For everyday, she settled on an ice blue jacket and
unmatching trousers. As orange as rust these trews were.

They float before me as I write, a U-tube of weak tea. Shirts, it was determined, should have frilly fronts. A bunch of those were bought, one grass green, I remember, one purple (a colour that was discovered in those days, like black and turquoise), and there was another all the colours of a circus wagon. A three-quarter-length black coat was also part of the ensemble, tight-fitting, frock-coatish, priestly in a vaguely Protestant style. And for my crowning glory, Liz succumbed to velvet bell-bottoms, crushed and red like an old cinema seat. These were for special occasions, when *esse est percipi* was even more on our minds than usual, like Friday nights at Middle Earth or visiting friends of friends in hopes of acid. I gave the man with the tight black shirt and ponytail the money, and we left high.

Liz put on something Indian and spangly, a purple waistcoat with shiny metal lozenges, embroidered on the back with probably symbolic sequences of beads (she was beginning to focus with the third eye), and forth we sallied, as brazen as graffiti. The looks we got from staidsters in the tube were all our hearts desired. We saw in them that we were sartorial strobe lights, dancing in their darkness like episodes in an electrical storm.

Inside Middle Earth was warm, velvet dark, midnight blue, electric blue, dark of midsummer night, dark of desire, cosmetic, concupiscent, chthonic. Strobes wriggled like a partner peaking, danced on our senses like hits of speed, the machine already at the pitch the crowd aspired to. A ballet of bright bubbles on the screen behind the band held us in thrall. It shimmered like the hookah's peace and love, blisters of pleasure bursting on brain cells. It was like the chiming of a sitar from an inner room. It was like neurons speaking Elvish. No God but Bilbo! Sometimes the walls showed movies, rockets continually taking off (it was the infancy of space-cadetery), razor slicing eyeball from *Le Chien Andalou* (the Vietnam War was on TV in Sevenoaks and Pinner). We felt no pain.

We went to the Roundhouse for Pink Floyd and the Who.

Liz was trying to figure out how to make Limousine psychedelic. The erratic, automatic way Floyd had coloured light go on and off was really clever and, wistfully, 'probably quite expensive'. Pete Townsend raped an amp with his guitar.

Tomorrow packed a solid *chunka* in 'My White Bicycle', overture to situationism, hymn to Amsterdam of the options. The good old days, when Provo stood for carefree. Chris McGregor from South Africa led Brotherhood of Breath into post-Coltrane apocalypses. Notes flew like bullets from the hardly human trumpet of Dudu Pakwana.

Yoko Ono Cox performed a cabaret happening. She had a big bag, and invited members of the audience to come up and climb into it. Apparently, once inside one could see without being seen. For fear of slandering the artist, I'd better not say that the outlook improved enormously if the inmate undressed. I don't remember. It didn't seem to matter at the time. The point was to don the amniotic sac and be amazing. Behold the spirit of the underground, to gaze from a safe darkness into a cultic twilight. After a while, the bag was folded away and everyone applauded.

There was an above-ground spirit, too, sublimating daily doles. To this Liz now showed signs of being drawn. Not that she desired to be a squatter or began the day with herbal infusions. No sandals for her, much less bare feet, and she execrated Hobbity affectations. Image was not important, she decreed, what mattered was one's inner self. Those feelings to which she'd all her life been prone, and which profoundly impressed her by their urgency and accuracy, now appeared in public, all dolled up. Her organ solos obviously invoked the aleatory and the intuitive, the instrument itself real only as a pretext. She shook the mental hand of Gurdjieff. She'd found a fabulous reader of the tarot. Days out together, sitting in Lyonses wondering how to create 'contacts', trying to peddle those fabulous hits of ours, also included long trips to Indica, Southampton Row. There among the ascetics, dieticians and kindred holy heads, Liz pored over astrological blueprints in search of her true story. Aspects, cusps and houses twinkled in her mind's eye like gold discs. She loved the thought of reading minds. She wished she was a gypsy.

She should turn professional, I said, invest in a crystal ball and change her name to Psyche Delia. She should do her devotions in her own time, I said, not leave me in the lurch by the organic vitamins, where with a sullen jealousy I drank in the kinky personal ads in *International Times*. I said I knew exactly what was going on, I'd been there a thousand times before, only then it was known as a novena to Saint Jude, lighting penny candles. Whistling in the dark (good name for a group . . .).

But there was no group, now, really. Limousine was stalled. That was why Liz and I spent days climbing stairs trying to make appointments to see Kit Lambert, Tito Burns, anyone, everyone. Talent was priceless, surely, and we definitely had it, plus the material, so why the brush-off from Miss Courrèges Boots in reception? Tony Hall would not return our call. George Martin's number wasn't in the book. On our way down the stairs from Immediate Records in the Dick James Music building, New Oxford Street, we bumped into Jonathan King. He was with somebody and passed by, laughing. That was as close as we came to being in with the in crowd.

I took to the back of B52-sized butterflies, which zoomed eternally to ground. I was awash with dysenteric greens and reds and yellows. The walls I fell past wept cloying floods of blood and puke and weird amoebas, bringing me down, down, into a drowning. Lucy fled the sky. I feared for my life. It was exhilarating. But it was control I wanted, not technicolour latitude. Not possibility but purpose. The sputtering, sparking mind that I'd spent years trying to get used to would do, if I could only turn it on. If only Liz could turn it on for me.

But we were fighting now. All her old guff about synchronicity, the mandala, the whole house of superstitious cards in which she tried to hide, annoyed, unnerved.

'Well, why don't *you* do something, think something, moron-parasite!' Liz went.

'I'll fucking show you. I'll have a novel published before you have one shitty single in the Top Fifty!'

'You? Novel? Don't make me laugh!'

Sometimes we cried, hugged, and swore blind never to be hurtful any more. Once we scared each other so badly that we made love afterwards. The missionary assumed the position, had his little gallop and expired. The whole thing smelled as off, as instantaneous and as messy as our lives. Liz was right, it was overrated. We didn't talk about it. What was really needed was one good Limousine gig.

It was a good gig, too. It was midweek, but at Middle Earth. The crowd was small, but cheered more loudly at the end of Limo's set than for the headliners, who were, I think, the Nice. They were cheering John.

The set opened with Robin mashing the butt of his bass into the amp and moving like a stripper grinding, while the organ tripped through a kind of highfalutin hysteria. Five minutes into this, John leapt on to the stage, looking mighty dark and fierce, and dressed all in black. Beard became polo neck became shiny old tuxedo trousers, and the skirts of his long black greatcoat flew spectrally about as he did his thing. He didn't sing. He pulled a newspaper from his pocket and wrath-of-Godishly declaimed from it. He admonished, he excoriated, he boomed and made the spittle fly. Great is Limousine and Black John is its prophet. The crowd stood like the crowd in *Blow Up*, unable to believe their eyes or ears, stoned by excess and novelty. At length John sank to his knees, bent over, and was still. Someone killed the spotlight, completing his resemblance to the rock of ages. Talk about the Sunday joint . . . Robin and Liz rolled into the final frenzy, which definitely called for a barrage of drums, I thought. But I thought, too, standing in the shadows, what matter? Limousine had liftoff. They'd done it without me. It was just beginning, and it was just all over. Backstage, we all hugged under a bare bulb.

I went back to 'Ice' and Mrs Spiegel's.

There's these two old lags recruited into criminal stardom by a military type, Sir Matthew Garrison. The job's a doddle, just snatch some ice from a Hatton Garden courier. Then everything unravels. The murkiness of Sir Matthew's motives makes its mephitic presence felt, without ever becoming clear, exactly. One of the old lags, The Moper, is iced. It turns out in the end, the big surprise, that the story, told in the first person (I'sed), is a self-conscious retrospective by the surviving robber, now in prison – the ice house, as he calls it.

The novel opens in Finsbury Park. Sir Matthew has a spread in Wimbledon. Casing Hatton Garden was a replay of my lonesome Saturday walks. The plot was about failing to get away with something. But I never thought of 'Ice' as autobiographical. After all, its enabling conceit was a character who'd failed, writing on his own in a not very big room!

> There isn't much more to say ... I'm tired of writing this; and I'm tired to think this is the end. Putting it down on paper has helped, I suppose, but it makes it all so final, as if it has ended and everything afterwards went to contribute to happiness, and the final proof didn't have such a rough time after all. A happy ending. But it doesn't go like that – it didn't for me, anyway – because you bring your experiences with you. You spend one half of your life making them, and the rest of it paying. And it isn't possible to get rid of them by writing; it's only possible to make them big and grotesque and significant. For everything you do, there's something left undone; it must be, to keep the balance. And this is how you pay.

The remotest resemblance between the recidivist narrator and myself was inconceivable. Now, of course, the hint of one is just another fable of identity, part of the game called autobiography. I was happy. I had a room and time. In the words of the old Virginia Woolf number, who could ask for anything more? No people put in or out with me. Liz rang. I went limp. I had a schedule and stopped going out. *J'ai découvert que tout le malheur des hommes vient d'une seule chose, qui est de ne savoir pas demeurer en repos, dans une chambre* . Let Limousine fly high and the best of British to all who sail her. Writing was better, better than anything Liz and I had ever done in bed, better even than wanking. The driving pen, the field of white, the flood of words, the all-enveloping and engrossing silence with the odd little murmurs and climactic cry . . . I felt unembarrassed by myself, unashamed. I was innocent. I was the harmless, safe, small boy who didn't blot his copybook, taking himself by the hand down the big long page of the wide world.

Limousine crashed. No slightly shop-soiled cherub approached Liz with a business proposition. No A & R man booked studio time. Despite roughly a million calls, Immediate did not return the tape we'd left for Arthur Greenslade.

But the beat went on. Liz allowed herself to be recruited by a soul group. Denis played lead, Mack bass, on drums they had a sixteen-year-old giant calling himself Thor. I went to a rehearsal in a boy scout's hut in Harlesden. Liz had trouble doing the instrumental bridge in 'Mr Pitiful', but Denis had all Steve Cropper's licks off pat. They got a contract to play NAAFIs in Germany and to celebrate bought tickets for the Stax Show. Booker T. & the M.G.'s, Arthur Conley, Eddie Floyd. Green suits and purple shirts, suits of powder blue, shirts of cerise. *'Aaaw . . .'* That sweet soul music. Sam and Dave did vaguely suggestive callisthenics during 'Hold On, I'm Coming'. And finally, the absolute guvnor and king himself, 'Mistah O-tis *Redding*' (the emcee was Emperor Rosko), crooning like a lonesome broken hinge, creaking like a forest while painstorms raged, but never, ever, falling. I-can-take-it, I-can-take-it, Good-God-a'mighty-I-take-it, I-take-it . . .

Nothing in my London life felt easier than being a glad

spectator, then, to stand with everyone at the end, clapping, swaying, chanting, laughing at the ludicrous simplicity of simply being present. Such strange sufficiency. Merely being a white man in Hammersmith Odeon was a name for happiness. 'Fa Fa Fa Fa Fa.' This was some kind of family. And I belonged. I even thought I got the taste of that knowing innocence from the Gauloise-and-mint in the kisses of my new love, Linda.

OLIVER!

Lyndon Dykes was waxing choleric, even though all we'd
done was answer the ad in the *Standard*. 'Unique sales
opportunity.' Just the ticket, I thought, something vague
but classy. And, reassuring me that I was their man, 'no
experience necessary'. Caxton Press. A publisher (be still my
beating heart)! But the address in Fitzroy Square was
shabby, with stacks of half-opened boxes lurching against
grimy cream walls and the artificial smell of newness. There
were a dozen of us, but no interview. There was only being
virtually shouted at by gaunt, dog-faced Dykes.

It wasn't salesmen he wanted us to be but technicians of
insecurity. We had to flog what people, judging from the
cluttered hallway, didn't want. Encyclopedias. They didn't
know they wanted them. We had to tell them. There was
a two-pronged strategy. One was to lurk outside super-
markets in the afternoon and intrude on, or rather interview, housewives. Are you interested in your child's
education? Great changes are taking place in *education* these
days, the new maths, for instance, mention of which was

absolutely guaranteed to freak out concerned mother of two, West Acton. The poor dears, our quarry, would be so punch-drunk from morning radio, so relieved to have someone talk to them, so put-upon by their fretful nippers, so dying for a cuppa, that they'd agree that you could come round later when hubby was home to confide further in them about the sex drug of the future (intimate whisper), *education*.

If after inserting prong two, the evening visit, paterfamilias signed up for the high pressure treatment, as only he could legally do – *bingo!* you got a tenner. ('And conversely' – as was suavely noted – 'if not, not.') Shortly after dear old dad signed, a suit appeared and charmed him into x payments over y years. Eventually, no doubt, Lyndon himself would tool round in the gold-painted Van of Learning to deliver the volumes of life everlasting in their plasticky forest green buckram. I stuck the job four days, got as far as three living rooms, failed to bingo, told a sub-Dykes he could stuff it. It wasn't the money, or the no-money, that put me off. I enjoyed acting the part, up to a point, spreading my gaudy information sheets on never-never Axminster, occasioning the telly to be turned down, trying to refer to Darren, Wayne and Tracy by name. But then there always came the point when wife looked at Dad and Dad scratched his head, moments of scepticism and rejection more true to life than anything I could sell.

I packed my kit and left, more pleased by my failure than by my performance. It was the first time failing felt like the proper thing to do. It felt like choice, like power, like action. I was saying No. No to Dykes's drilling and to so-called easy money. Not because of ethics. I still lived largely thanks to fears and fancies, no values required or desired. The *fuck you* feeling of dropping rather than being dropped was a simple pleasure, nothing more. A small thing, but mine own. It felt great.

And here was Linda – ample, generous, young, unbossy, promising another new life (the best yet, needless to say).

She had long blonde hair and shampooed it with cans of Long Life. I asked if that was what kept her hair blonde. She laughed immoderately, thinking I must be joking and wanting to humour me. I was serious, or rather, excited, which felt like the same thing. It was intimate, seeing hair being washed, the tossing and plunging, the refreshed emergence (we were in the kitchen), and I wanted to know more about it, to prolong what was so ordinary to her but to me was privilege.

I think, *wanting to humour me* . . . I'm happy. Now she's asking me to put up the ironing board. She's stretching her hair along it under brown paper to be pressed, she's daft. I like her. She's knocking something over and going 'Shit!' within earshot of her parents. She takes them for granted. I badly want to be persuaded that she's free to be that way. I keep having a dream. Linda and I are crossing Hungerford Bridge. She has a blanket. A young dosser accosts us, entreating. Linda gives him the blanket. I protest, half-marvelling. She'll be killed when she gets home . . . She laughs insouciantly, which is how I know it's her. I look back over my shoulder. The dosser is me. She's ebullient, generous, restless, melodramatic. There was a largeness to her. Her big brown eyes open wide after we've hugged. I smell her large, scented breasts and think this is how home must smell; think, she could make being an orphan fun.

Being very much in like was ten times better than being in love, a desperation I was cured of now. No more false fingering, or kiss the girls and make me cry. This time I was going to enjoy. But Linda favoured those damned culottes. And there was Dad, though perhaps he wasn't such a bad sort, he'd had a novel published, even if fathers were all old bolloxes really. Things between Linda and Dad were complicated. She'd written a profile of him for a *Sunday Times* colour magazine competition. It came third, was published, someone she referred to as God Smith heaped high praise on it, on her. Oh, Christ! – she was a writer. She had a future, was already in the anteroom of big time. I gnashed my teeth, mad jealous, and asked to see the piece. Dad was a beast when boys came calling. Dad knew boys were trouble. Bad weather and no money, and the fact that Linda was leaving home for Trinity College Dublin, found us surprisingly quickly on the bed at Mrs Spiegel's. We were there all of five minutes when suddenly Linda began to scream and scream, as though in pain and stuck. She'd lost her locket. (The bathetic truth, so help me!) Mrs Spiegel loomed large in the doorway the following morning. 'I thought you were murdering the girl.' I didn't think that she meant murder. Flattered but offended, I volunteered the true story. Mrs Spiegel, saying nothing, didn't think that I meant locket. Her hooded eyelids slowly lowered into a glare of bleak dismissal. I must take up my filthy metaphor and walk.

The move turned out to be the favour I was looking for. The new room was in Randolph Avenue, Maida Vale (my last address alone in London), a dim, damp box in a basement. But Linda's was just on the other side of Little Venice in Westbourne Terrace. And that was where I really moved to, believed I had because I so badly wanted to, craved like an orphan the moreness of that place, those people, Dad and all.

Time out of mind I roamed through that home alone. Light filled the living room, made the hospitable table gleam. Bouquets of fine meals hovered like attentive hosts. There were more books than even in my father's house. Constance Garnett's Russians, pre-war Penguins, *Finnegans Wake*, books of poems inscribed by Mum and Dad's poet friends, Linda's Livres de Poche, German books in which language looked like an exploded view of a wooden juggernaut. Half-finished bottles of grappa stood out on the sideboard, Glenlivet also, and some lighter-fuel brandy Linda brought from Spain. Some evenings after dinner I was able to watch the Vietnam War presented by Robert Dougal. This was the Bourgeois Free State, the old firm of Creature Comforts. Randolph Avenue, by the gas fire,

Sunday evenings, say, I gave my sentimental fetishism free play, saw myself tiptoeing gladly through the open door of that unpoorhouse, Oliver Twist, begging the question, with a bowl as big as himself.

I dare say I wanted to seduce Linda. But it felt nicer that her family seduced me. Her home's open door became one of her greatest attractions, and her largeness a mere scale model of her family's openheartedness. Their apartment was possibility, protection and Paddington Station, a home that was a street, a street that was a haven. Even when Linda and I took to her room to listen to her Incredible String Band records (she has a record-player in her room!) and abortively to snog, we were not alone. Shouts would go up from small brother Charlie, who loved answering the phone, for sister Sonia, second eldest, to come assuage her swain, Ed Blood. Charlie talked like that. He was nine. Brother K.D., second youngest, who was forming a group, an amp and a Hendrix poster his life's sole necessities, would in the room next door rev up his bass to mock us. Dad could be heard from the study belabouring Baskerville, the household's hat-eating bulldog, for scoring another 'symphony of gaseous effluvia'. Dad slammed the door. Dad raised his voice. Dad put his foot down, which to Linda was the same as putting his foot in it, and the boot in. Dad was Donald Wolfit doing Lear. Then Archie Rice. Dad's friend, the poet Robert Greacen, dropped by, and edgily they scouted each other's situations, both bearing the scars of small success, clearly past it, I thought. Their being from godforsaken Belfast proved it.

Terence Gervaise White called often. He's named in the acknowledgements of Ellmann's *James Joyce*. Saliva ran unaccountably down his unshaved chin. It was hard to think of him being young once and Paris-inclined, with goatee, briar and foulard. It never crossed my mind that something awful could have disturbed him. I drank gallons of headless Tankard in the Albion with Sonia's Ed, and agreed that indeed Sonia was the second coming of Miss

Marmaledov. Ed, *âme damnée*, demanded purification. Ed was a painter, in his second year at Camberwell. He showed me his self-portrait. He wore the headdress of an Indian brave and a haughty stare. To either side of him, bombers lay in flames.

Saturday afternoons, K.D. jammed with his pal Golly, who ached to be Jimi and who had the looks, who hour upon hour mimicked his master's flurries, pain and all, who later played with Osibisa, who died of heroin. Yes, and Charlie, all grown up, dead of AIDS and not much more than thirty. Our only ailment way back then was innocence.

Happiness had its discontents, however. I *quite* liked Linda (we were three months old now). With her I was sixteen again, for the first time. My overriding ambition may have been sulkily detumescing, but there was still any amount of sweet, wet kisses. It wasn't Linda I wanted, but everything she had, all that family ebb and flow, the hugs, the shouts, the pride in what she'd done, the Sunday joints with good Bordeaux from Dollamore's. It all aggravated me. I wanted more than the mere pleasure of it. My need was greed, my happiness a form of anxiety. I wanted to be the man who came to dinner.

Without quite realising it, I began to resent Linda, as though she were upstaging me. Alfred Marks, bad cess to him, had landed me a clerkship in miserable Benham's, Judd Street, where the sun never shone, just by King's Cross, next door to the Salvation Army supplies shop. She had pocket money and didn't work (*a record-player in her room* – Christ!). I wanted to play happy families. She wanted to be away out in the world. At Trinity College. Dublin. I might have tolerated Cambridge or Salamanca or some other foreign fortress. But that place! Was she trying to show me up or what? All I was and wasn't came to me again, as though now Linda had invented it. Neither son nor student, intimate nor loner, ghost here, exile there (*sniff, sniff*) . . . She didn't even mean it. But that was what made it worse. Real.

I saw striped blazers, straw hats, *deux-chevaux* spanking merrily along the minor roads of Meath. The aqueous air was split with shrieks of 'Darling!' I saw Linda surrendering her maidenhead to Rupert in a Morgan, to Julian in a Wolsey Hornet, to – oh, my God! – some couth youth from the Six Counties. Even if it was to just a plain Paul in an unheated room over a shop in Anne Street, I didn't have a 'No' for it, and couldn't look away, stood outside the gates, cap in hand. I sat alone at Benham's during lunch time, trying to scour my mind of the Dickensian morning with *Brideshead Revisited*. Loagy Eric from the desk adjoining sauntered in from the greasy-spoon and went salaciously, 'Ow, *Bride's*-head.' I hid in the gents most of the afternoon to finish the chapter.

With Linda in Dublin, I feared legitimacy as a caller, so I thought I'd play up to Dad. He could think me Free State, pre-condom Man, the horrid present, all flotsam and jissom. But I would reassure him I was an as-new, second-hand virgin, my pencil leaded by great books alone. We'd sit with brandy in the study as beech logs danced in the grate. He'd tell me how he wrote *The Man from Madura*, and go on to laud 'Ice', refuting Linda's allegations of his do-the-boys proclivities, I'd even probably forgive him for being from the North.

Not that that would be necessary. He'd already done that for himself. The little house in East Bread Street, by the ropewalk, was virtually romantic, seen from the end of a road which had begun at Queen's University. 'Rounding the corner by the abbatoir, Dostoevsky singing in my veins,' he'd say, reliving the important bits. He was his daughter's Dad, an unremorseful leaver. And how he loved to rhapsodise. Hemingway at the Ritz, of old Lisbon and the *fado* of the fisherfolk, of Clichy, Ischia, poor folk and white nights in Petersburg, all his talk an aria of restlessness, addressed to no one in particular, a mulling over of a menu of hungers.

'In my younger and more vulnerable years my father gave me some advice that I've been turning over in my mind ever since. "Whenever you feel like criticising any one," he told me, "just remember that all the people in this world haven't had the advantages you've had," ' he'd go, grinning a superior grin. His voice was nasal, drawly, full of surprise whines and strange contractions, a collage of colonial vocables. Leaning on those zinc-topped bars in Place Pigalle, while evening like a stream of peonies slid along Las Ramblas, he didn't hear himself. He just threw the stick of himself into the air and swaggered on again, citizen of the epic, all-engrossing world, consort of Madame Mammon, siren, mistress, muse.

Was that the way that I should go, too, then, Dad – hit the road, fight a war, fall for some Lola in a Coimbra café (she of the jealous husband, the docker with a knife)? Was I wrong that my insipid journeys, my no Spanish and less French, led me more inwards than onwards? I supposed so, dazzled by Dad's colours, longing to have a friend in Stockholm to call. But he only showed me the boastful post-cards, never took me with him, not even down the Shankill. He'd left everything behind, kept insisting that doing so was the only way to go. How could he forget our common origins in political squalor and the *apartheid* of the sect? I began to hear his foreign phrases as mere rain drumming on tin chapel roofs, and in his vowels the sound of fife and con-certina came to air out my prejudices. He was the one who was wrong. *Father* . . .

All selves instantly available always, none less worthy or of more use than another, that was me. I was impossible. But sooner that impossibility than another's escapism, I decided (that dogged pride). Nothing would compel me to sample *tapas* or to swill the raw *rioja* like a man. My own was by far a superior restlessness, all internal and domestic, where the real challenge always was. All my novel-reading told me so.

Without Cousin Susie, however, I might not so readily have added a full stop to the resounding No I felt I could give Dad. Or rather, I had Susie and her Kenyan novelist boyfriend, James, to thank. They'd met at university in Leeds, where Susie studied sociology. Both locale and subject, Dad implied, had a black-sheepish hem to them, Kenyan or no Kenyan. Not that James's presence came as a surprise, he stoically sermonised. Here was fear for daughters growing up come home to roost, winds of change growling through the generation gap. But I was thrilled that there was such a side to be on.

I ate James's novels skin and all. They were all about people who had nothing but the big intangibles, fear, hope, rage, pride. Their lives were all their own, yet not, because there were authorities. Church and State. How well I knew them. I walked the dusty roads with old Ngotho. I ached all over again with Njoroge's dream that schooling would transform and validate him. 'Mugo felt nervous. He was lying on his back and looking at the roof.' He was the informer. I even felt that I was close to his confusion. In these vulnerable villages, in this plain prose, I found myself more at home than ever I did in Denmark Street or Ionesco.

Most important of all, James had an agent, address in Mayfair, name of the agency, London International. I uttered the name slowly, every syllable a key unlocking. It was open-sesame time again. (I had my book.) Out of my way, reactionary old-timer. You're Dad but you won't lie down. I felt as young as in the early days of Liz. Again I had an excuse to go AWOL from work, to don the velvet breeks, to ride a silent lift, up, up and away. The offices were plusher and more hushed than even those at Calor, Cavendish Square. Carol, the assistant, glided out to greet me, smiling. David was on the phone but he'd be with me shortly, would I like some coffee? Heaven (that is, attention). I was in heaven. And the snares that hung about me week to week – unbearable Benham's, melancholy Maida Vale – didn't matter now that I sat cheek to *chic*. I understood why in musicals the principle ambition is to dance on top of things.

Then there was David, holding the door, shaking hands,

offering a Gold Leaf from a lacquered box on the glass-topped coffee table. David, with curls close-cropped, patrician style, and an unfamiliarly unassuming accent. David, handler of money and law, citizen of the big world, W1. He moved to the sweet Avon's flow, to the current of Danube and Seine. Soon he would have his powers work for me. I looked across the desk at him and saw Culture, god of Class.

I tendered him 'Ice', my jewel. He said it could do with polishing, but added casually that he'd send it round, one never knew one's luck. I heard a carillon peal out my triumph. Oranges and lemons, said the bells of Saint Gollancz. Taut thriller in original début. Poor James, I thought, still stuck with blood, blacks and Brits. There was no money in that. But I'd post him a few bob in the bush.

I began a play, 'The Hammers of Felix'. David raised a quizzical eyebrow.

'It's a one-man Brechtian concept of a musician who's more played upon than playing,' I explained.

'Ever thought of writing for television?' David asked mildly.

'I want to make music with words,' I replied, mighty offended. Here was an educated man, yet he seemed unable to appreciate my saga of voices in the head, of the guilt of yesterday and its ghosts, of the fundamentally alienated, spiritually desiccated, disinherited-mindedness of midcentury man at the fifty-ninth minute of senescent capitalism's eleventh hour! How extraordinary that somebody so clearly in the know would be out of sympathy with my poor hero, raging for harmony but drowning in the psyche's essential atonality. The talk drifted to New Authors, a Hutchinson innovation, publishers of *The Furnished Room* by Laura Del Rivo, which David thought I might take a look at. I already had. A piece of shit, I said (too close to home, in other words). David just didn't understand. It wasn't kindness I wanted. It was salvation.

I hardly noticed myself biting David's hand, however,

because I was receiving such fine feeding from the hand of Mum. Not just free fags and endless Maxwell House. Hearing the phone ring and my name called and Mum saying cheerily, 'It's just pot luck, I'm afraid, but do come round', obviated mind and all the worlds it had to win.

There always had been Mum, of course, cooking, coping, foraging in her purse, holding variously her family's various hands, bustling out to work (she was a part-time Miss Lonelyhearts for a woman's weekly), tower of strength, house of plenty, ceaseless cartographer of adequacy. I took her totally for granted, like a family member, and wanted her to do the same for me, for fear of obvious mothering. As usual, however, all there was to be afraid of was myself. Mum didn't hug or lullaby me out of my defensive independence. Kindness for her lacked theatre. She just talked to me. I took to doing the drying. She wondered if I'd help lay some lino-ish tiles, and didn't angrily call me useless when I botched the job. Eventually it dawned on me how regularly she rang.

When I remember those calls now, it seems they always came after a bad day at Benham's, which is a fond memory of her fondness and of the sweet delight of appearing to be singled out. No day was good in that mental blacking factory. No buses passed through Judd Street to remind me of alternative destinations. No natural light came into where we were (only managers had windows). Instead of Pakistanis and birds of passage for colleagues, I had ardent, thirtyish girls from Walthamstow and Forest Gate, who worked without laughter or a bun at coffee break, and who made me work. My ice-blue King's Road jacket turned navy with neglect and I spent lunch time in the lavatory, reading ('If I am out of my mind, it's all right with me, thought Moses Herzog').

Onions, pepper, liver, bacon, lamb chop, pâté on melba toast, real coffee ground by hand in a box with a drawer . . . These were my salvation. Not only in the eating, which I carried out with few slices and much dispatch, wordlessly, with unasked-for seconds, but also in the aftermath, when there was talk. My very ordinary opposition to the Vietnam War was welcomed. It was possible to begin to wonder if the Labour Party had no shame. Other evenings, although it was a busman's holiday for her, Mum would listen without a hint of yawn, as I tried to put together bits and pieces of my past, pretending the whole story bored me so as to disguise the difficulty of telling and my excitement at having an audience. At Christmas, I stood next to her in All Saints, Lancaster Gate, singing Protestant hymns and proud to do so, then sitting on the edge of my pew, hearing in amazement my own puny No to war endorsed, as Canon Anthony Bridge unwittingly rehearsed the politics of the coming year by glossing peace and love anticolonially.

Linda and I went to bed that Christmas, but peace and love eluded us, so we made vague plans to travel in the summer. Better to remember the spring of the new, revolutionary year. Mum sometimes brought home work, sheafs of desolation from Hull, Bootle, Luton, Crewe, too intimate to publish, too painful to ignore, dire lives in places made of Judd Streets. How desperate they must be, I said to Mum, to talk to total strangers. They weren't even Irish, even lived at home. It felt as though I knew something about those letters, as though I'd once been blank paper on which such aches and frets had been inscribed.

But that feeling presents itself with unaccustomed sluggishness. I have to force myself to go along with it. The past seems a long way away. Mainly I feel that I've just eaten and this is a safe room. The evenings are getting longer. Weak spring sunlight sneaks in the patio French windows. Mum and I are sitting in the living room. In point of fact, it seems unlikely that we'd be alone, but memory won't have it any other way. I'm reading the sports pages of The Times. Manchester United are looking good in Europe. I'm as relaxed as if I were the man of the house. Mum asks me what I think of something in a letter from a brokenhearted

Brighton fireman, inclines her head attentively, comments kindly on the little I can say. Later she gets up to put on the kettle. Let me, I say. With a little laugh at being attended to, she does. These foolish things . . . I'm not the waif with the begging bowl any more. I'm home.

II

There was no sign of the rain stopping, or of a car stopping either, and I was in the middle of nowhere, a roundabout outside Uxbridge, hatless in my parson's cutaway, and this was stupid. It was about half eleven now, and I'd been at a sodden standstill for over an hour, cursing the world and blaming everybody. Ed Blood had promised me faithfully that thumbing to Oxford would be no bother. He'd been hitching home to West Hartlepool for years without a bit of trouble. But he was a real student, looked the part, denim jacket, eloquent sideburns. I, on the other hand, was what the commercial travellers' Cortinas splashed by, a lamppost for Rovers, there only because the world at large thought me not to be. I'd get that Ed when I got back to Westbourne.

That is, if I ever did go back, if I ever did forgive Mum for making me be here, stuck, for abandoning me generally between coming and going. Making much of me, applying to Ruskin, had been her idea. *The idea of it*, I heard ancestral voices mocking. Exactly! I replied, forthrightly, my head singing with the merest glimmer of the possibility (could there be such moreness for me?). But the hoary hoarse ones had been right. I heard their voices now again, sounding like teeming rain, making me cold. And I thought Mum was hardly any better than them, her kindly, 'But you *must*', leaving me as vulnerable as the non-encouragements of the past, beset by the world's mud and traffic.

I don't remember how Ruskin first came up. Mum had been at Oxford, but she only spoke of it in passing when a familiar name caught her eye scanning *The Times* or the very odd time when she indulged in reminiscence. She was so accepting of the present that it took me quite unawares to hear her refer to a different life. And she was so little of a Dad that it disconcerted me to hear her speaking foreign – Isis, Carfax, OUDS, Port Meadow. At least Lady Margaret Hall had a familiar English sound like Arthur or Lionel, like Barker or King. I saw a stern beadle-ette in twinset and pearls hovering lankily over little misses in ankle socks. And Ruskin did sound exciting.

It was the 1930s, years of hunger, days of strength. New places appeared on the moral map. The old Norse name of Jarrow entered the mind like cold iron. From ruined Welsh valleys men walked to Cowley to make cars. Mum and her mates tasted modernity and took to the streets, shouting to do good. Shouting was a good in itself, solidarity the new clerisy's one choir. Mum took a deep breath and linked arms with atheists. I saw as though in the grainy light of an old photograph a crowd of toothy boys and girls in cloche hats lined up together across a width of street, scarves flying like pennants, big banners flauntingly aloft, a tableau of naïve but indispensable worldly faith. Ruskin was somehow at the centre of all this hope and ardour – green room and kitchen, hospice and library, a prototype of home in Westbourne Terrace.

I had to have it. I knew that when the application came and I saw the snapshots of the Rookery, of bearded swots playing ping-pong, and read of lectures and tutorials. I knew it as I wrote my essay of application, violently dissenting from an *aperçu* of Henry James (something about 'the terrible *fluidity* of self-revelation', no doubt). My head was on fire with the prospect of an audience (the idea of it!). I knew when my stomach turned to water and my mouth ran dry as I memorised the invitation to the interview. And here I was, demanding a lift, as though that alone would prove the viability of my raging need, the need I hugged and feared, my sustenance, my hunger.

I slogged back to Uxbridge, tube and Paddington. I knew this was a day I must live out. In Reading poor Wilde, the Irishman, came to mind, and Clapham Junction (that other roundabout). I accepted that I had to serve those sentences, that form, to which I'd put my name. For Mum, I thought, at least. I owed her that much, and that rationalisation proved relaxing, returned me to a familiar mode. Nervousness offered itself up as duty. That was the way I went, obsequious, resigned, impersonal, suspended, the ghost in the Clapham Omnibus. The train pulled out of Didcot, scampered through the placid, saturated fields as though the world was nothing but normality.

There was no Rookery. There were no pipe-smoking beardies. There wasn't even, as with the other colleges, a big wall. Instead, the premises on Walton Street resembled a smallish town hall, opening off the street with just a pro-forma flight of steps, disarming but disappointingly demotic. No tower, no flag, no carpets, no log fire, no ancient portraits peering through companionable gloom. And instead of Basil Rathbone to escort me to the proper chamber, a typist in spectacles and pink cardie led me up the stairs, parked me in an easy chair outside a door on which a modest plastic sign in black and white said PRINCIPAL, and wished me luck. Everything was so un-assuming and ungothic that I could have screamed with anticlimax. But yet there would be dentistry, I told myself, yet would my masochism be served. I scanned unseeing the insiderhood of a *New Statesman*, an escapee at the border. The cast-iron radiator by the chair made evil-smelling steam come from my coat, unmistakable aroma of cooked goose. The door was held. I passed through.

The dentists, the doctors, the eminent men of letters – a Treadwell, two married Hugheses, and another Hughes, the boss, Billy. – sat around a table looking full of lunch. I sat down stiffly and the talk began – the talk that hasn't stopped since. Background first. The difficult part. I wasn't Labour, I was Irish. But I hadn't laboured. Invoicing had kept my small hands soft as carbon paper, not calloused or contorted by McAlpine or t'pit. So how was I entitled? It soon appeared, however, that Independent Status suited me down to the ground and the cloth cap of Mature Student was a snug fit. Willy-nilly, I turned out to be a fully-paid-up member of the Welfare State, had been taxed and insured for the requisite three years, and heard in wonder that this would have its own reward. They foresaw nothing to prevent me getting a grant. Being Irish was no barrier. They'd seen me, it seemed, disguised as a Belfast seaman or a Derry fitter. Did I know George Johnston?

Interview wasn't a synonym for oral surgery, but for chrysostomy. Mrs Hughes talked about the writer and commitment. The writer *was* commitment, I opined. My words emerged with unfamiliar ease, as though some second nature was released in me. I didn't know I thought that. Other words ensued, all mine, big words, long words, pretentious sentences, asides, concessive clauses, possibly even a half-baked witticism or two. Everything that I had never said aloud in those various bedsits on interminable weekends, immobilised by Goncharov, brained by lapidary Mann, rushed out, blurting and bragging until it was impossible to distinguish between my talk and my happy clatter down the stairs, between the percussive, tiresome rain and the day as, miraculously, a rite of spring. The quartet round the table looked at each other. Moved some paper. Smiled.

I found my way to George's in the market. The man who stood proprietorially by the urn had a face like a plate of corned beef, a lantern jaw and a grim look. But I was ready for anything. I'd have a meat sandwich and a mug of tea. Harsh steam from the urn, gruff orders to the slatternly milkmaid of a counter hand, soft burr of Oxon brogue. 'My duck,' I heard them say, endearingly (*moy dok*), for all the world like farm folk transposed from the old country. The market was festooned with game, like Billy Baldwin's shop a thousand years ago. Grouse and pheasant, their breasts the mottled hues of muted rainbow, hung down the front of

Hedges'. Butchers in straw boaters and striped aprons put steel dramatically to carving knife, bisected carcasses with clinical cleavers. They loved their broad gestures, accompanied them with high-pitched patter. There was sawdust on the floor.

This was the circus. The fruit stall with the glowing mounds of green and red and orange was the feast of Christmas. The encampments of the cheesecloth vendors were images of old fair days, the cheap material and gaudy colours a celebration of the loony belief that things can keep us going. Their stock, the very stalls themselves, seemed replicas of memory's harmless trivia, evocative and transitory, the make-up that mocks the makeshift day and renders it a festival. The bovine help who'd served my tea and sandwich had kindly muttered that I'd get my death going round like that, I would. But the butcher, the baker, the cheap jewellery maker told me, on the contrary, that I would not. Here, smiling, I believed I could get anything but the old familiar blues.

The rain stopped. I emerged on to the Turl and its palaces of Exeter and Jesus. Their strange names and tawny façades made them as distant and as dear to me as Yokahama or Connemara. I might have been visiting a diorama. I might have been on a day trip with authoritative Daddy, waiting with a child's impatient patience for word on what Lambay Island or the Tholsel in Kilkenny stood for. Except now I was father to myself. Mature. Independent. Those were the labels I'd been told to rejoice in. I could face up to these big Englishnesses, not go by scowling on the other side, as on Westminster Bridge. I was as legitimate as any learner, asking what these ancient unruins really meant. I even felt that 'really' could be a term I might be using confidently soon, as though there was an innerness to things, a core behind appearances to believe in, as though the recent hour spent spouting was the undoubted making up of me.

The colleges were peaceful and at rest, shrines to Saint Sanguine and Blessed Reconciliation. That's how history looked when it was good. The stones were warm and light (a watery sun beamed from behind the railway station) because that's how learning was. How everything fits together like a fate, stone upon inevitable stepping stone! By Radcliffe Camera and Sheldonian Theatre I would lay me down at last, and look dirty Dublin and grey Trinity in the eye.

And Linda said, 'Let's go to Cuba!' Looking back, the idea of such a trip seems a virtually promiscuous pursuit of more light and a wider world. But at the time it seemed no more to penniless me than confirmation that my revolutionary day out in Oxford had made me Linda's equal. Besides, I knew that everything would be all right – her inspiration was an ad on the back page of the *New Statesman*. As for money, I could always slow things up at Benham's and get overtime, I could return with confidence to barkeeping at weekends some place in Kilburn, I could make a novena to Saint Joseph, patron saint of novel and remunerative redundancy. I'd heard there was a world to win – 'London! Paris! Rome! Berlin!' – and what on earth could come between me and my share of the spoils?

Cuba, si! It had been the first to prove there was a world to win. And those who'd held pigs at bay in Grosvenor Square and Berkeley had looked on Cuba and seen that it was good, had looked on Che and seen the real thing. And I agreed that Che's beret was brilliant. His lonely and unguileful eyes were hippyishly *simpatico*. This was what a real big brother looked like. What a great doctor he must be ... What bracing medicine he dispensed! (And his mother was a Lynch from Argentina ...) In his name I would practise the strange sound of 'we'. We all would. For his sake I would sweat out five summer weeks in an insect-ridden camp in the interior, though I was neither mad dog nor Englishman, and abhorred the midday sun.

We were in the embassy, in deepest Mayfair. I was undergoing another Oxford overwhelming. After my first colleges, my first revolutionaries. Two sallow young men in olive-green gaberdine suits stood by the door watching us would-be workers without batting an eye or the hint of a grin. Endearing disciplinarians! They were the exact same as university subjects. Their surname was Power. And the spokesman looked the part as well, Groucho moustache, brow crinkled from deep thought, tinted spectacles masking restless, doleful eyes. The ardent don. A lucky man, living an ideal. I called him Energy. With them I could willingly form another Westbourne family, a 'we', and work, and know the joy, as earlier when the rain in Turl Street stopped, of something to say yes to, of living out the bequest of my various No's.

But I made the mistake of not praying to Saint Joseph. I was as badly broke as ever, and there was a ticket to be bought. The prospect of working Saturdays and Sundays, no bother to me, I presumed, with temperatures above a hundred in far Oriente, was sickening in the ordinary way of things. If Cuba meant anything, if it truly was an Oxford in the sea, it was because it would immunise me from the mind-numbing and regressive norm. I refused to consider myself forced to spend evenings moving yet more intractable paper as daylight fled from Judd Street in the desert. I was talking liberation here!

I vaguely thought of worrying aloud to Mum, source of more. But to ask for an extra Oxford would compromise my state-sponsored independence and maturity. Instead I went to my other powerful symbol of the higher meal-ticket, agent David. His job was seeing people right. And after 'Ice''s marketplace meltdown I reckoned he owed me something.

It didn't sound like much. There was a woman by the name of Ware, Literary Something at 20th Century Fox. David dialled a number. Yes, by all means go round to Soho Square and she would have some reading for me. *As for reading, our servants can do that for us . . .* I felt vaguely offended. Didn't David recollect that I had been to Oxford, was virtually a student, a revolutionary and (dream child of those two) an intellectual? But once inside the Fox building all resistance melted into air that was essence of Havana, was swept up the broad, shallow-stepped staircase on which stars must surely dance. Chauffeurs paced the terrazzo acres of the lobby with furtive cigarettes, so many Rafts and Bogies. And I had business here in Soho, just like a grown-up.

Not only did I have to read, I had to write as well, plot summaries, recommendations, reports. The books were new as infants, without dust jackets or hard covers, and I took them home intending tenderness. But a good spanking was what most of them called for and a solemn promise never to lie to me again. The degree to which they declined to be revolutionary, intellectual, study-worthy was simply shameless, almost made me glad I wasn't being published. Life was a lonely woman, they declared, small gains and painful pasts, Acacia Avenue, gardening, tea and fitful sleep. And even when something ostensibly more promising came along, D.H. Lawrence's *The Plumed Serpent*, a potential Burton–Taylor vehicle, I was told, its men with pert bums and dark blood and mystique's clotted thought just made me madder. *We had fed the heart on fantasies . . .* Fuck that, even if it cost me five quid a go to say so.

My free-thinking, terse candour and great wit clearly made an impact on the industry. The book supply dried up, leaving me somewhere west of Shannon, waving and drowning. But I was forgetting that everything now was for the best in the best of all possible worlds. The Fox drought led almost immediately to the Charing Cross Road branch of City of Westminster libraries and to Daniela from Bologna and to bed.

Decent David had dispatched me to compile a bibliography of new translations from the Portuguese (ten quid). The lady librarian gave me strange looks. I knew I didn't have the appearance of one of nature's bibliographers, so her scepticism agreed with me. And whenever I looked up, clerking Daniela was looking too, and smiling. It took me about an hour to smile back. Then I closed the reference book and sauntered out. I heard footsteps behind me, turned and waited. I was not afraid.

She was kind of short and kind of plump and wore cool cotton and a flowing skirt. Her eyes were big and brown as chestnuts, eager in their friendliness. She had a mane of sloe-black, curly hair. Her skin was creamy, pimpleless. Ah, she's the real thing, I said to myself. And yes, she'd like a cup of coffee. She was doing a dissertation on Alan Sillitoe, my instantaneous old favourite, whom I at once extravagantly praised. Here comes Saturday Night at last, I thought. But I planned to make special reference to the allegorical resources of *The General* later on. The thought of her was in my trousers too, though. I wasn't interested in pretending. (*Not timid!*) I said that the tube for my place was handy at Trafalgar Square, like. Daniela cocked coquettish eyebrows and shrugged enthusiastically.

Long, slow, delicious kisses did Daniela kiss, with tender tongue. Long, hard, delirious kisses then we gave each other, tongues turning into firebrands. I unclawed her bra. She didn't say a word. Large breasts fell into my glad, trembling hands. I ate them the whole afternoon.

There was no rush except the one that we delighted in, and just a little blood. Daniela said she was okay, really, and after that we lay a long time silent, breathing in the savoury odours of our sweats and slimes, the effluents of peace. I was on an island, safe. I'd flown to Cuba. I used to dream there might be more. Now in this dim, dingy, room, I had a dream that there might be enough. At six we strolled down to the pub on Warwick Avenue corner and drank halves of lager, shy and smiling. And at the tube, Daniela said, 'I come to you on Sunday.'

She did, too, twice, I think. The rusty, rhythmic bed springs echoed the marching and chanting in Grosvenor Square. My generation. Daniela went away, leaving me strangely liberated and not in love. I spent a few lingering,

148

narcissistic moments staring at the stains on the sheet, feeling with pride a long way from Highbury. Then it was Easter. Prague was springing as though from the grave, offering new, plain-spoken heroes. Bobby Charlton scored against Benfica with his head. Manchester United redeemed history. I saw on television at Westbourne Terrace de Gaulle being robbed of the virginity of *la gloire*. The French were going out of their minds. Paris was a white's Selma, a speechifier's Saigon. *L'imagination prend le pouvoir*, said the walls, and I, laughing, thought, Why not?

Ruskin wrote to tell me I was in. I lay on the bed in the lightless basement clutching the letter as though it was Daniela's bright, delivering flesh. Mum said, 'Oh do come round for dinner.' Harvey's Bristol Cream, taramasalata, lamb chops with champ . . . Dad went, 'Oggsford', Gatsby-ishly approving of the sound but aloof to the meaning, as surprised, amused and incredulous as myself. I didn't mind a bit, for once, if he was being patronising. That evening I may even have kissed Mum on the cheek.

One Friday afternoon in early June, just after suave Paul Muttonchops had brought around the pay, I ran away from Benham's. I skipped along the pavement grey at the peculiar hour of two, every step a glad adieu to the dreary steeples of King's Cross and St Pancras. I had a world to win. Or at least the nothing that I had to lose seemed at last sufficient fuel and motor for me.

It was that kind of year.

III

The guards were wearing guns.

I didn't notice that till I was in the terminal lining up to have my passport controlled and they were staring at me. What had caught my eye crossing the scorching tarmac from the Skyways Fokker was their almost gaudy crimson shirts and sky blue trousers. *Ma foi!* I thought, vaguely recollecting the same colour combo from the centre pages of the *Eagle*, these lads look like demobees from 'Luck of the Legion' (where I'd learned my French from Legionnaire Bimberg). This must be one reason why old soldiers never die. They tog out as tourist tenders. And evidently their orders were to preserve and protect such vital national interests as the way to dangle a fag at the angle of maximum cynicism and how, by wearing sunglasses, to look dressed to kill.

I didn't care for the guns, however. And I could have done without the stares as well, though I'd been years in training for them. My reckless hair, my discoloured pee-green naval duffel bag with matching (as to colour, material and age) Lawrence's Corner jacket earned me the happy right to other ranks' disdain. I was the image of a No! and didn't care who knew it. But something like a shiver went through me as cold, dark eyes, with all the arrogance of arms, raked slowly over me. I would have felt offended if my landfall had gone entirely unremarked. But guns . . .

I couldn't understand them. Big things, not in holsters but resting talismanically at chest height from a cord slung round the neck. Black things. Bare, burnt prototypes, or skeletons, of some abortive variety of bird, fish or fern. Guns meant that things can blow up in your face, a reminder of which I didn't need just now, *merci beaucoup*. Guns were simplistic, like a missioner roaring, theirs the excess of honesty that belies experience. It made only comic-opera sense – especially when I saw now, close-up, that those fetching uniforms were actually far-fetched, remnants of *le tricolore* rendered as the blouse and pantaloon of authority – to swing lead here as bald-faced as police in Belfast. For God's sake, this was only Beauvais, Dungarvan with an airstrip. I badly wanted the queue to move and to get on the bus and the bus not to stop till it crossed the ocean to Havana.

Those French guns brought me down to earth. What with the exhilaration of departure and flight, a kind of ultimate post-Benham's skip, I had forgotten to bear the way things really were in mind.

It was the worst of times.

It was Beauvais because it was not Havana. It was Beauvais because of a misfortune by the name of Phil. Pill, I pronounced him, and Ed Blood said he knew and bought me another pint.

Phil was a fabrication of Linda's, meaning that he wasn't a bit like me. He looked young, for one thing. And he quite possibly was young, except that his youth was most unforgivably compounded of rosiness of cheek, shortness of clean hair, demureness of presence, and Trinity education. The unexceptional but provocative sight of him in *my* Westbourne kitchen that Whit Saturday almost put me off my dinner. He said little, flinched when Dad boomed gambits at him, and ate so little that Linda had to rescue him before dessert. Out she flounced with him, banging the front door.

Of course they were lovers. Phil was studying biology, which I took as proof. He possessed knowledge and possibly technique, a thought which pained me as much as Linda's letdown. And as if that wasn't proof enough, Phil was going to Cuba. I said I understood, and put on a masterly little show of self-seeking sentiment masquerading as sincerity. Bless you, my children. Don't mind me. I'll just sit here in dark Maida, vale of tears. Off with ye now to yere Trinity Ball and yere exams, yere happy-ever-after. Call themselves students? I muttered witheringly to my *Guardian*. Why aren't they off to Paris?

The bus bowled happily along. I knew it was a far, far better thing I did than I had ever done before. It was the best of times. As the cliché of memory decrees, the sun shone all afternoon and late into the night as well. Beyond the window, a gallery of Penguin Classics covers slid effortlessly past, shutters in Utrillo green, a faded café in a shady *place*. Wind belts of plane trees stood out against flat fields, as planned as paintings, as planned as what I knew in Ireland as avenues leading to invisible big houses. Avenue – my mind dinged the little triangle of itself – that must be French. A venue. Must mean place, I thought. And there was *bienvenue* at Beauvais airport. I knew no welcome, just 'good place', and made out it spoke my language. At once I loved those beige fields, those deep green distant hills. I loved driving deeper, ever deeper, without map or plan, trailing clouds of glory and azure exhaust, having no idea where I was.

I marched boldly down Sebastopol and Turbigo. These were my father's footsteps. That was the shady door in Rue du Temple where he had entered for the assignation he'd been promising himself all year in widowers' Dublin. These were his sunglasses and Gitanes on a table at Aux Deux Magots. In Boul' Mich' bookshops I, in loving memory, fingered the uncut pages of cream-coloured Gallimards. At holiday times together, he'd let me slit his with a ruler, ten at a time if I was good, part game, part act of homage to his essential foreignness. I'd leap-frogged England into his big world. He was that tanned man in beret and shirt sleeves on the open end of that ancient single-decker that truffled through the traffic like a bumpkin. He was that Montande-que figure speaking volubly, intimately, to a woman sheathed in something sheer and crimson by Balenciaga, about whose lips, as the romances say, there played an almost imperceptible smile. All those centuries ago, when he brought back the Eiffel Tower ashtray and sang with fake, excess emotion and nasality, 'La Vie en Rose', I'd longed for us to run away together. Now it felt as though we had. He was ahead of me, of course, and still elusive. But I felt no need to catch up. At least – at last – he led me. That was enough.

The dreadful Goriot girls began debouching from lithe Citroëns in Rue de Rivoli, and every café was packed to the doors with Daniels and Iviches. And there were even more improbable fictions. I spent the best part of a day circling the Dôme, but Poulou and the missus didn't turn up (they were probably en route to Cuba . . .). I passed an afternoon neither coming nor going under the walls of la Santé, waiting for Beckett. A *flic* eventually moved me roughly on, groping for his night stick, a real Frenchman, not a bit like Montand or the man on the Neuilly omnibus, though to get me on my way he'd have done better merely to murmur, 'No pilgrims where none intended.'

The whole city was a fabulous read, with its unintimidating rhetoric of pale stone Palais and Hôtels, its vivid gazetteer of street names from opaque, colourless schoolbooks, its Nation and Bastille and all the rest that brought to life the three graces of democracy in a way no monument I'd ever seen did. This was an Oxford *extraordinaire*. This was a place to be a foreigner in, and welcome.

I was sitting on my duffel bag on Pont Neuf, writing a postcard to Mum, when a spindly lady of uncertain years accosted me, essaying the tongues of Europe. After a few hapless flurries, she settled on English, spoke smilingly of Stratford-on-Avon, assuming it to be my own fair bailiwick. Unlike the diffident neighbour of la Santé, I didn't have the wit to demur, *'au contraire'*. Instead, I satisfied honour, if that's the phrase I'm looking for, by raising my voice and adjusting my accent. 'Ah,' said her spindlyship, 'Yames Yoyce.' Aye, very like a whale. Whereupon, she dug in her purse to press a ten franc note on me. I was rambling down Rue Gay Lussac, going nowhere *avec plaisir* and all the time in the world, the evidence of recent battle in the broken street a voyeur's delight, when Wolf of Ulm stopped me, bottle in hand and looking wild. I would take a drink with him, yes? So, to be international and solid, I swigged his inky Nicolas. In next to no time, the pair of us were capering around the street like cossacks, singing tuneless songs and talking seriously, two likely loners all set to scandalise Wimbledon.

Wolf was in a bad way. By day he worked in the architect's office of his Uncle Martinet, and by night lay down without conviction in the same relation's fabulous apartment, not far from Franklin Roosevelt. And I? I threw my heavy, semispastic head back and roared up at the stars in so-called song, 'I ain't got nobody!' Wolf narrowed his mad eyes and turned his jaws to iron. I suspected him of thought. 'Come,' he commanded, detaching me from the all-important railings. Tonight I would bed down in uncle's spare room. Wolf's glee at the idea was just the same strange mixture of the grim and the immoderate I'd noticed when earlier he told me an incoherent, revolutionary anecdote about his gymnasium, complete with shattered door, and a thickset head going purple in the face with rage. At times like that, he intimated, it was good to be alive.

There was a night under chestnut trees beside the river learning the words of 'Bandiera Rossa'. There was an evening being taught in dumb show by an Algerian girl what *copain* meant. I met Antonia. I met Pam. I even met, behind the Opéra, looking for the American Express office, Helga, the Scottish student temp from Calor, sporting a bald man not her father. They were heading for St-Germain-en-laye, though, couldn't stop, so nice, do drop a line some time. I grinned and waved and let them go, feeling as detached as she from old acquaintances, as free as a graffito. Far better to stay up most of the night on the fringe of groups whose languages I couldn't understand, and to nap, in preparation in the grand gloom of Saint Sulpice, as delighted with a life of transience as though it was what I had always wanted.

Antonia was Linda's young cousin. She had a notion that she should be seeing the sights and going without a phrase book, what with A levels coming up next year. We visited the Louvre and Notre Dame, yawning and dutiful. Impatiently, I took nothing in, saw nothing except mausoleum and plunder. She translated from an Odéon wall, *Soyez sales, pas sucres!* and we agreed that was more like it. She met Tom West of Oak Park, Illinois. He offered me floor space in an *atelier* he'd borrowed in Rue Descartes, near Rue Mouffetard, beyond the Panthéon. But word came from

154

Mum of Susie and Mbella. She wrote care of American Express, forwarded a fiver too, I shouldn't wonder.

I only had to hear that Mbella was a novelist from Cameroon to move in with them. They had a minute room in the Marais, and when Antonia and I sat cross-legged on the floor with them, soaking up spicy meat sauce with wads of semolina, this was living. I ate until I turned into a tree, causing amusement and vague anxiety, Susie scolding me enjoyably for going so long without a proper meal. 'Proper' was very good, Susie, though I wasn't laughing just at her but at the strange sound of English briskness, as old hat as old pals from Calor.

Susie knew what she was talking about, however. It was all a question of using one's loaf, basically. Les Halles wasn't far away. Therefore, to eat, one merely had to prowl from stall to stall enquiring sweetly, 'Des jetés, m'sieu?' Meat, fruit, cheese, vegetables, all the perfumes of the casbah came Susie's way. Before my very eyes, the bazaar of Bayswater turned into a work of art, and Oxford market became an epic. Admiring the peaches and the pale asparagus, the aubergines whose bloom and volume made them seem Cézanne's, was drug enough. But to bring them home and gorge on them felt like being la vache qui rit. Even when Susie went back to England and Mbella drifted off after Swedish girls, I spent nights happily quaffing truckfuls of the warm south and rummaging in cast-off crates and cartons for yet one more fine feed of beautiful, bowel-crumbling produce.

As for accommodation, Susie said I should be able to find that in my sleep. Mbella took me to a hostel on Rue de Vaugirard, Sorbonne end. The name of this place was Bedlam, though the inmates were a grand bunch of lads. White teeth twinkled in dark, friendly faces. Italian situationists argued in English, to be safe, about the ideological acceptability of hostels. Some compañeros from beyond the sea sat with sad eyes singing up-tempo ballads. But when I went and had a shower, all hell broke loose.

It was only nine in the evening. There was a thunder of doors slamming and bolts being shot, a clatter of authority's big boots ascending the stone stairs, then a fierce *tatarara* altogether on the frail door of my stall. I didn't budge, being naked and afraid, but that only made the hammering worse, the voice louder and what I could only imagine to be maledictions more numerous and no doubt more specific. Then silence. I wasn't dry or anything near it, but I decided that I'd nip back to the bunk now before the lunatic came back with his extended family. Of course, as soon as I came out the bathroom door he pounced on me. I still don't know what I was doing wrong, but wrong I very definitely must have been because I well remember stumbling through the shuttered dormitory, accusations snapping at my heels, my wet fluster feeling like a fit of guilt. I reported back to Mbella. 'Drowning in the bed,' he said musingly. 'Iss baedt.' So he threw me a life belt called Geoffrey.

At first, that is, for an hour or two, everything went swimmingly with Geoffrey and I. He was a translator from Patagonia, he said, and worked betimes for *Présence Africaine*, where Mbella had put in the good word for me with him. I first met him in a café called Le Celtique, alongside Sèvres-Babylone, where we eventually entrained for Lamarck-Caulaincourt, a bulky, boisterous party in a loud check suit. His chin was weak and his cheeks were putty-pale and puffy. He laughed like a road drill at his own jokes, the laughter of a man who's had more than his share of also-rans at Goodwood. He downed *demis* like billyo. The deluge of *bonhomie* was not necessary. I took it for granted that he was superb company, and had planned to grin whatever he said, laying on the exaggerated sincerity I reserved for all my benefactors.

The show wasn't for me, however, but for an old Vietnamese at the far end of the zinc. To him was raised each glass of Stella with the toast, '*À la lutte continue!*'

The shabby, toothless, toothpick raised his glass in return and gave a complex smile which seemed to translate as something like, 'White man, you're fucking loony, but I forgive you, just this once!'

Geoffrey sighed. 'I've been drinking with this old coot for six months now,' he said, 'and I still can't get a word out of him.'

Ah yes, I nodded with a swimming head, this definitely is life. Nothing becomes it like its funny foreignness.

Notre-Dame-de-Lorette was tough going enough, but St-Georges was tougher, and the way the train ground up the hill suggested that it was a *mutilé de guerre* and should immediately be given a seat. I was almost as done for by the time we got to Geoffrey's, but in no time he had his floppy slippers and an apron on and was busy breaking baguettes, opening tins of ratatouille and sloshing plonk into bamboo beakers engraved with atolls, palms and yachts.

Exoticer and exoticer, I said gladly to myself. I drank the wine. For this was I born, I told myself, feeling all-powerful, for this came I into the world. Geoffrey buzzed busily about, plying me with toothsome goodies, aping to perfection the ample aunt who, delighted to be visited, overdoes the mothering at tea time. And as if food was not enough, exotic names kept floating towards me too – the great Senghor, Aimé Cesaire, the fab Fanon, about whom I tried to say a few approving words, believing that I'd earned the right to do so by being a part-time wretch.

But Geoffrey wouldn't hear of it. Fanon was a fuck-up, '*mon ami*', Fanon wasn't art. I can't swear that he didn't then go on to exclaim, 'Give me poetry. Give me life!' and pirouette, but I see him plainly in the kitchen, leering, limp-hipped, arms aloft in deliquescent joy, and to follow, a lengthy disquisition on negritude.

I fell asleep. Geoffrey must, I figured groggily, have been trying to help me from the table. But Geoffrey wasn't trying to get me up at all, or at least not in the only way I thought made sense at the time. 'But!' he expostulated as I woke then in a hurry, angry to discover that not only had the whole evening not been innocent but that I'd never once imagined what Geoffrey had in mind.

It was cold. I felt queasy with the drink. I'd been looking forward to a cosy bed, a long lie in, a wash. Still, the city remained. The thing of nothing which had just taken place seemed worth it, somehow, for the view I had now of the illuminated veins of its illustrious body from high Montmartre. And had I not said, simply, No, and walked away, unscathed and unthreatened? For some reason, such simplicity struck me as a great accomplishment, enjoyable, almost, a big improvement on being legless in Wimbledon and of the fear of the worst that used to feel so sexually menacing there. Sage as a drunk, I told myself that I was getting on all right. My footsteps led me into a replay of the credit sequence opening *Bob Le Flambeur*. I made my bed in the great whited sepulchre of Sacré Coeur.

Other anecdotes suggest themselves, mainly about money. A woman, lightly and unsuitably attired, with hair astray, rushed up to me quite early one morning as I was breakfasting on rejected melon in the Tuileries Gardens, thrust a five franc note into my rancid battledress, then rambled on at a sedate trot towards Place de la Concorde. Pam gave me money. Pam bought me coffee. Pam gave me priceless attention, listened patiently to my impassioned nothings about Gogol and Godard. She liked *Pierrot le Fou*, too. I liked Pam, although she was American. She fixed me up with a room in Zella Silverman's snooty sublet out Boulevard Malesherbes, of which she'd heard on the survivalist grapevine which flourished where she lived, the YWCA, Rue Cambon, beside the Madeleine. Zella thought more of the apartment than of me, and with frowns and silence bade me do the same. That was the end.

Not that a good address and a bossy landlady had sent me packing. Paris had raised me above such pettiness. By now I'd had my kidneys truncheoned once or twice, nothing serious, the cops' casual swipes just what everyone wants to give tramps. And in the smell of piss and serenaded by the rattle of ruined lungs I'd had my three or four nights camping out on Métro steps at Les Halles, Temple, Arts et Métiers. I'd been on the fringe of knots of happy, stamping, chanting demonstrators when the CRS had rushed up and waded in and made heads go *crack!* as though they were mere Dylan albums. I had no problem saying No to whatever Zella thought she represented.

It just felt like time was up. Whatever I had come to do seemed done, although it was hardly a matter much of doing. These Paris manoeuvres were simply a more colourful and concentrated version of playing out the inventory of selves that had kept me going in London. It helped, of course, that here all the world was Westbourne (which must be why most of my memories are of meals and money), and life was all hand-me-down and pick-me-up. All I had wanted, it seemed, was to know I could survive. Now I had proof. Mum, Ruskin, Paris . . . It was that kind of year.

So when in years to come our boys Ben and Nick ask, 'What did you do in the revolution, Daddy?' all I'll be able to say is that I played the hobo and met Pam, their mother. For a long time having so short an answer used to embarrass me. I'd feel more or less ashamed, depending on the questioner, that I'd been neither a worker nor a student and that the revels all had ended by the time I got my *bienvenue*. I'd don something of S. Dedalus's hauteur ('Paris, you know, Boul' Mich'') or dissipate my discomfort with a nod and a wink, as though there was something unbelievable, or even wrong, in seeming on the inside while remaining an outsider all the time. I'd been there, but not properly there. I'd been down, but not out. It seemed beside the point that the revolution hadn't lasted but that what happened to me was permanent. I'd hum 'My Back Pages', and let it go at that.

The buckled wheel of myself had come full circle, a recycling which felt like a reclamation, a repossession. Not that it described anything as integrated or stable as a pattern. Instead, what came to mind was something like a series of subterranean impulses, reminders of at least a psychic continuity, some drive or current as invisible and incessant as biological activity, and as impossible to do without. I was no Orwell, but I knew now I wasn't Eric either.

'*Revolution*: the locus of a moving body which, describing a closed curve, successively passes through the same points' (*Dictionnaire Larousse*).

SOLDIERS

I

'Paris,' said Mrs Fox, and the match she held before her lips
blew out. She lit another and said, 'Parh-ee.' This time the
flame stayed put. We were doing French at Ruskin. Barry
Carpenter, Sheffield and BRISAKTA, was there, also Jack
Sleight. Tony from Belfast and the ETU was having a small
problem pronouncing words like *mur* and *heure*. Mrs Fox cir-
cumflexed her lips the proper way for him. Mrs Fox was
wonderful. I was dying to be noticed by her, mimicked
somewhat maniacally her grand cuisine of sounds. When
asked to read, I could do so only at the rate of a cataract.
Anything slower, less affected, might dilute my unBelfast,
non-Don River internationality. Basically, I couldn't tell my
dont from my *donc*, but stuck my chest out mouthing *l'usine*
and *la grève*, as serious as somebody who knew what he was
talking about.

Mrs Fox's office was in Bowen House. That made sense.
Bowen was best. Not because Barry, I and Tony lived there.
It was where the revolutionaries lived, Ron, the Dundee
Maoist, also George Armstrong from Clydeside, who after

closing time made doleful moan through the chanter of a bagpipe, Paul Kneafsey too, in whose room there was always tea. We stayed up all night enumerating the ways trade unions had merely begged questions of the world. The point was to change it! If Ron was in the mood, we made midnight cauldrons of Vesta Chow Mein. The aroma of a fry came from Mac Reid's. John Sheldon, John Schild, Jim Tattersall from Batley, the self-styled ''umble lad' ... I should name them out in a song.

And Martin. He was the real thing. He'd been to Paris in May. He bought the *New Left Review*, had heard of *La Pensée*, thought the *New Statesman* moribund, mortifying me. He lauded Gramsci, worried about Bernstein and the Second International, did brisk tattoos on the graves of Webbs and Coles, which caused some of his teachers to see nothing in him but outrage and anarchy. Years before, Bessie Braddock had hugged him at some Labour youth do. Now, as though in response (he spoke fluent dialectics), he insisted we go every Friday afternoon at four to St Anthony's Common Room to hear Chimen Abramsky discourse on the Bund. There were, perhaps, eight of us. Martin chain-smoked Disque Bleu, grinning shyly, enthralled, eyes gleaming with vistas of knowledge and of struggle. 'Mandel,' he'd begin, later, at the Welsh Pony, or, 'Tariq ...' He approved of Geismar, that tendency. 'Hey, Mandel had his car set on fire during May. He was at the Odéon or somewhere and when he came back, there it was – *gutted*. Mandel takes one look and goes, "Fucking brilliant!"'

I remember how rumpled his sweaters always seemed, his chortling laugh. I remember the names of the concepts, the theorists, the groups he floated past me, just out of reach, like solutions of crossword clues I couldn't understand. All my classmates at Ruskin were wonderful, even those I never really knew or couldn't stomach, but Martin was the one I loved. He was from Nottingham. He believed in Forest and in Workers' Control. He could tell a Pabloite in his sleep.

They were wonderful because they were so exotic. I'd

never knowingly met workers before. The nearest I'd come to them were emigrants, and that had been back in Lismore. And immigrants had always seemed stained, somehow, by the sweat of their brow, as the soul was said then to be blackened by sin. Neither powder nor paint, court shoes nor signet ring could purge the moral stench of labouring. (Thus sin, despite confession, was said to bequeath a virtually indelible rime of remorse. Thus to be born unknown into an ideology.) To those at home, the emigrant could never do enough to justify himself, or especially, herself. So they weren't workers, really. They were estranged family members, sheep blackened by the endless, fretful machinations of an inexhaustibly sectarian culture. As for English workers, the inmates of the Jolly Gardeners qualified, no doubt. But I'd seen them just as colourful topers who drifted off to lives unknowable when we closed, the pub their sole collective, my view conditioned by a wish that they seemed just as lonely as myself.

The vital expression of my fab new worker friends' exoticism, however, was togetherness. At first it was all theirs, and took a bit of getting used to. My Ruskin comrades struck me as insiders to a man. They were used to being with their own kind and to that being adequate. I was strictly a parliament of one. Although before going up they'd never met, most of them already knew each other in a generic sort of way and were able to relate thanks to that awareness's fortifying fabric. And I had to learn their language. There were more venerable and more virile terms than togetherness for their common properties, such as 'solidarity' and 'union'. Those terms' strength asserted itself only when there was stress and threat. But with bosses about, it seemed there was no telling when that would be. Better to be on the safe side, best to learn sceptical hope. Tend the seedlings of that strength, the lesson said. It was as though I'd happened on some kind of providential vibe or vein of warmth.

I was embarrassed, though not surprised, to find that all

I knew of my comrades' lives came from the weary gnashing of editorial dentures in the *Guardian*, from squads of marchers traipsing intermittently through the nine o'clock news, followed by men in studios and suits politely vilifying them. That was why, I supposed, I'd first seen them as emigrants' vague kin, virtual tinkers, alien to classiness and culture, noteworthy only when available for belittlement. Yet, on a point of order (as I was learning to say), they were all great families – NUM, NUR, DATA, NUPE, and the daddy of them all, the T & G. They provided help and protection. They created brotherhood. They cherished and supported membership (most students came to Ruskin not on grants, like me, but on union scholarships and bursaries). The family feel was what all these wacks, mates and marrahs had brought to Ruskin with them. It was there in the endless making of tea, the vicious ping-pong friendlies, the dialectical derring-do long after Gladys turned the light out at the Black Boy. And there was unimaginative me thinking such treats were exclusive to Westbourne and Paris. 'Sup up, lad,' I said to myself, as I saw myself dance with delight on the grave of O. Twist.

A much less childish version of this wind of change was available as well. Objectively – a new word, with which I instantly fell in love (it signified the happy presence of worlds not invented by my hunger) – I saw the brothers were neither the wretched of the earth nor cast-offs from *The Titfield Thunderbolt*. Admittedly I loved it that they had the accents and vocabulary for the latter role, gorgeous north-country accents, cutting and grinding and grating as though in sublimated mimicry of machine tools. And I delighted in acquiring something of that lingo. Bliss was it in that dawn to apply 'pillock'. And to pronounce 'prat' was very heaven. But that didn't tell me who they were. Besides, I spent too much time and pride denying stereotypes of myself to be content with thinking there was nothing to my siblings but cloth caps, mufflers, tripe and clogs. They had to have a history. They had to have *something* to come from pit and foundry so quick, so confident, so convincing.

Soon I had the understanding that I wanted, a nice repertoire of big words. First, *identity*, *tradition*, *struggle*, which quickly were transformed into terms richer, stranger, apter. Alienation. Militancy. Left. I pictured marchers and banners as solemn and self-righteous as long-forgotten Children of Mary. I joyed to sing of workers and their slumbers, considered myself one of the original citizens of want. It made my chest expand a proud extra inch to note our anthem didn't pull intellectual punches. If the Age of Kant could complete a rhyme, well then, by all means let it. That was what I called freedom.

And I saw that what I had christened families, in my first flush of sentimental solidarity, might just as readily, and with more purpose, be called regiments. Vivid images sprang to mind of Victorian rank-and-file returning from the colonies to find conditions much the same in Trafalgar Street as they had been among the natives in Amritsar and Fermoy. The rows of back-to-backs which I'd seen in Woodfall Films seemed themselves colonies now, and their bossed, uprooted, downtrodden people a breed of Irish. Super Irish. Dare to struggle, dare to win! Won they had, too, not often, no doubt, certainly not often enough, and always inconclusively. Yet they'd taken on not foreign invaders but their own intolerable fellow countrymen. And their achievements were plenty to be going on with.

The heart sang in me to the sound of Peterloo and Tolpuddle, as once to Vinegar Hill and Aughrim. All this without adding prayer to shivering prayer or claiming that their history was a pilgrimage and penance. They'd just locked arms and kept on saying No! as loudly and as long as they were able. They were doing it still. Nothing of my forbears' faith in freedom moved me as much. This was a world to try and be at home in.

That year, E.P. Thompson's *The Making of the English Working Class* was turned into the one-thousandth Pelican. I had tutorials with Raphael Samuel. But I skimmed the book and didn't pay attention to my gifted teacher. I was too immersed in my latest romance of arrival, this better Cuba, this village of belonging. At the history workshop in November, Alun Howkins threw his long blonde locks back and gave out with passion a great, sad-spirited song about when Jones's ale was new. The blessed secular spirit of the everyday came through the way 'me boys' went in the chorus. I sang 'The Wild Rover' and imagined that my raucous fervour and the hall's applause meant that every word of it was true.

Even geography affirmed what a brave new world we'd found. We didn't have to bother with Oxford or be confused about whether we denoted town or gown. Not being members of the university, it suited us to remain in the pretty enclave presided over by the Rookery, Old Headington, safe from the irritants of posh accents and plush pubs. Christ Church and Balliol could forever be other parts of the forest. The rumblings of bulldogs, JCRs and proctors were so many unintelligible noises off, as long as we had Bowen and Stoke and Bowerman as green rooms. We did go in to take the Latin oath always to enter the Bodleian minus incendiary devices, giggling lest we appear to be counter-revolutionaries. Tony and I tried the cavernous English library at St Cross, but it was way too echoey, too underpopulated, so we spent our afternoons in the basement drinking vile vending-machine coffee and bitching about how unintimate the big world of learning seemed. St Cross was where Sean Gervasi's five-thirty economics lectures were too. Bowenite buddies doing the Dip., the Diploma in Social Studies, couldn't miss these 'shit-hot' happenings. Tony and I went, to be sure of a lift home. We didn't understand a word, but emerged as dazed and as delighted as if we'd seen *Potemkin*. The lecturer's flamboyant style conveyed to perfection what we were looking for, an Oxford more dramatic than Oxford itself. It was a question of the seizing of the power (*ceteris paribus*). So screw Schumpeter!

We roared back through St Clement's, six of us squeezed

into Alec Irwin's Mini-Cooper, every one of us an intervention in the making. We didn't even pause for cynical reflection upon Chateau Maxwell on the Hill. We were ravenous from overstimulation. We were stars because we had an audience. We had Miss Oates's brilliant pan-fried pork chops waiting for us, and civil coffee from the silver urn afterwards, and sociability with the girls who slept all, all alone in Stoke House. We were out of our minds.

Some knack of surpassing sophistication was required, I knew, to make an impression on those Stoke girls. We were so many, they were so few, and since talk was not my goal, my talk needed to be extra rare and fine. But when Sally, who had a background in the theatre, asked me if I actually knew Harold Hobson, I could only splutter that at times one almost felt as if one did. Ariel was from Geneva, so I tried to discourse knowingly of Paris with her. But I never even got as far as Beauvais. Ariel only had eyes for Martin, and he was going out with Sally, proving thereby (as I slunk away) how worthy he was of my admiration. I remember Sue, who went out with Bob Elliott, and her pal Margaret. They were studying social work. I reckoned they would turn out to be severe. They each had friendly smiles, but I backed away. To think there was a time when I'd have gladly been a case . . .

Heather made more sense. She was from the newish semis down the road at Marston. There was a hop. It had been so long since I'd danced with anyone that I felt almost innocent as I squirmed about to Wilson Pickett's 'Midnight Hour'. Almost. No to dreams of chocolate lips and gymslips (Heather was seventeen). Heather may have come to bop, but I took it that she remained to lay. Nothing else would do me now, what with the independence of my status and having risen to the occasion with Daniela, and the general triumph of experience over hope that life was turning out to be. Pigs were being offed, but not male chauvinist ones. It was the revolution.

I was writing to Pam. She was back home again in Indiana, at university, suffering withdrawal from Paris and without a Ruskin. I said she should see me now, and asked if she could forward me something by Leroi Jones. I met Rosemary. Her skin was white as Wonderbread and fish suppers. She wore fine white lacy shifts, a total menace. Our kisses were the true epoxy. Hurtful. Bliss. I saw red (it was the revolution). But Rosemary believed in saving herself. One night after a feed of cider, a tired and emotional Heather and I encountered the nothing about which there had been much ado. And I didn't respect her in the morning. I should have kept to that straight and narrow leading to distant social workers. They would have saved me from embarrassment. But I didn't want saving. Saving is for now, strictly for the face and the phenomenon, writing trying to paper over cracks which it alone reveals. Ruskin was freefall time. I liked the idea of being boss, imposing my will and acting the prick. As for responsibility, my victim could assume that for me and for that little one-dimensional man of mine. Messing with, or up, Heather was nothing like the fucking we revolutionary worker students would give to whoever tried to fuck us up. For peace and love, cry Fuck! cry War! 'Smash the state!' Joe, a member of the Irish Communist Party and a former hurler with Holycross, used gleefully to hiss. At the midnight hour, baby . . .

The sound of violence – what a glow it gave, what a sense of purpose! How much more inspirationally praxis fell upon the ear than *mauvaise foi*. And how ego-boosting of my peers to teach me that I'd outgrown at last my sophomoric, Simon-and-Garfunkel existentialism, luxury of white boys self-confined to single rooms. No man was a rock, much less an is-is-is-land.

Never were new selves more necessary. For today the struggle. Right here, right now. For, shockingly, even at Ruskin there was a system to oppose, complete with pale pink (true-coloured) bosses. We had an uneasy sense of having been done the dirty on. College (Power) had supplanted Ruskin (Life). Ruskin we gladly knew to be all fraternal greetings and late night stand-uppery at Club

Iskra, Bowen kitchen, the coffee house of everyone's tomorrow. College, however, the Hughes *junta*, was nothing but conceptual analysis and compulsory statistics. College was just a variation on have and have-not relationships. Classroom chimed disconcertingly with class. Knowledge bore an intimidating resemblance to network, inner sanctum, member of the board. Study felt like a special mode of ignorance. There were embarrassingly theoretical impasses. 'Keynes is a cunt!' The family romance of Labour revealed its rancid origins in someone getting fucked.

Lads began to feel adrift. Futures seemed less obviously than hitherto the fiat of pasts. There was a claustrophobic sense of being on one's own, veiled off by sheets of lecture notes, embarrassing and inopportune, like inexperience. Smash! was often heard, describing tutorial wrangles and what would happen Hobbes once hands were laid on him. And smash this system we would as well, and history would see what a strategically invaluable rehearsal our so doing would prove for the ultimate, inevitable triumph, the whimpering away of the state. But today the struggle. So comrades, come rally! We will hang the last bureaucrat with the guts of the last priest. *Venceremos!* What is now proved was once imagined. Kiss me, Hardy.

When fears of mind transplants first started scooting anxiously around the Bowen kitchen, my one smug thought was, This is what you get for doing the Dip., the course for which most opted. I couldn't understand how these sound men could identify with such cranky tools as sociology and economics, aiming to claim that the world was understandable, or even more bizarre, that they understood it. Students have tried to comprehend the world. The point is to enjoy it. Had I the interest or energy to come up with a slogan of my own in those days, it would have gone something like that. Dip-heads should have been a lot more like us literary coves, who started out with flitches of flat Crabbe and then went bravely and impatiently on to Blake the loony, enviable doer of his own thing and sometime man-er of the visionary barricade. 'In every cry of every Man/The mind-forg'd manacles I hear.' Aye, aye, we went, and felt vindicated. With Blake our comrade, we didn't mind that it was poetry we were being asked to read, or that it was a woman who was teaching us. We didn't even feel particularly patronised when she threw well-meaning Hoggartly looks at us if we came up with anything interesting to say. Such, such were the joys.

They didn't last long, though, the same joys. Soon I, too, was declaring myself fit, if not to smash English, to kick its arse so hard that it would need its head examining. Top and tail of William Wordsworth was what I had primarily in my sights, but it was no accident, as the saying went, that English in general was my target. The generalising, or paranoid habit of the time demanded that attack be all out, leaving attacker in no doubt of his militancy. Soldiers were taught to roar when sticking bayonets into bags of straw, weren't they?

This William Wordsworth was supposed to be a revolutionary. He'd been to Paris, and he changed men's thought. The latter was what *Lyrical Ballads* was supposed to be about. Don't make us laugh. There was no history here, no epic on enclosures, no Jacobin energy, United Irishmen, maddened Luddites and Captain Swing. Hosts of a lot more than golden daffodils were blowing in the wind, and here was yer man acting the scholar gypsy, his ear to the ground for the language of men, acting the innocent, with his Michael and Lucy, solitary reapers and rustic ruins. 'The idiocy of rural life.' *Maven* Marx put his finger on it. Again. 'Earth has not anything to show more fair.' Well, where's your actual working class, reactionary twatface? It was the wrong romance for the right time of year, mate. And anyway, the tigers of wrath are wiser than the horses of instruction. Plus, speaking personally, Wordsworth is way too autobiographical . . .

Well then, let there be novels! And there were novels. But

they were as void as verse of images of us. Jane Austen, the Wedgwood Wordsworth! The very idea of Mr Knightley having something to say for us was drearier than even the still sad music of humanity, even if the depiction of Emma was all too convincing. We knew her type, playing hard to get, imagining it was a flowerpot for growing hair she had between her legs. We were not hair-conscious Frank Churchills, or Fred Vincys either, though Fred, at least, played snooker. But the length of *Middlemarch* made us want to run away with Sleary's circus. We got jumpy with impatience at it, like so many Ladislaws coming hotfoot home to roost, though redder than pale Will by far. And as for pathetic Stephen Blackpool . . . Nobody dared hold a mirror to the nature that was us, clear evidence of how the course, the college, literature itself conspired against us, having in mind merely to make us consumers of their constructs. Well let us in the name of freedom have a nature not yet imaged, inscribed by ourselves alone.

We would not, we would not be moved. For today the struggle. English would somehow have to be struck. Occupied. Its files and identity cards needed jumbling up a bit, reordered along class lines, in the interests of democracy and relevance. Down the town, there was talk in *Oxford Left* of revolutionary logic. Only a craven class traitor would not make a similar intervention on, objectively, his own behalf. Or so it seems from the fact that I prepared a document. There it is, unread for twenty years, stuck between the sheets of a Leicester University RSSF pamphlet, five smashingly cogent points set down in what looks like the orthographic equivalent of severe constipation.

The transparently repressive tolerance of the weekly essay needed to be exposed. The naked and insidious ideological manipulations of the bureaucracy would have to be unmasked. The essentially anti-democratic paternalism of the structure of education should be overcome immediately, if not sooner. The smelly tenure of H. Wilson in L.B.J.'s hip pocket must be denounced as a matter of pedagogical

171

urgency. And, not least, I called for much more French, the tongue of theory and of all our futures. *Ne changerons pas d'employeurs, changerons l'emploi de vie*. In the Leicester comrades' unforgettable words, 'Thus the structure of learning in universities is illogical, just as its content is barbarous.'

It was a matter of the posing of the question. Martin could do it. Martin marched from Queen's Lane to Carfax in a demonstration which with one voice went, 'Structuralism IN, Historicism OUT!' At the history workshop, Martin followed E.P. Thompson to the bog (I was there), and as we sluiced the porcelain together, asked if the great one planned to reply to Perry Anderson's (magnificent) attack on him. E.P. unflinchingly kept straight his patrician profile and said, 'Oh, I may address it in a footnote.' Martin energetically pushed his spectacles into place a time or two and grinned his endearing, slightly goofy grin, as much as to say, 'See? See? I told you...' Whatever he meant, I believed him.

II

Our true Penelope was Trotsky. *Student Power* (A Penguin Special) was all very well, with its eloquent, pictureless red cover and its invaluable directory of intellectual enemies, bourgeois apologists and the fifty-seven other varieties of establishmentarianism. Being militants, however, we were not to be placated by a mere verbal smashing of cultural bossism. However crucial critical consciousness was, there was also the clear, nay ineluctable, need to materialise thought in action, to fashion *is* from *ought* (as war does). The point is to change it. For this we needed not only Theory but its objective manifestation, The Party. Furthermore, comrades! We must purge ourselves of the political defalcations implicit in the intellectual solecisms of certain stern, inadequate, European fathers, or rather running dogs. As for the generation of '56, what had it accomplished? A bibliography (coarse laughter courtesy of Karl Kraus Laboratories). Thompson, Williams, Hill, Labour's clerisy-in-exile, yesterday's men... It only stood to dialectical reason that an alternative source of authority be found.

It had to be Lev Davidovich. He was so like us. He liked literature, but he could be tough. How tough all depended (there was a pamphlet war going on about the Kronstadt), though in the last analysis didn't matter, now that we had his historical vindication in hand. His daring heresy would be seen for the inspired vision it was. His exile was the drama of our birth. We didn't need Peter Weiss to write a play, much less a Losey movie. We knew about persecution, alienation, vilification and the other strangely stimulating penalties of being right. And his assassination placed the seal of certitude on all conspiracies. We'd never heard of Hochhuth or Sikorski, but the way one linked the name of Churchill with the other came only as a shock, we smugly noted, to the hacks of the bourgeois press. Look at the Chicago Seven. Think of Fred Hampton!

Trotsky was an ideological virgin (inviolate), a martyr for the cause, a Peter the Hermit, a John d'Arc, and a general, all-round prince of materialistic and dialectical enlightenment. Even his paternal prowess was the stuff of legend. Stalin's offspring was the sclerotic, simple-minded and, most unforgivably, vulgar CP. And Mao had only sired the CPGB(ML), an infantile disorder. But Trotsky contained multitudes, with two families, IS and IMG, and his own international.

He wasn't perfect, mind. The International Socialists were bastards. Their whole analysis was illegitimate. The Soviet Union was simply *not* state capitalist (this was very important). Anyone who even for a moment considered that it was had to be out of his fucking tree. We, the International Marxist Group, proponents of the degenerate-workers-state thesis, were objectively correct, and that was all there was to it. Like all pretenders, IS always seemed to have more rabble to rouse and louder voices to do it in, cadres in unions and a theoretical organ. We didn't let such affectations, with their unseemly taint of populism, make us feel small, however. Indeed, they attractively confirmed that there was something pure, true and bolshevik about being *un groupuscule*. To be considered puny, marginal and insubstantial had, after all, been our Father's fate. Think of Alma Ata. Think of Norway! Okay, so IS had Cliff and Kidron, able dialecticians both. But we had Mandel the cantsmasher. Enough said. They had *Socialist Worker*, we'd *Red Mole*, which was a lot more colourful to look at, plus its name came from holy revolutionary writ. They had Paul Foot. We had Tariq. We had Martin, who staged an in-house seminar on Althusser, who stood his ground against an old CP shop steward accusing him of preaching 't'negation of t'fucking negation'. We were making the world an open mind.

But I often felt I lacked the right credentials, that I was always thereabouts, never quite there. I kept wanting to live the life I was being given, as well as the one I'd made for myself. I wanted sex, or even love would do, when revolutionary discipline was obviously more important. It was manifestly true that there was a world to win, but always restless as soon as I'd found home, always aware that others meant self-obliterating power, I wondered if I'd find that new world more inhabitable. Maybe I was just dressing in the drag of militancy, selling out to the commissar's shilling, mimicking a march to a different drummer. I reproved myself for petit bourgeois individualism. Yet, I did bite that iron shilling, and found it less counterfeit than others, and was glad. I just wasn't able to swallow it. The escapist in me delighted in the essential puppetry of belonging. And the only permanent revolution that interested me, really, was my own.

The closest my fellow-travelling took me to conscription, or volunteering (I loved the rhetoric of there being a war on), involved the Circle Line as far as Aldgate. It was the Christmas vac. I'd considered it no more than my revolutionary duty to overdraw on my bank account, and now was broke. (I nicked books in Broad Street in the same guerrilla spirit, escaping detection, prosecution and disgrace I don't know how. The thought of it now is almost a model of the past. Excessive, wasteful, cocky, risky, vain...) Disoriented by being demobbed, I could only act the Oliver again, and found floor space with Ed Blood in Herne Hill. Ed fed me pints at the Brockwell Tavern, even found some nurses for us to serenade on Christmas Day with old Everly Brothers' numbers. 'All I have to do is dream' . . . This, too, fraternal. This, too, a sign of the times, when seemingly just to be around evoked generosity. Except it was not what I had in mind at all. This outing to the innards of my bedsit past made me desperate to rejoin my new life. No sooner had Ed given me a base than I began to go cold turkey for warmer places and more fitting anthems. I found Ariel's number. Better yet, Martin was in town. Martin was the security I needed now. Martin took me down to Aldgate.

We had to go via the Roundhouse, however. There the RSSF annual conference was in full spate. The platform was in the central pit of the place, and revolutionising around it were socialist students of every stripe. It was as difficult to know what, if anything, was going on as it had been between sets at the Chris McGregor–Who–Pink Floyd concert on the same floor twelve months earlier. Then it hadn't mattered what was happening. Scented air and smiling faces said something was. Its very vagueness was the signature of its reality. But this was a Federation! Comrades, come rally. All I could hear, however, was sound and fury, ragged cheers and whining microphones, exhortations, execrations, stormy exits, a birthday party at which everyone wanted to have his cake and eat it. I felt like a parent, mystified, distant, vaguely anxious. Martin fraternised, I imagine, though what I remember best is spending a good deal of time prowling the galleries above the mêlée with him, looking for Fawthrop.

Still, this was the Roundhouse, not a satirical bequest to us from the proletariat but the future's omphalos. What if there was an air of slouching to be born about us, birth awaited, sure as we slouched. We must be significant. Were we not gathered where late the Dialectics of Liberation conference had uttered its Orghast? And I loved the place itself. Its murky galleries and gangways were an ideal backdrop for the various backstabbings, cabals, public executions, invitations to self-criticism, table-turnings and war crimes tribunals being staged below all at the same time. As usual, my impressionism could only synthesise an image. I had to be content with that, having absolutely no idea what I was supposed to be doing there.

The room in Aldgate was off the main thoroughfare, away from rhetoric's glare, up a down-at-heel staircase. It was the kind of place that smells of dust, with a name adverting to the import–export line, a cross between the Emerald Staff Agency and the old Irish Film Society's premises, North Earl Street, Dublin. I listened for the Harry Lime theme, but it was only the telephone in another office. The man we were to meet, according to Martin, was definitely Lime-big, though, had been ordered hither posthaste by, I think, the International Secretariat. I saw in black and white a brotherhood of Sydney Greenstreets at table in a Zurich side street, smooth-shaven jowls as grainy as old film stock, postprandial best Havanas clamped in stone, Churchillian jaws. Plots and prognostications mushroomed under clouds of turbid smoke. Men and materials marched across implacable, graphlike minds.

Our host had lately organised in Canada, Martin said, a fact which seemed as good a way as my imaginings to emphasise the mystery of these dim stairs. He would be lithe and coiled and have a brush-top haircut, a shirt of lumberjack plaid, a tan despite the midnight-midwife nature of his calling, spectacles . . . Nervous and excited, I thought of joking about Canada and cold war, but Martin was right. This was serious. This was eyeball to eyeball, much realer than

Roundhouse runaround. This was my big chance to impress. Steady yourself, idiot! So instead I asked what was the name. Steele? Armstrong? There was no *nom de guerre*, however, but a Northern Irish accent disconcerting me. Since when had anyone from there espoused the name of brotherhood or international or the cause of freedom?

But then, everything about The Organiser was unexpected. I was only right about the spectacles. He was pale and pudgy. I have an impression of a beige sweater and a paisley tie, but that's probably a gloss on how his impassivity struck me. I'd have passed him in a bus queue. Martin introduced me as an Oxford comrade. A twitch of cheek muscle acted as his smile. I felt he must have known me from my previous lives, he ignored me so comprehensively. It was as though I wasn't there. I began to think I shouldn't be. He and Martin swapped some desultory gossip about comings and goings, aims and issues, faraway places and strange-sounding names, and Martin laughed immoderately at his soft-spoken comments. I looked intently out the window, wishing that some Paris graffito (*Je suis marxiste tendance groucho*) would spring up on an Aldgate wall and show I spoke the language. But all that happened was I stood there, outsider, insider, soloist, groupie. Later, Martin and I went to Ariel's aunt's house, where there was food of the best, choruses of 'Pie in the Sky' and other novelty numbers, and funny stories from the life and times of Palme Dutt. I was back again in the best of all possible worlds.

Besides, The Aldgate Organiser didn't seem to matter. Trotsky had a much more likely vicar on earth at home in Oxford, name of Bob. He impressed on all fronts. He was older. He was married, had a family, had a house out by Wheatley, a suit, a tie, a day job running the British Society for Pneumatology or some such. He had a long lean face and a goatee, a few bad teeth and a few gold ones, and eyes with a devilish glint. He looked like everything the romance of our principles could promise – pirate, grandee, mobster, gambler. Other Ruskin students, average shop-floor alumni, were used to the intensities of, say, a Bert Rammelson. But Bob was different. Bob was fun. He didn't show his age at all, and in everything he said he was on our side, revelling in our amazement at finding someone over thirty who didn't seem emasculated by what, in their false consciousness, they called responsibility.

Most of the revelling took place in the King's Arms, by Wadham, during lunch time. Here Bob regularly held court, gossiping and guffawing and sinking pints like he was bottomless. He lent authority to our positions, picked arguments to see what we were made of, made bold to say that we should get up off our theoretical arses because at the end of the day the only thing that made a difference was action. Then, after closing time, he'd saunter grandly up the Broad for a dose of Welsh rarebit at the caff in Elliston and Cavell's, with a 'Ta, luv' to the waitress, suddenly the unassuming shopper.

We knew how dangerous he was, though, from the way he thrilled us with predictions of how dangerous we could be. Loud, colourful, daring, resourceful (I think he even had a photocopier we could use), and always with the price of a pint on him, he was the voice of experience, Bob the *Zeitgeist*, his name a cryptic anagram of our potential. For him we stood outside Pressed Steel Fisher when the night shift came off selling *Red Mole*. For him I leafleted Cornmarket in the rain. For today the struggle. Had he not existed we would have had to invent him, the perfect parent, second only to Lev in verve. Bob would free me from Aldgate anonymity and bid me don the dungarees of relevance and commitment.

But there was trouble at t'mill. Holycross Joe might know these grimy men emerging into the cold, pale Cowley morning. He was familiar with what work they did and how, why unskilled were segregated from skilled, the lines of demarcation and the piecework rates. He lived what I knew only as vocabulary. I could only see my would-be brothers through what I'd heard and read, under my nails no grit or scum and in my hand nothing but sentiment. Yet I hoped that might be something to go on, my admiration for them, my fantasies of family. Their fathers had been quarrymen at Headington, winning stone to build the common rooms, the chapels, the whole walled city by the pleasant river, from which they were for all their days remote. How was it possible not to want more for their sons than dirty faces and the going rate? How not to want them to want more for themselves? Emblems of survival, infantry of history, mascots of a new world in the morning! If you could only see that it's all (this world, your place in it) a matter of consciousness . . . Look – see those spires? Knowledge is power. (And imagination is its conscience, but that's beside the point at present.) Do yourselves a favour, brothers, buy a little know-how from me now. Be like me. Read all about it. 'Red Mole! Red Mole!'

But all trooped by unseeingly, nothing on their unforgivable minds save food and bed. And when a couple of the younger ones stopped, I had nothing to say to them beyond a nervous thanks. In my less than half a dozen trips to Cowley, I suppose I sold twenty papers. 'Ne' mind,' Bob went, with a breezy cackle. 'From each according to his abilities, to each according to his needs, eh?'

I wasn't organised, that was the trouble. I lay on my bed in Bowen, trying to read *The A.B.C. of Communism*, but taking nothing in except the authors' names. Bukharin, Preobrazhenskii, might have been a pair of South American volcanoes, and I was an evening spread out upon a table. Useless romancing suffocated me with its glut of impressions, kept me going in its unceasing swirl. Spire became rifle became spiral onion-dome became red flag flying here. I should have been able to mount the platform and roar to the distracted world like all the others. I should have been able to talk to Martin in the lingo of matrix and nexus, base and superstructure. I thought of switching to the Dip., and losing myself among real models of actual worlds. I wanted to do labour studies, to leech good stories and the stuff of dreams from generous Raphael Samuel. I told myself that I should be like Joe. But I could only watch. In the halls the comrades come and go/Talking of strikes and Uncle Ho . . .

There was no world. There was either home or nothing. There was just the promiscuity of things, their atmosphere, their ineluctability (evocative rain shrouded all Shotover). And there was the task of naming. That had to go on regardless. The familiar, ever-new, uncontrollable activity of place becoming name, and name place, back and forth, back and forth, Penelope's mourning shuttle . . . That was restless me.

The Anglia rode the bridge at Horse and Jockey, County Tipperary, going south . . . Twenty miles down the road, in Cahir, my Aunt Chrissy was in childbed, was at prayer, was doing I didn't know what, living a life. The thought of her invaded me like the refrain of a soldier's song. Goodbye Piccadilly, farewell Leicester Square.

There was no material, only memory. There was no history, only texture. From each according to his abilities, to each according to his needs . . .

There was a place called Jericho. I'd heard of it already. Ruskin in Walton Street had its back to it and its cap set at the university. I'd almost been there when I sloped off by myself to watch Miklos Jancso's desolate, engrossing dreams of history (*My Way Home*) at the Scala. The streets were chock-a-block with small, unOxford houses. In the Carpenter's Arms the Double Diamond was warm and Keith Moon rampaged through 'Pictures of Lily'. This was the poor quarter. We went there after dark, along wet pavements shining like knives under the streetlights. It was good. It intimated blue angels and red lights. It was Cowley without being embarrassed by workers. But I wasn't able to see Jericho properly until *Jude*, which was the idea of the place.

The past being more a place of mood than fact, more ambiance than almanac, I can't say what the practicalities were of getting *Jude* going. There were smoke-filled rooms, no doubt, and certainly, though I can't remember them, girls frenetically typing. I do remember loud get-togethers in Alun Howkins's room in St Bernard's Road. A tall non-student from the *Oxford Mail* lent a solid hand. There was something about comrades from *The 1/- Paper*, Cambridge, who either came over to encourage or were visited, though quite possibly I'm imagining that. Where the money came from is beyond me. There was no La Passionaria of the piggy bank that I know of, no Zelda Curtis of the *Morning Star*. It's as if the name is all I can recall, as if the echo of Hardy's ballad of the addled, redolent of poverty and scholarship, a room in Jericho and blind, blithering need are energy's only residue.

The idea was that the obscure not be forgotten. The city's outlying estates with their English names and treeless concrete made lead stories. Blackbird Leys and Minchery Farm sprang off the front page with lives and histories to instruct and chivvy. Old fields despoiled by new developers were pictured, their plight as communities indignantly set down. Old photographs of bargees and brewers, of Edwardian hands outside Lucey's iron-works, and bygone St Giles fairs, were dusted off and given dignity. The city council tried to pull a fast one at the planning stage. *Jude* sounded the alarm. Tenants' meetings, school activities, all that never saw the light of *Daily Information*, *Jude* defined as our beat. The university was relevant only when it proved a poor employer. Speaking the language of men, and in a common cause, would bring crashing down all walls unworthily policing us. *Narodniki triumphera*.

There were probably some leaders and a manifesto to that effect. And I suppose *Jude* did have stories about Jericho. I don't remember. I didn't particularly need them, though what they said, forgotten now, meant all the world at the time. In *Jude*, Jericho came to stand for what I had lost sight of and could now begin to see anew. This place denoted what I'd first indistinctly heard of as Church Lane, Lismore. Also Drimnagh, the Liberties, Lambeth, Ballyfermot,

Ballybough, the many Irishtowns, the Shannon in Enniscorthy, all those homes where I belonged in spirit, where the
citizens of want lived. They were what couldn't be rational-
ised away, the drag, the grind, the narrow round, the making do (or not). They were where Ruskinians belonged, what
they defended, what they were being not very subtly coaxed
from. They were society's mirror of itself, my tutors in moral
politics and imaginative sympathy. For once, through *Jude*,
I listened.

Maybe the gay ex-busman with the squeaky voice and
blonde, crinkly hair bought a *Jude* as he flaunted by. And there
was a type of Nuffield postgraduate who had to have the set.
There was a core of loyalists, too, not all by any means from
Ruskin. But in George's in the market, men in the uniforms
of the railway, the buses, the Post Office still preferred the
pink 'un. Their wives, hurrying to Queen's Lane to get home
with Littlewood carrier bags and cakes from the Cadena,
barged past, if accosted, with a cluck.

I still was largely a Prufrocky spectator ('Full of high
sentence, but a bit obtuse'). But that wasn't all. As a newsboy
on the corner, at least I knew where I stood. I had my portrait of the artist. And I did sell more *Jude*s than *Red Mole*s,
perhaps as many as twenty of each issue. But the paper only
lasted six issues or so. That was bad, and all concerned were
sad. But all knew, too, that it had been right to raise the flag
of it. It had felt like action. Our hearts were pure, like those
of young people. And now, if anyone invited me to 'see the
midnight march of the proctors, so stately, so antique, past
the quarrelsome Irish scaffolders in the doorway of Old Tom'
(Jan Morris, *Oxford*), I'd know what I would look at, would
even say a few words in the language of their quarrel.

III

The point was it was so difficult to change it! Interpretation
might be our second nature, but still the powers that be

unnaturally resisted. Even inside Ruskin, their world was too much with us. We all knew how culturally dislocated we were, how far from home, how driven way out of our minds by enforced responsibility for utilitarianism and supply curves. But there seemed so little we could do about it. Motions were proposed and amendments, too, conveners covened, deputations marched aloft to the bureaucracy on the second floor in Walton Street armed with participation, democratisation, the legitimate aspirations of we, the people. And marched back down again.

Then ranks wouldn't stay closed. Genial former engine drivers turned into Stalinists. Trotskyites developed extra backs in order to be stabbed in them. There were fucking social democrats who wouldn't shut their cakeholes and who, besides, committed the solecism of coming from Kent. Meetings broke up in anvil choruses of points of order. The intellectuals amongst us declared that the proletariat made poor dictators, being much too fond, when up against it, of appealing to fair play and *Roberts Rules of Order*. That was not the way to smash the state. So there had to be tyranny, I thought, cast-iron party discipline, dogma's righteous writ, the remorseless Caesarism of Cromwell in the field, the self-denying, self-defining suffering of the Long March. Anything but this fruitless pantomime, free speech. No wonder power came from the barrel of a gun. And with it, brand-new, mind-forged manacles. And, in short, I was afraid.

What our education said it meant created insecurity too. Even we unworldly ones doing English were made to realise that our two years at Ruskin were merely a rehearsal for university proper, by means of Terry Eagleton. When he arrived at Wadham, it was put about that applications to go on with him would be most welcome, obligatory almost. This signal honour, evidence of the classless society which the quality newspapers kept trying to project, thrilled our tutor. Steve Kelly, Ernest Parkin and myself were designated to compete for the one place.

It was an interminable hour, a wet afternoon, a large, gloomy room overlooking Holywell Street. A pursey oldster politely endured my persecution and assassination of Wordsworth, while my would-be benefactor tried to be encouraging. It seemed a long, disillusioning time since that other wet-day interview and the going on I'd imagined it to promise. Wadham, sod 'em, I consoled myself. No! If I couldn't beat them, I wouldn't join them.

The lads doing the Dip. were coming to feel the same way, only more so. English was strictly the surplus value to what they had to set their minds to. And brain-changing confrontations with new idioms and strange conceptual devices were not the worst of it. The comrades had to change their lives as well. They had a new identity now. Mind-worker. It didn't altogether oust the old one, but there was no denying its much greater pressures. They were being given tools to master the system. They had instruction manuals for remote, abstract controls. They could expect power surges. There was every anticipation, though they didn't share it, that they'd prove worthy of the means that remade them. That was what going on meant.

A suspicion of selling-out hung in the air like halitosis. They would line up to sit Schools and feel more naked than ever on a picket line. Who'd have thought that the readiest means to serve the membership was going on to yet more foreign parts named Oriel, Corpus, Balliol, PPE? But they'd never go back, not even the rare few who did return to the shop floor. Goodbye Rochdale Hornets, farewell Wigan Pier . . . It was a long, long way to Transport House, and now that they were inevitably on the road to it, a trek so different to the one from Jarrow, not one could say his heart lay there.

It wasn't only Ruskin that, by appearing to blend fraternity with Big Brotherhood, made us wonder who we were and what exactly we could do about it. Oxford seemed astray as well. We were reliably informed by comrades from obscure locations in New Inn Hall Street and Wellington

Square that the place didn't know its class-ridden arse from its ideological elbow. But how to rectify this anomalous anatomy? Not easily, it seemed, particularly with, as we were fond of saying, a guvnor who'd published lives of Hitler and Ernest Bevin.

Walls could be written on (DON'T TAKE IT TO HART), marches organised, massive resolutions moved at JCRs. It was possible, and a lot of fun, to cause uproar at Union debates, to chant and harangue plutocratic apologists delivering after-dinner drivel. All these activities were well and good and had significant victory's tang, while they lasted. Action kept us in the picture, tore up a cobblestone or two from the cultural straight and narrow, alerted us to worthwhile items in pamphlets from Hornsey and Hull, gave us Gestetner stencils to type for *Oxford Left*. We in Ruskin were not the only spancelled ones. There were neighbouring minds in chains, forbidden their legitimate fathers.

> For us this refusal to consider anything more novel than Aristotle stems from enmity to Bertrand Russell, who has in recent years been so active in social action, be it against the war in Vietnam, interference in San Domingo or American Imperialism in Cuba. It is probably felt that, if occupation with formal logic, and foundations of mathematics, leads to this sort of thing, we had better not expose young men to these modern, new-fangled ideas. (*Oxford Left*, II, iii, p. 25)

There they were inside the All Souls parlour, cracking walnuts and smugly relishing the world, as though they hadn't made an utterly unjustifiable balls of it. The horrors perpetrated by power were, objectively, their responsibility, but their sole commitment was to covering up the fact, bellowing in *The Times* about barbarians, pretending to remain unmoved when hearts and minds were torched in obscure villages and burning children ran down a road to nowhere. Fortunes of war. Dear boy, do grow up ... A touch more port? Imperious fingers snapped, and a faceless servant buttled forth from Jericho. They hated us as clearly and unreasoningly as our fathers. Only self-sacrificing obedience could placate them, they were old and tired and fundamentally fucked-up.

Well, we didn't need them.

> We disdain, for example, to work out the labyrinthine relations of Hebdomadal Council, Congregation etc, and the arbitrary arithmetic of token representation . . . (By feudal we mean the paternalistic form of relationships between students and teachers, and the diffuse sources of authority as embodied in colleges.)

The Oxford Revolutionary Socialist Students' manifesto got it right. Let our self-styled, self-deceiving masters intone, As it was in the beginning, is now, and ever shall be. No glory be to fathers sinning thus. Not while there was a cattle prod or cop's snarling Alsatian left in Alabama.

They wouldn't keep on Sean Gervasi at the Commonwealth Institute. We protested. Sean Gervasi left. They had themselves the Craig affair at Lancaster. We protested. Would they listen? So what could a poor boy do except liberate books from Blackwell's? That, at least, struck a blow for academic freedom, hit them in their only living part, the pocket. Hesse and Marcuse were not their property. Selling books was spiritual theft! Nor was that all. Classics were appropriated too. *Macbeth* became a blast of floodlights in the audience's face, with upstage the evil couple dry-riding. We would take our freedom where we found it. *Venceremos!*

We would rip out the poison that was Powell. He was given the City Hall to speak in. Of course. And Thames Valley's finest were on hand to ensure he did. Naturally. His was the speech whose freedom had to be protected. The brazen buggers. This was more of their fair play.

Ruskin hardly needed telling how to act. Opposing Powell, taking to the streets in the name of the family of man, the voiceless and unwanted ones, was second nature.

A former Ruskin student called Dave Kitson was rotting in a fascist cell in South Africa for being a colour-blind trade-unionist. Every year in spring lads marched from Oxford to London and rallied in Trafalgar Square outside fortress Boer to show that he was not forgotten and that no more was there clean getting away with that kind of thing. Unions came out solid for us that day, too, and even anti-apartheid liberal humanists were welcome, and vaguely tolerable Labour Party fathers; Eric Heffer, say, addressed the earnest and exhilarating carnival of principle, confirming us in what we already knew. We were no petty people. And now the politics of exclusion and denial, the grotesque face of all that power had taught us, the imperium's most bare-faced instance of its imperative, was being brought home to roost from Jo'burg and the mines. Well, we'd see about that.

Meanwhile, how thrilling it was to be busy and not alone in saying No! Just organising for the demo brought a rush of voltage. We dashed around for days, putting up posters, scurrying from St Cat's to Nuffield, receiving vows of brotherhood from total strangers, making sure in public bar and JCR that we'd be there in force, feeling the vehement excitement and all minds humming with the certainty of uproar and of not being moved.

We assembled at the bottom of Longwall Street and marched up the High, a couple of hundred strong, arms linked, with a sea of sentiment waving over us in black and white and all in single voice. Unite and fight! 'Enoch! – We Want You . . . DEAD!' we went, and it was hard to stop from laughing. 'Racism, out, Out, OUT!' Pure adrenalin, pure purpose. Mind became body as we marched, which was the plan. And plan there had to be, because we were revolu-tionaries and because we knew our enemy. The enemy of the people spent its life planning. Its idea was to grant us a permit to pass by roaring, allowing us to hang around a while and heckle before disbanding for our toast and tea. Patronising fuckers! Well, we'd make sure it had another think coming.

We wheeled into St Ebbe's not merely to denounce but to confront. Powell should not speak. City Hall could not disguise itself as private property. Down with the charade of contradictions! Occupy the people's forum! No to Tory opportunists! In other words, we were in fine fettle when we hit the line of cops. Or when it hit us, rather, which with a whoosh of gaberdine it all too suddenly did. Their job, for which the fucking bourgeoisie was probably paying them a special rate, was to break our ranks. We'd told each other that. They'd try to act the immovable object to our irresistible force. One by one, they'd try to pick us off, because they hated our togetherness. In the unlikely event of their succeeding in lugging us to their wagons, we should remember to kick and scream and give the right salute, like John Carlos and the comrades at the Olympics. We agreed, without talking about it much, that it was just as well we weren't taking on the Mexican authorities. But we vaguely regretted not being like our Japanese brothers, with their staves and crash helmets, sashaying in a snake. We did have, though, the inestimable electricity of our righteousness. If we remained really solid, toe to toe and arms confidently locked, we would overcome.

But however much we rehearsed approach and attitude, it was all different when it began. A moving barricade of solid bone, all tentacles and messing, was a bit too much like the real thing. Comrades pushed forward from the back, cops pushed back from the front, smell of their Old Spice and our sweat, bodies squeezed and jammed and wrenched about, small cries of pain and danger, shouts of solidarity and renewed effort, blood a chaos in the head, and the tongue all dry and tingly . . . The only thing that seemed at all like true to form was how the cops detested us. Their stony eyes glinted with readiness. Come on, you little shits. Their clamped jaws told us they were boulders in a cliff and we were sod. They were the pillars of the establishment, we were noisome rubbish, fit only for disposal. And they were trained. They went for the groin, knowing that we'd have to unlink arms to kick and stop them. If we let an arm loose they'd haul us away. If we caught their shins they had an excuse to wade in swinging, pretending that they'd lost control, like the angry and malevolent fathers of our worst fears.

The tearing and dragging must have lasted a good half-hour. We were getting nowhere. We were getting tired. We were dying for a smoke. We could do with half a mo under the old thinking cap. Some comrades in the rear came up with a diversion, ran down the street a ways and began attacking the police wagons with their placards. Dave Youlton was arrested, one of ten. Enoch spoke. No problem, and a full house. We paid five bob a head for Dave Youlton's fine. Thirty quid for breaching the white peace. I think a couple of police wagon windows were smashed.

But, 'One man, one vote!' we shouted. We were in the Northern Ireland Civil Rights Oxford Campaign now. Praise Marx, *la lutte continue*. Bob was right, the Irish thing was going to be huge.

Not that we needed Bob to tell us that. This one had everything. It was maggoty with history, a good start. A seven-hundred-year-old saga of exploitation and repression had at last festered to the point where its internal contradictions, its familiar and jealously policed morality of divide and conquer, could only articulate corruption. Blessed change, turbine of unity and just action, beat on your drum, march, take us to your moment!

And as well as the mystique of possibility, there was also concrete analysis based precisely on locating the historical macrocosm within the microcosm of the contemporary, and vice versa. In other words, Northern Ireland was England's Vietnam. A sturdy citizenry in a backward and untouristy land was rising up against (objectively) imperialist aggression and its vile clients to claim its democratic due. It was a classic instance of the unquenchable revolutionary spirit of the people, and thereby vividly instructive of how the margin could characterise the centre, the outside the inside, the colony the metropolis (cf. Algeria). Moreover, and concomittantly, Northern Ireland conditions spoke explicitly to the essence of Powellism, revealing the machinations of bigotry in the appalling regalia of its true economic colours. This revelation, in turn, obviated the obdurate and benighted ideology of Orangeism, which had made of its home a mini Dixie, a South Africa without sun. We'd lay it bare in all its idolatrous recidivism, our minds exquisitely poised to foreclose for ever on such bankruptcy and the mainland interests which lent it might and right.

Clearly, then, given the decayed and panicky condition of the autocracy and the sustained enthusiasm of the people in their cause, this was potentially a revolutionary situation. And our analysis was proved additionally plausible because those in the vanguard of Northern Ireland consciousness and organisation were students. History might indeed be a nightmare, but they were awake. Their energies received our joyous welcome. Devlin, Farrell and others (names forgotten) appeared in vehement and uplifting concert in the patrician pages of the *New Left Review*. The idea of CS gas virtually intoxicated us, acted as a kind of ideological nitrous oxide. Britain was a cop in riot gear with baton raised to strike defenceless Ireland on the cover of *International Socialism*. But the only hands across the sea that mattered, we'd make sure, were those of solidarity. Now we'd found our citizens of want, the real thing. We'd fight and no surrender.

The NICROC marched from The Plain to the Martyrs' Memorial, from Folley Bridge to Gloucester Green. Women from Marston with Sunday hats and eager smiles took part, and so did sober, lost-looking men from Rose Hill and Kidlington. The Irish community. It took me aback to see them. I had forgotten that their normal life meant invisibility. I had forgotten my own past. But thanks to them, town, for once, outnumbered gown. If Ireland for the *illuminati* was too obscure, religious, far away, well, let the people speak. Their doing so, after all, provided an unprecedented opportunity to forge links and raise consciousness. Old dream of unity, shine once again, shine on . . .

After the marches they packed Ruskin for the speeches. My pal Tony told what life was like in the Ardoyne and was questioned as though he were a traveller from an antique land. John Hume came, and there wasn't a dry eye in the house. Gerry Lawless bowled them over with some excellent left spin deliveries. When United Ireland came up, some solid fellow at the back took the pipe from his mouth and almost smugly asked, 'Who's going to pay for it?' The smugness expressed not so much the speaker's enjoyment of his common-sensicality but rather a shy pleasure of having got a word in after all these years. Old-style republicans tensely and at length corrected what they heard as misplaced emphases, their points hinging on some momentous but insignificant incident that their fathers witnessed on a summer road near Bandon or Bunclody in 1921, their lust for accuracy ill-concealing the landscapes of loss and bitterness in which they'd spent their time.

Those were the days. All agreed that Stormont was no more than two vast and trunkless legs of stone, imposing right enough, but a thing of the past. Nobody had heard of Armalite or Semtex, the Abercorn, Bloody Sunday, La Mon, the murdered Miami.

Joe made friends with a lame old fatherly tailor from Skibbereen.

I had dreams of Mum marching up the High with us, and Dad our halt companion, separate but in all that mattered, one. Oh, yes, those were the days . . . Even being Irish could be a source of optimism.

Nothing beside remains . . .

When I was recalling my five-point analysis of Ruskin English and its cramped writing, I wrote at first that its thinking was as constipated as its hand. But I couldn't let the cynicism stand. Not merely to save face. What face? The only worthwhile one I have is the one writing restlessly creates by effacing and reconstituting all the random features, weaving inside with out. So I crossed that snideness out, not because it speaks inaccurately or even untruthfully, but because it's too easy. It conforms too neatly to a conventional belittlement of how we were back then, as if times are better now or we ourselves are. The view from twenty-five years on isn't automatically more sensible or reliable by virtue of being recent. It can all too mindlessly exploit those great times' openness, protecting the present by pretending that our hot youth was, at best, a time of harmless but immature distraction, an episode in nostalgia's repressive kitsch.

I've not been able, haven't wanted, to eliminate all the snideness. Did I say we were naïve? All that sloganeering. Our Panglossolalia of causes. Our Duke-of-Yorkist marching. Unity, our kingdom come. We were out of our minds with theory. Our actions were artifacts of sand. We sallied forth highheartedly from the suburb called the fifties, reached for the apple and were stunned to find rot. Presumably we never stood a chance. When we asked what our country could do for us, we were told what we could do for our country. Sit down, stay in, give thanks, identify with distant death as vindication of just cause. Skip murders in Memphis and Meridian and My Lai. Long Kesh and Shankill sounded vaguely Vietnamese, but that was as far as we got, despite the death there too. Death was not what we had in mind at all.

We only wanted our say to count. But the powers that be, their one-track minds as paranoid as our own, thought participation meant apocalyse. So we broke furniture, scattered files around, were called criminals, a lunatic fringe and, ultimate anathema, 'politically motivated'. We were the gods that failed. And sarcasm merely masks my disappointment. We had it in our minds the world should want us as we were. We favoured common ground and not enclosure, not property but resources. Our every No was Yes to betterment. Some strange idea, increasingly unfashionable these days, told us it was worthwhile to oppose aloud, in numbers, and if possible permanently. We wanted to be generous. And in that 'we' I found complete acceptance, of others first, and then, at last, myself. Through it I got my Oxford education. I'm still learning how I might live up to it. I wouldn't have it any other way.

THE KNACK

It was a misty morning in raw March and I was late. The wedding was to be at eleven and here was I having to hoof it from the pre-nuptial bed off Botley Road to Headington, hoping to coax a change of sheets from the bossy cleaning lady in Bowen. Who wouldn't be there. Who'd be too absorbed in her Player's Number Six and cup of tea to be disturbed. Who'd see that I was the one who was disturbed and laugh at me. And why not? I definitely was out of my mind. Plus, it was Thursday. Ever since boarding school, Thursday was the most unlucky day.

I hadn't thought of boarding school in years. Its sour aftertaste had been more or less rinsed out by Mum's proper coffee, and the plonk and watery spaghetti bolognese of much more recent times had finished the job. Nevertheless, running for a bus that obviously wouldn't come, humiliating Thursday scenes of drill under Jack Fraser rose before me, archetypes of other rituals I'd be damned if I'd perform. The acrid aroma of cabbage boiled to blackness seeped through the day's poor visibility. What if Pam couldn't cook? It would be just my luck. But I would be calm. I would put on my thinking cap. I would walk to the station, buy a single ticket, and so long.

With one and thruppence bus fare. With – talk about luck – a rare number five trundling through the murk at me. I stumbled up the stairs and lit a horrible pre-breakfast Piccadilly. I crossed my legs, my heart, my fingers. My loose foot flapped incessantly. No, yes, I was in it now. All the letters had been written. My importunate entreaties, my essays in emotional solidarity, were now flesh. The scramble to help Pam buy a plane ticket, a fiver from this comrade, a tenner from Martin, twenty on loan (but already with inverted commas round it) from Sally Thaw had been cashed in. The paranoid wait at Heathrow had turned into long brown hair, tweed trouser-suit, banjo. I had the ring somewhere. We had a flat, two single beds, a stove. Life was turning into things, the last magic, the ultimate threat. The real thing.

Romance by letter had been fun, kind of, at any rate less frustrating than, say, courtship *chez* Dad. All its emptiness could be written off, creating for me, thanks to Heather and Rosemary, a perverse excitement. It was theory, all text and sublimated narrative. Like dreams, like rhetoric, like the future. It spoke like my past to me, a deferment that felt like enhancement, a distance that seemed the principle of iden- tity. We got pretty good at it. Or so I thought, until the terminal wait in Terminal 3. Then Pam began to matter. Each sequinned or seersuckered stranger emerging from the flight brought a pang of doubt, a pang of love. She's lost. It's all a hoax. She's been arrested. It was as if I hadn't known I cared till then. I fucked and blinded the authorities and my reject's luck.

But as luck would have it, the authorities married us. When Pam presented herself at immigration, it seemed at first she had committed countless bureaucratic mortal sins. Thick fingers leafed through the ledger of her inadmissabil- ity. Walls of impenetrable official serge and waffle rose around her. It must have been terrible. I shivered even at the telling. But Pam just laughed her gentle laugh. She was like that, extra calm and quite secure of aim. So when HM's inspector asked, 'Kindly state the purpose of your visit', she simply said she was coming to get married and was given a month's leave of land.

Then I laughed too. We were a book of fairytales. First, meeting in Paris, now clemency from the Queen. We were Ray Brooks and Rita Tushingham speeding in a double bed through Knightsbridge in *The Knack*. It was the revolution! And, by way of proof, Pam brought me a cup of tea in bed next morning and kissed me on the cheek.

Women! I was still wearing the ratty military surplus jacket that I had in Paris. Pam threw it out. Also, a pair of old pyjamas to which I was attached (seedbed of memory . . .), though I was more inclined to cede it to her. That jacket, though, was me, its cowdung green my unvarnished presence, its stench my uniform. Who was this neat *couturière*? I could only hope she didn't think I had the money to be buying clothes, and that she wasn't going to go all bourgeois on me. No. She just wanted to be nice. Unbefuckinglievable!

And then there was the hit she made at Ruskin. It fazed me in a different way. She was American. But she didn't have that much of an accent. So the comrades felt pretty much at home with her at once. She'd been to university, but also had dropped out, went back, dropped out again, loved England, which all found fascinating, brooding on their own indenture. As a teenager, she'd lived in Arlington, Illinois, and so was able to place lads in The Loop while cops broke heads for Daley and the Democrats. Crazy judges were no news to her. She could translate strange acronymns like SNCC and CORE with ease, demystifying, remystifying them. We'd hardly heard of militant Madison, Wis., or the Port Huron Statement. She spoke about the good McCarthy, Cleaver, Kunstler, Seale, heroes all who made us shake our heads and fists once more at quisling Wilson and putrid Powell. Pam hadn't been to Berkeley. 'Ne' mind, luv', she was one of us all right.

All this and France as well ... I had the ill grace to be jealous, vaguely threatened by somebody so travelled and so free. I wished I could have been an *au pair* in Angoulême, or chambermaided like a slave at the Grenoble Winter Olympics. But I had heard no Sartre at no Sorbonne. It should have been my *Paris Match* album of Mai and me supplying the insider's commentary to the smashing, yet already strangely distant, pictures. And she just a woman ... And then there was this steady stride in which she took things, her unassuming grasp of where she was, this air of there being not a thing to doubt. It had to be some kind of knack, some act. I couldn't figure it out.

But it was hard to stay defensive when I kept on falling for that style of hers, loving it. The banjo had been made for her by Keith Craddock, Bloomington. It rang out with the sound of tin cans tied to a runaway jalopy. That was bluegrass ('Foggy Mountain Breakdown'. Ah, willst thou be Bonnie to my Clyde?). Bill Monroe invented bluegrass. He lived in Bean Blossom, Ind. There was a professor of jazz at Indiana University. Pam took voice lessons there, also a course in swimming. That was when the family lived at Meadow Ridge and brother Barry shot the copperhead snake. She drove to class in the only Morris Minor Traveller south of Muncie. It was called The Spook. Her father's Lancer was The Rancid. The family lived in Monticello then. Pam water-skied on Lake Freeman at Indiana Beach and the same evening went to the Frankie Avalon concert, or cruised through the humid, velvet night listening to Dick Biondi on WLS, Chicago. The call sign meant World's Largest Store (Marshall Fields, at State and Randolph). Dick was pretty swift and really neat. Adlai Stevenson was beaten and her father hurt like hell. Her father worked as a crop hail adjuster. Mom was a homemaker. They visited Granma and Aunt Lois in Hebron. Sometimes we talked through the night. And when we made love it was as friends, with more a sense of fun than passion.

Then Pam said she had to see a doctor. *H'nn?* The Pill. She thought it best if she were on it, what did I think? Oh my America! my new-found-land, I quailed, this is virgin territory. Liz had been blunt, but that had been so she could shun or blame or keep a distance. But what I had now was involvement. This was virtually the irksomeness of the blood relative.

I tried being cool. It's your thing, baby, do what you want to do. It's only some mechanical chemistry, like having the brake fluid of your Spook topped up. Talk to your mother. I badly wanted to sound casual, but everything I said came out rough and sullen. Very soon it was, No, since you ask, since you deign embarrass me, I'm not planning to use anything. It's obvious I've given up going to barbers. As for Boots, with shop girls sniggering at me, you must be joking . . . Not that that's the point, I quite agree. I hate the bloody things. Using them is swimming with your socks on. Sorry, and all that, but that's the way I *feel*, okay? Now that I've had *experience*, I don't *need* protection, see?

A long, cold silence followed, which I broke by falling back on self-effacement, preferring nullity to being responsible. Look, it's okay. It's just that I don't have getting kids in me. I considered myself marked, somehow, not necessarily infertile but definitely infertilised. It was all psychological (she wouldn't understand). But this line proved more upsetting than the rest. So, there was nothing for it but go all out on the soft sell. We were great the way we were, why change it? The sheer unlikelihood of our being together was surely prophylactic enough. Pragmatism, admirably Yankee in its way, without a doubt, would in this case, alas, just break the charming spell, turning pillowtalk to oestrogen. Let's be the last romantics, okay?

Whether I liked it or not, however, we were way beyond deferment and the picturesque. It wasn't just the Pill that I was trying to fight off but the revolutionary change brought on by being more intimate than I'd ever been before. I'd spent the best part of a year shouting for institutional informality. Now I wanted my own patriarchy, and I couldn't be convincing, and it shook me. All that had happened so far had been so simple, so open, so miraculous. Pam and I had met in Paris. Pam and I had corresponded. Pam and I were going to get married. Nothing became the times like such magical directness.

And that wasn't all. What was happening was not just on the outside. I was wanted. I'd evidently been chosen. Freely. I was being asked to participate. I was being thought worth the risk. I was being seen as tantamount to purpose. It was altogether too much like the real thing. And still there was no knack that I could see.

Pam sickened on the Pill, moaned and retched. I sat in the other room, 'reading'. This was the body and its rotten fate, I thought, God damn it, let me out of here! And yet she was prepared to weather even this. I made a cup of tea, perhaps. 'Ta, moy dok,' said Pam.

In that small moment I imagined myself able to accept all that scared and sickened me. It was as though I needed something as visceral and distressful as Pam's fake, but very real, morning sickness to concentrate my mind. The Pill, or, What I Learned at Oxford. Here, at last, was what I couldn't walk away from. Here was trust, even if I hardly knew enough to recognise it. I'd woken up, it seemed, and found I was, in fact, aged twenty-four, and it was time. Pam and I could evolve a form and live in it. It would have to be out of our minds. I was broke, was headed I didn't know where. But still we had our faith. We'd let each other in. There was this chance of home.

I visited the St Giles Registry Office and named the day. Pam found the flat in Alexandra Road. She got a paper-moving job at Pergamon Press. We went to that Lawrence's Corner of domesticity, the Oxfam shop in Broad Street, and got a ring there for two pounds ten. Pam paid.

Martin clutched the Sainsbury's bag of sheets. Joe, gig-gling, pointed at his watch and screwed his face up into a gargoyle of shocked disappointment. I knew. It was almost five past eleven. The mist had turned into a miserable drizzle. There was no Pam. Maybe if we buggered off now to a pub where no one knew us, the damage, whatever that was, could be controlled. But I lit my sixth, stomach-turning cigarette of the morning and made myself wait. The idea of having as witnesses a Trotskyite and an Irish Communist was too good to be abandoned lightly. If all came to all, maybe a marriage could be arranged between the pair of them. I could think of a few suitable words.

A taxi pulled up. Out stepped Pam. She had nice legs. But she seemed smaller, or something, than she had the night before. I gestured truculently at her much too stylish transport (those things cost drink, you know!).

'I wanted to be on time,' she explained.

'Yeah, well, you're seven minutes late.'

'And fourteen seconds,' Pam said.

We entered the stone cold hall, received a sad look from a desk clerk, climbed the stairs to where two bureaucrats were fidgeting and freezing. There was a plump one, who looked saturnine, and a tall, thin, bearded one with the timid, puzzled look of a padre in a porn shop. Plump was the man of legal words. All my worldly goods I thee and thou. Take this man. Poor Pam. And blah, blah, blah. Come on, chum, move it. It's not as if we actually need your fucking permission. I rummaged for the ring, and handed it to Joe. He promptly gave it back to me. It loosely fit. Martin's face was as rigid as a bucket from trying not to laugh. Beard hovered over us with extreme unction. We signed the lines.

The drizzle had given way to wintry grey. Joe pulled out a camera. Pam and I posed in a doorway. The reception was held at the St Giles caff, bacon, bangers, beans, and when we said we were just married, the management did us an order of fried bread, special, well worth the shilling extra.

We rambled across the street to the Lamb and Flag. I felt as ample as an animal now, and my cigarette tasted proper, mixed with the tin flavour of the caff's red tea. The sky was brightening. From out of nowhere, Martin produced his Ornette Coleman *Free Jazz* album, long coveted by me. We didn't have a record-player (we didn't have a thing). But even now when I listen to its improvised unorthodoxies, its non-stop jumpiness, I can't imagine a more inspired wedding present. I stuck it in with the sheets. Joe bought a round. We all had something ludicrous, brandy and pineapple, whiskey and bitter lemon, and acted like we were going to get as pissed as underdogs.

Paul Kneafsey turned up. He'd bought a record too. Everyone was laughing. After a while we all went really mad and ordered ploughman's lunches. We laughed some more. Joe took pictures of us laughing. The drink no more affected us than rainwater.

At closing time we ambled up the Cornmarket with Joe. He wanted to have tea at Fuller's. The pubs would be open again soon. But Pam and I were keen to start our honeymoon. She had to be at work in the morning. At Carfax, Joe bumped into the lame tailor from the civil rights campaign, and guffawed, 'These two are just after getting married', by way of introduction. 'The best bloody wedding I was ever at!' Then, feeling pretty pleased by the day's demystification, he shook our hands and winked, as though we were his kind of conspirator, all atheistic and unafraid.

Pam and I looked at each other and grinned. We walked along Westgate Street, Park End Street, past jewellers and florists, saying nothing. The sun was brightish over Nuffield and the jail. She gave me her hand. It felt as boneless as a bird. This was the hand that, time out of mind, was going to touch me. This was the hand which wouldn't go away. This hand would clean and wash and hold Ben and Nick to swollen breasts with joy. This hand was on my side. We strolled along, going west, restful at last, no longer needing witnesses, smiling shy smiles, under the railway bridge, past Osney Mead and out the road to Hinksey, Swindon, Cumnor, Kingston Bagpuize.